••••••••••••••••••••••••••••••••••••

LAUREN *takes* LEAVE

A NOVEL

Julie Gerstenblatt

••••••••••••••••••••••••••••••••••••

To Jen →
Dear Steph,
Enjoy! It's always
great to spin @ soul
with ya.
xo
Julie

Lauren Takes Leave is a work of fiction. Names, characters, e-mail addresses, places, and incidents are the products of the author's imagination or are used fictitiously. Any resemblance to actual events, locales, or persons, living or dead, is entirely coincidental.

Cover concept and design by Brett Gerstenblatt and Gary Tooth
Illustrations by Liz Starin

FIRST EDITION

www.juliegerstenblatt.com

"The truth is rarely pure and never simple. Modern life would be very tedious if it were either, and modern literature a complete impossibility."

—ALGERNON MONCRIEFF, FROM OSCAR WILDE'S
THE IMPORTANCE OF BEING EARNEST, ACT 1

"Hey, Cameron, you realize if we'd played by the rules, right now we'd be in gym?"

—FERRIS BUELLER, FROM JOHN HUGHES' *FERRIS BUELLER'S DAY OFF*

PROLOGUE

A Confession or Three

NOW, THIS IS GOING TO SOUND CRAZY, ladies and gentlemen of the jury, but it's true. All of it. Except for the parts that I made up, of course. Those are false.

My first confession is this: I *wanted* to get placed on a jury. Yes, bizarre as it sounds, I longed for it.

Only, I didn't know how badly I wanted it until it was almost too late.

Fact: I received a blue jury questionnaire in the mail in January of this year.

Fact: I filled out the form and sent it back to the return address, promptly forgetting all about it.

Fact: As luck, fate, or divine intervention would have it, in April I was called for jury duty at the county courthouse in Alden, New York.

This one act led to several random incidents, including a bit of travel, some outpatient cosmetic procedures, and, of particular note, a brief adventure with a cross-dressed burlesque dancer named Dixie. It also led to my so-called incarceration.

I am standing before you now to beg your forgiveness. It is my desire to explain, with almost complete candor, as much about the past week as I can recall. Those bits from when I was inebriated notwithstanding, I will do my best to piece it all together for you.

Why you? Because, dear reader, by picking up my story and cradling its contents in your hands, you have become my jury.

Unwittingly, perhaps, but isn't that how all jurors come to be? One minute you're in your office cubicle, playing Scrabble against the brain in the iPad, or running on a treadmill somewhere, trying to will your thighs into submission, and the next, you're responding to a summons from the local courts and deciding the fate of a schoolteacher who may or may not be guilty of the types of wrong-doings that we're all guilty of, to a degree.

And so, please read without bias. The decision lies in your hands.

Fact: I am mostly innocent.

CHAPTER 1

Monday

"BEN, YOU NEED TO CHANGE. Those pants are way too short," my husband, Doug, says, passing Ben on the stairs.

My nine-year-old son checks himself out by looking down at his feet as he reaches the bottom step. "They're fine," he concludes. "I'm not changing."

Doug appeals to me, calling down from the second-floor landing. "Lauren!"

"O*kay*," I say, wondering for the thousandth time why it is automatically my job to clothe, feed, and bathe the offspring we produced together.

"And did you get to pick up my shirts from the dry cleaner's yet?"

"Yes!" I shout. But then I remember a small detail. "They're still in the trunk of the car."

Silence.

"Dad, I *like* my pants like this," Ben calls up the stairs, daring Doug into a full-on, 7:30 a.m. brawl.

There is a heartbeat's length pause as the house holds its breath, waiting for the next move.

I, for one, know what will happen next, because this conflict occurs between them in some variation every weekday morning. Doug puts on his glasses after showering and his critical eye wakes up, begins to focus.

It's the hair not brushed, the dishes unwashed, the frogs unfed. The bed unmade, the shoes untied, the homework incomplete.

I nod and smile, brush the hair, clean the dishes, feed the frogs, make the beds, tie the shoes, finish the homework. (Which is hard, by the way. Since when does third-grade math include algebra?)

The conversation between them goes on over my head, and snakes between my chores. It always boils down to "You didn't do this or that" from Doug and "Why do you care? You're never home" from Ben.

Both have a point. I referee. I acknowledge to Doug that Ben is a bit spoiled and we're working on it, and then, when Doug is out of earshot, whisper to Ben that Dad's stressed out because his start-up company isn't doing that well in this economy and we have to be understanding. I try to make peace by cheerleading for both sides.

It's almost enough to make a person want to run out of the kitchen to go teach middle school.

Almost.

"Lauren? Did you call the electrician yet? And Ben needs to apologize."

"No," I call up the stairs.

"No, what? Electrician or apology?"

"Yes," I shout back, emptying last night's clean items from the dishwasher.

That should be sufficiently inconclusive. There's no word from Doug upstairs. Ben just shrugs and saunters into the kitchen for breakfast.

Like in a finely choreographed ballet, the next dancer comes onstage just as the other one exits. My kindergartener, Becca, yells from her room at the top of the stairs. "Everyone be quiet! I need my sleep so the monsters don't come into my head!"

"What does that even mean?" Ben asks.

"Not sure," I say, following him.

Ben sits at the kitchen counter and waits, like this is a restaurant and I'm serving up his favorite.

"We've discussed breakfast, Ben. You are old enough to get it for yourself," I say, as I set up his breakfast for him—bowl, spoon, milk, Cinnamon Toast Crunch—the irony of which is not lost on me, and move on to the making of lunches and snacks—mine, Ben's, and Becca's.

Becca stumbles into the kitchen moments later, her hair a testament to her fitful sleep; it looks like she was caught in a wind tunnel. Oblivious to her appearance, she slides onto a stool at the island. "Kix, Mommy. Now."

"Now, what...?" I lead.

"Now, *please*," she says, rolling her eyes. There's a dormant teenager living inside my five-year-old, like an ancient volcano that could explode at any moment. These days she just rumbles. But in a few years, I'm going to have to move out of the house in order to protect myself from the hot lava that will be Becca.

I scan the shelf of cereal boxes to find that, although we own approximately forty-two kinds of General Mills and Kellogg's varieties, we are fresh out of Kix.

"How about limited-edition Froot Loops Sprinkles?" I say.

"Kix."

"Berry Berry Kix?"

"Regular!" she says, clearly not amused.

I know how this is going to end, and it's not pretty.

"Bec, I'm all out of Kix." I make a pouty face, to let her see how devastating this moment is to me. Maybe if I feign distress, she won't have to.

Her mouth opens wide, but no sound emerges. Her face wrinkles and contorts. Ben takes his bowl and moves to the other side of the room with it, so as not to be caught in the path of whatever tornado is about to be unleashed.

A piercing wail breaks the silence and reverberates around the room. Fat tears sprout fully formed, running down her pink cheeks and drenching her pajamas in seconds. She is a tsunami, a typhoon, a series of natural disasters from around the globe bottled and unleashed in my kitchen.

"*Mommy!*" she hollers. "Ooooouuugghh!"

Little people, little problems. I try not to laugh at her need for drama, then I console her, as I do every other morning when I can't give her exactly what she wants. If I have plain bagels, she wants sesame. If I have apples, she wants pears. If I've made pancakes, she wants waffles.

Today, I offer up all the other cereals like they are contestants in a beauty pageant. "Look, Bec, Lucky Charms has swirly horseshoes! The unopened Frosted Flakes holds a prize inside! *Don't you want to know what it is?*"

I'm all slick gloss on the outside, and I know that I'm supposed to be the one in charge here, but my heart is beating a million miles a nanosecond. Just to be clear: I am a tad bit petrified of my five-year-old.

Becca considers my overwhelmingly enthusiastic response. Her puffy eyes meet mine and, for a moment, I think the storm is blowing over. There may be a spark of reason there, behind the psychotic glaze.

Instead, she reaches over and grabs the opened box of Lucky Charms, sniffing its contents like a fine connoisseur. Then she takes a handful of the sugarcoated puffs, slides off her seat, and considers me. She opens her fist and pops the entire contents into her mouth, chewing thoughtfully. A stray purple star ends up on the floor, where Becca steps on it, perhaps accidentally, on her way back to the sunroom's television.

That poor Lucky Charm is like a fine dust now, and Becca is trailing it with her sock across the white kitchen tile.

"Miss Rebecca Eliza Worthing!" I say. As if what? The use of her full, formal name will whip her into shape? "Shake that off your foot!" She does. "Now, please come help me clean that up or I'll..." But she's gone before I can come up with a suitable threat, perhaps to work through the rest of her displeasure with an unsuspecting Barbie.

"Good job, Mom," Ben says, deeming it safe to approach the kitchen island once more.

He places his empty cereal bowl in front of me and mocks my parenting with a thumbs-up signal and a sardonic grin.

"What? You can't put the bowl in the sink, twelve inches that way?" I snap at him. "Or, God forbid, *inside* the actual dishwasher?"

"Whatever," he says, heading to the den to watch cartoons. "You and dad are both in bad moods this morning."

Amidst deep, cleansing breaths, I write sweet little notes on paper napkins and slip them into my children's lunch bags, hoping that by doing so, I will actually feel the scribbled sentiment.

After I finish putting Ben's and Becca's lunches and snacks, in their color-coordinated containers, into their rightful pockets of the correct backpacks, I place my lunch in my school bag along with a folder of graded essays and three folders of not-graded essays. I move it all to the door, ready for launch in eight minutes' time.

Becca sheepishly re-enters the kitchen, fully dressed for

school. She leans against the doorframe and looks up through long lashes. "Can I have some more of that cereal? It was good. I'm sorry. Please?"

"Sure, honey," I say, biting my tongue. *She's only five, Lauren,* I think. *She doesn't know any better.* I pour some cereal into a plastic cup and hand it to her for breakfast on the go.

"Laney, could you find Ben and make sure he brushes his teeth, please?" I call. "Laney?" There's no response. I try a few more times. "Laney?" My mantra eventually brings Ben in from the den.

"Where's Laney?" I ask the kids, looking around. The already cluttered kitchen is now covered with breakfast detritus. Laundry is piled by the basement door, ready for washing. "Where's dad?"

"Dad said he had to go make money," Becca replies. "Is that what he doos at work? Makes things?"

"That's not quite what he *does*, Bec. He's trying to start a new company, a graphic design start-up. All by himself. It's very hard work."

"Dad says it's risky, but it's better than working for someone else," Ben adds sagely.

"And dad is right about that," I say, trying to sound optimistic as my brain focuses on the adjective *risky*.

"Which is why it's good to have a teacher in the family!" my kids say in unison.

I roll my eyes. "Doug!" I call up the stairs. My husband believes that if he brainwashes our children, I, too, will eventually fall for his propaganda surrounding the necessity of my stagnant career.

"He went to work, I told you that." Becca goes to the front door and licks the glass heartily, like it's an ice-cream cone.

"Ew, stop! Gross!" I pull her away and wipe the saliva with my sleeve. "Ben, where are your sneakers?" He stares blankly at the floor, as if they will materialize in front of his imagined Darth Vader–like laser-beam eyes. "Find. Them. And. Put. Them. On."

I rummage through my pocketbook and grab my cell phone. My husband picks up on the first ring, and I can hear him panting as he walks briskly down our street and toward the Hadley train station. He's probably trying to catch an express train into Manhattan, which only takes thirty-eight minutes on Metro North.

"You left for work? Without saying good-bye to me?"

"Maybe?" he asks, his voice an octave higher than usual.

"You are *never* supposed to do that! September eleventh!"

Step, step, pant. Step, step. "Sorry."

"Sorry accepted." Out of the corner of my eye, I see Ben putting on his sneakers. It's starting to drizzle, so I help Becca into her raincoat and Hello Kitty boots, then shrug on my own parka.

There is still no sign of Laney anywhere.

Doug continues. "It was crazy in the house and no one was paying attention to me after the pants episode, so I just made a break for it."

"Nice move. Detonate a bomb and then clear out."

"You don't get it. This deal with Nickelodeon could be huge, but I've got to stay on top of it, every moving piece. Today was a chance to head into the office early."

I'm a working mom with two children, a largely absentee husband, and a flaky babysitter-slash-housekeeper who, I'm pretty sure, steals my clothing, and *I* don't get it? "I'm deeply sympathetic to your hardship, Doug, really. You should file a complaint with the management."

"I've tried," he says half-jokingly.

"You're dying to go to work and I'm dying to take a break. What's wrong with this picture? Why can't I just quit my job?"

"Because you love it."

"I do, or I *did*? Which verb tense are we using?"

"Well, I sure as hell do, present tense, Mrs. English Teacher. The salary, the benefits, the lifetime tenure. I'd kill for a job like that."

"You can have mine without murder," I say.

"Lauren, not now." It's a running dialogue, a continuous loop day after day, and it always ends with "Lauren, not now." I wait four seconds, knowing he will deftly change the subject. One, two, three... "Is that rain? I forgot my umbrella."

"Sucks to be you, I guess."

"I guess. Love you."

"M-hmm," I mumble.

"I could die today in a horrible terrorist attack, remember?" Doug says.

"Yeah, yeah. I love you, too."

Only half-listening now as Doug tells me about a meeting he has later today, I scan the messy kitchen and locate a pile of what looks like art projects of Becca's and old homework of Ben's, corrected and returned, that I never know what to do with. I'm about to move on when I uncover some legal-size envelopes.

"What's this?" I ask, holding up the mail as if Doug can see it, too. "Did you know about this?"

"Oh. Um," Doug says, which isn't an answer, so I give him a hint and wait for more.

"Mail."

"By the toaster?"

"Yes, by the toaster!" I say. "Which is *not* where we keep bills and other important-looking papers."

"I must have put them aside to show you and then forgot."

"How convenient of you."

He sighs. "Better check the dates. Some of them are probably past due. You're going to have to call."

Great. Bad credit is just what I need to make this day even better. "Why am I the one who has to call? This was your mistake!"

"I don't have *the time*, Lauren."

Like I do. "I detect some condescension in that statement," I say. "And I don't appreciate it."

"There is no 'condescension,'" he says, in a definitely condescending tone. "You're being dramatic."

"At least say you're sorry! And...argh, I am not being dramatic!" I slam the pantry door closed to prove it, but since the hinge is broken, it bounces right back open in my hand.

"It's mine," Ben says, his voice floating up from the basement playroom. "Mom!" he calls. "Becca won't give me back my Bakugan!"

"But we traded!" Becca says.

"Laney!" I say, knowing that she won't answer.

Fuck! I want to scream. Sometimes I feel like walking out on them and never looking back. *Here's the instruction manual*, I would say, flinging a blank spiral notebook over my shoulder, to the surprise of the entire Worthing contingent. *Have fun figuring it out without me!*

For the second time this morning, my pulse is racing. I'd love to blow up at someone, anyone, really, and just relieve the pressure mounting in my chest.

But it's 7:52.

I take a deep breath and turn back to the phone.

"Doug, I've gotta go. Before the kids kill each other. And before we do, too."

I put down the phone and check the time. "Kids!" I say. "Bus time!"

I really need Laney to appear this instant and take the kids to the bus stop so that I can get to work before the first bell rings. I mean, it's nice to live in the same town where I teach—my commute contains only four traffic lights, and if I time them right, I don't have to stop for any—but still. Cutting it this close is not my style, even if I am feeling more lax about my job since that fateful meeting with my principal last month.

"Laney!" I try one last time, her name echoing off the walls. Where the hell is she?

I hustle the kids out the door and down the driveway, still clutching the envelopes in my fist.

"Mom, you never take us to the bus!" Becca says. It sounds like an accusation.

"There's a first time for everything, Bec!" I chirp.

Ben runs ahead and calls out to some of the boys waiting at the curb. "Look at my new baseball cards!" he brags, pulling them out of his backpack. The small crowd of elementary school kids parts to let him in. They all seem immune to the light rain, while I huddle with Becca under her small pink ruffly umbrella.

Three moms in black workout leggings and different Lululemon jackets are standing together and laughing, each with a dog leash attached to her wrist. I look down at my tan pants, fancy raincoat, and ballet flats that pinch my toes.

When and if I ever quit my job, I'll celebrate by getting a puppy and a wardrobe filled with expensive, glam sweatshirts and matching spandex pants.

I should be friends with these women, but I'm not. Stay-at-home moms and working moms exist on different schedules, like humans and vampires. We inhabit the same world, but go about our business pretty separately. Sometimes I worry there will be blood when we collide.

"Hi!" I call out to the women, who break apart and look at me blankly. Then they return to their chatter.

"I'm Ben and Becca's mom." No one says anything in my direction, so I add, "Lauren?"

Still no response.

Anyone? Anyone?

This is getting embarrassing. I hide back under the umbrella.

Becca tries on my behalf. "This is my *mommy*!"

"Oh, hi!" one of the women says, coming forward. "We weren't ignoring you, sorry. We were just talking about someone, but now we're done." She's the tallest of the women, and she speaks very fast. "I'm Lisa," she adds.

"O...kay." I smile. "It wasn't me you were talking about, was it?" I glance over my shoulder in semi-mock paranoia.

"You're so funny!" Black Leggings Number Two adds. "But no." She has wild red hair and big thighs. "Patty." She points to herself. "And this is Pam." The third in the group is bone thin. She waves in my general direction, thereby using up four calories and getting a jump on her daily exercise.

"We're not talking about you unless you kicked your kids out of your car and left them alone on the streets of Alden to fend for themselves," Lisa adds by way of explanation.

"Not recently, no. Haven't done that for years, not since the kids were in diapers."

"She's a hoot!" Pam declares. One of the dogs barks in agreement.

I smile somewhat painfully.

"Lauren!" Lisa chastises. She takes a step closer to me; she's clearly the leader of the pack. "Don't you read the *Hadley Inquirer*? It was the front-page story this weekend. This working mom who was just completely overwhelmed decided to..." She trails off.

They all look at me expectantly.

"Um...I didn't have time?" I begin. "I'm a working mom who is completely overwhelmed?" It's meant as a joke of sorts, but it hangs in the air between us like a challenge.

Good way to make friends, Lauren.

"Well, you're missing out." Patty sniffs. On both the local gossip and the camaraderie forged by spreading local gossip, it seems.

"Too bad," Lisa adds as the bus lurches around the bend and stops in front of us.

They turn away from me in what can only be called a collective diss.

Let's just add this to my morning tally of Ways in Which My Life Sucks. Not that I'm keeping score.

"Bye, kids!" I call, the stack of mail fluttering over my head in my grand farewell gesture.

Ben and Becca smile and wave. My heart swells with love just as the school bus door closes and my children disappear from view.

The bus pulls away and a hearty gust of wind blows past me, Mary Poppins–style. I feel a definite shift in the air.

Only then do I notice the blue envelope.

After I wave to the departing school bus, that particular piece of mail gets separated from the others, caught by the wind and released from my grasp. Instead of flying away from me, however, the envelope drifts slowly and deliberately to the ground at my feet.

It's almost as if the letter is *daring* me to pick it up and read it.

CHAPTER 2

WHICH, OF COURSE, I DO.

It's a jury duty summons addressed to me.

How do I know this? Because written on the outside of the baby-blue envelope, in bold type so I won't miss it, are the words *Jury Duty Summons Enclosed. Immediate Attention.*

Damn Doug.

Hands shaking, I remove the tri-folded paper from the envelope and begin to read aloud, scanning the words quickly. "Your services are requested...yadda, yadda, yadda...County Courthouse ...yadda, yadda...ten a.m. on Monday, April tenth."

That's today.

"Failure to show up on appointed date...yadda, yadda... incarceration or fines. Fucking fuck me!" I cry out, sprinting back toward my house.

I explode into my front hall and race to the phone, jumping over Laney's coat and bag that lie in a heap in the middle of the floor. I try to find the substitute-hotline phone number pinned somewhere to the bulletin board at the small kitchen desk. "There it is!" I say, dialing furiously.

"Good morning to you, too," Laney scoffs in her lilting Spanish accent, passing me with an armful of laundry and attitude.

"Seriously?" I shout.

She whips her long black hair around the banister in response and disappears into the basement.

The substitute-service answering machine beeps. I leave the most frantic, discombobulated message known to man, pleading for a substitute to arrive by 9:30 this morning and take over my classroom for the remainder of the day. Then I grab my school bag, stuff the jury summons inside it, and clamber into my minivan with six minutes to spare before I'm officially late for work.

Weaving in and out of traffic, I pretend I'm playing Mario Cart Wii and get to school in less than four minutes.

The middle school parking lot is jammed with cars and I can't find a spot. "What the hell?" I ask the air, as if it will know why my day is already so royally screwed.

People are heading toward the gym en masse, and I remember that it's a local election day. Knowing he's still out on sick leave, I park in the assistant principal's space and sprint toward the building just as the first bell rings.

I take the steps of the turn-of-the-century schoolhouse two at a time and narrowly avoid bumping into one of the voters streaming out of the building.

"Excuse me," I say, wasting a half moment on pleasantries. The woman's perfume trails behind her, carrying the scent of hope mixed with summer flowers. She's dressed expensively, and her long ash-blond hair is bohemian perfection.

"Lauren?" the woman calls.

I turn back. "Shay?" I say, surprised that this specimen of flawlessness remembers me. We've only met a couple of times at PTA functions, where Shay Greene is an officer and I am an underling underachiever barely holding up the T in PTA.

I say the first thing that pops into my head. "So, who'd you vote for?" My heart is hammering in my chest and I'm silently counting down to the second bell. If I could have any super power, I'd want the ability to beam myself instantaneously from place to place at the snap of a finger.

"Myself, of course!" She laughs.

"Of course!" I say, pretending to know what the hell she's talking about. "Good luck, then! Gotta run!"

Shay waves good-bye. I watch her graceful descent, amazed that someone in four-inch heels can make walking down stairs look like floating.

And then I see the sign: VOTE HERE TODAY! SCHOOL BOARD OFFICERS ELECTION! POLLS OPEN 7 A.M. TO 9 P.M.

I push past a few more voters and dash down the hall like I'm really, really excited to be here.

....

My mailbox contains nothing except a small, handwritten note scribbled on our principal's personalized stationery, reading: *Please see me.*

Now, that can't be good, I think, leaving through the nurses' office door so as to avoid bumping into our fair leader, Martha Carrington, before homeroom.

I should probably inform her that I'll be leaving for the county courthouse as soon as my substitute shows up, but that will have to wait until I'm on my way out the door in an hour's time.

Usually, I would stop by Kat's classroom to say good morning, but since I don't want to be spotted and I'm running exceptionally late, I head directly to the middle school wing, slip inside my own classroom, and close the door behind me. *Safe,* I think. *At least for now.*

A nanosecond later, the bell rings and my homeroom students start pouring in. I take a deep breath, put on my happy teacher face, and say, "Welcome!"

Let the games begin.

A few minutes into a one-on-one reading conference during first period with a kid named Martin, it hits me: *He has not read this book.*

Problem is, neither have I.

It's a novel called *Ice Glory.* While I read tons and tons of young adult literature, this is one that I have missed. In fact, now that I think of it, when we were in the library last month and the kids were taking out books, Martin kept asking me about titles. "That's a good one; I think you'd like it!" I had said about *The Westing Game,* and, when he put it back on the shelf and picked up a Gary Paulsen novel instead, I had said, "He's my favorite author; I've read all of his books!" Finally, Martin found one I hadn't read. "It looks good," was all I could muster. And that's the one he selected.

And now he's bullshitting me with bizarre details that just wouldn't make sense in a story about ice hockey.

"Then the dad, he's the brain surgeon, gets into this car accident and is paralyzed from the waist down," Martin says.

"Wow," I say. "That's so...unexpected."

"I know!" Martin says, like he just can't believe it himself.

"So, how does it end?"

"With this huge alien invasion." He doesn't miss a beat, this kid.

I take the book from his hands and flip it over to study the blurb on the back. The story centers on a boy from a small town in Montana who wants to skate his way to fame and fortune. It's based on the true story of an Olympic gold medalist.

"Extraterrestrials, huh?" I ask, my eyes locked on his.

Martin squirms in his seat.

"Did you really read it?"

Martin makes an I-don't-know-don't-ask-me-I'm-just-the-messenger face, but he will not speak.

I believe Martin is pleading the fifth.

I look past Martin to where my New York State Middle School Association "Teacher of the Year 1998" plaque hangs forlornly on the wall, crooked and in need of a dusting. There had been a ceremony in Albany, a new dress, champagne filled with bubbles of hope. I shook hands with the governor, who suggested I come work for him, help overhaul the failing schools across the state.

But I had just met Doug, and I didn't want to move upstate and away from him and from the middle schoolers that I loved, for a job in educational policy.

When I first started teaching, and for quite a while after that, education was a field full of promise and excitement. I spoke at conferences nationwide and planned on using my classroom research to write books on educational theory. I created a writing inventory checklist now used by every teacher in my school district.

There was so much to do, to look forward to.

And now?

I still have that folder filled with research notes in the top drawer of my desk, and occasionally I revisit it. When I do, I get inspired all over again and promise myself that during the summer I'll write up a proposal and send it to an educational journal for review. But then I never do.

I shouldn't be so hard on myself. I mean, I recently bought a small notebook to carry in my pocketbook and jot down ideas for classroom research. But most of the pages are filled with lists of things I need to buy at CVS.

The fact is, I'm rooted in the great countdown of tenured life. In twenty-four years, I can retire at eighty percent of my salary and with sixty-five percent of my sanity, with a gold watch and a gray head of hair.

I turn away from the plaque to study the rest of the sixth

graders in my first-period class. They are quiet, hunched over their books, but are they reading? And how much do I care if they are or are not? Is everyone just going through the motions and faking their way through, trying to coast?

Or is it just this one little asshole?

I look back at Martin, his eyes too big for his face, his head too big for his body, his hair cut unevenly. At the open house last fall, his father insisted in front of one hundred other families that I should be teaching the composition of e-mails, not essays, because that's a skill these kids are going to need in the real world.

I decide, *Nah, it's just this asshole.*

What is the appropriate sentence for Martin, book faker, in this particular case?

I'm thinking about one of three punishments. I could make him reread *Ice Glory* and we could conference again in a week. Or, better, I could select another book, one that I know inside out, and make him read that one. In fact, I could take that one step further and say that for the last three months of the school year I will handpick all of his reading material and get written as well as oral reports from him each time he finishes a book.

I know what will happen here. Instead of reports I'll get phone calls from Martin's parents. I'll have to defend my point of view to the guidance counselor. Next thing you know, I'll be roped into spending more time with Martin than I do already, giving him help after school and during lunch recess, eating at my desk instead of with friends in the teachers' café. And all the while, he'll continue to look at me with those bulging eyes and that crooked hair, stressing me out with his inherent awfulness. Eventually, I'll fantasize about running him over with my car in the parking lot, and I'll end up in jail.

Whose punishment is that, I ask you?

"Hey, Martin," I say, snapping back to attention.

"Yeah?" He looks at his watch. There's only a minute left in the class period and he's counting down the seconds.

"Good job." I smile, giving him a thumbs-up. Like a rabbit freed from the jaws of a raccoon, he darts from the room, bewildered but not unpleased.

The other children file past me and I wave good-bye, wish them a nice day, remind them of the homework.

A weight lifts from my shoulders. Like Martin, I feel like I've just dodged a bullet.

My substitute is nowhere to be found. Neither is a pen. I scribble an unimaginative lesson plan for the remaining sections of sixth-grade English, using a hot pink highlighter, and leave it in the center of my cluttered desk, hoping the sub can find it.

Then I call down to the guidance counselor's office, explaining my situation. "So you're going to miss the lunchtime grading session for the state exams?" she asks accusingly.

Oh crap. Forgot about that.

"It looks that way, Shirley," I say.

"Well, that's not fair to the other members of the English Department, who are going to have to work longer now to grade your papers as well as theirs. They'll probably have to stay after school."

I picture the seven other members of my department silently cursing me for my absence while they sit, hunched over test booklets, trying to decipher chicken scratch and determine whether the responses are worth a random score of a 3 or a 4. I search my brain for a solution. "Maybe...I can...how about if I come in early tomorrow to do it?"

"You know they have to be completed today. The state needs them by the end of the week." She sighs.

Like I've planned this or something. Like I've concocted a lame excuse to get out of my responsibilities.

"Shirley, I have *jury duty* for God's sake! It's not like I'm going on a tropical vacation! I've had a tough morning, okay? So just...let it go!" I slam the receiver back onto the phone, knocking the whole thing off the wall.

"Jeez!" I cry. My hands are shaking as I pick up the phone and reattach it. Now I'm going to have to buy Shirley some Lindor truffles. From experience, I know she likes the peanut butter ones.

I'd like to crawl under my desk and hide from the world for a while, but there's a knock at my classroom door.

It's my principal, Martha Carrington.

Of course it is.

And she doesn't look happy to see me.

Naturally.

....

"Come in!" I say with fake enthusiasm, pulling the door open and making a sweeping gesture with my hands.

Martha's neat hair is brown and her small eyes are brown and her fuddy-duddy clothes are brown, and I can't for the life of me determine how old she is. Fifty-five? Seventy-one? A hundred and forty-three?

She enters my classroom stiffly and does a lap around the perimeter, like a general surveying his conquered territory after battle. I see the disorganized space from her point of view and cringe inwardly. My classroom is a safe haven for abandoned items that never make their way to the lost-and-found box at the end of the hallway. Currently, I am providing shelter for a homeless sweatshirt, soccer cleats, a football, and several textbooks from other classes. There is a pile of newspapers in the right hand corner; glue sticks and scissors are scattered on desks.

"We're just wrapping up our journalism unit," I say, by way of explanation. I pick up some loose feathers and tuck them into my pants pockets. She wouldn't understand.

Martha turns and studies me, left eye twitching.

"So...?" I begin, as a way of politely asking, *What the hell are you doing in here, when I could be having a cup of coffee with Kat and chatting away my free period before heading off to the courthouse for the rest of my awful day?*

"You don't seem ill," she states flatly.

"That's because I'm not," I counter.

"Then we have a serious problem here, Mrs. Worthing."

"Martha, call me Lauren, please." I say this every time we've spoken since she first arrived at our school five years ago. I think she does it so that I'll call her Mrs. Carrington.

You see how well that's working.

She crosses the room to my desk and begins typing furiously at the keypad of my computer, logging me out and logging herself in without asking my permission. Then she actually sits down in my desk chair. I stand awkwardly at her side, looking on. Her beady little rodent eyes meet mine. "My records tell me that you have been absent from school nine times this year."

"Nine times?" I ask, with actual surprise. I thought it was more like six.

"Yes, Mrs. Worthing—Lauren—*nine times.*"

Indeed, the blue screen staring back at me does reflect that information. "Wow. I guess I really *have* been sick this year." I pull up a chair and sit across from my own desk.

"I *guess,*" Martha intones, trying to match my vernacular. I feel like throwing in some "yo's" and "whatev's" just to hear her repeat them back to me.

The thought makes me stifle a chuckle, but it still doesn't explain why she's visiting me in my classroom, or why she seems to be upset with me. *Again.* Thinking back to our last meeting, I tuck my clammy palms under my thighs to keep my hands from wanting to strangle her.

"Yet this morning's notes from my secretary show that you have called for a substitute for later this morning."

"Oh!" I say, understanding now. "Did she not show up?" I ask. "I need her here by nine thirty."

"The substitute is not the problem." Here she stops, seems to consider what to say, like plotting her next move in a game of Battleship. She tilts her head and raises a finger to the side of her face, stroking a grotesquely large mole just under her right ear. I try to stay focused on her eyes, but she doesn't make it easy. "The problem is...where are you going?" Her voice deepens as she leans across my desk and enunciates clearly. "*Ten* absences is your legal maximum as stated in the bylaws of the latest contract, and today *will be your tenth* unexcused absence for the year. It is only April, and I fear..." I let her go on for a while, thinking of the way her inner computer wires are probably getting all crossed and creating sparks that are shocking her ankles.

I love to think of her spontaneously combusting.

Only then do I speak. "But Martha, this is *not* an unexcused absence."

There is momentary silence. "But why ever not, Mrs. Worthing? Lauren."

I try not to smile. "Because I've been called for jury duty!" It's the first time I've been able to admit this with actual enthusiasm.

"Oh!" Her tone changes immediately. The American flag in the left corner of the classroom seems to wave at me. I imagine that a fastidious, rule-loving person like her is all about public service to one's country. She leans back in my chair, pleasant now, good cop

and bad cop all wrapped up in one suburban middle school principal. "I didn't realize."

Milking it for all it's worth, I smile coldly and say, "No, it
seems you did not." *Ha, ha, take that! Ka-pow! Right back atcha!*

I stand, willing this to be over. Maybe I can make it down to
Kat's classroom after all.

Martha shoots me a look. "We're not finished here, Mrs.
Worthing. Lauren."

Immediately, I sit. *Heel, good doggie.* I return to staring at the
tiny pulsating blue vein next to her eye.

"As I mentioned to you in our last meeting, you are, in general,
a disappointment to me."

This registers in my stomach before it hits my brain. I lean
forward just enough to cover my belly from any more blows.

"Have you nothing to say to that?"

"I'm not sure," I say. "I'm not sure I understand."

"Typical," she responds, clearly offended.

"Typical what?" I ask. Blonde? English teacher? Frazzled
mother?

Actually, now that I've asked it, I'm not sure I want to hear
her answer. I just want to get out of this classroom, much like
Martin must have felt a few minutes ago under my gaze.

"Mrs....Lauren," she begins, tapping my hot-pink highlighter
against the linoleum desktop. "You need to be *clear* when you are
calling for a substitute. You had me quite distraught for nothing! I
wasted seventeen minutes of time on you this morning, all because
of your lack of *precision*. Plus, do you think I haven't noticed how
your performance has dropped off in recent months? You arrive
just moments before homeroom and leave just moments after dis-
missal. I notice. I *see*. You refuse to serve on the committee for
children with—what's it called..."

"Differentiated Learning?"

"No, no that one..."

"Allergies and Asthma?"

"No, no, no..."

"Same-Sex Parenting?"

"We decided against that committee..."

Although, now that I'm mentioning them, I realize how many
opportunities I have turned down this year.

And then she remembers. "Homework Aversion Disorder!"

"That's a thing?"

"Yes, and you reneged at the last moment! You never signed the paperwork. The committee folded because of your irresponsibility."

"That wasn't me!" I say, truly concerned. "I've never even heard of such a committee."

"You gave me a verbal commitment, Mrs. Lauren. And then you missed the meeting and never filed the forms."

Wouldn't I remember giving her such a promise?

It's gaslighting, I'm telling you. She makes me think that I'm crazy, remaining calm as I come undone.

"That's not true—" I begin, but she silences me with her palm.

"The point is..." Here she stands, stretching her long torso across my desk to get as close to me as she possibly can. "I. Am. Watching. You."

"O...kay," I say. I've never in my life hit someone, but right now, I wonder what it would feel like if my fist made contact with her aquiline nose. Better to do that than to burst into tears.

"Which is why *I've* decided to be your substitute teacher for the day." Martha tilts her head upward, the steadiness of her chin challenging me to disagree.

"Excellent," I choke out. "Let me just grab a few things before I go."

I quickly take the hastily written lesson plan and stick it inside a folder of essays that I clutch to my chest. Then I speed walk my way the hell out of there.

Martha's so confident, I'm sure she'll think of a brilliant assignment with which to fill the time.

In fact, wouldn't it be fun to get placed on a really long court case just to spite her? Okay, fine. I'll take that back. I'm desperate, but I'm not delusional.

I call Kat's classroom from my cell phone as I'm getting into my car. I can instantly tell that her kindergarteners are within earshot.

"Where the truck are you?" She never says hello like a normal person. "You bailed on coffee talk time."

"You cannot even *imagine* my morning," I say. "Look out your window and wave. I'm in the VP's spot."

Five seconds later, a wrist loaded up with silver bangles emerges from a window on the second floor. Instead of waving, she points her middle finger at me.

When she's back on the line, I say, "Classy."

"Why are you getting here so late?" Kat asks.

"Nah, Kitty-Kat, I'm just leaving." I put her on speakerphone and explain as I drive through the suburban, tree-lined streets of Hadley and into the city of Alden, where the county courthouse is located. "And the kicker is, Martha's my sub."

"Love it!" She laughs. "I'm gonna have my students call over there all day and keep hanging up when she answers."

"Kat," I say. "I thought we talked about prank calls."

"What? *Someone* has to teach these vital lessons to the younger generation. In the age of the Internet, phony phone calls are going to get lost, unless, of course, I work my tass off to keep the ancient art alive."

"Whatever," I say. "At least *you'll* be having fun today."

"Whaddaya mean? Jury duty's the best!" There is a muffled sound on the line, and then I hear Kat talking to a student. "Lexie, stop pinching Jane or else I'm going to have to pinch you so you know what it feels like and, therefore, develop empathy."

"Kat," I chastise.

"Empathy is this year's district imperative," she explains, back on the line.

"Not what the Hadley School Board meant."

"Live it up today, Lauren. I'm telling you, JD is *the bomb*. I went over to the courthouse last month to volunteer for service, after a particularly rough day in the sandbox. I was like, what could be better than a few quiet, contemplative days in a municipal courtroom? *Anything* is better than kindergarten. Only, they didn't want me."

"Imagine that." I navigate my way through the downtown streets and turn into the parking lot for the courthouse. "Tragic."

"Speaking of which, I really need to talk to you. Can you swing by on your way home? I'll be here late, filling out report cards."

"Will do, Kitty-Kat," I say, slamming the door to my minivan and pressing the lock button on the remote. "Over and out."

....

With only five minutes to spare before my summons blows up in my hand, or whatever, I hightail it across the street, cursing the fact that I didn't have enough quarters to feed the meter for more than two hours.

Inside the front entrance, I follow the snaking line of visitors through the metal detectors.

"No cell phones, Kindles, iPads, laptops or other electronic devices allowed inside the courthouse," a security guard drones. He must say the same thing a hundred times a morning. Then I realize what it is that he's actually saying.

"You're kidding me!" This catches the attention of the people directly ahead of and behind me. "I can't have my cell phone? Not even on vibrate? Like, at all?"

"Best thing to do is take it back to your car," a man in a suit and tie says, nodding sympathetically. "They can hold it for you here, but I'm not sure I'd trust them."

What are they gonna do, play with my Barbie Dress Up app all day? I want to ask, but I am too busy running back across the busy street in my own game of Frogger, my giant shoulder bag banging against my hip.

Total hassle.

Two minutes and forty-three seconds later, I skid back across the polished marble, phoneless. The suit is now at the front of the line; he catches my eye and waves at me to join him.

"Thanks," I pant, pushing some hair out of my eyes.

"Have a great day." He winks. "And relax. You look guilty of something."

I manage a half smile and look around for directions. A sign marked JURY DUTY points me down a corridor and into a waiting room.

"Summons, please," a bailiff requests, hand outstretched. He yawns.

I tear off the top portion of the paperwork and hand it over to him.

"Now just have a seat and wait. You may be called today, you may not."

"Really? Because I was kind of hoping..."

"To get it over with today, I know," he says.

"To get some change for the meter, actually, so that I don't get a ticket and wind up back in court!"

He shrugs, letting me know how deeply unmoved he is by both my pressing need for quarters and my sad attempt at irony.

I enter a rather large lecture hall, like the kind of place where college Psych 101 would meet. It's all blond wood and modern in feel. The open, airy quality is not what I was expecting from a county courthouse. I select a spot in the very front section of the room to seem more eager for service and, therefore, less likely to get picked for it. I expect to get some direction from a judge, but none is forthcoming. So I reach into my bag and start chipping away at the paperwork.

During the first hour I grade an entire class set of ridiculously depressing essays, rife with grammatical inventions, and write out checks, including an overdue payment for our electricity. For the first time in a long time, I feel productive, ahead of the game. The room has a soft hum about it as people go about their work. It's calm and silent, buzzing with thought like a library.

I stand and stretch, taking a look around. About fifty people are scattered around the room, heads bent over books and notebooks. Not having cell phones and computers inside the courthouse has a curious effect on us all. Without the ringing, beeping, and pulsing of an immediate connection to the outside world, it's almost as if there is no outside world at all. Real time is suspended.

I have nothing I have to do, nowhere I have to be, nothing I have to worry about. I am unreachable, unfindable.

I kind of love it.

I dig in my faux-leather school bag, remembering the chick-lit paperback I've been carrying around with me for the past few months. Good thing I don't own a Kindle or I'd be staring at the ceiling tiles right about now. Finding my place in the story, I settle back into my seat and disappear. The next time I check my watch, another forty-five minutes have flown by.

That's when it hits me: Kat may have a point about jury duty.

This may just be the best day of my entire life.

CHAPTER 3

IT'S JUST SO *QUIET* HERE. Like a spa. Or an ashram. Too bad they don't serve organic unsweetened teas and let us walk around in terrycloth robes and slippers.

A worrisome thought pops into my head about ten minutes later, as I'm finishing another chapter of this awesome book about absolutely nothing. What if this is it? What if I get excused later on and I have to go back to school tomorrow?

That can't happen. It just *cannot*.

I must find a way to stay here, in this tranquil place, with all these peaceful people, and hide from real life for as long as is humanly possible.

The truth—absurd as it may be—is this: I need to get placed on a jury. I *want t*o get picked for a jury.

A baritone voice breaks my trance. "Jurors 203 and 204, and all jury summons numbers 211 to 221. Please come to the front and enter the juror waiting room to my left," the judge says, pointing with his gavel.

My heart is beating fast with anticipation. I want to jump up quickly, but now I have to think of appearances in the opposite way that I had previously. *Take your time, Lauren, look like this is the last place you want to be.* I catch one woman looking my way and roll my eyes at her, like, *ain't it a bitch?*

But, really, I'm like, *juror waiting room, hooray*! That's one step closer to reaching my new goal. I've made it to the next round! Feeling a bit jittery, I collect my belongings (slowly) and follow people out.

The juror selection process is kind of like being a contestant on *American Idol,* only without any talent other than being American.

The waiting room is aptly named, with lots of seating and several clocks. I grab a chair around one of the circular tables and smile to a woman across from me. Then I open my book and scan the first page again: *Three women step off a plane. It sounded like the start of a joke.* A guy named Josh watches this scene unfold at the airport, thinking it might be a nice way to start a short story. Please, Elin Hilderbrand, take me with you to Nantucket, I beg. Conjuring up the smell of hydrangeas in July, I find my place on the bottom of page seventy-six.

Two pages later, a different bailiff enters the room and clears his throat. "Will those people just called from the jury selection room please follow me."

"Where are we goin'?" some guy calls out from the back.

"Voir dire," he announces. "Room 704. Please stay together as we approach the elevator banks."

"I cannot believe this," a woman complains as we step onto the elevator together. "Just my luck. You ever get one of those feelings, like something is supposed to happen? No matter what?" she asks me, running her hands through her cropped blond hair. "As soon as I got the summons, I just *knew* I'd get picked." She shakes her head slowly back and forth, almost talking to herself. "I just *knew* it, goddammit."

"Me, too!" I say, framing in a new light the magical moment this morning as the bus pulled away from the curb and the blue envelope floated toward me. She looks at me questioningly. "I mean, *me, too*. Goddammit."

"I have so much to do at work," a young guy in a suit pipes in. "I just started this job and can't afford to be out."

"Take it up with the judge," comes a monotone response from the bailiff, staring up at the lit numbers. He must hear this kind of babble all the time.

"I did," the suit replies, sounding defeated.

"Well, maybe you won't be right for the case," I add.

"Yeah," the guy from the waiting room agrees. "To get out of a case, I plan on being a total *ist*," he confides.

"An *ist*?" several of us echo back.

"You know." He gestures, his right hand raised, pushing against the air for emphasis. "Racist, sexist, communist, whatever it takes. I'm goin' in as a total asshole."

"Shouldn't be too hard," the woman with short hair sings under her breath.

"What was that, sweetheart?" he asks, moving toward us as the elevator doors open. He's a stocky guy, wearing ripped jeans splattered with paint. Seven hundred keys jangle from his hip as he pushes through the crowd.

I turn and smile. "Oh, it was nothing! She just hopes that strategy works for you!"

"*Sweetheart!*" she adds. We power walk to keep up with the bailiff as he takes us down a long hallway.

"By the way, I'm Lauren."

"Carrie. Glad to meet you." She makes a little wave in the air as we are ushered into a big room with modern windows. A few rows of white folding chairs are neatly lined up in the center of the room, but the bailiff instructs us to sit in other chairs around the perimeter of the room for now.

Entering behind the bailiff are two men in suits. One is tall with sandy hair and the other is short, with jet-black, slicked-back hair and a goatee. Right away, I don't like him.

I'm so impartial.

Think like a juror, become a juror. This little mantra enters my mind and I hold fast to it. *Think like a juror, become a juror.* No one is guilty until proven so. No, wait. That's wrong. Put it in the positive. Everyone is innocent until proven guilty.

The tall guy speaks first. "Ladies and gentlemen, good morning. I am Mr. John Silvan, and to my right is Mr. Thomas Parnell. We are the lawyers on this case. We are here to speak with you this morning because we need to assemble a jury."

"And we need to do it quickly," Parnell adds.

Silvan nods his head. They both clutch clipboards with little pieces of paper attached to them. I feel like I'm in *CSI: Alden.* That's why, in my head, I've decided to call everyone by their last names. I am imagining the crisp television theme music playing in the background as these guys speak.

"This is a civil case in which a mother is suing a daycare for neglecting her child," Silvan explains.

Oh shit. Really? I sink back in my chair, instantly deflated. Of all the voir dires in all the world, I have to walk into this one. Child neglect! I bet when the lawyers sat down this morning to imagine an ideal jury, they were like, *You know, what we really need to balance out this jury will be a mother of two who is also a teacher.*

Someone really on the inside, with lots of experience and bias. As soon as I open my mouth, I am so getting kicked out of here.

Parnell picks up where Silvan left off. "Now, whether the accused did or did not do this, and to what extent the law is in the daycare's favor or the working mother's favor, is what you will decide if you are placed on this case. For this trial, you will merely look at the facts, hear from several witnesses, and examine the law to decide if the facility and its owners are at all guilty of any wrongdoing."

"Now, I am going to call forward a few of you to sit here, in the twelve seats in the center of the room," Silvan says.

I'm the fourth one called. Carrie is also called, as is Sweetheart. Before long, there are twelve of us seated, two rows of six, with a circle of others looking on.

There are a lot of people here trying to get *out* of jury duty, but I am not one of them. I take a furtive look around the room to size up the competition.

There's one. She's a gray-haired black woman actually *knitting* in the corner. She's got all the markings of your typical juror—old, domestic, with time on her hands—and I scowl at her, trying to will her away. She looks up through her bifocals, probably having felt my death stare. I turn away just in time.

Today she's going down.

Because I have to get put on this case.

I have to get a leave of absence from my life.

"Please raise your hand if you have children." Up goes my hand.

"Please raise a hand if you have ever spent time away from your child or children. Perhaps you have traveled overnight on a business trip, or taken a vacation without them. Perhaps, like the defense in this case, you are a working parent who has put his or her child in daycare or preschool." Not all of the people with children raise their hands, but several do. Including me.

This is kinda fun.

"Please raise your hand if you work full-time, outside of your home." Two women do not raise their hands, but the rest of us do. *Stay-at-home moms,* I think.

Just for the fun of it, I wiggle my fingers around in the air, like the A-plus students in my classes do, so that I can really be seen and remembered.

But, instead of noticing me, the lawyers start asking those women questions. Things like: "Do you work from home?" "Do you work part-time?" and "What is your primary occupation?" As I expected, both are stay-at-home moms. They are so off the case. I picture them walking out of the courtroom together a few minutes into the future, honking good-bye to each other from identical minivans.

Sayonara, I think.

"Please raise your hand if you work with children," Parnell asks, and suddenly, it's show time. I will make this work to my advantage. I push my hair from my face, raise my hand, and meet his eyes.

"Ms...." Parnell scans his clipboard for my name.

"Worthing," we say simultaneously.

"Yes, Ms. Worthing. Could you tell me what exactly it is you do?"

"I try to teach eleven-year-olds where to put their commas," I say. Good-natured laughs are sprinkled around the room. Parnell joins in, sport that he is.

"Yes, well. And for how long have you been...teaching English, I presume?"

"Fifteen years," I say, shaking my head at the ridiculousness of it, at the way time has passed, at the fact that my students have moved on, growing and changing, while I am still in that same classroom year after year, the same *Harry Potter* posters clinging to the walls, without anything but a Teacher of the Year plaque from the last century and a trophy of a golden apple to show for it.

"Ms. Worthing, are you all right?"

"Oh, great!" I shout, too loudly for the cramped room packed with hostile potential jurors. *Keep it together, Lauren*, I chastise myself. *Keep your eyes on the prize.*

"I was just wondering...how are those commas coming these days?"

"Great! Love 'em!" I say.

"Really?" he asks.

I sigh and think about the last pathetic quiz I gave. I know that I should be upbeat and firm about my commitment to education if I want to get a coveted spot in the jury box, but I just can't muster the energy to lie like that. Martin and Martha already took all the lying I could dish out.

But I really need this case.

Don't I?

I look around the room and into the eyes of these two lawyers in their cheap suits, and I just feel tired. All these people get up each day and do their work and come home and fight with their kids and make love to their spouses and fall asleep only to do it all again the next day.

Life is boring, predictable. And no amount of jury duty is really going to change that. Not in the long run, anyway.

I open my mouth. What comes out is the truth, the whole truth, and nothing but.

"No one knows where to put the commas. Ever. Did you know that there's something like eleven uses for them in the English language, and that sixth graders can't think of more than three? And the great irony is that just when you've actually taught the children all the uses of commas, it's June and they leave you, only to be replaced by children *who do not know where to put their commas*! My life is like a broken record, playing the same verse over and over again. I'm Sisyphus!"

I notice the hush that has fallen over the room.

Parnell gives Sylvan a look. The he approaches me. "So, Ms. Worthing, would you say that overworked teachers—good, decent people like yourself—might not always be recognized and appreciated for all they do? Might, in fact, require mental-health breaks from time to time?"

Voir dire. To speak the truth.

I sigh. "In fact, that's why I'm hoping to stay here, to get put on a jury. For a little break. From grammar. And...my husband, my kids...other stuff. I'd kind of like to volunteer for service." I'm so fucked.

"Jury duty as a break from life..." Parnell looks up at the crowd. "Now, *that's* a new one!"

Suddenly, the guy's a comedian. This is the jolliest voir dire on record at the Alden County Courthouse. Everyone's slapping their knees and wiping their eyes, it's all so funny.

To everyone but me. *Hey, people,* I want to call out, *this is my life. I have to use jury duty as an excuse to get a little me time! You should all be sobbing at my feet, it's so pathetic.*

After asking a few more questions, the lawyers take a five-minute conference break, absenting themselves from the room. I stand and look around, preparing to move back to my seat by the window, and possibly to the parking lot, since I'm sure to be dismissed. But then the bailiff is asking us to sit again and Parnell and Silvan are back.

"Ladies and gentlemen, we'd like to do just one more thing here with the twelve of you before moving on."

The lawyers call out some of our names and have us rearrange ourselves accordingly. "Yes, Mrs. Worthing, please take the fourth seat right there. And Mr. Grady, seat five, and Mrs. Anglisse, yes, right there..." He scans the seats in front of him before finishing his thought. "And that makes ten of you, correct?"

Parnell looks at the two rows of us, and we look back at him. The two stay-at-home moms have been ousted and are fidgeting awkwardly in the corner, like the last ones picked for kickball.

"That's it. Eight jurors and two alternates. Ladies and gentlemen, thank you very much for your time and patience. We have our jury."

Okay, maybe it is a little bit funny.

Actually, hysterical is more like it. It's 12:30 on Monday and we've been dismissed for the day. "Report back to the courthouse tomorrow morning at nine thirty sharp," the bailiff tells us, handing out our special parking passes. "Place these on your dash and you'll get in to our jurors' lot. It's located directly under this building, where the spots are not metered. No need for quarters!"

"Great!" I exclaim.

Carrie is not amused. "I'm on a case. I knew it. This sucks."

"Indeed!" I add. "Wanna go shopping? Get some lunch?"

She studies me hard before responding. I meet her eyes, which are rimmed in too much black eyeliner. She's older than me, by about a decade, perhaps. End of her forties. "Lauren, I gotta get back to work. If this case is going to go on for a full week like they say, then I need to use this time to get set in the office."

"Oh, of course!" I nod in agreement. "I just thought, you know, something quick before heading *back* to work." I look at my watch. "I guess I should just go now, too. If I hurry, I can be there in time for sixth period."

We head down in the elevator together, Carrie checking her watch and me pushing back some cuticles on my right hand.

In the glossy marble hallway on the first floor, we part ways. "Well, see ya tomorrow, I guess," Carrie says with a nod, half-distracted by thoughts of work.

"Yeah...see you then." I wave, turning the other way and pushing through the heavy glass doors of the modern high-rise.

The crisp sun surprises me, and I look up to see that the clouds have disappeared.

My mind knows that I should return to work, to the over-achieving students in my sixth-period honors class, all of whom read more than I assign, even though I ask them not to. Do you know what it's like to read the rumble scene of *The Outsiders* aloud to an audience that has heard it all before?

It's a drag.

I find my minivan, drop some more quarters into the meter, and keep on walking.

Bye-bye, sixth period. So long, Ponyboy. It's a beautiful day indeed, I think, as I head down the street in search of a salon and a deluxe mani-pedi.

CHAPTER 4

"NO, YOU DID NOT!" Kat screams in my ear.

"Yes, I so did!" I scream back. The ladies in the nail salon are shooting me dirty looks, so I cradle my cell phone under my ear, collect my stuff, and head outside. "I got on a civil case. For an entire week."

"I hate you."

"I know. I would hate me, too, if I were you, stuck in school. Kat, you were *so right*."

"Now, that's a shocker."

"They also selected jurors for a criminal case today, manslaughter or something, and that one's supposed to go on for like two or three weeks, but, you know, the one I got on is still pretty good."

"Manslaughter." Kat sighs. "What a beautiful word." There is silence on both ends as we let this sink in. "So, where are you now? At the courthouse?"

"Nope. Salon! Got out at twelve thirty," I say, finding my way back to the parking lot behind the county office buildings.

"Will you come visit me in my prison cell later, like you said you would? I've really got something to tell you."

"Why so mysterious?" Gingerly, I reach into my bag for my car keys, trying not to smudge my nails.

"Because the Oompa Loompas are on their way back from art."

"Catchy. You should use that term at the open house next year."

"I should find a new job, is what I should do."

"Yes, I believe we've been over that one before. Maybe teaching isn't your calling." I start the car and pull into traffic.

Kat is quiet for a minute and I switch to speakerphone. When she speaks again, her voice is barely above a whisper. "Maybe it isn't. But then...what is?"

I sigh, thinking about my own questions and uncertainties, my own life's dilemmas. "I don't know, Kitty-Kat. I really don't. See you in an hour or so."

"Where you off to now?"

"Sophie's."

"Ooh...have fun."

I pull up Sophie's long, winding driveway and find a space between the Porsche convertible and one of the handyman's trucks. There is always commotion at Sophie's. Today, several workers are on the flat-topped roof of the contemporary glass fortress that is Sophie's home, calling out in Portuguese as they pass tools and supplies to one another. The gardeners are here as well, their mowers drowning out the sound of the four dogs of different shapes and sizes barking on the other side of Sophie's front door.

I think I ring the bell, but actually cannot hear it, so I wait, waving and talking to the anxious pooches pawing the other side of the glass. "Where's your mommy today, huh? Do you have lots of goodies to show me, doggies? New merch?" They jump on top of one another and push one another out of the way, nails alternatively clawing against the floor-to-ceiling windows and tapping against the marble entryway.

"Hold on! Hold on! I'm *coming*!" I hear Sophie call as the churn of the lawn mowers die. She glides across the landing from the far side of the house, a brown toy poodle nipping at her heels.

Sophie is about fifty years old and very round. Because of her amorphous size and shape, she tends to wear lots of black, flowy clothes that carry the breeze in them and balloon up around her, so you cannot tell where she ends and the fabric begins. On top of the outfit is always a colorful shawl or a scarf or a wrap of some sort that adds a bit of gypsy flare. Her hair is permanently helmeted into a stiff, glossy black bob. She wears bright lipsticks to match the shade on her long fingernails.

"Lauren!" she cries. She hugs me with one arm while simultaneously using her boots to kick back the dogs and close the door behind me. "Long time no see! What a nice surprise! It's not even time yet for your annual birthday purchase, is it? When you called, I was like, *no way*! And then I looked at the time and wondered why you weren't teaching. Not that it's any of my business." One penciled-in eyebrow is cocked as if to add, *but of course I'm hoping you'll tell me why anyway.*

I delay answering her by asking about her daughters, Gigi, Bebe, and Coco, all of whom I taught at some point in middle school and none of whom I can tell apart.

The girls are all doing well at college, and we continue making small talk as we head up the stairs and into Sophie's expansive living room. The entire thing is done in crisp white, from the couches to the brick fireplace to the shelves lining one wall. The far wall has the same floor-to-ceiling windows as the foyer, beyond which lies the recently manicured lawn and a pool, not yet open for the season.

But what makes the living room unique is not the all-white décor or the breathtaking view beyond. It is the handbags.

Covering every nook in every couch, covering every inch of every shelf, lined up neatly across the glass coffee table and against the fireplace, and propped atop, astride, and next to the Mies van der Rohe chair and ottoman, are handbags.

Sophie's pristine, high-ceilinged, light-filled living room is holy.

Here is where rich ladies come to pray.

Gucci, Prada, Chanel. Amen.

Judith Leiber, Louis Vuitton, Ferragamo. Amen.

Balenciaga, Chloe, Bottega. Amen.

And, every once in a while...Hermès Birkins and Kellys! Can I get a *Hallelujah* from the crowd? Amen.

Sophie, who used to work in fashion, had been searching for a way to work from home when her kids were small. She contacted some fab friends looking to trade their bags for cash, and the next thing she knew, her living room was open for business.

Sophie gives an entirely new meaning to the concept of the mom who works from home.

"I'm the bag lady!" she boasts whenever I introduce her to a new client. "Look at me. I have bags under my eyes and bags under my chins. I even have bags under my arms that I won't show you for fear of scaring you away. I do not have a body made for clothes." Here, she always pauses dramatically and takes a step closer to the newcomer. "I have a body meant for handbags. And I want to share my love of bags *with you*."

Women melt at those words.

I am not one of Sophie's most devout clients, but I do like to, you know, pay my respects every once in a while. Once a year, I celebrate getting older by spending some of my hard-earned teaching salary on a gorgeous designer bag. And the rest of the time? I buy regular bags. Lots of 'em. Doug likes to joke that I was born—or, at any rate, bred—in a handbag.

As I come fully into view of the living room, I am overwhelmed, as usual. There is just so much to see, so much to touch. All of it is sexy, and all of it comes with Sophie's testimonies. There is soft, tan, fringed suede ("isn't that *luscious*") and bumpy black leather ("it's ostrich, you know, ridiculously high-end") and slouchy and quilty and patent...oh my!

Sophie picks up a large red bag with interlocking Gs splattered all over it and a wooden shoulder strap. "Now, I know this is not your style, Lauren, but isn't it just *fierce*?"

I make a face and tilt my head. "Not so sure."

She shakes her hairsprayed helmet at me. "How long have we known each other? Eight, ten years? You always go for the safe bag. The classic. Everything about you is sort of..." She looks me up and down. "*Conservative*. You need to break out a bit. Try something messy, less structured, more...fun!" And with that, she throws me a shockingly purple Balenciaga motorcycle bag covered in hardware.

For good measure, I sling it over my shoulder and pose in the mirror against one wall. "Yeah, nope."

"Today's the day. I can just sense it," she says, clearly not deterred. On tiptoe, she weaves in and out of the piles of bags, wiggling her fingers over them like a magician conjuring a rabbit from a hat.

And then she stops, bends over, and grabs one. It is a large, somewhat slouchy, dark blue Chloe. I actually gasp upon seeing it.

"Ta-dah!" she announces triumphantly.

"It's so...rock-and-roll!" I gush, immediately taking it from her and putting it over my arm. "It's seriously glam." I turn one way, then the other. "I love it." I size up my reflection, as if I'm another woman. "I'm just not sure it's me."

"It's *so* you," Sophie concludes. "The new you."

As I stare at my reflection, I think, *Maybe it's actually the old me. Coming back.* In high school and college, I used to dress sort of funky. I used to be playful and edgy and...interesting.

What the hell happened to me? When did I start to equate "growing up" with being dull and conservative? What's the big deal about breaking out a bit, being a little glam, a little fun?

I smile and tell Sophie I'll take it.

I eventually end up with the Chloe bag tucked like a poodle at my feet and a cup of tea in my hand. From time to time I reach down and stroke the soft leather as if it actually is my new pet: dead calf. Sophie and I have taken a break from posing in front of the mirror with the bags (which all look great on her; she's the best model for her merchandise) and are sitting cross-legged in an available corner of her living room floor.

"This just occurred to me...how do you entertain?" I ask, looking around. Even her dining room table, on the other side of the fireplace, has bags piled high across it.

"Oh, I don't!" She laughs. "I don't like cooking. And because of my business"—she gestures around the room—"I feel like I am always entertaining. It's a tad exhausting, actually."

"So is my job," I say.

"Yes, work is...work." She shrugs. "Otherwise it would be called something else. Speaking of which, you never did explain...why aren't you at school today? Mental-health day?"

I look at her and nod my head yes, then no. "What I mean is..." I drift off, considering for a moment spilling the story, telling Sophie how I purposefully tried to get selected as a juror. But then I'd have to explain why, and I'm not really sure I have a clear answer for that one. I look down at my new purchase and stick to the basic truth. "I'm on jury duty."

"Ugh, poor thing," she concludes, and I let her believe it.

Ten minutes later, I push open the heavy, spring-loaded classroom door and step inside. The lights are off, and a hazy afternoon sun leaks through the windows. Finger-painted animals cover one wall, while a giant calendar with movable felt pieces hangs on another. A blue shag circle rug sits empty in the middle of the room. Spider plants hang limply over the teacher's desk. I hear a scratching sound and remember the hamster. What the heck did this year's class name it? Hammy? Something original like that. A low, muffled sound belonging to a human voice startles me.

"Kat?" I whisper loudly. Something about empty classrooms creeps me out. I flick on the lights and try again, louder this time. "Kat! C'mon, I know you're in here. You've called me three times since twelve thirty!"

And then I see it—a curling black telephone cord vanishing into the supply closet at the far end of the room.

Inside, Kat is crouched on a wooden, three-legged kiddie stool, like a teenager on a toilet seat in a bathroom stall hiding from the principal during math class. She has the phone cradled under her left ear and a cigarette clamped between two fingers in her right hand.

"What the hell?" Kat calls out, squinting into the sudden light. She momentarily loses her balance on the stool and has to put out her right hand to steady herself.

"Kat, I think the question is 'What the *fuck?*' and I'm supposed to be the one asking it."

She rolls her eyes and speaks into the phone. "I gotta go. No, it's not the administration. It's just Lauren. Yup. Me, too. TTYL."

Kat emerges, brushing a stray black curl from her eyes. "Hang this up for me, will you?" Then she gestures with the cigarette. "Do you have a light?"

"Is that a *candy* cigarette?"

"Insert second eye roll here. Duh, Lauren. You really think I'd smoke around those frigging five-year-olds?"

"Such colorful language."

"I'm outta matches is all. I'll be golden once I take a puff."

"Fine." I move my thumb across the knuckle of my pointer finger and hold it out to her. "Use my lighter."

Kat presses the dusty white sugar stick to her lips and closes her eyes. "*Much* better. Thanks."

"Who was that on the phone?" I ask.

"Just...no one." She takes a bite of the hard candy and starts chewing.

"It was Varka, wasn't it?"

"Maybe yes, maybe no." Chew, chomp, puff.

"I thought we talked about this. I thought we agreed that a ten-dollar-a-minute psychic was not the answer."

Kat is complete nonchalance. "Depends on the question. Mercury is in retrograde right now, and Mercury rules travel and communications, among other things. It means things are gonna be kooky for the next few weeks." A smile plays on her lips. "Lauren, Varka has me worried for our safety."

"Oh puh-leeze! You know, I don't need this. I'm 'off duty' at school this week. I promised myself I wouldn't step foot into this building unless completely necessary."

"Technically, this is the elementary wing, so you're not *really* in the middle school, you know."

"Technically, go to hell."

"Such colorful language."

There is a break in our banter, neither of us knowing what to say next. I meet Kat's eyes and see for the first time that she must have been crying. Her eyes are red-rimmed and puffy. I wait.

"Psycho Mom is at me again."

"What's the complaint this time?" I ask. "Air toxins? Not enough visual stimuli in the kindergarten? Too much?"

"Gluten in the finger paints." She tries to say it with a straight face but can't help breaking out in a smile of sorts. It's not a happy smile, more like the kind that says, *My life is ridiculous and I'm in on the joke.* I know the feeling.

"But who eats finger paints?" I ask.

"Son of Psycho Mom does, actually. This little fucker loves the green. Licks it off his fingers like it's candy! And he's allergic!"

"Well, that's not funny."

"But his mom is the one who *bought* the paints for me in the first place because they were 'environmentally friendly.' She tried to petition the school board about it, remember? Get the whole district to change over their art supplies?"

"Okay, *now* it's funny."

The woman stresses me out and I don't even *know* her. It should be illegal to carry a reputation like that. Poor Kat's taking this really hard. I mean, she's a tough one, generally speaking, but here she is, laughing so hard she's crying.

Like, hysterically.

After a minute or so, she still hasn't stopped. It's the kind of laugh/cry combo made by a sociopath in a movie right before he cuts out someone's guts and eats them, so I'm starting to get a little uncomfortable. I scan the room for the blunt scissor caddy and am glad to see it's safely on the art cart, on the other side of the room. Next to the finger paints.

Kat is now rolling on the carpet and clutching her side. Snot and tears are everywhere. If I didn't know any better, I'd think she was rabid.

I check. "Have you recently been bitten by a squirrel?"

Kat goes on making this "he-he-he" sound from the back of her throat.

"Shall I call 911?" I ask in a British accent, trying to sound authoritative.

She shakes her head, now tucked in the fetal position.

"Varka, then?"

Again, she shakes her head.

It's good that she's responding. But I'm still freaking out. I mean, I've been drunk with Kat and high with Kat and I've even grieved with Kat when her mom died. But I've never seen her like this.

I tentatively approach the blubbering blob on the circle-time carpet. "Are you *on* something?" I ask. "Is this, like, a *Pulp Fiction* moment? Do you need me to shock you in the heart with a hypodermic needle?"

I reach out and touch the curve of her protruding backbone. She's so thin, I think. Since when?

Kat takes a deep breath. It rattles her whole body, but she seems calmer suddenly. She's probably too exhausted to respond to me, but I try again.

"So..." I begin. (I didn't say I try *well*.)

She uncurls herself and sits up. I hand her a tissue from the nearby box. She blows her nose.

Again, I wait.

At some point pretty early on in our friendship, I discovered that pushing and prodding and asking lots of questions causes Kat to clam up. The trick is to wait.

Which takes some getting used to.

I stroke her back and hand her another tissue while trying nonchalantly to glance at my wrist and see what time it is. I've got to get back into my own classroom soon and sort things out for tomorrow's substitute.

As I begin to go off into a daydream about the joys of jury duty—sleep late, eat lunch out, meet new friends, read a cheesy novel—Kat clears her throat. I snap back to attention. Her bloodshot green eyes find mine.

"Peter wants a divorce. For real, this time."

I am momentarily startled. I was in Psycho Mom mode, and so this is surprising. Although, in most ways, it makes perfect sense. I shake my head, shifting gears, and manage to get out some words of support. "Oh damn, Kat. I'm so sorry."

She produces another candy cigarette from a pocket in her blazer, holding it out to me with a shaking hand.

"You sure he doesn't want to work it out? That he isn't just being hotheaded like usual?" I ask, taking the sugary stick.

She shakes her long black ringlets back and forth emphatically, like a woman selling shampoo on TV. "He bought a Maserati with our retirement savings. He's moving in with a younger woman named Carly."

"*No!*" I groan.

"*Yes!*" she cries.

"But that's so...stereotypical! Like a caricature of what a forty-year-old guy would do. It can't be for real."

"What can I say? Peter always did lack originality. It's the friggin' truth."

We sit like that for a moment, smoking and taking bites in the still classroom. No wonder she is losing her mind. "This sucks," I offer as encouragement.

"The candy or my life?"

"Um...both?" That gets a half chuckle out of her.

I have a momentary image of Kat, hiding on her wedding day. She disappeared before the ceremony, but I eventually found her hiding in the back of the florist's van her dress bunched up around her. She was pulling the petals off some discarded daisies.

"Can I just say something?" I ask, and Kat nods. "Without offending you, I mean?"

"Now my interest is piqued."

I speak quickly, in one short breath. "You never really liked Peter all that much. You didn't want to marry him."

"Not the point."

"Kind of is."

She stares at a blank spot on the wall, between all the kid art. "Still...it hurts. I should have left him a long time ago."

"I'm sure it does, Kitty-Kat." I rub her back and we chew on our candy cigarettes. I feel like a sixth grader suddenly, helping my friend through a breakup with a boy who beat her to the punch.

"Consider it your starter marriage," I try.

"As in: I have to start all over because now I'm broke?" She attempts a wan smile.

"As in: Practice makes perfect. Next one's a guaranteed Prince Charming."

"Can you put that in writing? Guaranteed in under five? Cause my eggs are getting hard-boiled as we speak."

"You're fine. You're what? Thirty, thirty-two?"

"Thirty-three next month."

"A mere babe in the manger. A wee lass." I dismiss. "I didn't have Becca until I was almost thirty-five."

"I won't think about it."

"That's the spirit!" I encourage, because, really, what else is there to say?

We make plans to go drinking after school with the gym teachers, which brightens Kat's mood significantly. "I hope they are all sweaty," she pines. "Even the girl ones."

"You're disgusting."

"I'm hurting."

I glance at the clock over the door and stand, stretching. "How can you sit on this carpet all day? Doesn't it kill your back?"

"I'm not old like you, remember."

"Ha."

Kat turns to me, her green eyes intent. "Seriously, Lauren, I know I'm the one who's an emotional wreck, but can I be honest with you?"

I consider her request. "Actually, I'd prefer if you lied."

"You *really* look like shit." She gets to her feet and gives me the once-over. "I've been meaning to tell you for a while, see if you wanted to get your makeup done at Nordstrom's or something. On you, thirty-nine is like the new fifty."

"And on that note..." I start heading for the nearest exit. I pull the handle on the classroom door and say, with fake enthusiasm, "Thanks!"

"It wasn't a compliment!" she calls back.

I give her the finger. "Call down to the gym, please. See you at Flannigan's. Three fifteen!"

There are still nine minutes left before last period. In teacher time, that's like an hour. I figure I'll sneak into my classroom once my students vacate to attend their foreign language classes at the end of the day. That way I can set up the lesson plans for the rest of the week and leave them on my desk for the sub. Which reminds me: Better call the sub service and secure a real substitute through Friday, since I'm sure Martha won't be interested in keeping the job past today. My ballet flats squeak against the glossy linoleum tiles as I make my way purposefully down the hall.

I duck into the nearest girls' bathroom and examine my face in the cloudy mirror.

Kat has a point.

I don't know how or when the change occurred, but staring back at me is not the *me* I picture in my head. Instead, I have been replaced with one of those poor, unsuspecting women pulled out of the crowd at the *Today* show for a miracle makeover.

Over the winter, my hair has grown very long, and it's now too heavy around my face. And though technically the color fits somewhere on the blond spectrum, my mousy natural-colored roots are showing themselves in a thick racing stripe down the center of my head. My blue eyes lack spark. Worst of all, the skin around them seems swollen and slightly black-and-blue. And forget my forehead. All those creases and lines. Put it all together and I look...what is the right word? Haggard? Harried? Haggard and harried?

Oh hell, who am I kidding? That assessment is kind. In truth, I look like a woman who has just had her mug shot taken and is next in line for fingerprinting: Dazed.

"Mrs. Worthing. What are you doing here?" The monotone of Martha's voice simultaneously shakes me from my reverie and scares the shit out of me. "Is that a *cigarette* in your hand?"

"Jeez, Martha!" I clutch my chest. "You trying to give me a heart attack?" I realize my error as soon as the words escape my lips. I mean, not that Martha necessarily *caused* our assistant principal's heart attack last month, but still. Faux pas extraordinaire. Her always brown-lipsticked mouth is set in a straight, tight line. I smile wide enough for both of us. "I mean, hey there!"

She points to my right hand. "Explain."

There are benefits to being on jury duty. Not having to teach anyone anything for several consecutive days is one of them. Knowing that the world is bigger than the one in which your principal reigns supreme is another. Which is why, in the bathroom with the fake cigarette, I decide to have a little fun with her and simultaneously throw a kid under the bus.

I take a deep breath and gather my courage.

"Oh, Martha. I'm so glad you are here. A little miscreant was pretending to smoke this candy cigarette when I walked in to use the facilities a moment ago. I, of course, immediately confiscated it, and sent her right to the principal's office. You probably passed her in the halls just now."

"Really?" Martha asks, clearly intrigued but not yet quite believing me.

"Abso-lutely." I begin wild gesticulations to add authentication to my tale. "She's, like, yea high and she has, like, brownish-blackish-blondish hair that's not too long or short and is basically straight when it isn't curly. I think you know her. Her mom's on the board of ed, maybe?"

"Lucy Williams?" She is really getting into it now, going through her mental Rolodex of faces. "Fourth grade?"

"Perhaps. Could have been third or fifth, though. Here. Evidence." I put the remainder of the slightly damp confection in her hand. "But now, if you'll excuse me, I have to run…I have a parent meeting in five," I add, pushing open the bathroom door.

"But wait! Mrs….Lauren. Are you back from jury duty?"

"Nope…case starts tomorrow. Could be a *really long* trial. Don't you worry, though; I'll call the sub service. Unless you want to continue filling in?"

Martha's brain is still catching up, and I'm not about to let it finish processing.

"Nope? Then, see ya!"

And with that, I am off across the quad and through the double doors of the middle school building.

"That is hi-lari-ous!" Kat declares from her bar stool perch. She swivels around a few times, beer glass in hand. "Jim, isn't that hi-lari-ous?"

"Yup," Jim concurs, handing each of us another Jell-O shot. Kat takes one, but I decline.

"To the *di*ministration!" Kat toasts, holding the small paper cup high over her head before sucking the contents out in one giant slurp.

"You sure?" Jim asks me, still holding the extra Jell-O shot. The three of us were hired by the Hadley School District around the same time, in our twenties, when Jell-O shots were a fun diversion from grading homework after school. At some point, I stopped joining the fun, but Kat and Jim still go out at least once a month.

"I've got to get home to the kids soon, relieve the babysitter. One-eighth of grain alcohol a day is plenty for me, thanks."

"Always so responsible, Lauren is," Kat pipes in.

"Wise for someone so short, Kat is," I reply.

"How's that babysitter working out?" Jim asks. "The one you found on Craigslist last summer?"

I shrug. "Oh, you know. Same. Horrible."

"You haven't fired her yet?" Kat laughs. "I thought you were going to get rid of her at, like, Christmas. That was…" She counts on her fingers. "Four months ago!"

"Yeah, but who can fire someone at Christmastime?"

"Scrooge!" they both call out together.

"Jinx!" Kat adds, clearly tipsy.

"So why don't you fire her now?" Jim adds.

"Because I need her. I hate her, but I need her. Otherwise, I can't go to work."

"So, don't go to work!" Kat says, taking the last Jell-O shot from Jim's hand and inhaling it. *Like it's that simple,* I think. "Hey, speaking of work, where is Jim Number Two?"

"You mean James, the other physical education teacher?" Jim asks.

"Yup," Kat hiccups. "And Bo, the sort of lady one?"

Jim leans in close, whispering conspiratorially in Kat's ear. His short-sleeved T-shirt stretches tight across the Hulk muscles in his chest and arms. "I told them they couldn't make it."

Kat's momentary confusion is replaced with a knowing smile. "Ah! Very crafty!"

I wink, then wave in their general direction as I leave Flannigan's, though neither one is looking at me. It might be Kat calling out "See ya tomorrow, Lauren!" over Def Leppard, but I don't reply.

CHAPTER 5

ON MY WAY HOME, my cell phone rings. *Moncrieff* comes up on the screen, so I answer and put it on speakerphone. "Jodi!"

"I can't talk right now," a husky whisper responds, wrapping my car in her distinctive voice.

"Then why did you call me?"

"I mean, I want to talk to you—I *need* to talk to you—only I've gotta go."

"Why is everyone doing this to me today?" I ask no one in particular, since Jodi's already hung up.

Two minutes later, Jodi calls back as I'm pulling into my driveway. I idle in the car to listen to her tirade.

Jodi, like Kat, is one of my good friends. I met them both at Hadley Middle School, though Jodi stopped working right before her first daughter was born. "Why would I want to be with some-one's else's children when I could just be with mine?" she'd said one day in the teachers' lounge, rubbing her diamond-encrusted left hand across her protruding belly. No one could come up with a sufficient retort, so we all just shrugged in her general direction and let her go.

Actually, no one ever can come up with a sufficient retort to anything that Jodi says, *ever*. Not her husband, her mother, her best friends, her kids, or any poor worker bee forced to deal with her wishes at any hotel, restaurant, or store of any kind. It's all in her delivery. That, plus the fact that she's disarmingly gorgeous. Suffice it to say that, in this universe at least, Jodi's always right, even when she's completely wrong.

Some people find this behavior of hers shallow and aggressive. I find her self-absorption wholly refreshing.

In small doses.

I tune back in to her drama of the moment. "What was that? Is this about *shoes*?" I ask.

"*Ugh!* Yes! Aren't you even *listening*? I was in *Palazzo* Shoes and I was just *trying* to return a pair of *Manolos*, but the woman was giving me such a *hard* time," she moans.

Jodi has a way of elongating words so that they sound, well, naughty.

"But that's not why I'm calling. Let's meet for lunch. I have something important to discuss. Oh, PTA call coming through."

We agree to get together soon, and then she disconnects midsentence.

Inside the house, the kids are glued to the television set and Laney is nowhere to be found—again.

I actually panic for a moment: Did she leave early? Could the kids have arrived home from school without her waiting there to open the door? Child neglect! I think of the court case I've been assigned to.

I will have to prosecute Laney.

But then I will be prosecuted for hiring an illegal. No good.

I know she didn't arrive until after the morning rush, because I had to put the kids on the bus. Then she gave me some attitude and disappeared into the depths of the house. And after that? My mind flashes to a terrible scene: Laney lying dead somewhere, our immigrant babysitter, with no identification except her Planet Fitness membership. How would I describe her to the police? As a beautiful, twenty-two-year-old Latina who chose to tramp herself up with long blond Shakira hair and really tight stretch jeans? A man in blue would come to my door with just a diamond belly stud in his palm, and I would burst into tears.

"Laney!" I shout. "Donde esta?"

She emerges from the basement slowly, with her head down. I can tell instantly that she's in one of her black moods, but I don't care. She's not dead! My children were not neglected, exactly. I practically hug her.

"Hola," she mopes.

"Hola!"

Laney sighs. "There is so much laundry."

"Yes!"

"I just couldn't..." She gestures toward the kitchen. I turn and see that nothing—and I mean *nothing*—has changed in the kitchen since I left the house at 8:00 this morning. Some dishes are piled in the sink and some are holding firm at the spots on the island where the kids ate half their breakfast. It's like a ghost-town kitchen, or something dug up from Pompeii, abandoned yet completely intact. It's an art installment at the Whitney: *Still Life with Sour Milk*.

"What the—?" I crush an enormous ant underfoot for emphasis.

"I just couldn't..." She trails off. Because really, what is there to say? We both know that she hasn't cared about her job for a long time.

We stand in silence for a moment, evaluating the tangled mess of the kitchen and the inertia in our respective lives.

Then I remember Laney's text from earlier in the day, which I never responded to. She perks up considerably when I tell her that, yes, she can leave a half hour early tonight to catch a train into the city for a concert at Madison Square Garden.

She consults her watch. "So, I go in...twenty-seven minutes?"

"Sure, Laney. Knock yourself out." She does mental calculations. That gives her roughly seven minutes to clean the kitchen and twenty minutes to style her hair—no doubt with *my* ceramic straightening iron.

"Okay!" she decides, clapping her hands together like, *now I'm really going to get down to work*!

When Laney calls out her good-byes a few minutes later and the screen door slams behind a trail of spicy perfume, I breathe a sigh of relief.

My house, my kids, my little world. "Ben and Becca! Time for dinner!" I sing, imagining the nice family conversation we will have huddled around the table.

"Ow!" Ben cries from the sunroom.

"Give it back!" Becca wails.

"No! It's mine!"

There is a crashing sound. I reach the sunroom in time to tear my kids apart, yelling something asinine like, "Stop it this instant! One of you could lose an eye!"

When that doesn't get them to lay off each other, I reach deep into my bag of mom tricks for more powerful weapons. "No television for the rest of the night! No dessert! No stories before bed?"

Not working. Ben is now kicking Becca and she is pulling his hair.

I throw a biggie at them. "If you don't get off each other *right now*, Jackie won't come to babysit this week!"

Instantly, they jump apart. Becca smooths her hair back from her face, and Ben sucks his lips in tight. Both are straight-backed and at army-like attention, with their big eyes on me.

My kids love Jackie more than they'll ever love me. She's an education major at a local college who is so popular with neighborhood kids that I have to book her sometimes months in advance. If she didn't come to sleep over on Thursday night, they'd be devastated.

"Now, that's more like it," I sigh. "Come have dinner."

"What is it?" Ben asks.

"Mac and cheese and chicken nuggets."

"Again?" they complain in unison.

"Laney was supposed to make meatloaf, but she didn't. Sorry."

"You could make something else," Becca suggests, "like a call for sushi."

"Maybe tomorrow," I muse.

The kids are tucked into their beds and I am nursing a headache. I can hear Doug in the shower when I come up from the basement, having just folded the laundry that Laney left in the dryer.

I go into the bathroom and knock on the glass wall. "Hi!" I call out.

He wipes away some condensation so that I can sort of see him in there. He waves.

"How was your day?" I ask.

"Whah?" he answers over the running water.

I try again, louder. "How was...nothing," I say. "Forget it." I already know the answer.

I turn to the bedroom door handle where I have hung the dry cleaning, and begin removing it from its plastic wrap. I open the closet and push aside my cheerleading uniform from high school. Laney borrowed it for a costume party and actually returned it. Surprise.

Doug opens the shower door. "Hey, Lauren? Where'd you go?"

"I'm here," I call from the bedroom.

"Is that a new pocketbook I saw downstairs?"

"Not new!" I yell. Technically, this is true. Sophie said it had been used once for a Chloe ad.

After a moment's pause, Doug says, "Really? Because I haven't seen it before."

"That doesn't make it new."

"The blue one?"

"Right."

"Huh."

"Also," I say, "if I may point out, I am working hard. I know that my paycheck is needed for real stuff, like our electricity, for instance. But sometimes it's nice to...break out a little bit. Splurge on something. To make me feel..."

"Can you hand me a new razor?" Doug interrupts.

I go into the hall closet and come back, still talking. "Just to make me feel...special." I pass the razor through the mist. He closes the door behind him and we go back to raised voices.

"Lauren, those 'special' items are things like college funds and 401Ks! Not Gucci bags."

"Chloe," I correct.

"Who's she?"

"Nobody new, that's for sure." I'll have to bury the new Chloe dustcover that the bag came with in the back of my underwear drawer. No need to invite further suspicion.

I've tried to talk to Doug about my feelings, really I have. It's not like I want to lie. I'd love to be able to come home and say, *Look at my gorgeous new pocketbook! Don't you just love it?* And he'd sigh and say, *It's just what you've always wanted. I'm so happy for you.* But anyone with a husband knows that that's about as realistic as a Disney princess movie. And so, the big purchases get hidden. They come into the house when he's not home, the shopping bags magically disappear, and then the items get seamlessly added into the rotation as if they were there all along.

It doesn't matter if the conversation is about shopping, or about traveling, or, most recently, about feeling these urges to party like it's 1999. He always shuts me down. *We don't have money. We don't have time. Can we talk about this later? When I'm not exhausted from work?*

I finish hanging the dry cleaning and raise my voice over the shower. "I'm going downstairs to watch TV. You coming?"

"In a few. I have to return a call from my client at Bank of America first."

"Okay."

"What's for dinner?" Doug shouts, as an afterthought.

"Nothing!" I say. Since returning to work when Becca turned two, I have sucked at making dinner, and Laney has not been a great help. Why is preparing dinner nightly *my* job? Why are all the things I did when not working—like scheduling doctors' appointments, getting presents for birthday parties, going to the supermarket and dry cleaner's—still *my* job exclusively now that I work full-time again, just like Doug? Sometimes I wonder who put me in charge.

And then I wonder what would happen if I just decided one day *not* to be.

CHAPTER 6

Tuesday

I ROLL DOWN THE WINDOW of my car and pull up to the security booth at the courthouse parking lot. As instructed, the special juror permit is on my windshield, and I motion to it while saying good morning to the guard. He barely looks up from his newspaper as he waves me through. "Thanks!" I call. "Have a nice day!"

Making my way up to the main entrance, I'm feeling rather cheerful indeed. My first day as a juror! I have purchased a new notepad for the occasion, as suggested by the bailiff yesterday, to jot down any technical notes from the case that I might need to recall during deliberation. While waiting in line at the metal detector, I sip my coffee and imagine the jury deadlocked. Flipping through my notebook, I will find the one loophole to knock the whole case wide open. Juror number four saves the day!

Law & Order has messed with my head.

I enter the juror waiting room attached to our courtroom on the fifth floor. "Morning," I say to the group.

"That it is, doll," Sweetheart says. No one looks up. Carrie gives a little wave, but her eyes are glued to her BlackBerry.

"You smuggled yours in, too?" I ask. She nods faintly in reply, not looking up from her screen.

It was a risky move, but I really wanted to listen to a new mix I made off of iTunes, so I hid my phone deep in my pocketbook and told the security guard that I didn't have my phone on me.

I thought I was being such a rebel. Apparently, I was only following the herd.

No one's chatty this morning, so I take out my iPhone and pretend to be busy. Something catches my eye as the incoming e-mails unroll down the screen. There's a message from "lkatzenberg."

Lenny. I scroll back through the uploading messages to find it, but just then a bailiff enters and clears her throat. I drop the phone into my pocketbook.

"Hello, jurors, my name is Delilah and I am the bailiff assigned to this case." Delilah is such a feminine name for this woman standing before me, with no makeup on her cocoa skin and her black hair pulled back tightly into a bun. Women in uniforms always look like men to me, even if they are wide hipped and big bosomed like Delilah. She fingers the gun in her holster and I snap back to attention.

"The judge and the lawyers for the case are in chambers right now, preparing for the start of the trial. Until the judge tells me to call you in, you will stay here. In this room, you may eat, you may talk to each other, and"—she looks my way—"you may use your cell phones, as long as the other jurors don't mind." She then tells us how to find the bathrooms on the floor and warns us to be prepared to wait for a while. "Could be up to an hour, give or take, depending." She shrugs before leaving the room.

"Depending on what?" Sweetheart asks after she's gone. "That doesn't make no sense!"

"Any," Carrie says emphatically. "Doesn't make *any* sense."

"Exactly." He nods in agreement and smiles at her. Carrie returns the smile hesitantly. Then she looks my way and rolls her eyes.

One older woman takes out some Sudoku puzzles and another one picks up the novel she's been reading. A young guy gets up to stretch and tells us that he'll be on a call in the hallway. "Come get me if the judge needs us, okay?" I remember him from yesterday, the guy with a new job. Poor thing. He thinks work matters.

Then I remember the e-mail. Leonard. I can't remember our last exchange, exactly, except that I had the feeling I'd somehow pissed him off. In the midst of all the junk e-mails from department stores, I find his note:

```
Subject: New Video
From: lkatzenberg@yale.alumni.edu
Date: April 10
To: laurenworthing@gmail.com
```

```
Hey All,

I have posted my new video on YouTube. Please
take a look, and share the link if you like
it. (If not, forget I ever mentioned it.)

MC Lenny
```

I'm a little bit disappointed that this isn't a personal message, a shout out or joke just for me. But the video intrigues me, as always. I plug my headphones into the phone and click on the link, which takes a moment or two to load.

Leonard is a friend from high school with whom I reconnected last year at our twentieth reunion. The regular rules of high school were suspended for him. While I was stuck in my B-plus crowd of above-average-but-not-quite-awesome people, Lenny was allowed to move effortlessly between cliques, from the cool varsity basketball team to the hip jazz band, from the geeky honors society to the even geekier Stock Market Club, and back again. No questions asked.

Good looks combined with athleticism, wit, and smarts can do that to a person, catapult them to unfettered popularity. Everyone wanted a piece of him and was happy with whatever time or attention they got from Lenny. Including me.

Only, I didn't get much.

Until senior year, when luck had me working side by side with Lenny as coeditors of the yearbook. I used to cancel staff meetings and "forget" to tell him, just so he and I would end up alone in some science classroom after school, talking about nothing and everything at the same time. There was one intense month of work—March, I think—when we had to finalize all the photos and cram to get all the layouts done and submitted to the printer. We pulled a bunch of all-nighters at my house, the cut images and graphics spread out before us in a jumbled mess, the soft glow of basement light making the damp, unfinished space seem almost romantic, and I'd think, *Now he's going to kiss me.*

But he never did.

But then he'd look at me and smile, and our hands would touch just the tiniest bit as we passed the Scotch tape back and forth, and a current would pass up my arm. And then I'd think, *Now he's going to ask me to the prom.*

But he never did that either.

Which is why this online attention I've been getting from MC Lenny Katzenberg since the reunion is most unexpected, although not, in fact, entirely unwelcome.

Lenny's video comes up on YouTube. He is dressed in jeans and a graphic tee. He's this tall, kind of nebbishy Jewish kid from Westchester, who went to Yale and now spends his days as an accountant. He spends his evenings and weekends putting together rap lyrics with synchronized music. Then he records himself and edits together an iMovie to put up on YouTube. Sometimes his skits and songs are performed alone, and sometimes with others, like random New Yorkers, or an on-again, off-again girlfriend. A few have been politically charged. Others have been crude or somewhat sexual. Sometimes these mini-movies involve rather complicated choreography. They are always really funny and cutting-edge.

This one doesn't disappoint. It's about the latest health care bill being voted on by Congress. It's typical Lenny: left-wing and liberal, with clever rhymes and a touch of Justin Timberlake.

I'm slightly distracted by Lenny's companion. A woman with the longest legs I've ever seen is wearing a tight, white, short-skirted nurse's costume and gyrating her hips around him while he raps his way around HMOs, PPOs and HDHPs ("How the fuck am I supposed to know which one is right for me?"). I wonder who this "nurse" is, and if they're more than friends.

But then Lenny's hazel eyes shine, and I'm back in the moment with him. He looks right through the camera and into my eyes, like this is all just an elaborate private joke between the two of us. A playful smile turns up one corner of his mouth, into his trademark impish grin.

I forward it to Kat. This should give her another needed pick-me-up.

"Who knew a smart dweeb could be so friggin' hot?" she had commented the first time we watched one of Lenny's videos. We were huddled together in the back corner of the middle school's computer lab during a free period, staring thirstily at the screen as Lenny shook his ass at us.

"I did!" I had exclaimed. "Always! I had the best time on those temple retreat weekends!"

"Yeah, well, I'm not sure I'd brag about that." She'd then grabbed one of her curls, pulled it out straight, stuck it into her mouth, and sucked on it. She turned back to study the screen in contemplative silence. "Although, that guy does have something. I just can't put my finger on it." Silence, except for the sucking of hair. "Wait! Is he married?"

"No. He's thirty-nine and single, never been."

"I got it! He's gay!"

"Kat, he's not gay. He's just funny and unafraid of busting a move on the international Internet circuit."

"Yeah. Children, are you listening?" She had pretended to address a class of kindergarteners. "That spells g-a-y."

Lenny breaks out the Michael Jackson pelvic-thrust-with-hand-cupped-over-genitals move, and I snort heartily in response. Kat is going to die when she sees this.

Someone is suddenly tapping me on the arm. I look up from my phone and notice that all the jurors—plus the bailiff—are staring at me.

"Having a good time, miss?" Delilah accuses.

"Yes! I mean, sorry. Just a funny video on YouTube. I'll turn it off now."

"You do that. Then follow me."

"Why? Am I in some sort of trouble?" I panic. "I know I'm not supposed to have my phone…"

Several jurors chuckle. Delilah does not. "No, miss. Every one of you is supposed to follow me. Judge Banks has called you into the courtroom."

"*Oh!* Great. Guess I didn't hear." I gather my belongings and line up between jurors three and five. Then Delilah opens the door and we file through.

The judge is standing before us in her black robes, and so we remain standing. "Ladies and gentlemen of the jury," she begins, "I am Judge Banks." She looks to be about sixty or so, with the kind of Hillary Clinton hair popular with power-women of a similar age. "I would like to thank you for your time. This case has been settled. You are free to go."

"Yes!" Carrie hisses under her breath. Others clap.

Crap! This can't be happening. But here we go, being led like sheep by Delilah, back out of the courtroom and through our waiting area. "If you'll all follow me downstairs, I'll hand you the official paperwork saying that you've been dismissed after two days of service." My heart is beating out of my shirt. My mind is a tornado of thoughts, a whirlwind screaming, *Disaster, disaster!* Delilah keeps talking, but I can't make out the rest. We follow her down the elevator and to the administrator's office. I think I might faint.

All around me, people are smiling and congratulating each other for getting out of trial. I stand frozen in place and have to be nudged by Sweetheart.

"Whatsamattah, honey?" he asks. "This is a great day! You look spooked."

"I..." I glance up at him and meet his eyes for the first time. They are round and blue, and actually seem to be emitting warmth of some kind, maybe even sympathy. In that moment, I decide to trust him. "I just don't want to go back to work, is all," I exhale.

But now that I've said that much, the rest pours out of me. "I got passed over for a promotion I really wanted—head of the English Department, which I've been working toward for *years*— and someone from the outside got the job. Apparently, she's the superintendent's niece or cousin or something illegal like that, and she hasn't even finished her master's degree yet! Now I can't face my colleagues. I'm completely humiliated. I'm kind of lost. And so, I pretty much hate my job. Every time I step foot in that school, I want to puke."

I'm feeling better now, as if someone opened a window and let in some air. I keep going. "The principal flat out *lied* to me, said I'd get the position, that I was the natural next choice. I jumped through all these hoops, took extra grad school classes to get the right certifications. Got all dressed up and sat in the hot seat, was interviewed by parents, community members, *friends of mine,* for God's sake, with classrooms down the hall. She even made me teach a demo lesson *in my own class,* even though I've been tenured forever! And then, the committee didn't choose me." I shudder at the memory of myself in heels and a tailored pantsuit, squirming as

Martha called me into her office to break the news—delivered cold, of course, without emotion. I had to picture her in flesh-colored granny panties to keep myself from crying. "I can't go back. Not right now, anyway."

"Talk about your verbal diarrhea!" he jokes. Great. Of all the people in the world to confess to, I pick this asshole.

My husband doesn't even know the truth. I keep putting Doug off, telling him that Martha hasn't made the decision yet. He kept talking about how my new salary would help take some of the financial burden off of him. The plan was to sit down and tell him over dinner, except that in the past six weeks we haven't had one of those dinners. And the more time slips away, the harder it becomes to remember what the truth is anyway.

Sweetheart's eyes suddenly look confused. "Wait a second...did you say, go back to work?" He laughs. "Who said anything about going back to work? My boss thinks I'm on trial for the whole week!" He leans toward me and I smell the tobacco clinging to his clothing. "And what he don't know..." The rest of the sentence lingers in the air between us. He winks. Sweetheart grabs his walking papers, waves them theatrically over his head, and starts walking.

I grab mine and do the same.

CHAPTER 7

CLEARLY, I AM NOT GOING BACK to work *today*. That much I know. It's ten o'clock in the morning on a beautiful Tuesday and I am free to do as I please. Leaving my car in the juror's lot, I walk around downtown Alden. When I pass the new hair salon in the Ritz Carlton hotel, I decide to go in.

Jodi texts me while I am sitting with streaks of white hair color under the hot lamps.

Free 4 lunch?

Yes, I text back, looking at the time. *NM at 1:15.* She always forgets that I work, and usually texts me like this once a week.

Good. I need to find something to wear Sat nite!

C U there, I write, finishing our conversation for now.

I put the phone down and try to rip a page out of a magazine without anyone noticing, but my hairstylist, Brandon, catches me in the act. I tear the page out just as he tears it from my hands.

"What have we here?" he lisps, even though that sentence doesn't have any S sounds in it. Unlike Lenny, Brandon is definitely g-a-y. "Botox! Juvederm! Fabulous!"

I turn bright red and shush him. "I'm just, you know, *thinking* is all."

"I see that, honey," he says, touching the protruding frown lines gathered like Mount Kilimanjaro between my eyebrows, waiting for someone to climb them. "Looks like you think *too* much, I'd say. Botox will take care of your forehead in less time than it takes to count the candles on your birthday cake."

"Yeah, but...my husband would kill me. He likes me natural, you know, no plastic surgery, very little makeup..." I trail off.

"Sounds like a real scumbag." When my eyes widen, he adds, "Hard to debate that one, huh? Truth is—and I'm sure he's very nice, in that vacant way straight men have, don't get me wrong—but he won't even *notice* if you do a little maintenance. Do you know how many of my clients have had minor work done? Injections, mini lifts, whatnots to their hoo-has? These dimwitted husbands just think their wives have had pedicures and facials. That all the exercise really *does* lift foreheads and shape butts. They are none the wiser, and you are all the better. Olé!" He strikes a final pose, clippers in hand.

"Dear God, Brandon, put out the fire. She's new here and you're scaring her!" another male stylist sings, coming to my rescue.

"Hush, Priscilla," Brandon sings back. "This woman is in need. I can sense it. I'm channeling my inner diva to help her find her own diva, lost deep down inside, hidden under years of mediocrity." He looks at me. "How'd I do?"

"Not bad. Pretty fair assessment, actually."

"You and I are one and the same," Brandon sighs, leaning over the back of my chair to look at us side by side in the mirror. "We're stereotypes. I'm the flaming gay male, and you're boring suburban mom." He pumps some mousse into his hands and re-fluffs his spiky hair. "It happens."

"That's kind of harsh!" I balk. "Suburban and mom, yes. I wouldn't call me boring, necessarily."

"But you'd call me flaming, right? Just what you'd expect from your hairdresser?"

Of course, he's right. But being honest seems mean, especially to someone I've just met. It's like the Jewish American Princess principal: I can call myself that, but if anyone else does, I'm offended. So I give a tentative smile and continue on, not answering him one way or the other. "I'm just used to things a certain way. The rhythms of my day have become predictable, regular. I'm just living the way I think I'm supposed to, the way people around me do."

"Well, then, if mediocrity is what you're used to, I'd suggest bangs to cover that forehead. But if you're looking to break out of the same old ho-hum, I'd say take this card"—using sleight of hand, Brandon produces a business card from up his sleeve—"and go for Botox."

"What is this?" I read the typeface on the card and see that's it's advertising my very own dermatologist. "Dr. Grossman? He's the ancient guy who burns off my warts!"

"Now, that's the kind of thing one shouldn't be 'out' about,"

Brandon notes, checking my hair under the lamp. "Dr. Grossman is a genius. And look! So am I. You're a blonde again. Let's go wash and blow."

Jodi passes by my table at Neiman Marcus several times. I actually have to call her over, and even then she's not sure whom she's walking up to.

"Holy Mother of God, you look gorgeous!" She leans across the table to kiss me hello. "Bitch," she adds, grabbing a clump of my hair. From her, that's the highest level of compliment. "Who did this to you? It's a*maz*ing."

"This guy at the new salon at the Ritz." I shrug.

"Brandon blew you?"

I chuckle. "You *know* Brandon?"

Jodi tosses her long hair dramatically. "Lauren, I know everyone."

We sit back to chat. "Did you notice anything else about me?" I lead.

Jodi's doe eyes, always framed in mascara, bat once or twice as she thinks, taking me in. "No," she concludes. "Other than your hair, you look the same."

"It's not my looks, dork. Try again. I'll give you a hint. What time is it? What day of the week?"

Then it clicks. "You're not at work!"

"Shh...I could be spotted by a mom of one of my students right now! We're in dangerous territory here. That's why I'm facing the wall."

"You could just lie, you know, if anyone saw you. Say you're at a conference, on your lunch break."

"A conference for what? Cashmere?"

"Shakespeare, cashmere, same thing," she dismisses. "Ugh, I'm so hot." She peels off her sweater to reveal perfectly skinny arms and bony clavicles that make her fashionably gaunt.

"You get those arms from Pilates?" I motion.

"No way! You know I'm too lazy to work out." She takes a sip of her water through a straw, leaving a ring of sparkly pink lip gloss on the plastic. "It's just the way I'm built. It's hereditary."

"Jodi, we've been over this. Just because your grandparents were Holocaust survivors does not mean you are meant to be thin."

"Say what you will. My grandmother always had weight issues before the war. After? *Never.*"

"But..." I trail off. Typical Jodi. Her logic is so flawed. And yet it's delivered with such confidence that I don't even know where to begin to untangle it and set her straight.

Jodi motions to the waitress, who nods her head and comes our way. "I'm *starving.*"

"The mandarin orange soufflé is great," I suggest as Jodi opens the menu and looks it over.

"Jell-O mold? Gross." She shivers theatrically, then looks up at the waitress. "I'll just have a bacon cheeseburger with fries. And a Coke."

"Diet?" The waitress asks.

"Ugh, no. Regular. And two pickles, please."

I order the so-called gross lo-cal Jell-O mold and pass the waitress our menus.

Jodi continues our conversation. "Anyway, it's spring and I'm bathing-suit ready. Even got waxed by my bikiniologist. Now, *there's* someone with true talent. You should see what she can do down there."

"I'll just take your word for it, thanks."

"True artistry. But that's not why I called you for lunch." She butters a popover, bites off a piece, and rolls her eyes skyward as she chews. "Ah. Strawberry butter. So good." She finishes that piece and tears off another. "Here's the thing. I need your help with something."

"Yeah, with what to wear Saturday night. You already mentioned that in your text." I stare at the basket filled with warm, crusty popovers and consider what my thighs would have to say about them. Instead, I unwrap the world's thinnest breadstick and try to savor its crunchiness.

Jodi waves her hand in the air. "The outfit is a diversion. I need to talk to you about something *serious.*" She leans in close, across the table. I lean in, too.

Jodi whispers, "I want to go back to work."

"What!"

"Quiet! Lee can't know that I'm thinking about this."

"Why do we have to whisper? Is he here?"

"You know what I mean," she says, relaxing a bit and moving back to her popover. "He'd kill me if he knew."

I have to process this for a second. Why would a husband *not* want his wife to work? "Because he likes you at home."

She echoes it back, nodding solemnly. "Because he likes me at home."

Oh, the irony of my life and hers. "Unbelievable!" I state.

"Isn't it, though," she adds, thinking only about herself. "I mean, I like making dinners and everything, don't get me wrong. I've become quite the little homemaker in the eight years since I stopped teaching. And it's been great to watch the kids grow up, finish preschool, go off to kindergarten...but before I know it Jossie will be in middle school..." She trails off.

I think about all that carpooling, all that tennis. "You're bored," I guess.

She pinches her thumb and index finger together and makes a face. "Little bit."

All I want in this life is to be a little bit bored and a little bit too skinny.

I dig in my pocketbook for my small notebook and quickly scribble down a thought before it vacates my mind completely: *work v. stay-at-home dilemmas*, with an exclamation point and a question mark following.

"What are you doing?" Jodi asks.

"Research," I say. The beginnings of an idea are forming. It could be an interesting academic topic, if I could find some existing research, test some theories, build on the body of literature that already exists in the field, and write it up for a scholarly journal. Maybe I really should start thinking about advancing my career in education.

While I'm at it, I could become Miss America and start growing my own hemp, because that's how likely it is that I'll act on this notation. I close the notebook and push it to the bottom of my handbag.

"You can have my job," I offer.

"Ha," she spits, spraying popover pieces across the tablecloth. "Been there, done that. Teaching is *way* too hard. I want something part-time, where I can come and go as I choose."

"Like Sophie the Bag Lady," I say.

"Exactly!"

I throw out some ideas. "You could tutor. Or walk dogs."

"Or tutor dogs!" she adds.

"Or become the local Lice Lady!"

"Lee always says I'm such a nitpicker." We laugh as she reaches for a second popover. "Plus, I really miss dressing up."

I stop chewing midchew. Suddenly, her desire to work makes perfect sense. *That's* really why Jodi wants to go back to work, not because she's bored. Jodi longs for a cool, new, employment-worthy wardrobe.

"You're not serious." I don't ask this as if it's a question. I declare it outright.

She shrugs like it's no big deal. "If I worked, I could buy *so* many great outfits. Like those new wide-leg trousers on the mannequin on the second floor. I covert them, but I don't need them."

"Covet," I correct.

"See? You like them, too. Only, I would look silly wearing them to a PTA meeting. For that setting, I'd look much better in my skinny jeans and a Vince asymmetrical tee. That says, like, 'I'm chair of the book fair' without overstating my own importance."

"Spoken like someone who doesn't have a job." You know your life is unfulfilled when you spend inordinate amounts of time plotting outfits for meaningless occasions.

But as much as I joke about Jodi's logic, the thought of stay-at-home motherhood makes me sigh. "I'd love to be a PTA mom in a Vince asymmetrical tee."

"No, you wouldn't." Jodi shakes her knife at me. "You have *no* idea, Lauren. None. The PTA is like the mob. Once they get you in their grip, they won't let you go. First it's 'Oh, won't you please help out serving pizza lunch?' and then it's 'Could you chaperone the band concert?'—all smiles and friendly camaraderie—and finally, it's 'We've signed you up to chair the multicultural lunch, the staff appreciation day and the charity auction, and if you cancel, we'll blacklist your kids from getting the best teachers.'" She sighs. "I kind of want to go back to work just to avoid having to make any more excuses to the PTA. I mean, how many herniated discs can one have when the annual fundraiser rolls around? How many sinus surgeries coinciding with the school fair? I joined the PTA to see my kids more often around school, only I got so busy working for the PTA that I never see my kids anymore."

Hands shaking, Jodi reaches across the table and snatches up my untouched popover. She rips off a chunk and chews it sensually, with eyes closed. I almost feel bad for her.

Almost.

"Lauren, you just want what you can't have. Trust me, it's all of the work—or more—without any of the pay, or any of the glory."

"What glory is there in teaching?" I want to know.

She puts down her cutlery so that she can create grand hand gestures. "You know, being loved by your adoring fans."

"They're eleven-year-olds."

"And they love you, and think you are so cool, and tell you all their problems, and want to be just like you when they grow up. Students are so much better than one's own children that way." Now it's her turn to sigh.

We are both quiet for a minute, lost in our own reflections. When I started teaching, people used to tell me that I picked the perfect career to balance with eventual motherhood. "You'll have your summers off, and you'll vacation when your children do, and you'll get out of work just as they end their day in school," yentas at the nail salon would say. And I would cringe, because I thought, *That's so small-minded of them. I'm not going into teaching in order to pick a career that works for a life I don't even have yet. I'm going into teaching to shape lives, to change the world.*

And now, you know what I think? I think all those yentas had it totally backward. Because, yes, I have school-age children now. And when they go to school, I go to work. And when they are home from school, I am home from work. Their vacations are my vacations. Their free time is my free time.

Do you see the inherent problem, here?

I never get time off without them. I never have a vacation day that is not also their vacation day.

I can't just take a holiday whenever I want to, because I already have something like fifteen weeks off a year built in to my schedule. And so, on my teacher's salary, I travel during the most expensive black-out dates, with my children, natch, and wherever I go, other school-age children and families are there, because everyone in the free world is on school vacation concurrently, yelling out "Marco" and "Polo" and annoying me while I'm trying to read poolside.

Teaching has become a kind of vacationer's prison.

I shudder at the truth of that and tell Jodi, "Yeah—teaching's not the right move for you anymore."

"Actually, I do have *one* idea," she hints theatrically.

"Okay," I say.

"I'm thinking this." She pushes herself back from the table and sort of makes a frame with her palms. "I'm thinking...that I should become *famous*."

She stops. I wait.

Famous for what, I wonder?

Then I realize I'm supposed to respond.

"Famous! That's an...interesting idea." Is there such a thing as being just famous?

"I *know*!" She pours some ketchup and digs into the burger that has been gently placed in front of her. Between bites—and during them—she continues.

"It's just that when I go to the city, I feel like I'm *somebody*, you know? People *notice* me. They think I'm in fashion, working for a magazine or for a mega-designer like Balenciaga. They ask me if I'm *in the art world*."

"And...are you?" I ask, wondering if Jodi has some secret talent in design. Maybe she's set up an artist's loft above her garage and is going to become this new, self-taught, amazing painter. The mother of postmaterialism. Maybe she's been scribbling poems day and night like Emily Dickinson, and has drawers filled with tiny scraps of brilliance.

I take a bite of some melon on my plate and wish I had red meat instead.

"No! I'm not there *yet*. So, to help me along, I'm going to hire paparazzi. To follow me around and bother me and take my picture! Only, I'm not going to know *when* and *where* they're going to strike, just like a *real* famous person. I figure I'll hire photographers to surprise me one day—I think I need a bunch, right? Because one is kinda lame—like, when I'm walking out of lunch at the Modern or on the steps of the Met or something, and then I'll be, like, caught off guard and have to duck into a cab while the cameras are flashing, and then people will notice the commotion and wonder who I am! Next thing you know: boom. I'm famous."

"And to think, I'm wasting all my time teaching sixth-grade English, when I could just become famous!" I joke.

"I know!"

I shake my head to clear the confusion from at least one of us. "Wait. This is your *real* idea? You don't think this is sort of...ridiculous?"

"Why?" she asks, all doe-eyed innocence. I look at my longtime friend and debate: Do I burst her fault-filled bubble? Do I squash her dream right here and now by saying, *Look, you are beautiful and ballsy, but that's not quite enough to catapult you to fame, paparazzi or no*? I try a softer tactic.

"Maybe...you need to come up with a business plan or hone some skill or talent *first*. Then you could hire press to help you advertise and market all your brilliance."

There. I think that's a fair compromise. Plus, it's not quite as pathological.

She's shaking her head. "But I don't *have* a marketable skill or talent. I just want to be *known for something*."

"Something other than being a wife and mother," I say.

"Yes! See? You get it." She nods, satisfied. "Because *you* want the same thing."

Underneath all the bullshit, and minus the paparazzi, the girl has got a point.

"These fries are a*maz*ing. They have, like, this garlic-y coating. You should try some."

"Okay, Seriously? How do you not put on weight?" I ask.

She stops chewing and looks at me like I'm as dense as her burger. "Lauren, we've been over this. Warsaw, World War II."

"Seems too good to be true, is all. It makes me kind of hate you."

"Oh please." She gulps down some soda. "Hate Hitler."

We debate a few more non-work work options with a high fame quotient for Jodi, and settle for the moment on television personality, wardrobe consultant, or publicist. Then we switch to discussing Saturday night, and she tells me what kind of outfit she's looking for. "It has to be somewhat conservative," she acknowledges. "Since the dance party is at my temple."

"I can't imagine you wearing anything conservative," I say.

"Well, the rabbi pulled me aside at Friday night services last week and told me that my outfit can be strapless, backless, *or* short, but not all three," she explains. "I saw something great online that almost meets the criteria."

I describe the dress I'm planning on wearing, a black sheath with silk trim at the neck, and side pockets below the slightly dropped waist.

She nods. "Yeah, that sounds like you." I know it's not meant to be an insult, but for some reason it stings.

After lunch, we prowl the different departments for a while, but Jodi can't seem to find what she's looking for. Instead, she ends up buying some new skinny jeans and a few sexy tops.

She digs around her bag as the saleswoman rings her up and announces the total. "That will be six hundred fifty-two dollars and seventy-five cents. Would you like to use your Neiman's charge?"

Jodi looks around slyly as she proffers a wad of bills in a crumpled envelope as her form of payment.

"What is that?" I ask.

"Cash back," she says, counting twenties. As if I know what that means.

Jodi produces more and more random wads of bills from the depths of her purse. Some twenties are crumpled little balls, while others are folded together into neat stacks bound by rubber bands. One or two bunches of cash come organized in Ziploc baggies.

"What the hell, Jo?" I ask, by way of clarification.

The sales clerk seems less surprised, merely shrugging as she takes the bills. Then, with expert precision, she turns them so they are all facing the same way, tugs on the pile so that it's nice and crisp again, licks her thumb, and begins counting.

"Come into your trust fund?" I add.

"No!" Jodi says, rolling her eyes at me. "It's like I just told you: *cash back*."

"You mean, you earn dollars back from Visa, or get points on your AmEx that mysteriously turn themselves into random twenties at the bottom of your pocketbook?"

She laughs at me and shakes her head. "I can't *believe* I never told you about my cash-back program."

I shift my weight to one hip and lean against the counter. "I don't think I would have forgotten this. Sounds even more intriguing than your I'm-tired-of-my-Manolos exchange program."

"It's the funniest story, actually," she begins. Then she turns to the saleswoman and says, "I bet you know all about it."

"Indeed I do," the woman responds, a little smile playing on her lips. "I see a lot of customers just like you."

"See?" Jodi says triumphantly. "I thought I had invented it, but then I started noticing other women doing the same thing."

We wait for the saleswoman to get the right size shopping bag from the back. I am no clearer about this than I was a few minutes ago. The only thing I know for sure is that if Jodi thinks she invented it, it can't be good.

"I had this idea last year to throw a surprise party for Lee, for his fortieth birthday," she begins. "I didn't want him to know about it, but that was a problem because I didn't actually have any *money* to pay for the party. So, I thought: Jodi, how are you going to get money without Lee noticing?"

This part of the story has me more than slightly worried, but since she is smiling, I smile right back at her.

She digs through her bag for some lip gloss and starts applying, leaving me hanging.

"*Anyway.*" She moves over to look at her reflection in a nearby mirror. "I was standing in the checkout line at Target when the solution came to me: cash back! You know how the bill at places like Target is always huge? Like two hundred dollars?" She doesn't wait for my response. "Well, I figured I could easily tack on a little cash back and Lee would never know! So whenever I shopped at places like that—the supermarket, Costco, Trader Joe's, whatever—I asked for cash back at checkout. I got forty bucks here, and sixty bucks there, and that money, combined with what I get from Claudine, added up pretty fast!"

She smacks her shiny lips together in satisfaction.

"Wait a minute," I begin, trying to get my mind to catch up with her story. "You just gave me so much to think about!"

"I know!" she agrees.

"I don't think you do, since I'm being sarcastic. But, first off, what money do you get from Claudine?"

"Oh, I tell Lee that I pay her four hundred dollars a week for babysitting and housework, but I actually only pay her three hundred." She takes out her phone and scrolls through e-mails while talking.

"And the rest?"

"Is for me. *My* salary, for making sure that Claudine does what she's supposed to do, for driving carpool, for, you know, being a mommy."

"That is so twisted." I laugh at the absurdity of it.

"No, it isn't."

"It's wrong, Jo," I try to emphasize. "You're stealing from Lee. From yourself!"

"Nu-huh!" she responds, sounding like one of my students. "Plus, remember, I was doing this *for* Lee. To throw him a party!"

"Only, I don't recall a fortieth birthday party for Lee," I counter.

"Well." Here she pauses and puts her phone down on the countertop. "Turns out, he didn't want one." We let that sit between us for a moment. "So, suddenly I found myself with, like, a thousand dollars in cash that Lee didn't know about. And I couldn't tell him, because he'd be furious."

"Why would he be mad?" I ask pseudo-innocently. "You weren't *stealing*, after all. You were doing it *for him*."

"It's hard to explain," she says, trying to look serious. "You wouldn't understand."

"That you're full of shit? Oh, I understand, Jo. I love you dearly, but I know you're completely full of shit."

Just then, the saleswoman emerges with some shopping bags and tissue paper in hand. As the items are wrapped, Jodi explains the rest of her sordid tale. You see, she decided, the best thing to do with the money was to get rid of it. By spending it. On herself. And then, she got used to having that money and spending it on herself. So, now, almost a full year later, she routinely asks for cash back pretty much everywhere she goes. And then she takes that money and shops. Like right this minute, at Neiman Marcus.

"That's stealing!" I call to her from a pile of jeans that I'm flipping through. "Why don't they ever have my size?"

"I prefer to think of it as embezzlement," Jodi says matter-of-factly. "Which I learned from an expert named Lee Moncrieff."

See? So hard to argue with her logic.

"Not to mention, you're involved now, too," Jodi adds.

"Me?" I ask, looking through a pile of short-sleeved T-shirts for a white scoop-necked Splendid in medium.

"How did we pay for lunch?" she asks, coming closer.

I stop what I'm doing to give her craziness my full attention. "Um. You paid with a credit card and I gave you my half in cash." As the words leave my mouth, I realize what I've done. "Ohmigod! I've just contributed to your cash-back program!"

Her full smile flashes its perfect white teeth at me. "See how easy? I'm *always* the one to collect for someone's birthday. I can make a cool two hundred *at least*, every time one of my good friends passes another milestone!"

"And what, you charge the gift on Lee's credit card instead of using all the collected cash?"

She nods. "I'm like my very own rewards program."

"That's intense."

Jodi merely shrugs like it's no big deal and saunters back toward the register.

You think you know someone, and meanwhile, they are lying, cheating and stealing right under your nose. The thought makes me shudder slightly, like I did yesterday at the bus stop, as if a cool breeze just blew through the climate-controlled mall.

While Jodi is finishing her transaction, I meander around and try to process the amorality and simultaneous brilliance of Jodi's cash-back program.

Something shimmery catches my attention and I walk toward it, almost possessed. I grab this gorgeous Missoni sweater from the rack and see that it's on sale, but of course it's not the right size.

I've never worn anything like it, but suddenly I must have it.

Thoughts of Jodi's thievery fade into the background as I talk to the saleswoman about my conundrum.

"Let me see if I can locate that for you in another store," she offers, taking the item from my hand and moving to the computer to start searching.

"It's not like you to pick that." Jodi nods toward the top. "It's see-through!"

"That's only because of the knit. It's the whole point of Missoni stuff! You wear a tank top under it, and then it won't be see-through anymore."

"Duh," she says, like she knew this all along.

"Excuse me, miss?" The saleslady interrupts. "I found that sweater in a size six in our Boston store. Would you like me to have it sent to your home?"

"Um, yeah, I guess so." I say, walking back up to the counter. She asks for my home address, which we locate in the computer.

"It should arrive in five-to-seven business days," she adds, ready to complete the transaction. That's kind of a bummer. It would be nice to wear that sweater tomorrow night, to Leslie's fortieth birthday party.

"W-wait!" I stammer. She lifts her hand from the computer. "How much does overnight shipping cost?"

"From Boston? Let's see...fifty-nine dollars, plus tax."

"That's ridiculous," I say, mentally erasing the sweater from my wardrobe for the time being.

But then I think again.

Boston.

It's not like Boston is all that far away. People travel there and back in a single day all the time, for business. There's the Acela train. I could get there pretty fast.

Georgie's in Boston.

And I have nothing to do tomorrow.

Everyone thinks I'm on jury duty.

What's more ridiculous? Overnight shipping or a random day trip?

I look over at Jodi, who seems perfectly content to lie to her husband, to get one over on him and do as she pleases.

But come on, Lauren, I think. *You're no Jodi. You can't just lie to everyone around you and have a good time while doing it. You have a conscience and morals. Besides, you feel guilt exquisitely.*

Boston. I test the sound of it in my mind.

Jury duty.

Take a little leave?

Just for one day, I muse.

Nothing big.

I turn back to the saleswoman and smile.

"You know what?" I ask. "Can you put the sweater on hold for a day? At the Boston store, I mean?"

The saleswoman nods, but seems confused. I lean over the

counter to whisper my plan. "I think...I think I'll go get it myself tomorrow!"

Just then, Jodi walks over. I worry that she's heard me, but she's too busy shopping to notice. "Ugh, all the clothing here is so cute! But I have to go get the girls at school, take one to tennis, one to art, and one to tae kwon do, then roast a chicken and plant some pink impatiens by the front walk before stuffing envelopes for the PTA." She gives me a quick hug and is off. "This was fun! See you Saturday!" she calls.

I wave in her general direction, but am distracted by my own slightly deranged thoughts, which are now moving quickly.

Boston. Georgie. Road trip! I leave a voice-mail message to see if Georgie is free for coffee, then check the Amtrak schedule.

Wednesday is shaping up to be quite an adventure.

CHAPTER 8

AS I'M GETTING INTO MY CAR, the phone rings. "Hello?" I ask, not recognizing the name or number on the screen.

"Mrs. Worthing? This is Lila over at Dr. Grossman's office. I know I told you it would be impossible to fit you in today, but I've just had a cancellation. Can you be here in ten minutes, at three o'clock?"

My throat falls into my stomach. "Absolutely."

On the drive over, I keep checking my forehead in the rearview mirror. This makes driving a bit complicated. People honk as the traffic lights change, but my car and I don't move. Self-obsession is a dangerous business. I don't know how Jodi does it.

And then, I wonder, is self-obsession what I'm really after? Isn't it enough to just take a day trip to Boston? Now I have to go and get my face pumped full of poison, too? I mean, yes, I want to look younger. But what is the cost and what the gain?

First thought: Doug will be mad. More than mad. He once said he would lose respect for me if I ever did any cosmetic alterations.

I wonder if he'd remember saying that. It was kind of a while ago now.

Anyway, isn't it *my* face?

My face, yes. But he has to look at it every morning for the rest of his life.

Except, not tomorrow morning, because I'll be slipping out early to travel to Boston. Ha!

Come back down to earth, Lauren, and deal with the decision at hand.

Okay, so Doug likes you the way you are.

Which is, you know, sweet.

But I could look *better*. Wouldn't he like *that* even *more*?

We haven't seen much of each other lately. I wonder if he

remembers what I really look like up close. Maybe this "tweak" of mine could fly beneath his radar?

I could just not tell him, I think, channeling my inner Jodi.

I didn't tell him about the pocketbook, and that went pretty smoothly, I rationalize.

Now that my hair is colored and cut in a new style, I could just insist that this is what's making me look younger. Jodi almost didn't recognize me because of my hair, after all. People don't have to know that I look better because I froze some really small muscles on my face.

But then I wonder, if he doesn't notice any change, does that mean the procedure was successful? Or, isn't the whole point of getting Botox done to have people gushing about how fabulous you look?

See, I'm already self-obsessed, and I haven't even had botulism injected under my skin yet.

I enter the elevator in Dr. Grossman's office building and hit "3." The back wall is covered with mirrored panels, so I turn and stare at myself some more.

I never really thought about my forehead much. If I do go through with this today, I know I'll examine my face all the time. I'll have to watch my forehead change, and then worry about it, and then run back to the doctor's office to maintain the perfection of it. Maintenance is expensive, and it's perpetual.

As it is, I have hair color to maintain, and we all know how well I've done at that. And let's not even talk about my bikini area.

I've heard that if you don't keep up with the Botox schedule, your face morphs dramatically overnight. Like, for a few months you're all smooth and glowy like a freshly picked apple and then, boom! You wake up on the morning after the expiration date looking like an apple-head doll. Wear a cloak and people will start asking you to perform voodoo.

Plus, there's cost to think about. I keep some of my teaching salary for fun splurges. Would I rather have new clothes or a wrinkle-free brow?

If I started tutoring kids after school, maybe I could afford both.

Tutoring for Botox? Is that crazy or inspired?

Though I'm still undecided when I reach the receptionist's desk, I give my name and wait to hear what Dr. Grossman's opinion will be.

In the waiting room, I check my e-mails and see that there is a follow up from Lenny. I am expecting it to be another group message, but this one's personal.

`So, what did you think? I'm waiting.`

My heart lurches a little. I scold myself, but I write back immediately:

`Not bad.`

I'm about to write more, but a woman in teddy bear scrubs opens the glass partition and calls, "Lauren Worthing? The doctor's ready for you," so I hit "send" and take a deep breath.

As we walk the pale hallway, I imagine meeting Lenny for drinks in the city sometime in the near future. As I swivel toward him on my bar stool, he tells me that I look as great as I did in high school. No! *Even better than ever, Lauren, like you haven't aged a day.*

In the examination room, I hop up onto the giant reclining chair and wait. "Change into this backless paper gown," the teddy bear assistant directs. "And the doctor will be with you in a few moments."

"But I'm just having him look at my face," I explain.

"Still. We like to embarrass everyone. Please put on the gown." As she pulls open the door to leave the room, I catch a glimpse of the next patient being taken down the hall.

The woman is frumpy and in late middle age, with drab brown hair styled like the queen of England's.

Oh my God, I know a woman with hair like that. It's Martha, my principal! She turns her head toward the nurse walking beside her, and in that moment my worst suspicions are confirmed. She's here. I quickly close the door and duck out of sight.

By the time Dr. Grossman comes into the room I am an emotional wreck. "I can't do this!" I say, the tears welling up in my eyes. "It's just crazy! It's not who I am!" I tuck the paper gown under my butt.

"It's okay, Lauren," Dr. Grossman begins, sitting down on his leather-covered stool and then wheeling over to my side. "So many women feel the way you do when beginning treatment with Botox or other fillers." He scratches his balding head, displacing a tiny tuft of white hair, and smiles up at me. "But I think you'll find that, while the decision-making part of the process can be difficult, the rewards will immediately make up for any conflicted feelings you are experiencing right now. In only two days, results may be visible!"

"I'm such a liar," I sob.

"*Lying* is a strong word for the most popular cosmetic procedure in America. I prefer to view this as an aesthetic fib."

"It's not just the Botox," I try to explain. "It's everything. I'm having some honesty issues. At home, at work, in general."

"Ah, I see. A midlife crisis, perhaps?" He opens my file and takes a look. "You're thirty-nine. Sounds like you are right on schedule for yours." He smiles wanly.

"Let me guess. If I just get Botox, all my problems will be erased?" I joke.

"Well, no. These lines right here will be erased." He hands me a tissue and gently examines the crease between my eyebrows. "But the rest is much harder to smooth over. Why do you think I became a dermatologist instead of a psychiatrist?" He shrugs, moving across the room to prepare the syringe. "I wave my magic wand and miracles happen. In many cases, I can instantly make my patients happy. Not so with psychiatry."

"So you're saying I should quit seeing my shrink and just come to you?"

The intercom beeps and a voice fills the room. "Dr. Grossman, call from Columbia Presbyterian on line two."

He puts down the supplies and takes off his rubber gloves. "If you'll excuse me, I have to take this. We've been playing phone tag all day. It'll just be a minute." He leaves me alone with my paper gown and some thoughts.

I haven't seen my psychiatrist, Dr. Joan, for about a year now. Maybe I should have gone to her office today instead of here, I consider, fighting off the nausea building in my throat. But then I remember: I always leave her office crying, and there are never any visible results. It's an endless loop. *Time's up, come back next week and we'll keep talking about your lame, upper-middle-class problems.* For years and years and years!

Time to try something new.

That's what Dr. Joan always wanted for me, after all, to break out of my rut. What would she say? *You suffer from Good Girl syndrome. Don't always worry about what other people will think of you, if they will approve of your decisions, your clothing, your actions. All those competing voices are keeping you from shaping your life your own way. Dig deep and decide what's right for you. Then you can go out and find it.*

Dr. Grossman coughs as he re-enters the room. He crosses to the counter to get a new pair of gloves from the box, then adjusts the glasses on the bridge of his nose. "So. Are we ready to do this?" he asks, handing me a mirror and scooting to my side on his wheelie stool.

"Indeed!" I chirp, doubts erased, looking at my face as he continues. It comes out perhaps a bit louder than necessary, making Dr. Grossman jump a little.

"Okay, then. I'd like to start by just injecting this area between the eyebrows, called the glabellar lines. They are creating this number eleven you've got right there, and they tend to make one seem angry. Botox is really good at freezing these muscles and smoothing them out. You're young, still, so this treatment might be enough. If not, as a second line of defense, I'd have you come back and I'd use a filler like Restylane to plump it up. Okay?"

To me it sounds like *blahblahblahblahblah*, followed by a cash register opening, cha-ching!

"Yup!" I gush. "Okay!" My heart is beating wildly. This decision has released so much adrenaline that I have to mentally try to slow my insides down. *Deep breaths, Lauren. In and out.*

The needle advances.

"Now, you're going to feel a pinch. There. And another, there. And one more. And...done."

He hands me some gauze soaked in alcohol and tells me to hang tight for a while, holding the swab over the sight of my former elevens. "Remember, these are surface changes, Lauren. They will help, but they won't solve what's really bothering you. I've been removing those warts from your feet for thirty years." Dr. Grossman removes his gloves and clasps his hands together. "And so *I* know that *you* know what really matters. You'll figure it out," he adds, opening the door and waving a good-bye.

A mellow old sage, with all the confidence in the world that I will do right.

Dr. Grossman is like my very own Yoda.

I try to pay the (very expensive) bill quickly and without bumping into Martha. I locate a pair of slightly crooked sunglasses in the bottom of my handbag and put them on. Martha's voice carries down the hall, and, just as it gets louder, she turns the corner and I pass through the wooden office door and out of sight.

I hope there is some confusion about Martha's insurance that significantly delays her exit.

I consider taking the stairs to ensure a fast departure, but get sidetracked by my appearance in the elevator bank's wavy silver doors.

My forehead looks pretty normal, though there is some stinging at the precise points where the toxin was injected. It's hard to tell exactly how much bruising there is, since it's kind of dark in the hallway. When the doors open, revealing the mirrored back wall of the elevator, I press "L" and go stare at my reflection under the fluorescent light.

A voice calls "Hold that door!" just as it's closing. It's Martha, goddammit! Her sensible right shoe is about to encounter the sensor. The doors will push back to let her in.

And if that happens, I shall be screwed.

I frantically hit the "close" button and try to push the doors shut with sheer mind strength.

And, magically, it works.

But not before Martha gets a good, clear look at me and I at her. "Lauren?" she whisper-asks. Her brow wrinkles in a way that mine may never do again.

And then she's gone.

I collapse against one wall and cough out nervous laughter that ricochets around the empty elevator, making me sound like a mentally unstable cartoon villain. My heart slows to a gallop.

Martha was so surprised and confused to see me out of place like this just now that she actually used my first name. Unheard of! Revolutionary!

This cannot be good.

I start moving as soon as the doors separate. I'm across the lobby and pushing around the revolving glass doors when I hear her behind me.

Damn you, stupid revolving doors! You are a death trap for errant schoolteachers everywhere.

"Mrs. Worthing?"

Lauren, I coach myself, *be invisible. Be deaf, blind,* and *invisible. And pretend to talk on the phone. Yes! Be deaf, blind, invisible* and *distracted, and move your ass as fast as you can across that parking lot and into the safety of your vehicle.*

I move my ass, move my ass, move my ass across the parking lot.

Using the remote start button on my keychain, I prepare my minivan for immediate takeoff and hop inside.

I put my foot on the gas and accelerate quickly, only to be stopped by a red-and-white-striped gate at the end of the parking lot. "Hurry, hurry!" I say, searching through my wallet for the white paper ticket and inserting it into the credit card slot. I inspect my rearview mirror, scoping for signs of Martha, feeling very much like Marty McFly when his flux capacitor isn't fluxing. Time is running out. "C'mon…c'mon!" I pray.

The barrier pulls up and lets me through. "Yes!" I exhale, bumping my palm against the steering wheel in a sort of high five. The victory music from *Back to the Future* plays in my head like my very own inspirational soundtrack. As I make a left turn, I check the rearview mirror once again. Martha's car pulls up to the exit kiosk, just as the arm of the gate drops in front of it.

Ha! Take that, lady! You and your moles are no match for Team Worthing.

I'm figuring it out, Dr. Grossman.

Really.

At a red light, I take a deep breath, letting go of any tension from my narrow escape. I need to mentally toughen up before driving the next half mile back to my house.

I wonder what today's welcome-home surprise will be. No

baths? Homework not done? Piano teacher pissed off? Something on fire?

My phone vibrates, letting me know that a text has come in. It's Georgie.

Glad to hear from you! I'll be in my usual place, 11:00.

I write back quickly, before the light changes to green. *It's been a long time. C u soon.*

Looking forward to it bubbles back her response.

CHAPTER 9

MY HOUSE IS UNNATURALLY STILL when I enter. "Ben?" I call out. "Becca? Laney?" I move cautiously into the kitchen, hoping my family hasn't been massacred.

Sometimes I get macabre.

A yellow Post-it is attached to the refrigerator, reading *Gone to park 3:30.*

Huh. Laney took my kids outside. For physical activity. Some vitamin D. Astonishing.

She must want something.

A raise?

Complete ownership of my ceramic straightening iron?

I riffle through the possibilities while heading back out the front door and down the block. At the curve in the road, I take the shady dirt path through the woods, which opens onto a baseball field and playground. There, on the blacktop basketball courts, with their bicycles (their *bicycles*!), are my children. Laney is standing by, cheering them on. She's not texting on her phone, listening to her iPod, or even chatting it up with another babysitter in the park. She's actually paying attention to my kids and having fun with them.

It's been a while since she's done that.

Come to think of it, it's been a while since I've done that.

"Mommy!" Becca calls, seeing me emerge through the trees. "Look!"

I watch as she pushes down hard on the pedals and gets the bike to move steadily forward without needing a shove from behind. "That's super-duper, puppy!" I call, feeling warmth spread through me. Who knew such a small action could inspire me to cheer so loudly? And when did Becca get so big?

Ben gets off his bicycle and comes over sort of shyly, pulling a tennis ball from his jacket pocket. "Wall ball?" I ask.

He merely nods his head as we walk over to the racquetball wall set up on the other side of the park. Wall ball is a third-grade phenomenon. The rules seem to have been passed down through the ages, from out-going third-grade boys to incoming third-grade boys, perhaps through some sort of formalized, recess-based ceremony that only they know about. Keeping the traditions of this ritual alive in playgrounds and blacktops of this great land is critical to the culture of nine-year-old males.

In September, when I asked Ben how he learned about this game with all its very many complicated (and sometimes contradictory) rules and regulations, he shrugged. "I just did, that's all." I pictured him being sworn to secrecy behind the jungle gym before being handed a neon-yellow ball.

I love playing wall ball with Ben, talking about our day, laughing about nothing.

Even if he does keep changing the rules and I always lose.

"Mom, I have to tell you something," Ben says, concentrating more than necessary on the wall and the ball.

My mom-gut clenches in automatic response, but I keep it breezy. "Sure, pup, what is it?"

"You didn't put my homework in my folder, and I got a zero for the day." He eyes me now, accusingly.

"I didn't?" I say, emphasis on the "I," as in "Why would I?"

"No," he agrees. "You did not! And I missed recess to do it over and now I have to do a whole extra packet of work just because!" He stifles a sob. "And it's all your fault!"

Missed recess? Assigned a whole extra packet? *Well, it's not my fault that your teacher is a bitch,* I think. I take a deep, cleansing breath and say, "Putting your homework in your folder is *your* responsibility." Though the fine line is quite wavy between his list of responsibilities and my acts of indentured servitude.

"I'm not doing it," he shouts, hurling the tennis ball at me and trudging over to the swing set. "You can just write a note to my teacher explaining what you did."

And you can just go to hell, my friend, I think, *'cause I'm not doing that.*

"Don't talk to me like that!" I call after him.

"Ay, Dios mio!" Laney exclaims from the blacktop, where she is standing with Becca.

"What?" I ask, jogging to their side. "Becca, are you okay?"

She nods from under her bicycle helmet and silently points at Laney.

"She *bit* me!" Laney says, clutching one hand in the other. "Like a dog."

"No!" I say. But I'm not really sure of that, so I ask my very quiet five-year-old. "Becca, did you bite Laney?"

"We were playing a game called Cats and Dogs!"

"Becca!" I yell. "You never hurt someone *on purpose*. Only accidentally!" Which might not be the best way to explain what I mean, because Becca's nodding her head in furious agreement.

"I didn't mean to, Mommy! Really!"

How many times have I heard that from her, I wonder, trying to catalogue the most recent examples. Last week, it was a boy down the street who she didn't mean to punch, and the week before that it was a teacher's aide on the playground who she "accidentally" kicked in the shins. Since she started kindergarten, I've spent more time at Becca's school than at my own.

"How did this happen?" I say, looking to the sky for an answer.

"Well," Laney begins, "first, we pretended that we were at a kennel…"

"No, Laney, not *this*," I say, gesturing to the small, jagged teeth imprints in her flesh. "*This*!" I say, sweeping my hands across the playground in a generous motion. "My life! The way things are fine and then, suddenly, *bam*, they aren't! They are very not fine!"

"Oh," she says. "That's like, what do you call it…existential, right? I am going back to the house to clean this and put on a bandage."

Everyone else has left the playground now that the sun is setting. Metallic creaking from Ben's swing and the chirping of a few birds are the only sounds besides a roaring in my ears. I sit cross-legged on the blacktop and rest my head in my hands, trying to still my pounding heartbeat.

We were having so much fun, I think. *Why does my time with them always have to slide into chaos and stress?* I try to flood my mind with serene images: a turquoise ocean, a palm tree, the hot sun.

It helps, a little.

"Googly's here," Becca says, gently tapping me on the arm. "And I'm sorry."

"You'll have to apologize to Laney back at the house, Becca," I say, sighing. "But I thank you for saying it to me, too."

I stand up and walk with her toward our favorite little pooch, a gray Poodle who always has a pink bow in her hair.

"Hi, doggie," Becca says, petting the sweet animal.

"Wearing your sweater today, I see," I say, talking directly to the dog.

"Yes, we've just come from Miami, where it is so warm, and she loved it," Googly's owner, an elderly man with a French accent informs us. "But here, the evenings are still chilly, and Googly is very sensitive to cold."

"Aww..." We nod, petting the dog and making a big fuss over her. Ben ambles over slowly. He doesn't acknowledge me, but he has picked up the tennis ball and now throws it for Googly. She dashes after it and grabs it but won't give it back. My kids think this is hysterical.

Their laughter lightens the mood and helps me start breathing again.

Maybe all we need to ensure family harmony is a dog with a sweet personality and comedic flair.

"She's not much of a retriever," her owner acknowledges. Googly wags her tail in agreement, eventually giving up the ball.

"My turn!" Becca shouts, throwing the ball for the dog, who looks lazily past it and decides instead to chew some dandelions. Ben runs after the ball and a game of catch ensues.

"So, Miami, huh?" I say, by way of conversation with this man who I see all the time but whose name I do not know. At this point in our relationship, it would be sort of awkward to ask, so I let it slide.

"Yes. It was splendid," he says, nodding at the memory. "Such an easy trip, you know. So many direct flights from New York, so many wonderful, dog-friendly hotels in South Beach. The best little getaway I know of," he sighs.

I sigh too, wrapping my arms around myself in the crisp evening air. "Sounds perfect."

It's getting late. I announce that it's dinnertime, and we wave good-bye to Googly and her owner.

The kids spend the entire walk home—and most of dinnertime—pleading for a dog of their own.

I'm thinking about Googly, too. How nice it must have been for him to get away from chilly New York for a few days.

Right before Laney leaves for the evening, I remind her of tomorrow's schedule. "You will need to take the kids to the bus in the morning, so be here by eight." She nods. I don't tell her why, that I'll be on a train to Boston to pick up a sweater and then meet a friend for coffee. Even in my own head it sounds crazy. "And I have that party to go to at night, so I'll just be home to change around dinner time before going back out. I'm not sure what Doug's schedule is," I say, unsuccessfully trying to keep the annoyance out of my voice.

"Okay, then. Bye, mis amores!" Laney calls out, blowing kisses to the kids. "I had fun with you today!"

Later, as I'm cleaning up in the kitchen and overseeing Ben's homework, I panic. *Homework*, I think. *What's my homework tonight? Tests to grade? Lesson plans to write? Reading, to stay a chapter ahead of the class?*

The rolling seasickness passes as I remember: I'm on leave. No tests to grade this week. No lesson plans to write, no books to read for class, no parents to e-mail. Relief washes over me like warm rain.

"Hey, Ben?" I ask. He looks up from his homework. "Wanna have a family game night tonight?"

"Really?" The surprise in his eyes tells me all I need to know. "With a championship round and everything?"

"Indeed. Championship round and everything. The World Series of board games."

"With me, too?" Becca asks, coming out of the bathroom. "I can have a family game night, too?"

"Of course! That's why it's called 'family.'"

"And Daddy, too?" Ben adds hopefully.

I pause. "Um...sorry. It's Tuesday, Daddy's tennis night. He won't be home until ten or ten thirty."

Ben looks down at his homework and scratches his head.

"I know, pup. I probably won't see him tonight either, if that makes you feel any better."

He finishes his math worksheet and begrudgingly follows me into the den.

"Yay!" Becca calls, pulling out all the games. "Which one first?"

After an hour of board games, followed by baths and stories, my kids are tucked in and the hallway feels sleepy. I tiptoe down the stairs and into the darkened kitchen. Doug won't be home from his tennis match for two hours.

Time for Facebook.

I loved high school so much that, sometimes, I miss it. Doug thinks I teach middle school in order to help me recapture my youth.

I tell him he's crazy.

But I also think: Is it so bad to want to recapture your youth?

Nothing brings me back to high school faster than a status update from a person I haven't seen since 1988.

The pale glow of the computer screen is welcoming. I sign in and check my home page for updates.

Jamie in California is making challah.

On a Tuesday? I think. That woman is always making challah. It's like she's trying to out-Jew the rest of us in cyberspace.

Liz has another gastrointestinal bacterial infection and has been in the bathroom for two days. Liz shares way too much.

John in DC sent out another invitation to an online political rally tomorrow night. This one is called Who Cares? The answer is Not I.

Photos of the Wallin family. Ugly kids, poor things.

Ellen has beat her high score at Bejeweled Blitz! Challenge her to a game and see how you do. Or don't.

And then there's one from a person named Ninth Wonder. He wants to know if I have any used contact lenses that I could send to him for an art installation he's working on. "I live in a tent now in the Adirondacks, so you can just send them to my PO Box," he advises. Huh?

I scroll through my list of friends to try and figure out who this could be. When I see that he and I have Lenny Katzenberg as a friend in common, I send a private message to Len.

```
Who the hell is Ninth Wonder and how do we
know him?
```

While I'm waiting for a response, I decide to stalk some more long-lost high school and college friends. Tonight feels like a good night for Dan.

Dan's this one ex-boyfriend from college who is particularly fun to follow. He lives in Colorado with his wife and three kids; naturally, the whole family is really outdoorsy. Dan spends all winter uploading great images of kids bundled in ski parkas and helmets and masks coming down the slopes. The only way to tell the kids apart is by the colors of their jackets. There's Romy, in pink, riding on a lift. The boys, Parker and Hunter—though I don't know which is which—together with their snowboards. Dan and his wife Lynn, with their big, Chiclet-white teeth, at the top of a fake-looking, white-capped mountain.

I hate the outdoors. But sometimes I like to pretend I'm Lynn, married to Dan, living in Colorado with my three adventurous, mountain-loving children. Tonight we are sitting by the fire in our huge log cabin. Romy has just come back from mucking the stalls in the stables (I've added horses to the fantasy, though in real life I hate them, too), and all the boots and hats and layers of a life spent in nature are piled in the generous-sized mudroom off the kitchen. Dan has made his famous homemade popcorn, and we are playing charades in our waffle-weave long johns. I don't celebrate Christmas, but in this reverie, every day is just like the Hallmark greeting card version of that holiday.

There's an open bottle of wine in the refrigerator calling my name. I pour a large glass, put away some dishes, turn off the kitchen lights, and move back over to the computer.

By now, Lenny has written back to me:

```
I think "Ninth Wonder" is Sean Mallory, from
high school. He's finally gone off the deep
end. What a freak. Hey—that wasn't much of a
response to my video today. You've let me down.
```

His video! My Botox! I forgot. I type in a response as fast as I can with my self-taught, three-fingered technique.

```
Am such an idiot! I'm so (with like ten million
```

o's) sorry. I was in the doctor's office and
didn't have time to write more. But I thought
it was brilliant. Truly. Hilarious.

And maybe just a tad bit sexy.

I hit "send" and immediately regret it. I am e-freaked out by my
own e-forwardness, which requires several sips of wine to wash away.

Lenny writes back.

Can we chat somewhere more private? I hate fb.

Score one for e-forwardness.

We switch to our own e-mail accounts and continue our conversation, the online version of moving into a dark corner of a
crowded bar. I can almost feel Lenny's hand on my elbow as he
steers me away from the masses of potential onlookers.

I only get up from the computer once, to refill my wine glass
and to grab a handful of chocolate kisses, which I pop like...well,
like candy, actually.

From: lkatzenberg@yale.alumni.edu

Better. Now, what was that you were saying
about my video?

From: laurenworthing@gmail.com

That it's hotter than one of Jamie's freshly
baked challahs? That I like how you shake
your moneymaker?

I can't believe I just wrote that.

From: lkatzenberg@yale.alumni.edu

Yeah, moneymaker is pretty cheesy. I prefer
the term "booty." Also, there's nothing
wrong with a good old-fashioned "ass" now

and then. Yours, for example, I remember it being a good old-fashioned, nice little ass.

From: laurenworthing@gmail.com

Not true. I have a terrible ass. In fact, you once criticized my ass in high school for not being as round and perky as Lila Cummings' was, like I could just go to the mall and buy a better J-Lo. FYI.

Actually, I saw Lila recently. Two kids later, and she still has a fabulous behind. It's not natural.

What kind of a moron debunks a myth in a guy's head about the shapeliness of her ass? *Really, Lauren,* I scold myself. *Flirt wiser. He can't see you, so what's the difference?* Honest at all the wrong times, I swear.

I surf through Amazon while waiting for Lenny's response and order a new thriller about this guy who stalks women through Facebook.

From: lkatzenberg@yale.alumni.edu

Lovely image of you with Lila's ass. Did you touch it at all? Maybe rub up against it accidentally on purpose with your arm or something? Could you at least just pretend for me? Give a lonely guy something to work with?

Hey—are you going to be up for a while? I have something I'd like to show you.

From: laurenworthing@gmail.com

I'm not sure I want to see that.

From: lkatzenberg@yale.alumni.edu

It's my new video, douche.

From: laurenworthing@gmail.com

You didn't just call me that, did you?

From: lkatzenberg@yale.alumni.edu

What? Great '80s term. I'm bringing it back.

From: laurenworthing@gmail.com

Okay, but I think it's like totally grody to the max to call a woman a douche bag. Maybe this is why you don't have a girlfriend. Just a guess.

From: lkatzenberg@yale.alumni.edu

Speaking of which, it's too bad you and I never dated. Could have been hot, going south of the border together.

Where was this offer in 1988, I want to know? I get up from the computer and stretch, digging through the cupboards. There is solace in chocolate-covered gummy bears.

I chew through a few potential responses before deciding on one that doesn't make me sound like my inner wounded, prom-dateless teenager.

From: laurenworthing@gmail.com

Yes, tres mal. I often wonder how my life might have turned out if only I had let you into my pants.

From: lkatzenberg@yale.alumni.edu

I detect sarcasm.

From: laurenworthing@gmail.com

Really? Can't imagine why.

From: lkatzenberg@yale.alumni.edu

Lauren. Maybe I'm being serious.

I physically pull away from the computer, my face flushed. I need to remember where this is coming from. Lenny Katzenberg, awarded Biggest Flirt honors in high school, who has been engaged twice and gotten cold feet both times. Lenny, who used to scan the room at high school keg parties, looking bored, while I tried to make him laugh and he ignored me.

From: laurenworthing@gmail.com

You only want what you can't have.

From: lkatzenberg@yale.alumni.edu

Debatable. But in any case, I need your help with my latest project. I need your Aegean blue—I mean, honest and insightful—eyes to critique it before I post. Will you do that for me, no strings attached?

From: laurenworthing@gmail.com

What if I hate it?

From: lkatzenberg@yale.alumni.edu

You won't. It's awesome, like I am in all things.

From: laurenworthing@gmail.com

Hubris: look it up. You are not supposed to declare greatness at anything, lest the gods smite you with their wrath.

From: lkatzenberg@yale.alumni.edu

I thought if I came on strong with machismo,
you'd fall at my feet. No?

Next time, I will go for sensitive, poet-type
come-on.

Video's going to be ready for viewing in two
hours. You up for that? What's your ETS?

From: laurenworthing@gmail.com

Not up for it. Estimated time to sleep is in
about 10 minutes, max. Too bad we're not in
the same place. Then I could roll over and go
to sleep and you could nudge me awake when
you're ready for an audience.

From: lkatzenberg@yale.alumni.edu

Don't even put that image in my mind. How am
I going to work now?

From: laurenworthing@gmail.com

Alone, I guess.

I erase and destroy all the e-mails from tonight, then log off,
slightly embarrassed that I could be so forward. My online persona
just kind of took over there. I'm like some kind of modern-day Cy-
rano, whispering all the great lines from behind my computer
screen. If faced with flirting with Lenny face-to-face, I'd turn about
a thousand shades of purple and choke on my own tongue.

Still another hour before Doug gets home.

Just before quitting out of the computer, I decide to go back
on Facebook to update my status.

I click into the empty box, and the question "What's on your
mind?" stares back at me, waiting for an answer.

Everything? Nothing? I don't know *what*. Fill in the blank, I guess, like on one of my very own horrendous, multiple-choice grammar quizzes. I imagine scanning the page for the right answer, increasingly nervous as the minutes tick by and the correct choice eludes me.

I leave the space blank and log off the computer.

Then I scribble a friendly little Post-it note to Doug, like he's my college roommate, and stick it on the fridge. After dumping the empty chardonnay bottle in the recycling bin and hiding it under some soda cans, I turn off the lights and make my way to bed.

Only, I can't sleep.

Thirty minutes later, the mechanical buzz of the garage door triggers in me a mild but certain dread. Doug parks the car and enters the house. He moves around the kitchen a bit, and I follow the trail of sounds as he turns on the faucet for a drink of water, riffles through some papers, and searches for something to snack on in the cabinets.

Then I hear him set the alarm and climb the stairs.

In the darkness, I picture Lenny. And Dr. Grossman. And Sweetheart and Brandon.

I picture Doug's tennis league and wonder if he ever lies about where he's going and who he's with.

"You awake?" he whispers.

I feel him studying me as his vision adjusts to the darkness.

Playing possum, I keep my eyelids gently shut. I try to think of dreamlike scenarios the way a method actor would to convincingly portray deep sleep—I'm on the beach; I've won the lottery; someone's chasing me, only I can't run—*No, no, no, not that kind of dream, Lauren,* I scold myself—stay calm! Shallow intakes of breath, keep the rhythm steady.

"Lauren?"

When I don't respond, he pads across the carpeting and into the bathroom, shutting the door gently behind him.

Doug showers and changes into pajamas—boxers and a white Hanes T-shirt, I know even with my eyes closed—slides into bed next to me and promptly falls asleep.

Now the only sound in the house is the slight pounding of my guilt-ridden forehead.

CHAPTER 10

Wednesday

AS I AM WAITING FOR THE AMTRAK to arrive, a garbled voice comes over the speaker, announcing a thirty-minute delay northbound. I take a seat on a concrete bench and wait it out, hoping this delay isn't some sign from God that I shouldn't be making the trip.

Forehead feels the same, though there is some slight bruising that I covered with makeup. Don't know what I expected, but a little something-something would have been encouraging.

So far, no regrets about yesterday.

Except for the slight pang of remorse I felt this morning upon waking, recalling last night's drink-and-flirt session with Lenny. Did I go too far? I can't really remember what I said, which might just be for the best.

Instead of dwelling on anything potentially negative, like my marital malaise or my tendency to want to stray both physically and emotionally from all responsibilities—Ha ha! What a mess!—I continue reading that delicious novel about absolutely nothing. The train eventually comes, and I move, book open and eyes reading, into a seat, enjoying the cheesy pleasure of escapism for the better part of the morning.

Getting up to stretch around New Haven is a ritual with me. I used to ride this train all the time to visit my aunt, who lived outside Boston. It was an adventure as a teenager to take such a long train ride alone. I still love the feeling of watching the countryside roll by, glimpsing the New England towns and clapboard homes along the way. I would put something by Phil Collins on my Walkman, tilt my head against the glass windowpane, and let my mind be still. That train ride always felt like a mini vacation, and on this bright, April morning, it doesn't disappoint.

I take a walk to the dining car and scroll through a list of in-coming e-mails while waiting in line for a cup of coffee. There are about ten different messages from Facebook friends commenting on Lenny's latest video. Jamie in California has stopped writing about herself and her children for once, deciding instead to drool over Lenny. I feel a high school–like emotion rising in me as I read her gushing reports about how Lenny was "always so crea-tive, bright and clever—not to mention cute!" when we were teenagers.

How dare she act like she really *knows* Lenny? When was the last time she even spoke to him? I wonder. She didn't even make it to our twentieth reunion, thank you very much. There's a territori-al, nauseating, cheerleaderish feeling mounting in me. I try to push it away, but it just won't budge.

I'm jealous.

Ohmigod, I'm such a loser. Who gets jealous about a woman's comments about a man who doesn't belong to either of them? Why does being around high school friends immediately put me back into high school mode? It's like I've made absolutely no progress. I might as well be back in pre-calculus faking stomach cramps to go hang out behind the dumpster and smoke cigarettes with my best guy friend, Tom. Inhaling deeply, we would dish about everyone and scheme ways to get alcohol out of his parents' locked cabinet in the basement. Then we would go off campus and sit by the duck pond, tossing stale bread into the water and dreaming about get-ting out of this little town.

Needless to say, I got a D in precalculus.

And after college, I moved right back to this same little town, to teach kids who would then cut my class by lying about having stomach cramps.

Oh, the irony.

So, naturally, I do what any mature woman about to turn forty and married with two children would do. As the train pulls out of New Haven and makes its way farther north, I text Lenny.

```
Looks like the new video is a hit!
```

It's just a friendly little hello, like passing notes during science class, but it makes me feel instantly calmer. I've staked my claim on Lenny, even if Jamie in California doesn't know.

As I'm deleting spam, Lenny writes back.

```
Good morning, beautiful. You look lovely today.
Got your beauty rest, I see.
```

Playful and just slightly too familiar. Either his job is really dull or I'm the most exciting person in his gravitational pull.

I go with the latter.

```
Me: So true. I was mistaken for Gwyneth twice
already this morning. Speaking of fabulous,
how'd the video turn out?

Lenny: Ah. Wouldn't you like to know?
```

The compulsively charming bastard. Teasing and tempting me. My pointer fingers fly from key to key as I try to keep up the volley on my phone's small screen.

```
Me: Breathless with anticipation. I checked my
inbox when I woke up, but you weren't there.

Lenny: I like being in your inbox.

Me: I was going to respond with "and I like
having you there," but that just sounds wrong.

Lenny: But, oh, it sounds so right.

Me: Yeegads! Sometimes I can't tell if your
tone is tongue in cheek or molesterish.

Lenny: Yeegads? With tongue, definitely.
```

I am about to write back when Lenny interrupts me with another text.

Hey—just got an update from YouTube. 200,000
hits on my health care reform video since it
premiered yesterday. I think this thing is
gonna go viral!

Going viral? Who talks like that except for Internet hipsters
and their hacker counterpoints? Not being fluent in tech-savvy
lingo makes me feel old. I instinctively touch my forehead for con-
firmation of my age and find that the ridge between my brows
seems less pronounced.

Me: Congrats on maybe going viral!

Lenny: It's only happened one other time in
my life. Remember when I made out with Karen
Zinns after Homecoming and I gave her mono-
nucleosis and then she kissed some alumni
linebacker the next day at the game and gave
him mono, and then he passed it on to Coach
Bill?

Me: Now, that's a fun way to get sick.

Doug Worthing: Huh? Is that your response to
my text?

Did I just write that...to Doug? Where did he come from? My
heart drops in free-fall and I frantically scroll back to see what I've
just done. Then time sort of slows down as I prepare for the impact
of this mistake. It's the real-life version of the moment in the movie
when a kid on a bicycle is about to get hit by a car and an onlooker
runs into the street and screams "Noooooo...!"

How much has Doug seen? When did he replace Lenny?

I scroll up my phone to check the damage.

Meanwhile, Lenny continues our texting dialogue in ignorant
bliss.

And to think, it could have been you I diseased.

I know this is impossible, but I feel like Doug is suddenly in the room with me, reading over my shoulder. My cheeks are flushed like they were last night from the embarrassment of illegal flirtationshiping.

I once read that deep blushing was a sign of sexual arousal, and as that thought enters my brain right now, I blush even more.

To cool down, I peel off my sweater and consider the next move.

The best thing to do is to ignore Lenny's comment entirely while trying to get back on track with Doug.

I find Doug's text, which asks whether I've seen his glasses and if I think the eggs are too old to eat.

No and Yes! I write back. I try to be friendly but firmly dismissive. *Need to get into court ASAP—will be unreachable all day. Have a great one!*

I drop the phone on the empty seat next to mine and take a deep, cleansing yoga breath, stretching my head back to rest against the seat. I close my eyes and count to ten. Then I ask myself one question: What are you doing here, Lauren?

Talking to an old high school friend? Yes.

Escaping a little bit from real life? Indeed.

But is there more to it?

Or is this behavior innocuous? Just a married woman's reinterpretation of feeling like the childhood daredevil by going to an amusement park and screaming with terror and glee on the newest, craziest roller coaster?

And when the ride ends, you walk off the dizzy feeling, eat a Sno-Cone, win a stuffed bear, and head back home, tired but content.

Sounds plausible. Right?

I pick up where I left off and write back to Lenny.

Me: Viral? Define please.

Lenny: When a video or website gets over one million hits, it has gone viral. That's my goal— to knock one of these videos out of the park, and launch into a career that requires more singing/dancing/writing/rapping/ass-shaking than accounting does.

At age forty? I want to ask. Isn't that a bit, well, over the hill in the entertainment world? Not to be a killjoy or anything. But maybe it's different for guys, who can start families in their forties and become leaders of nations in their fifties and win golf championships in their sixties. For women, power comes from being young and glamorous, and so, as you age, you lose more and more strength every year. Unless you're Hillary or Oprah, in which case, even as you change policy and make the world a better place, people still remark on how fat and old you look.

Anyway.

I decide not to bother Lenny with my delusions of his delusions. He didn't sign on to this virtual courtship to be bogged down by a brooding midlifer with no sense of humor, and I didn't sign on to be the voice of reason. I read back our exchange from the morning and try to get back into funny mode before I hit Beantown.

Me: It's a shame that there's so little ass-shaking in finance these days.

Lenny: A lot of ass-kissing, though. And plenty of people still getting fucked by their banks.

Me: My train's pulling into the station. Literally. Gotta go. Good luck spreading disease across the Internet.

Lenny: You in NYC? Can I do you for lunch?

Me: In Boston. Got plans with Georgie.

Lenny: Who is Georgie? Am green-eyed.

Me: Friend from grad school.

I disembark and put my phone in my bag. Best to keep him guessing.

CHAPTER 11

GEORGIE IS ACTUALLY DR. GEORGINA PARKS, Professor Emeritus at the Harvard Graduate School of Education. She was the head of the Language and Literacy program when I was a student there, and from the first moment I heard her speak, I was inspired. Actually, I was inspired even before I met her, having already read her two seminal books on education, not to mention all of her related articles.

Georgie is one of the country's leading educational figureheads, a political mover and shaker. She's an inspiration to American educators everywhere, having influenced national policy and changed the way we think about teaching children to read. She's been on *Oprah*, discussing inequities in urban and rural areas of America. She's been on *60 Minutes*, promoting Literacy Speaks, her nonprofit program whose mission is to eradicate illiteracy in this country. She's larger than life, and she's my professional guru. Every speech she delivers carries with it the authority of the ages, as if she's speaking not from personal opinion bolstered by factual data, but from holy, ancient sources of wisdom.

You just don't mess with Georgie's ten educational commandments.

I haven't seen her in several years, since before I got pregnant with Becca.

There was this popular education tome from the 1990s, called *Other People's Children*, that I read in grad school and that prompted Georgie's first commandment, "Loyalty to other people's children first," so I'm a little bit nervous to tell her that I now have two of my own.

Another commandment is "Lying only hurts you in the end," though, so that one makes me feel more at ease. I mean, I can't lie to her and say I don't have another child when I do, right? Based on Georgie's philosophy, that will only come back to bite me in the ass.

Not sure what she'd say about my whole lying-about-jury-duty thing, though. Best to come up with an excuse right now about the reason for my trip.

By the time the train pulls into Boston's Back Bay, I have read half a novel, maintained the highly inappropriate level of my online flirtationship, and kept my husband from getting salmonella poisoning, while sidestepping a close call. All in all, I'm feeling pretty good.

I push open the heavy wooden doors to the lecture hall and quietly find a seat in the back of the room. Because of the train delay, I have missed most of this morning's lecture. The auditorium is filled with eager, fresh-faced twentysomethings, laptops glowing, fingers tapping to take down every word being said. Georgie is up at the podium. Her black hair is straight like Michelle Obama's, her body solid like Jennifer Hudson's during the *Dreamgirls* phase.

Working without notes, she discusses a recent intervention made by her team at Literacy Speaks, in which a whole school in New Orleans was saved.

Georgie's voice is filled with a deep, southern timbre that carries up the aisles like an evangelical preacher's. "These children were at risk of drowning *twice. Twice*. Once from Hurricane Katrina. And, then, after being saved from that deluge, they were almost flooded again by inequities in our educational system. These children were left to drown in their own ignorance. Right here in America, people.

"This is not okay," she says. "It. Is. Not."

She bows her head and the lights go down. An image of a black child reading a book is projected behind her, the last slide in her PowerPoint presentation. People close their laptops and stand to applaud her, and I join in.

In grad school, I was lucky enough to have been one of ten students in the program selected for Georgie's spring seminar, Reading and Writing as Empowerment. I took that opportunity to become Georgie's star pupil. I made sure that my research mirrored hers, that I quoted the right sociopolitical educational theorists at least three times in every essay, and that I read and reread the assigned texts so that I could recite important passages during class.

When Georgie said that children were stifled by tests corrected in red pen, I threw out my red pens. When she said that tests themselves were counterproductive to the real work of teaching literacy, I stopped giving children tests. When she said, a year later, that tests were the only logical measurement for reading comprehension, I brought back the tests.

I even started to sound like her during writing conferences, telling my students that their ideas were "so big," and that their writing "could change the world."

I had become a Georgie puppet. I wasn't sure the package was authentically "me," but it sounded really good, and made me seem really together, and for a while, that was more than good enough.

Because, having that letter of recommendation from the country's leading educational activist helped me land any job I wanted. And, at the time, there was nothing that I wanted more than to teach in prestigious Hadley, New York.

It took me quite a while to detox from all that Georgie-speak. To this day, fifteen years later, I still find myself using only green pens to grade tests. I use pencils to write on essays, believing that this will show students that, while their words are permanent, mine are erasable, mere suggestions meant only to help push their thoughts further.

If there's one person who can get me out of my run-fast-from-my-middle-school funk, it's Georgie. Hell, I'd even bet that she can inspire me on a personal level. If Georgie told me to have sex with my husband every night for the next two years, I would do it. Well, I'd seriously consider it, at any rate.

I wait for her to finish talking to some adoring fans before approaching the front of the room. She spots me and smiles, breaking away from the group.

"Lauren! So good to see you!" We hug and I get swallowed by her ample bosom. Georgie's just big in every way. "I was delighted when I got your text last night." She steps back to study me. "You look younger."

"I do?" I don't know if this is a good thing or not. My hand flies up to touch my forehead gingerly, unwittingly drawing attention there. I snap my arm back down to my side. It's the first time that anyone's noticed the Botox and I'm not sure how to react.

"Mm," she says, cocking an eyebrow knowingly. "I like it."

I relax. Having Georgie's approval still means something to me, even if it's unrelated to the field of education. I am a bit surprised, though, since I would have assumed surface changes were not her style.

She stops to speak to a few more students before we leave the lecture hall, then leads the way to her office, a gorgeous, loft-like expanse with casement windows, open to let the breeze in, overlooking the quad. On the way, we chat about life—hers, at any rate—her research, her travel plans, her life's goals being checked off the master list one by one.

"And you?" Georgie asks, once we've settled in to some chairs around a circular table in her office, each with a steaming cup of coffee in hand.

"And me." I say, considering the multiple-choice answers I could pick from. I go with A: Home Life. "I have two demanding, draining, life-sucking—although wonderful, the best ever, wouldn't trade them for anything!—school-age children. They've grown so fast, and sometimes I feel like I don't matter in their lives anymore, except as a chauffeur. And my husband is never really home until after I've put the children to bed, so I feel...lonely. Sometimes I feel like screaming for no reason," I say, feeling like screaming. The concerned look in Georgie's eyes is penetrating.

I don't want to lose my shit in front of her, so I switch focus. "However, I'm still teaching middle school in Hadley. And loving it, of course," I add as an afterthought. "You know me, I'll never tire of those sweaty, fidgety, ADHD middle schoolers!" Okay, maybe that went a bit too far.

She nods thoughtfully. "What about your interest in leadership?" she asks.

"Oh yeah, that," I say, wishing I had just stuck to the miseries of home life. I then have to explain to my idol how I was recently passed over for the chair position in the English Department for an outsider with nepotism on her side. "Despite my fine pedigree, exemplary teaching, and good rapport with parents," I add, with only a hint of sarcasm to my voice. "Despite the fact that I did everything right." I feel my eyes sting again and I fight back tears. Georgie doesn't do tears.

"It is something you still care about," she states rather than asks.

"I don't know what I still care about?" It comes out as a question. Maybe Georgie will answer it for me. That would be nice. She can just tell me what to do so that I can find my way back on course and do it. That's what I liked so much about high school, and college, and grad school, too, come to think of it. There was structure. I took courses and was handed assignments. Teachers just told me where to be and what to do. And as long as I followed the general rules and did my homework, I could coast through.

Maybe I picked teaching as a career because school was the only world I really knew. And maybe—it occurs to me fifteen-plus years too late—that kind of default thinking is lame and lazy.

"Hmm." She actually cocks her head to study me, as if I am some type of rare or exotic bird she's never seen up close before. As if I might become something for her to research. She picks up a pen and begins jotting some notes on a pad. "And, so, what brings you here today?"

I think about the excuses I came up with on the train, and pick the one that sounded best in my head.

Then I meet Georgie's gaze and mentally erase that idea. Who am I kidding? I can't lie to her, of all people. Besides which, I need to tell her the truth so that she can help me make sense of it.

"Because I'm cutting school like a truant teenager?" I smile.

"Interesting." Georgie nods, scribbling more notes.

"Which I'm doing because I'm experiencing a tad bit of a mid-life crisis?"

"Been there!" she says, holding her palms skyward as if I've just found God. I expect her to add an "Amen!" but she doesn't, which is kind of disappointing.

Bolstered by the freeing feeling of truth-telling and the enthusiastic support from Georgie, I'm on a roll. "Because I thought I could get a few days off from my life by sitting on jury duty, only the courts totally screwed with that plan and now I've got to come up with creative field trips to keep me busy and out of Hadley each day?" I say-ask.

"Mmm, mmm, hmm." Georgie is shaking her head at me with

a big fat no that actually means a hearty yes. She jots more notes on the yellow pad in front of her, definitely using a red pen. I call her on it.

"What, this?" she says, motioning to her hand. "It's just a pen. It's not devil worship or anything."

"But...!" I launch into my story of the complete and utter fear I have had of red pen usage in United States classrooms for the past decade and a half. "I don't even let the school secretaries order them from Staples anymore. I've tried to change the entire culture of my school to red-pen adverse."

"Well," she says. "That's just extreme, Lauren." She shakes her head and goes back to taking notes on me.

I am stunned into silence. Either Georgie's changed her tune completely or I really misunderstood my entire two-year graduate program here at Harvard.

"But...I thought...sacrilegious...doesn't honor the students ...demeaning...testing is very good...or is it very bad...?" I trail off, confused.

Georgie shrugs. "Testing is whatever you want it to be, Lauren, whatever you need in order to teach your children the things they must know. And teaching is not about the color of the ink in a pen! It's about the woman holding that pen in her hand. You should know that."

"But you used to say..."

"Used to. Not anymore. Now I'm all about the freedom to choose."

"The freedom to choose...what?"

"Exactly," she says. "The freedom to choose what. Only you know the answer to that."

"What about the ten commandments?"

She cackles loud and deep. "What am I, God? I woke up one morning about two years ago and looked at myself in the mirror. I looked tired. I *was* tired! I was tired of telling people what to do, of how to teach, of how to live, even if it was mostly good advice, mostly done to make lives better. I mean, it was all great at first. But over the years, something changed. I suddenly had a lot to live up to. People expected me to always have the answers, so I gave them answers, telling them red pens were damaging, that testing was the way or definitely *not* the way. Truth is, what did I know? I swear to you, that one morning, I said to my reflection, *Georgina Parks, you do a hell of a lot of preaching for a mere mortal. Maybe it's time to stop being in charge of everything all the time.* And, you know what? It felt empowering to let go."

"But this morning...I heard you. You sounded the same as always, powerful and sure. There were disciples taking notes!"

She laughs again, wiping a tear from her eye. "I know. People like to have something to believe in, Lauren. They need to have something to strive for. Don't you? Why did you come visit me today?"

My knee-jerk response would be "Because of a sweater," but that sounds insulting and empty.

Why did I visit Georgie? "For the same reason these students do, I suppose. To feel a part of something important. And," I add as an afterthought, "to have someone give their lives direction."

"And so that's what I do. But occasionally, it strikes even me as crazy to believe so much in me."

Something indeed is crazy. Georgie's ironclad rules about how to teach and what to teach and when to teach *just don't exist anymore?* Or they do, only she no longer really believes in them?

"Girl, listen to me," she starts. I love the "girl" thing. It's so familiar and yet so authoritative at the same time. When Georgie is addressing a crowd and is looking for the same effect, she'll use "people," like she did during this morning's lecture. And when she's got you one-on-one and wants to drive a point home, nothing is more effective than "girl."

With the use of "girl," I feel sure that she will settle this confusion once and for all and say what I need her to say, say what she used to say.

"No wonder you need a little break from teaching. You take it way too seriously."

Seriously?

Until this moment, there was an urn on a pedestal in my mind, reserved for all that wisdom gleaned from Georgie. Now, broken shards are all that's left of this vessel that once contained everything I found sacred about education, everything I thought was true in the world. I mentally begin the process of cleaning up a few pieces, avoiding the really sharp ones.

I think back to the way I just dismissed Martin on Monday

morning, letting him conjure an entire book plot from thin air. I think about the way letting him off the hook made me feel like I was also off the hook.

Then I look at Georgie's face and start to see her for the first time. She looks back, interested. "Yes?" she asks. "I know, I know, it's shocking! You thought I was a demigod, too, didn't you?"

"I guess," I say, not wanting to sound like the complete follower I have been. What are the right words for this particular scenario, the one in which your life's mentor reveals that she's not All That? "So...let me get this straight...you're like the Wizard of Oz?"

Georgie laughs good-naturedly. "I love it! Yes! Pull aside the curtain and see just how regular I am."

I watch her as she gets up and moves around her office, sorting through piles of mail and manila folders. "My point is, Lauren, that we're all fallible, we're all human. I still believe that literacy is power and that denying children access to that power will keep them down and keep this country from competing in the global economy. The opposite is attainable, though: healthy, literate Americans will change this world, you will see. But am I the only one who can provide structure, answers, plans? Is my word the be-all and end-all of educational opportunity? Hell no."

Hell no?

I don't think the Wizard of Oz was quite that fierce when he gave it up for Dorothy and the gang.

"So...what does all this 'freedom' of yours mean for me?"

Georgie smiles, her dark eyes warm and encouraging. "I think you know the answer to that."

I hate to look weak in front of such greatness, but this discussion is not going the way I had expected, right? So I might as well be perfectly honest, like Georgie. "Um. Pretty sure I don't."

"It will come to you. Just open yourself to the possibility that things can be different. That maybe you are not the master of your so-called master plan."

I'm totally not sure what that means, but I'm not about to argue.

"Don't look at me like that, little lost puppy!" she jokes.

I continue looking at her like a little lost puppy.

"Okay, fine," she sighs. "I *may* have an idea for a project that could involve you. I have to sort through some notes, first. I am switching gears, too, you see. I'm feeling a bit stale after spending twenty-five years on one cause. It's fun to mix it up! So, now I'm thinking about researching women instead of children. Still looking at empowerment. But now focusing on midlife issues. I have to sort through some notes first. No promises."

"Ooh! I'm a woman! I'm in midlife! I have issues! Plus, I've been taking some notes about a similar topic!" I stop to take a breath. "What's it—"

Georgie's palm silences me. "Enough for now. Did I or did I not just say that I am tired of being responsible for other people's lives?"

I nod my head like an obedient puppy.

Georgie comes back to the table and sits. "Lauren, I have always thought of you as one of my best students—particularly when it came to research—but you lacked your own voice, and your own passion and drive. In class, you hung on my every word, reciting me back to me. I worry now that what I saw in you was just a mirror of myself. So. Before I give you this opportunity, I need to know that it really is your promise I was seeing, and not merely my own. Prove to me that you can accomplish something meaningful on your own, and then we'll talk."

I think about what she's saying and I crack a half smile, an idea forming. "Would you like me to bring the Wicked Witch's broom to you as proof of my bravery?"

"Girl," Georgie says with a wink, "you do whatever it takes."

CHAPTER 12

"CHAMPAGNE?"

A very cute young man in a tux is standing next to me at the Chanel makeup counter, silver tray in hand. When I'm stressed out, trying on expensive makeup that I'm never going to buy, and/or painting my nails all different colors, makes me feel enormously better. In the last ten minutes, I have applied bronzer, liquid eyeliner, two different eye shadow colors, and a few other products to my face. I've fibbed to salespeople left and right, telling them that, yes, I'd love to buy their products. Next to one register, there's a pile of small boxes with my name—Dorothy Gale—attached on a yellow Post-it.

Georgie has driven me to the cosmetological brink.

I put down the newest limited-edition nail polish I have been trying and delicately pick up a glass flute.

"Thanks!" I say. "You read my mind!"

I didn't even know that you *could* drink alcohol at Neiman Marcus, much less for free, but I'm not going to question it. I down one glass and reach out for another, before you can even say "Bobby Brown."

I amble the main floor and collect my thoughts.

Maybe Georgie is dying.

She looked really healthy, though. No loss of hair, weight, energy, or bravado, that's for sure.

I remove the strawberry perched on the edge of the champagne flute and take a bite.

Sparkly jewels stare back at me from under locked glass cases. They seem sad, unreachable like that. I imagine them calling out to me like puppies in a shelter, *Take me home! It's so cold in here!* or *I'm the one you want!* I put my face up against the case, listening.

No one can hear diamond-encrusted distress calls from under the protective glass.

I pull back, considering Georgie again.

Maybe I'm losing my hearing.

Or maybe she just means what she said.

Maybe everyone's just tired of working so hard.

Maybe being a full-time grown-up just sucks that way.

Even if you're Georgina Parks, professor emeritus at Harvard University and head of your own educational think tank.

I do think I've learned at least one thing today. Perhaps we need to cut ourselves—and each other—some slack. Perhaps I have to figure out what's real and what's hiding behind the metaphorical curtain.

I finish the second drink and place it on a passing tray. The waiter hands me a postcard announcing the Christian Louboutin shoe event. Buy a pair today and receive a gorgeous faux-gold cuff bracelet, as shown in the picture. Also, if you purchase a pair, your name will be entered into a $5,000 Neiman Marcus shopping spree.

Well.

That just sounds too good to be true.

I wander over to the shoe department, you know, just to have a look.

On the train ride home, I'm feeling a little bit headachy and a little bit remorseful. But then I peek into the large shopping bag seated next to me and smile. Those black Louboutin spiky heels with the red soles are really hot. And now they are really mine.

I've never spent so much on a pair of shoes in my life. I feel simultaneously nauseated and empowered. Not in the way Georgie would use the word, but still. Like I could kick someone's ass in those heels. I'm starting to see why women have shoe addictions. I'm just not sure how they pay for this bad habit.

Unless they use creative cash-back programs like Jodi does.

I will say that opening a credit card at Neiman's was genius. It will allow me to acquire points toward future purchases while also hiding the bill from Doug as I slowly pay it off.

Jeez. That's some warped logic right there, is it not? I'm sounding a bit too much like Jodi for my own liking.

I yawn and feel the champagne mellow me out. The calming rock and roll of the train soothes me. *Vacations are exhausting*, I think, *and expensive*, my mind adds, before sliding into a gentle nap.

I wake to find a bunch of e-mails from Lenny, all of them asking about Georgie and hinting at jealousy.

From: lkatzenberg@yale.alumni.edu

```
Georgie Porgie, pudding and pie
Kissed Lauren and made me cry
When the boys came out to play,
Georgie Porgie pushed Lenny away.
```

And later:

```
I have searched through all your Facebook
friends. Of the 126 of them, there is no one
named George, first or last. Not even a maiden
name, like Alice George-Hamilton or something.
Who is Georgie?
```

And later still:

```
Darn.

It just occurred to me that I may not be your
one and only fling-relationship-flirting-guy
thing.
```

The last one makes me smile, even though the others are cringe-worthy and slightly stalkerish. I write back and tell him so.

Then I find my headphones and listen to another new mix I've made. It takes him the length of about three songs to reply. Eleven minutes. *Playing hard to get, I see*, I think as I open up his response.

Ah, yes, flirtationship is the perfect word
for what we have. Sorry to have accused you
of cheating on Doug and me. Still curious
about why you won't spill on the mysterious
Georgie, though.

Now that I know we're solid, I've got to join
in on a conference call for the next hour or
so. Will you be available again tonight for
some late-night witticisms?

From: laurenworthing@gmail.com

Sorry. Can't. Have a friend's 40th birthday
party to attend.

From: lkatzenberg@yale.alumni.edu

Perhaps it will be naughty nasty girl fun.

From: laurenworthing@gmail.com

Only in your imagination will it be that. ;)

Now that he mentions it, the invitation did arrive with a long red feather boa that I've been instructed to bring to the party. Not that I'm going to admit this to Lenny.

Although, suddenly I'm curious, and more than just slightly worried about what this party might entail.

Kat's been invited to Leslie's party, too, and, even though she doesn't want to go, I'm making her show up to keep me company. Leslie's husband is Kat's distant cousin ("From the drunk side of the family, not the alcoholic side," Kat explained when we both showed up at Leslie's 35th, surprised to see each other).

She'll know the scoop on the party. I pull out my phone and begin dialing. I don't want to annoy my fellow train passengers, but sometimes e-mail just won't do. Scanning the seats around me, I notice that most are empty. A few passengers are plugged into their iPods or have their eyes closed in a sleepy train trance. I think I'm okay for a few minutes of chatting as long as I keep my voice low.

She's not answering her cell, which means she's still in her classroom, probably working with kids after school.

I should wait a half hour and try her cell again. I could text her, or send an e-mail.

I decide to call the school line.

I expect to hear the voice system, giving me prompts, like "If you know your extension, you can dial it at any time." Instead, I get a real live human on the phone.

"Hadley Elementary School, this is Dara speaking," the office secretary answers.

"Damn—Hi!" I bark out, overly loud in my surprise, startling a neighboring dozer on the train. "Sorry," I whisper across the row. He makes a frowny face and then closes his eyes again.

"Dara, it's Lauren," I say in as low a voice as possible. I hunch down into my seat and move even closer to the window.

"Are you okay?" she asks. Which is weird.

"Yeah, why?" I ask.

"Because you don't sound like you," she says, cracking gum through the phone. How fresh out of precalculus are school secretaries these days? Didn't they used to have blue hair and dentures? "Are you sick or something?" she adds. "And how's your trial or whatever?"

And are you a pain in my ass?

"Dara, can you please just connect me to Kat's classroom?"

"Can't."

"Listen, I know the phone system *seems* complicated, but all you have to do is push three little buttons…" I begin.

"Ha!" she says, and I imagine a Bubblicious balloon protruding from her lips before she sucks it back in. "No, I mean, she's not there. She was in the office a moment ago, and she seemed really upset about something. But she just left."

"Oh," I sigh.

"Wait!" she says, and I hear her hand the phone over to someone.

"Kitty-Kat!" I say, relief filling my tone.

"No." It only takes one syllable to be sure: Martha. What is *she* doing in there? Martha never comes out of her office, even after school hours. She's always tucked away in the far corner of the building, yelling at some prepubescent miscreant or his parents. "Hello, Mrs. Worthing."

The sensation I have at this very moment is of riding on a train while also being hit *by* that very same train. It's meta, it's surreal, it's awful.

My first inclination is to hang up. But then I improvise.

This train's not stopping yet. Metaphorically speaking.

"So, Martha. How's the teaching going?" I swallow.

"And how is your jury duty?" I decide that her non-answer means she's sucking at my job big-time.

"Not as boring as you might think," I say.

"Same here."

Touché.

"That *was* you I saw at Dr. Grossman's yesterday, wasn't it?" she prods.

"Why, yes!" I fake-laugh. "I thought it might have been you, but I was in such a rush to get home to my children after that long day in court, I couldn't stop to chat."

Which does nothing to explain my presence in a medical building at 3:30, but whatever. I'm acting without a script here, people.

"Yes, but, that does not explain..." Martha begins.

"Oh shoot, Martha, my battery is dying. Gotta run!" I say, as cheerfully as I can, my voice on the verge of chipmunk, it's so high-pitched and strangled.

It's an hour later and Kat has not responded to my texts, e-mails, or voice-mail messages. I send her one more text for good measure. *IMPORTANT: What the hell happened at school? And what's the deal with Leslie's party tonight?!?!*

I check in with Laney. "We are fine without you," Laney states matter-of-factly. I am not sure if this is a purposeful dig or just something lost in translation, but either way, it makes me feel lonely.

"Can I talk to Ben, please?" I ask, rolling my eyes at my own desperation.

"It's piano lesson time," she reminds me.

"Oh, right!" I say, feeling like the world's most out-of-touch mom.

"How about Becca, then?"

"Playdate at Jane's house."

"Of course, I just forgot!" I say, startled by how fast I can move from knowing everything to remembering nothing about my children.

"I'll tell Ben you called," she says, like I'm a telemarketer that she's trying to blow off.

"Thanks!" I fake-chirp as we get disconnected.

I close my eyes for a few minutes and lean my head against the cool glass window.

I force an image of Lenny and me locked in an embrace, in some parallel universe where real life hangs in suspension, where it's okay to kiss someone new, someone who is not Doug. I try to make the fantasy work, but no matter what I create (on the dance floor of a crowded nightclub, by the fire in a hotel suite, in a hot tub), I don't feel any spark.

Has midlife robbed me of the capacity for both real *and* imagined passion? Instead, I find myself thinking about Doug, of all people. Of the way his hair curls up under his collar when he lets it grow too long. Of his dimples, which are most noticeable when he's laughing at something funny I've whispered to him when we're in a crowd.

I smile and send my husband an e-mail, reminding him of my plans to attend Leslie's party. Then I tell him that, after jury duty, I had just enough time today to run over to Neiman's and pick up something nice to wear on our date tomorrow night.

Some of that is true. For the record.

Next, I e-mail Lenny, explaining in full detail my day of leave and admitting just who Georgie is, in all her grand femaleness.

My phone rings as we pull into the New Rochelle station. I grab my bag and exit onto the platform while yelling into the phone, "Kitty-Kat! Where you been?"

There is a moment's pause before she answers, and I think the line has gone dead. Then I hear her faintly utter something. "Mygehfired."

"Repeat that, please. I got a train in my ear."

"I might get fired!" she says. "From my job! I friggin' met with the Heads of State at three o'clock today about *yet another* ridiculous issue I'm having with Psycho Mom, and they told me I have to apologize to her, and I told them that's never gonna happen!"

"Dear God."

"There is no God."

I sit down on a bench.

The call I made to school must have occurred right after that meeting took place. Martha knew. She caused Kat's emotional breakdown of the day, and yet she made it sound like Kat was upset about something unrelated to her. "Sadistic bitch," I whisper in disbelief.

"You hate me, Lauren, I know," Kat says. "You hate me for telling them off. But I finally stood up for myself against that Psycho Mom and the weak-ass *di*ministration and it felt damned good!" She sounds strong and together. She sounds feisty. She sounds like *my* Kat.

"First off, I don't hate you!" *I just think you're stupid for putting your job in jeopardy when your husband left you completely broke.* I want to add this, but, at the moment, I don't think it's the route to follow. So I mentally edit it out of my dialogue and save the sentiment for another time, like when we're figuring out how she can ingratiate herself again with the Heads of State.

I recently read an article about girlfriends who give each other a false sense of confidence, distorting reality for them by bolstering them up with the wrong advice in times of crisis. I don't want to do that either. I settle on something in between Disney Princess advice and Cold, Hard Fact. "You were one-hundred percent right to speak up about that mom, and the injustice of having to apologize when she's clearly at fault. But, Kat, I just have a feeling that you went a little bit too far in your own defense."

There is a pause. I imagine her pulling on a curl, chewing a fingernail, or otherwise fidgeting her way through her thoughts. "Perhaps."

"Okay, then. That's something. You don't want to lose your job, do you?"

"I don't know...maybe I do."

I worry that I've now planted a bad seed, given her an idea that I didn't intend would grow thick and weedy in her mind. "It was a rhetorical question," I backtrack.

"No, no...it's right. It more than right, it's brilliant!" Kat says. Uh-oh. I just gave her Varka-style advice, which only fuels the negative Kat.

"We should *totally* quit our jobs, Lauren. We should, like, head back to school right now and just go right in there and resign! Together! Take a break!"

Great, just great. I've created a monster. Now I have to find a leash big enough to rein in her unyielding enthusiasm for destruction.

One should never toy with the fragile mind of a cuckolded kindergarten teacher.

In response, I state the obvious, the fact that I'm the only one in my family with a steady paycheck while Doug tries to get some new clients. "It's not that easy, Kitty-Kat. There's Doug."

"So quit Doug, too!" she yells. I feel the comment like a blow to my middle.

Kat senses my hesitation and reconsiders. "I'm sorry. I didn't mean that. I'm kind of..."

"On the verge?" I offer, thinking back to Georgie.

"Off the deep end, is more like it," Kat clarifies. I can hear her exhale, and know that's a real cigarette this time, not one made of powdered sugar. Kat gives up smoking for Lent every year, and then celebrates Easter by buying a carton of Marlboro Lights.

"Me, too." I decide that a little of my own honesty might help Kat right now. Hell, honesty might even help me, for all I know. "Hey, Kat?"

"Yeah?"

"I kind of took a leave of absence from work. Went to Boston for the day."

"Wait a second..." Now I've caught her off guard. "But...what about jury duty?"

"They settled yesterday morning."

"Fucking lawyers!"

"I *know*. They totally ruined my week. Unlike you, I do actually like my job most of the time, even though it doesn't seem like it right now. I just needed a little...time off from it. To clear my head. To..." I run out of words to explain how I feel. "I don't know, exactly."

And then I come clean about MC Lenny.

"You little sneak!" Kat declares.

We contemplate that for a moment.

"Huh," Kat says. "But you're the rational one." I thought she'd be psyched for me, pulling that kind of a fast one, but she sounds upset. "I mean, if *you* go all AWOL, what does that mean for Jodi and me? You're our Metamucil, our prune juice. We count on you to keep us regular."

"Well, that's kind of insulting."

"It's a compliment to your normalcy."

"Kat! Really? Because it feels like a burden." I mean, I keep it together for Doug and the kids. I go to work every morning at 7:30, even on days when I don't always feel like it, to a tenured job with 100% family health coverage so that Doug can build his company from the ground up. I go into work when I have a fever so that I can save my sick days for days when I need to be home with my sick children. I work evenings and weekends, grading papers and creating new and exciting lesson plans for my hundred students. And, unbeknownst to me, it turns out that I have been holding it together for my best friends, too? Do I have to be everyone's poster child for stability?

"I'll see you tonight, Kat. We'll talk. We'll figure it out," I say, trying to sound strong and sure, but only feeling wrung out. I stand and begin to make my way out of the station.

"We'll drink, smoke and spin down a pole, is what we'll do," she says, by way of hanging up.

CHAPTER 13

I AM THE WORLD'S WORST MOM. No one else would be gone from her children all day and then blow them off again all night. It isn't right, and I feel a searing sense of guilt telling me to stop, slow down, play with them for a while, to be an attentive mommy.

Instead, I kiss Becca and Ben hello, pretend to listen to them tell me about their day, dash up the stairs, take a quick shower, and pile on the makeup.

When I went back to work, I found that leaving my children in the morning was hard, but that coming back at the end of the workday was even harder. This surprised me. It seems that I need time to transition back into the setting and the pace of my own home after a day of working with a hundred other children. I have to mentally switch gears, dump the work thoughts from my mind, and settle back in to being a good mom. This is almost as exhausting as the work itself.

But if I'm gone all day and all night, doing completely self-centered things, then there's really no need to worry about making that transition!

"Bye, everyone. I love you guys!" I call down to the basement, where the kids are playing a Wii game with Laney.

I grab my boa and leave, feeling both sick to my stomach about my behavior and sort of psyched about the night's upcoming festivities.

Although I took a cab, Leslie's street is jammed with suburban-mom vehicles of every shape, size, and color. It seems that everyone I know has huge cars for carpooling their three or four children—plus friends of said children—around town. I feel like a real underachiever having only two children, as compared with today's super-sized suburbia.

Leslie has four kids. Unlike most of the moms in Hadley, who lose their baby weight and then some, Leslie has proudly added ten pounds of padding for each child, which she wears much in the way some wear necklace charms for each offspring. At some PTA event a few years ago, she and I ended up seated at the same table and became what I'd call relatively friendly. In terms of ranking our friendship, I'd say Leslie is positioned in the front mezzanine of my life's auditorium. Not quite orchestra-seat worthy, like Kat and Jodi, but not in the nosebleed section, either.

Another cab moves off the street and I see Kat tottering toward me up the driveway on her fuck-me pumps, and I pause to wait for her. "Hug," I instruct, arms wide. She leans in and lets me rock her like a baby. Her head fits in the crook of my neck. "In those heels, you are almost normal size!" I pronounce.

"Nah, still Lilliputian." She shrugs. "Though smokin' hot, if I must say so myself."

I pull back to inspect her. Her tight black curls are shiny and set off her porcelain complexion. Her green eyes are bright and fierce, probably made more intense by some crying earlier in the day. "You actually look amazing. I think 'over the edge' really works on you."

"*Bitches!*" someone shouts, making us jump. We turn to see Leslie standing at the front door of her supersized faux castle under the glow of a red light bulb, waving us over with something in hand.

"Is that...a whip?" Kat asks, sounding more than a little bit afraid as we make our way up her flagstone walk and come face to face with the birthday girl. Four mammoth Grecian columns announce her "porch."

"Ouch!" I call out, momentarily stung by a slash of leather against the leg of my skinny jeans. "It's a whip all right."

"Bitchaaaaas!" Leslie calls again, making the word last for at least six seconds, like some kind of *ohm* or other mantra.

"Hey! Leslie! You look..." I begin, taking in the patent leather corset, fishnet stockings, and over-the-knee, zip-up stiletto boots. Leslie is wearing tons of makeup, with black kohl eyeliner and ruby-red lipstick. Her black hair is pulled back into a high, tight ponytail. She has an extension woven into it, so that the hair falls well past her back, grazing her generous bottom.

The complete effect is not flattering or sexy in any way. She looks more slut than high-end escort, more Britney than Madonna. I start again. "You look…"

"Completely fucked up," Kat concludes. I jab her in the side.

"What?" she asks, turning to me but speaking so Leslie can hear. "She does. She's dressed like a whore."

Leslie's smile cracks for a second, and I worry that her feelings have been hurt. She quickly blinks away any shame by batting her false eyelashes at us.

I get the sense that Leslie dressed this way in order to boss everyone around mercilessly and get away with it. It's like wish fulfillment, the way teenage girls dress like little Playboy Bunnies and act slutty for a night on Halloween without sustaining much damage to their real, pure reputations the next day in school.

I also get the sense that she has double-dosed on the drugs that control her manic-depression. She sometimes likes to do this when feeling festive, usually to negative effect.

Producing a wooden paddle from behind the bushes, Leslie leans in toward Kat. Her long, fake ponytail sways menacingly. "Bitch!"

"Yikes." Kat takes a step away from Leslie and leans into me. "Why are we friends with her again?"

"Bend over and let me paddle you, Katrina O'Connell. You must not speak negatively about Lady Hoochie. I rule. My word is law tonight!"

"Oh, no, it isn't!" Kat says, swerving out of the way in the nick of time and grabbing me as she heads through the front door.

She steals a cocktail from a passing waiter wearing a tight black T-shirt that says *Tasty*, and tries to regain her composure. "Leslie's a goddamned dominatrix!"

"Well, it is her fortieth," I smirk. My eyes focus on the large brass pole lit up in the center of the room, and I reach for a cocktail, too. "In a contest for crazy, between the three of us, I think she might win."

"Cheers to that," Kat says, swallowing the pink concoction in one gulp. "I'm cool taking silver or bronze."

We see some people we know and make our way over to them.

Like us, they are dressed nicely and are not decked out in any sort of costume. I am about to touch my forehead self-consciously, but stop myself just in time.

"I'm going to pretend this event isn't weird," a woman named Jen says, picking up a tube of K-Y jelly off the buffet.

"Good luck with that," Kat says.

"Is the K-Y for dipping the sushi into, or for use as a salad dressing?" I wonder aloud to no one.

"Maybe it's a condiment," Kristen says. She has a daughter in Becca's kindergarten class. "Like ketchup." She winks and pretends to use it on her mini-cheeseburger. She's kind of funny, actually.

I watch Kat as she drops some condoms into her clutch purse. She shrugs. "Nothing wrong with taking some party favors."

I manage to enjoy a few teriyaki salmon skewers and another drink or two while Kat and I mill around the living and dining rooms, chatting with people we know.

I feel my phone vibrate and check to see if the message is from Laney. Instead, it's Doug. I motion to Kat and dismiss myself from the group, trying to find a quiet spot in Leslie's office.

Not that she works. But still, it's nice to have an office, isn't it? For all that scrapbooking she does?

"Hey, Lauren, it's me," Doug's message begins. I haven't heard his voice all day, and the sound of it warms me a bit. He sounds tired. He must have had a long day. "Listen. I've had a really long day." See how well I know my husband? "There's a couple of really important issues that I didn't get to complete. I had to push a meeting back, with this guy who is only in town until Friday morning... So...I'm going to have to cancel our date night tomorrow night. I'm sorry. Just thought I'd give you the heads-up now, in case you want to make other plans. Maybe go out with some friends. Or spend some time with Ben and Bec." He tries to laugh, but it comes out more like a cough. "I'm sorry. I'll make it up to you. Promise."

And then he's gone.

"Those waiters are gorgeous," Kat mentions as I rejoin the group. "Did you notice?"

"Mmm. They must be models or actors for hire or something,"

Kristen adds. "Not that I noticed that one over there with the smoldering good looks or anything." He turns our way with an hors d'oeuvres tray and we all smile. His tight black T-shirt reads *Try Me.*

"I didn't notice him from the neck up. Too much to look at below."

I want to get back into the spirit of mockery, but after Doug's call, the party just doesn't feel the same. Disappointment clouds my vision. Instead of seeing a group of people to either make fun of or have fun with, I just feel tired of all this playacting that has become my life. I want to tell someone the truth: I haven't had sex with Doug in a long, long time.

"Damn, Kat! You need to get laid," Kristen challenges.

"Et tu, Brute. Et tu." Then Kat turns to me, looking for a reaction. "Why didn't you laugh at that? It was witty banter."

"Because." I explain the phone call, then pause and try to form a truth that won't reveal too much. "Doug and I never do anything together anymore. He doesn't see me. I'm like the secretary in the waiting room of his life. Purely administrative." I am thinking about crying some tears of the angry variety. But I try to will myself to keep it together.

"You should paddle him when you get home. Then he'll notice you."

I cock my head to the side and consider this. "Seems to work for Leslie."

"Although, as you may notice, her husband's gone a lot of the time."

"Wouldn't you travel for business any chance you could get if Leslie was your wife?"

And with that, we decide to down a few mudslide shooters and check out the rest of the eats.

"Bitchaaaas!" Lady Hoochie calls, signaling everyone to the living room.

"Never gets old," Kat says sarcastically. I roll my eyes as we reluctantly make our way toward chairs in the back row of the room, as far away from the dreaded pole as is humanly possible.

"Bitches and Hot Mamas!" Leslie begins again, now that the crowd around her has thickened like her waistline. "I am delighted to have you here with me this evening to help usher in my next decade of fabulousness!" She tosses her hair and jiggles her thighs.

There is a beat of awkward, embarrassed silence. Suddenly, people make up their minds to agree with her. Hoots, cheers, and catcalls follow.

"Am I a bitch or a hot mama?" I want to know.

Kat gives me a sideways glance. *"That's* your question?"

"I'm pretty sure that we're out of medal contention this evening," I add, as Leslie brings forth a woman of unknown origin.

"Ladies and bitches," Leslie slurs, raising a glass of something alcoholic and sweet, "I'd like you to help me welcome the first of tonight's entertainers."

"The *first*?" I whisper.

"Shh...this is getting good." Kat strains to see over the heads of people seated in front of us. I can make out orange-tanned flesh, red lipstick, and wrinkles on the entertainer.

"This gorgeous babe—"

"Not," Kat coughs.

"—comes straight from the Playboy mansion—"

"After a twenty-year detour," Kat adds.

"—to teach us all a little bit about...*sex*!" Leslie cheers. "It's the one and only...Candy Cox!"

"Woo-hoo!" Kat calls out to the silent room, standing up. "This sure beats ninth-grade health class, am I right?" Thirty women stare at her, bemused looks on their faces. "I mean, *bitches*, am I right?" The room explodes in applause and whistling.

After a good minute of whooping, Kat sits, delighted with herself. She winks at me.

"Some people just don't get your humor," I explain.

"Yeah. My kindergarteners, for one."

"Still, that's what makes it so beautiful to be around."

"To be *in* the moment and yet to make fun *of* the moment. That's where my true talent lies."

We turn back to the center of the room, where Candy Cox is holding the largest dildo I've ever seen.

"Is it my imagination, or did everyone just lean in a little closer?" the woman seated to my right jokes.

"That's all kinds of inappropriate," Kristen says, staring at the slightly floppy, undulating mass in Candy's hands.

"Now, hot mamas," Candy begins, "This is my show-and-share time, like in school."

"Just like." Kat nods. She cannot help herself. On a good day, she's compelled to create a snappy retort. But at an event like this? With such good material just waiting to be manipulated for her delight? I stop trying to restrain her.

Candy starts passing sex toys around the room. "Don't worry, ladies. Every one of you is going to get a chance to examine and feel these toys. And then I'll tell you where you can put them! Dildos, vibrators, anal toys, balls, lubricants, ticklers, and condoms are among the surprises in my bag."

"I've heard of condoms!" a woman named Lexie jokes, leaning against a wall on the other side of the room, waving her hand in the air like she's just won a prize.

"Good for you, sweetie. Your husband must frequent the clubs along the Jersey Turnpike," Candy replies matter-of-factly.

Ouch. Lexie slumps down onto the floor.

"Hey," someone calls out to Candy. "Didn't I see you on *The New Newlyweds*? You look so familiar!"

"Indeed you did, hot thing. My husband and I dabble in reality TV, when we're not making porn."

"Now, that's a nice career. You don't get stuck in a rut that way, like you do with tenure." Kat stands and stretches. "I'm getting a refill. Anyone?" she asks, glancing around to the group of women seated closest to us.

We shake our heads no and continue watching the entertainment.

"I don't usually start with the largest unit of the bunch, but I could tell that you wild ladies needed some stiff competition, if you know what I mean!"

The ginormous faux penis is coming my way. "What is that made of?" I ask. "Does it have veins?"

"I agree, it looks really authentic," someone adds. "Except that it's twenty times larger than my husband's."

The dildo is being passed around the room like it's a tray of turkey at Thanksgiving. It is *that* cumbersome. People have to put their whole upper torsos into maneuvering it around from person to person. My friend Susie holds it out to me, both palms extended upward. I mimic the gesture, and the thing sort of rolls onto my palms. It's heavy and clammy to the touch, like a huge dead trout. Not that I've ever held a dead trout. Or one of these, come to think of it.

"Huh," is all I can muster before passing it on to Kristen.

"Eyes up here, please!" Candy Cox sings, trying to tear us away from show-and-share time. A low hum of chatter fills the room as small groups of women giggle away their collective discomfort. "Ladies, if I could have your attention—"

"Biiiiitchaaaaas!" Leslie—excuse me, *Lady Hoochie*—cracks her whip against a sofa table, sending pictures of her children flying. Immediate quiet descends over the room. "Listen and learn, hot mamas, and give your undivided attention to Candy Cox! I will not stand for misbehavior. Anyone who does not cooperate has to see me outside!"

"Ooh..." arises from the crowd, on the verge of ridiculing Leslie. *Who does she think she is?* You can almost hear the partygoers ask it, souring the mood. But since no one wants to dare her to test her threat, we get mute pretty fast.

"Raise your dildo if you think she's taking this role-playing a tad seriously," Kat whispers to whoever is in earshot. "Scoot over, I lost my seat," she instructs. Susie moves down one and Kat settles in next to me again.

Candy has the floor once more. "Like to pleasure yourself on the go? Looking for something compact, something great for travel?"

Candy digs deep into her short-shorts and produces what looks like a lipstick.

"I don't see any pockets on those shorts," Susie says.

She has a point. Unfortunately.

"It looks like a lipstick, doesn't it, ladies?" Candy asks.

Several women nod their heads, trying to be diligent pupils.

"But not everything is what it seems..." She pulls off the top and flips some microscopic switch. A tiny buzz fills the room. Candy smiles and holds it out for all to see, rotating her palm this way and that. "Ingenious, am I right?"

"What is it?" Susie whispers.

As if on cue, Candy responds, "It's a lipstick vibrator! Carry it in your purse, take it wherever you go!" She sends it around the room as her lecture continues. "How many times have you been having dinner, bored by the company, thinking about getting off—"

"Every Sunday at Grandma's," Kat murmurs.

"But, with the lipstick vibrator, all you have to do is grab your purse and excuse yourself to the powder room—"

"*Okay*, it's officially time for me to leave." Kristen stands and gives a halfhearted wave in our direction. "Tell Hoochie I said good-bye, will you?"

"But...you'll miss the pole dancing!" I counter.

"Thank God for small favors," she says, and is off.

Susie is now in possession of one of the tiny vibrators being sent around, and is playing with the hidden switch. "It's kind of cute!" she says, watching it move in small circles.

Kat raises her eyebrows, turns to me, and mouths, "I might need one of those."

I can only hope she's kidding.

After twenty more minutes of pure shock value, Candy starts packing up her toys. "Well, that was sooooo much fun! I'll be here the rest of the night, in Lady Hoochie's office, for one-on-one consultations and to take your orders. I take all major credit cards and am running a special right now through AmEx. Double points."

"I wonder if she accepts Saks or Neiman's," Kat jokes.

"Oh, by the way," Candy adds, "lingerie is on display in Lady Hoochie's daughter's room, just past the stairs."

"Damn! I might have to buy something now," Susie complains. She heads toward the lingerie and I follow her. "I'm close to earning two first-class airline tickets through American Express."

"Where are Leslie's kids?" Suze asks.

"At their grandma's in Rye. And Steven is at a boys' night in AC."

We enter baby Bethany's room, which has now been taken over by racks of cheap lingerie.

"Baby Bethany's Bimbo Emporium," Kat declares, surprising us from behind. "I really like what she's done with the place."

We wander around and examine the merch. I'm kind of afraid

to touch any of it, since drunk women are trying on all manner of crotchless panties in the bathroom across the hall and then placing them back on the racks when they're done. Some, I notice, are just leaving the lace bras and nighties on. There seems to be a direct correlation between alcohol intake and clothing offtake.

A waiter passes by with a tray of Jell-O shots, and Kat and I eat a few. "I think this party wouldn't suck so bad if we were even drunker," I tell her.

"Okay." She shrugs. "Let's see how that works out."

"Hi, guys," a voice calls. Kat and I turn away from the Jell-O to find Shay Greene walking toward us.

"Funny, I just saw her the other day," I tell Kat. "She was running for some kind of office or something. Hadley School Board."

"No shit?" Kat asks, sort of rhetorically. She's too taken by Shay's entrance to utter any more. I know this because, well, so am I.

Shay seems to be moving toward us in slow motion, like a model in a diet soda commercial. Her long, golden locks sway like wheat in a field; her thin, perfectly muscular yogalates body is draped in shimmering, one-shouldered, pale-pink silk. Shay's husband, the renowned Hadley dentist, has created for her a perfect set of teeth, which she now flashes at us in a friendly hello.

They're the kind of teeth that look real and yet look too good to be true at the same time, which, before I knew about her husband's profession, always made me wonder if she'd just gotten the luckiest genes ever.

Because Shay is perfect. She's gorgeous *and* nice to everyone. She's even smart, with a law degree from Columbia. Shay and her husband have tow-headed ten-year-old twins—boy and girl, of course—and they live in a big (but not garishly huge) 1930s brick-front colonial with original crown molding throughout.

Not that I've ever been there. But that's the word on the street.

Shay works as a consultant to women starting their own businesses—when she isn't chairing some fundraiser for the schools, libraries, and local hospitals, that is, or running for the school board.

Kat and I gawk for the merest split second, because how can we not? Shay's our grown-up world's version of the prettiest cheerleader, the alpha girl. I always feel a bit awestruck in her presence.

So, Shay and Kat and I start talking about the district's budget plans, which, ordinarily, would cause us to roll our eyes at and stifle some yawns, like we do at faculty meetings. But when Shay talks, her brows lift animatedly, showing off a wash of silver eye shadow that sparkles so appealingly that I find myself nodding in harmony with Kat and learning a thing or two about the newly piloted foreign language program at the high school.

Then Shay says, "Hey, why don't we all do some shots of tequila?" Kat and I are really pretty drunk already, but we say, "Okay, Shay," because her charisma, intelligence, and flawless blend of custom-blended foundation compel us to.

While Shay is hunting for the necessary supplies in Leslie's pantry, Kat and I discuss. "Shay-sa-may-zing," Kat slurs. "It's *so* not fair."

"I can't stop staring at her butt," I admit. And I don't just mean tonight. I mean *always*. Whenever I see it around town. Her tush is perfectly high and slightly bubble-shaped. It's bouncy in her Lululemon spandex Wunder Under cropped pants, yet appropriately demure peeking out from under a Theory pantsuit. It's like the ass of a teenager, only Shay's got to be close to forty.

Not to dwell, but tonight she's wearing white jeans that hug the curve of her toned backside and look sexy without looking slutty. Not sure how she pulls that off.

Her butt is my butt's hero and, simultaneously, its archenemy.

So the next thing we know, Shay's back with some salt and limes and Cuervo, and we're preparing the shot's ritual. I put a line of salt on my right hand, ready to begin.

Here's where things go slightly left of center.

In one fluid movement, Shay reaches out and takes *my* hand in hers. Then she licks the salt off the pudgy part of *my* hand, downs her shot, slams the empty glass on the table, and sucks on a lime. "Excellent!" she cheers. "Who's next?"

I stare down at the damp crease between my thumb and pointer finger, stunned.

"Did that really juss happen?" Kat whisper-slurs to me. "Did she juss suck you off?"

It's not quite the phrase I would use, but I nod my head. Shay's tongue felt kind of warm and wet, not unlike a greeting from a neighborhood Labradoodle.

Though, clearly, this act crossed some line that doesn't exist when I'm saying hello to mixed-breed puppies.

I can tell that Kat's kind of into this round-robin lickfest, while I'm still mentally—and, fine I'll admit it, *emotionally*—catching up. She smiles at Shay and watches as Shay pours some salt onto her own soft, tanned flesh. I'll be damned if Kat doesn't grab that beautiful hand, with its manicured-in-Mademoiselle fingertips, and suck on it like it's the last spare rib at a Chinese buffet.

During this bizarre act of PDA, I can't help noticing the large (but not ostentatious) tennis bracelet on Shay's wrist, as it sparkles in the candlelight of Leslie's dining room.

Kat eventually releases Shay's hand, gulps down the tequila, and grabs the lime wedge between her teeth.

"Now this is starting to feel like a girls' night in," Shay says, embracing me with one arm and Kat with the other.

I'm wondering if that's innuendo or if I'm just being sensitive and stupid. "You mean, like, hanging out with women friends in a nonthreatening, college-like atmosphere?"

"I guess, if you're into that sort of sorority play," Shay says, in no way helping me make sense of what's really going on here.

Shay turns to Kat and presses her forehead and nose against Kat's forehead and nose. "Your eyes are pretty," she whispers before sauntering off, leaving the scent of tuberose in her wake.

"Huh," Kat says.

"That's it?" I burp theatrically. "Huh?" I take a shot of tequila sans salt, not wanting to put my tongue where Shay's tongue has just been. The alcohol warms my throat but also kind of makes me want to puke.

"I'm off to the bathroom," I tell Kat. "Be back in a mo."

Kat waves me off, distracted.

The hall bathroom is occupado, so I head upstairs. Either the entire second floor of the home was built on an angle or I'm drunker than I thought. Steadying myself by running my hand against the wall, I make my way down the carpeted hallway and into Leslie's master bedroom.

The room is dark except for the blue glow of the obnoxiously huge flat-screen on the far wall. Lots of women are piled together on the four-poster bed, watching an old-school porno on the television, laughing and talking animatedly.

I wave in the general direction of the crowd and find my way into the walk-in closet—oops, not it!—and eventually the bathroom.

Leslie has one of those huge, spa-like bathrooms copied almost tile by tile from the Ritz-Carlton, Naples. It's all crème- and brown-toned limestone and marble, with an oversized Jacuzzi tub and a walk-in shower big enough for a family of four grizzly bears. At one of the two sinks, I pump some soap into my palm and wash very, very well. Behind me there is a spaceship-like toilet and a porcelain bidet.

Being in the bathroom makes me realize that I do, in fact, need to pee. I sit on the modern contraption that must be a toilet, and am instantly pleased by the warming sensation of the heated seat. Leslie's rear end must be pretty high-end, blubber be damned. I sit a little longer than necessary, and then, just as I am ready to stand, I decide to push a button to the right of me on the wall, just to see what it will do.

A shock of cold water hits me in the privates.

"Ah!" I call out, surprised. Frantically, I try to turn off the device while instinctively looking toward the door, afraid that someone has heard my outburst. But instead of stopping the assault, somehow I hit a button that turns on a vent. Now cool air replaces the jet spray. Which isn't bad, actually. It's rather soothing.

I settle in for a good long moment, enjoying the York Peppermint Patty sensation of it all.

My initial distress now replaced with curiosity, I decide to touch another dial on the wall and mistakenly force the air up to Mach 5.

I don't think you're supposed to touch that particular dial while sitting, because my butt feels like it's in the eye of a small hurricane. It's suctioned to the seat and takes all the strength I have in my upper torso to oust myself to safety.

And, now that I'm sprawled on the floor, I can tell you that Leslie has radiant heat under her marble floor tiles.

Why does she also have a bidet when that Get Smart *toilet does it all*? I wonder.

The next thing I know, someone's pounding on the door.

"Just a minute!" I call, snapping to and quickly dressing. "Shit!" I slip on the tile while trying to stand and bang my knee. That's gonna leave a mark, I think.

I wash my hands so quickly that I spray soap and water everywhere. Grabbing a decorative hand towel, I begin cleaning up the mess as best I can. Then, with bionic speed, I manage to make myself somewhat presentable and swing open the door.

Leslie's kohl-rimmed eyes meet mine. "Who's in there with you?" she demands.

"Who?" I ask, trying to remember how to form words.

"Yes," she snaps impatiently. "Who. I was in the living room and I heard banging and shouting coming from above." She glances past me, her eyes sweeping the empty bathroom for clues.

I try to relax, but I can feel my cheeks get hot under her scrutiny. "Was it Tasty? Salty? Or Try Me?" she asks, referring not to Snow White's dwarves, but to the waiter/models serving downstairs.

I say nothing, merely trying to blink myself out of this situation.

"Well," Leslie concludes, seemingly satisfied with my lack of an answer. "As long as you didn't touch Eat Me, because I'm saving him for dessert, if you know what I mean." She raises one eyebrow to prove her point.

I cough out a laugh of sorts in response, move past her, and drunkenly saunter away, leaving her leaning against the doorjamb.

If you've never tried an elaborate, specially outfitted toilet, I suggest it highly. Aside from being a rather astounding force of nature, it leaves you feeling fresh and clean. Like a car wash for your hoo-ha.

I head back downstairs to find Kat, a spring in my step.

CHAPTER 14

MUSIC IS PLAYING PRETTY LOUDLY now in the kitchen and family rooms, and a lot of partygoers are dancing with the hired help.

"Have you seen Kat?" I ask a few women huddled around one of the possibly gay waiter/models. I don't know half of these women and they don't know Kat, so the whole effort is somewhat futile. "Petite, with black curls? Green eyes? No?" I have to shout to be heard, but the answer is still no.

Although I know I shouldn't, I grab a cosmopolitan from a passing waiter with his tray aloft, and enjoy it in a few gulps. I didn't realize how thirsty I was. Probably from all that alcohol. Very dehydrating.

In the living room, I spot that giant pole where Leslie's overstuffed couch used to be. Several guests are gathering around a really skinny woman with fake boobs barely encased in a shrunken black T-shirt. The rest of the outfit is comprised of tight, black boy short–style underwear, and chunky silver platforms. I'm hoping she's the instructor.

"Where does she *find* these people?" I wonder aloud. But without Kat beside me, there is no witty repartee in response.

The hottie blows a whistle and the group gets quiet. "Hi, girls! My name is Lola, and I'm from the Copa, Copacabana," she sings, imitating that Barry Manilow song.

Which answers that question, I guess.

Lola starts showing us some basic pole-dancing moves. She hooks her leg around the pole and then tosses her hair back theatrically.

I'm pretty sure I could do that.

Then she ups the ante a bit with slightly more complicated twists, turning her body around the pole while gyrating her hips. She dances around that thing ten, twenty times. Her moves are mesmerizingly sexy, especially with this heavy beat in the background, with some guy singing, "Come, my lady, come, come, my lady..."

Her legs are really long and perfectly toned. And she's so flexible! I suddenly understand why men like to watch this. *I* like to watch this! I feel both dizzy and embarrassed. I have to look away.

"Get in touch with your inner diva," Lola says. "Find your sexy."

This is misogynistic garbage, I remind myself, created *by* men *for* men who want to objectify women.

Stop being such a buzzkill, Lauren, I scold myself. *You're only upset because you lack the balls to get up and do something like this.*

But then another voice arrives to weigh in. *Where's your sexy at, girl?*

A third voice joins the party in my head, asking, *Why are you thinking in bad grammar? And where is Kat when you need her? She could get up there and then push you to do it, too. You'd get to be all shy and coy and like, "No, no, not me," and then she'd be like, "Yes, Lauren, you!" so you'd do it, secretly stoked. And then, if you look stupid or come off too slutty, you could blame it all on Kat and walk away clean.*

There are too many people in my head right now.

A few brave souls come up and spin while the rest of us cheer them on. One woman even manages to hoist herself up and spin right down like she's in Cirque du Soleil.

She doesn't seem objectified.

She smiles and high-fives Lola at the end of her turn. "That was a blast!" she tells us. "I'm totally getting a pole for my office."

I wonder what she does for a living.

I grab another drink from a passing waiter and watch the entertainment for a while, as three more women try the pole. It does look like fun.

Maybe even more fun than washing one's bottom in Leslie's bidet.

I mean, I'm not *completely* uncoordinated. I was a gymnast in middle school, for goodness' sake. *I can totally handle this.*

"Okay people." I stand, swaying slightly. "I've got some dance moves, and I'm prepared to use 'em!"

There are cheers all around.

Next thing I know, I'm up at the pole and pelvic-thrusting to the beat. "That's it," Lola coaches, "Now try to spin, one hand here, the other here." I follow her instructions, and...I do it! I actually spin around the pole. My hands are slippery from nerves, but that only seems to make my movements work better, faster.

I mean, not to brag, but I look *hot*. I can tell from the silence that has overtaken the room. The group is so jealous of my awesome moves, it has been rendered speechless.

After a few more turns, it's just so natural.

"Honey, let someone else have a chance," I hear Lola say, but I'm not ready to let go quite yet.

Leslie catcalls to me from where she has joined the group on the sofa. "Hey, bitch, it's my turn now!"

I wave to her, like, *just give me one more minute.*

"Plus, you suck," Leslie adds, standing up and coming toward the pole. A chill settles over the group.

Shut up, Leslie, I think. All night, she's been the killjoy to my good time, ruining her own party by yelling profanities and making me—and probably everyone—feel like shit.

I'm totally not giving up the pole now, partially to prove to her that I'm good at this, but mostly just to spite her.

For my next go-round, I have to pull an Emeril and kick it up a notch. I need something exceptional, something to make the crowd go wild.

Something that Leslie will always remember.

Unfortunately, there isn't much in my bag of tricks. *Think* Striptease, *Lauren. Find your inner Demi and let her loose on Leslie.*

Suddenly, I've got an idea. I look her way and wink, thinking, *Try to top this, bitch.*

Then I hook my left leg around the pole like I saw Lola do in her demo. An anticipatory "Whoo" comes from the onlookers. *Yeah, ladies, dat's right.* The feisty black-girl rapper in my mind is speaking to me, and she's gonna help me spin.

And right before I black out, I think: *Leslie is going down.*

There is just so much blood.

I'm not sure where it's coming from or how it ended up on my hands, since I don't see a cut anywhere on me and I don't seem to be hurting. I check my head, my legs, my arms. No signs of injury anywhere.

My legs are splayed at an awkward angle, though, so I try to move them. The spiky heel of one of my awesome Louboutin shoes seems to be caught in a net. A black net, like the kind to catch fish in. Yes, that's right—the word for that is fishnet!

The best way to get my shoe free from this fishnet seems to be by tearing a hole in it, which I do.

Ah. My black stiletto comes loose. I check to see if it's damaged, but it seems fine.

Right now my life is like a movie I'm watching on pay-per-view, except that the volume's on mute. Then someone comes into the living room and clicks the remote, bringing the sound back in full force. Noise is all around me.

"You bitch!" someone yells.

"Back off, get off her!" someone else says, not too kindly.

All these people bark directions my way. "Get off" and "move" seem to be the two most prevalent comments, so I figure I'll follow those commands and see if the noise stops.

I crawl away and something frees underneath me. The mass that I was resting on turns out to be a person, which strikes me at this very moment as sort of funny and also quite weird. How did *that* happen?

Then the person moves a little. And then the person speaks.

"Fucking bitchwhoreasshole!" It's Leslie, her voice muffled by the Oriental carpeting.

She really is rather awful, isn't she?

She sits up and turns toward me, clutching her cheek.

Ah! There's the source of all that blood.

I must have kicked her in the face with the heel of my shoe as I got airborne around the pole. Which is, you know, sobering news.

"I am so...so very...very sorry!" I say, reaching my hand out toward Leslie and standing up unsteadily, my wayward shoe tucked under my left arm like a football.

"Don't you fucking dare come near me, you fucking bitch-whoreasshole!"

What have I done? I am stunned into inaction as I survey the horror of the scene that's unfolding all around me.

I catch another glimpse of Leslie's beaten-up, pulpy cheek,

and I'm afraid of retribution both immediate and calculated. In this instant, a crowd of drunken women in lingerie could turn on me, like something out of Michael Jackson's *Thriller* video, and scratch me with their manicured fingernails, throwing their fruity drinks in my face. And tomorrow? What if this story leaks to the community and everyone at school finds out? I'll be known as That Teacher at the Sex-Toy Party Who Bashed in the Hostess's Face with the Heel of Her Louboutins. That's not the kind of title that inspires confidence in parents, right? I can picture them whispering about me on the sidelines of soccer fields throughout the county, saying, *I don't care how talented she is with iambic pentameter, just keep your kids away from that delinquent, pole-dancing drunk with lifetime tenure.*

Luckily, people ignore me as they tend to Leslie's wound. Gauze and towels and bandages of all shapes and sizes appear from the hall closet. A bag of frozen peas is passed in front of me.

"For the swelling!" handholding Pam instructs. "Put the bag of peas on your face, Lez. You don't want to end up purple and swollen."

"Let me help!" I plead. I'd really like to be useful in some way, instead of feeling rooted to the floor like another pole in the living room. Plus, maybe taking some positive action now will help soften their gossipy blows about me later. People might say, *She really screwed up, but then she came to Leslie's rescue like Florence Nightingale.* Or, *Lauren may be uncoordinated, but she has a gift for healing. I'm definitely going to request her as my daughter's sixth-grade English teacher, and I suggest you do the same.*

But it's like I've become invisible. No one pays any attention to me, or even seems to hear me. The sacred womanly wall of the Silent Treatment has been invoked, and it is impenetrable.

I'm dead to them, cast out of the tribe.

This absolute exclusion feels even worse than being screamed at. So I try again.

"I said I was sorry! It was an accident, people!" I yell to no one in particular.

"There are no accidents, only major fuckups," Kat says, materializing next to me and looking totally freaked out. Her hair is standing up funny, and she's missing one of her large hoop earrings.

"Thank God you're here!" I hug her. "To rescue me! I've got to get out—"

Kat cuts me off and grabs my wrist, giving a furtive glance toward the stairs. "Me, too. Like, *yesterday*."

"Okay. Let me just say good-bye to Lola..." I start.

"*No!*" Kat snaps, whisper-screaming at me. "There is no time for good-byes, Lauren. We've got to get out of here *now!*"

Her eyes are glassy, her skin pale and clammy. She looks possessed. For a split second I think, *Kat's been bitten by a vampire!* Then I remember that my life is not a part of the *Twilight* series.

"But I really have to pee again!"

"Squat outside," Kat says.

"Fine." I grab my purse and make my way to the front hall, Kat still dragging me by the wrist.

Word of Leslie's fate has spread quickly. Women are pouring into the living room from all parts of the house, including the master suite, proving that juicy gossip trumps vintage John Holmes videos.

There is whispering and mumbling and a sidelong glance or two my way. I'm nervous to stay, anticipating a barrage of insults, but I worry that leaving Leslie like this will only make it worse for me in the long run, like leaving the scene of a car crash and turning it into a hit-and-run.

I pull back from Kat. "I think I should just check on her one more time; it looked really bad..."

"Duck!" Kat yells.

I do, and narrowly miss getting hit by one of Leslie's lace-up boots. "Thanks for coming, *bitch*haaas!"

"Alrighty, then," I say. "Let's get the fuck out of here!"

"I've been trying to tell you that for the past three minutes! We need to leave *town!*" Kat says, clicking her high-heeled way across the marble foyer. I limp behind her.

"Ooh!" I say. Propped on a chair by the front door is a pile of small, pink Chinese takeout cartons. *Sexy-to-Go* is inscribed on hangtags in black ink. I grab two.

Like Kat, I can never resist party favors.

"Here, take this," I say, stuffing one of the favors in Kat's bag. "Did you see what happened?" We're hiding out under some evergreens, hidden from view of Leslie's house by a few huge bushes.

Kat's busy on her phone, tapping at keys, but she won't tell me what she's doing. She looks up long enough to answer.

"Um, which part? The completely embarrassing pole-dancing part? Or the tear-a-gash-in-the-hostess's-face part?"

"The..." I stop. "Wait a second. I've got talent! Moves!"

"And that's why you see so many men with bloody faces coming out of stripper bars. Because of the 'talented' pole dancers with their 'moves.'"

She returns to tapping her fingers on the small, glowing screen.

"You mean...Leslie was *right*?" I pause to consider this. What if, in general, I stink at things that I *think* I excel at? It's disturbing to contemplate that I might actually be delusional, and that I walk through this world posing confidently as others laugh. "I'm like the Elaine of pole dancing?" I ask.

"Worse. You're like the Elaine-meets-Tonya-Harding's-boyfriend of pole dancing." She shrugs, like it's a fact and all she's doing is sharing old news.

Figures. In trying to let loose, I come undone.

True, I may have temporarily misplaced my sexy, but pole dancing at Leslie's is not how I'm going to find it.

That is clear to me now.

"It wasn't nice of me. To hurt her and then leave like that. Even if she wasn't being...gracious. Who does that?" I ask the trees, the sky, the grass, since Kat's lost to her phone. "Who am I?"

Then, I remember the pressure in my bladder and go in search of a private spot behind a spruce. I squat as per Kat's instructions, trying really hard not to pee on my new shoes.

"Charming," Kat says, upon my return. "Plus, they totally saw you." She points to some teenagers leaning out a second-story window at the house next door and laughing.

We sit in silence for a few minutes, Kat still clicking away while I think of something to take my mind off my less-than-graceful exit and current humiliation.

"You were in a hurry to get out of there," I realize.

"Hmm."

"That's very descriptive."

"Yup."

I pull back and wait, but, in typical Kat fashion, she isn't forthcoming. "Done," she says, looking satisfied. "We're going."

"We've left," I point out.

"Not quite. We've left *there*," she says, pointing toward Leslie's house, "and tomorrow, we're going *here*." She holds the phone out to me, showing an image of white sand and turquoise water.

"I don't get it," I say to the screen. "It looks awesome, though, whatever it is."

"It's Miami." Her eyes look bright, in that same unnatural, vampire way. "I just booked two seats on the seven a.m."

"Two seats. To Miami. Tomorrow," I say.

Kat nods and finds a cuticle to bite.

"For us," I clarify.

She nods again, really digging into that nail with her teeth.

It's an amazingly stupid idea. I mean, it's easy for Kat to just pick up and leave, but how am I going to pull off something like that? I have children, for God's sake! A husband! A job.

"Nice try," I say, handing the phone back to her.

Well, a job that thinks I'm on jury duty. And a babysitter lined up for tomorrow night. And a husband who cancelled on me and is working late.

So, really, no one needs me. No one cares.

Maybe no one will even *notice* I'm gone.

"Give me that phone back." Kat looks surprised but passes it to me. I stare at the picture and imagine it's got smell-o-vision, as sea-salt air and balmy nights fill my nostrils. Coconut and pineapple mixed with rum. Suntan lotion spiked with aloe vera, silky to the touch.

And no children begging for me to build a sand castle.

"Something happened back there, at Leslie's," Kat says.

I know this; I caused it. "Duh," I say.

She shakes her curls at me. "No, with *me*, idiot. Me and...Shay."

I stare at Kat to see if she's joking. She's not.

I think of all that sexual tension in the house, all those women, all that alcohol and lingerie.

And Shay, beautiful Shay, licking my hand.

I want to say something funny, like, *You mean, like...a Katy Perry sort of thing?* "*I kissed a girl and I liked it / The taste of her cherry Chapstick?*" But I'm trying to be mature and cool here. This is about to be my first discussion about girl-on-girl action, and I want to do it right. I settle on "Could you *define* this thing that happened back at the house with you and Shay?"

"We kind of made out," Kat admits, making a face and confirming my fears. "Things got...interesting. I think she might have touched my..."

"*I don't want to know!*" I shout, covering my ears like there's a spoiler alert for a new blockbuster coming over the radio. I try to drown out her words with a "Lalalalalalalala!"

"I *know*!" Kat agrees. "I am fucking freaking out!"

"Shay is our girl-crush, dude! That means that you *admire* her, you don't...*fondle* her or whatever!"

"I know! It's like girl-crush gone wild!" she yells.

"Pervert!" I yell back.

"I am!" Kat agrees. "I don't know what came over me. I mean, one minute I'm asking her where she gets her hair color done, and the next minute we're rolling around like female wrestlers..." Kat trails off, thank God.

"Holy crapamoly," I say. The grass is wet from the sprinklers, and my feet and butt are starting to get numb with cold. I have to ask the next question now or I know I never will. "Did you, you know, like it?"

"Sort of." Kat takes out a cigarette and lights it. I hold out my hand and she passes it to me.

One drag goes right to my head. I cough out the nicotine and wait for more information.

"There were too many parts up top and not enough junk down below." I nod my head to pretend that I'm perfectly able to hear all about this without being weirded out. Kat continues. "I was, like, into it and watching myself at the same time, wondering stupid shit, like, *What's the name of that perfume she's wearing? I wonder if it would smell that nice on me?* But then again, her kisses were soft and her mouth was sort of exciting. And I'd had too much to drink, obviously, so everything was kind of askew, confusing, you know?"

"Uh-huh."

Kat pauses, takes a drag, studies me. "You're looking at me strange."

"No, no I'm not." Okay maybe I am. Maybe I'm worried just a

tad that my old friend Kat, who I thought I knew so well, who has broken up with her scumbag husband, is actually a coming-out-of-the-closet lesbian and now she's trying to take me away with her to Miami to seduce me on the beach.

"Lauren, I'm not *gay*," she says, meeting my eyes. "I'm just, I don't know, messed up right now. Plus," she laughs, "you're not my type."

I'm simultaneously insulted and relieved. "I know I'm not as hot as your first kiss," I say. "But what's that saying? Once you've tried Shay, you're always gay?"

"Start with Shay, it's the only way?" Kat adds.

I laugh, but tell her the truth. "I'm a little bit afraid of you right now."

"Get over it and come with me to South Beach. Separate beds. We'll just shower together."

"Ha," I say. "I need a minute. Just be quiet for one minute."

She leans toward me. "*You* were the one who suggested that we drink more to make the party more fun, if I may remind you."

"That's not being quiet." I close my eyes. I need to sober up and think clearly here. I need to make a rational decision.

Noise from the street causes me to open my eyes. Kat has her head sticking through an opening in the bushes and is talking to a small group of partygoers heading to their cars.

"You didn't hear?" one of the women asks us.

"Hear what?" Kat asks back.

"Shay Greene. Her husband called her just now to say the votes are *finally* counted. Someone was contesting the decision, but now it's all sorted out and...Shay won!"

"Won what?" I ask, fearing that I already know the answer. My stomach sinks in apprehension.

"Shay's the new president of the school board," the woman announces.

"Of course she is!" Kat says. Then she mutters to herself, "Jesus Fucking H. Christ."

"Thanks for the news!" I call, waving the group away although they can't see me doing it.

"Hey, Lauren, is that you hiding in the bushes with Kat?" I hear my friend Susie ask.

"Yes, it sure is!"

She bends down and catches my eye through the pine needles.

"You know, Leslie's on the phone with her dad. He's a partner at West, Hunter, and Harrison. I think she's planning to sue you. The whole incident was caught on the nanny cam; Leslie had them installed everywhere after that last babysitter, remember?"

Kat gives me a look. "Nanny cam?" she mouths. She looks like I feel: spooked.

Susie continues. "Just thought I'd give you the heads-up. Ciao, ladies!"

My pole dancing was caught on videotape.

I'm getting sued.

Everyone in town is going to be talking about me.

"Nanny cam?" Kat repeats, this time in an I-see-dead-people stage whisper.

"Do you think Leslie has cameras in the bathrooms?" I wonder, worried about my lovefest with the toilet.

"Lauren, focus." Kat lifts my chin and holds my gaze steady with hers. "Shay and I weren't in a bathroom."

Oh shit. I wasn't thinking about them.

Kat just kissed the new school board president. Kat just kissed the new married, *female* school board president, and, in a bedroom somewhere in Leslie's house, there's a teddy bear or a decorative ceramic object that saw it all.

I think back to Tuesday and that nice French man in the park with Googly the poodle, talking about his lovely little weekend getaways to Florida.

I turn to Kat, my heart beating fast. "Miami, did you say?"

She grabs my hands in hers, clearly freaking big time, her eyes glowing sort of crazy-like. "Two days, Lauren. That's it. Till we can figure out how to handle this. Just to, you know, get out of Dodge."

"We need to get out of Dodge," I say. What was an option a moment ago is now an imperative. There are just too many people to hide from in Hadley. I think of trying to have a few days of local fun while steering clear of Martha, Leslie, Shay. Doug. Kat's husband, Peter. It's just not possible.

Running away is our *only* way.

"But, we have to be back by Saturday night for Jodi's fundraising dance at the temple," I rationalize.

"I know. I thought of that. We're booked to come back on Saturday morning. We'll have plenty of time to do both."

My heart is in my throat, a sure sign that I've taken leave of my senses. Either I've had too much to drink or am making a scintillating, albeit potentially dangerous, decision.

Or both.

Kat and I lock eyes, making some sort of unwritten pact. It's now or never. *We deserve this*, I imagine her saying. *It will be a blast*, I say back. *Like skipping school when we were teenagers. No one has to know*, we agree. *There's no nanny cam in Miami.*

"I'm in," I say. Then, realizing what I've just committed to, I say it again, with excitement. "I'm in!"

"You're welcome!" Kat exclaims. I look at her skeptically. She shrugs. "I'm just saying. You're going to thank me for this later. You'll see."

"Thank you or kill you," I say. "We'll know by Saturday."

Kat and I have sobered up a bit but are not what you'd actually call *sober*. We get a taxi, which pulls up at the same moment as an ambulance with its lights flashing.

"Oh brother," Kat sighs. "You are so fucked." About that, I would have to agree. We watch from the bushes as Leslie is rolled down her driveway on a gurney, her black ponytail dragging behind her on the pavement. When she's hoisted in the back—with hand-holding Pam by her side and everyone else from the party rubber-necking—we make a run for it and dash from the tree line out into the street, and into the back of the taxi.

"Where to?" the cabbie asks.

"Just get us around this ambulance and off this street!" Kat directs.

As we pull away, Shay waves to our cab and mouths, with her fist to her ear, "Call me."

After the driver drops Kat off at her condo, I have an epiphany. I check the time, see that it's just past 11:00, and dial Jodi at home while the cab makes its way to my house.

Her sultry voice fills my ear, and I can tell I've either interrupted her sleep or her lovemaking. "Hi-yyy! Are you o*kay*?" She yawns.

"I'm fine! I'm great!"

"You sound high. Are you stoned?"

"Jo, I don't smoke pot. You do."

"Oh, right." She pauses and laughs. "*I'm* high."

So now I know what I've interrupted. "Are you with Lee right now?" I ask. "Because I need to confide in you; I need to talk to you in private."

"Well, I'm with Lee, technically, but he's passed out on the couch next to me, so I think we're cool for the deep, dark secrets," she whispers. "Spill."

"I'm...going away," I say, taking a deep breath. "I'm...taking a very small, much-needed, well-deserved vacation tomorrow, and I'm not telling Doug about it, and in case something horrible should happen to me—or God forbid to anyone I love—while I'm gone, I need to tell someone where I am going. I need to tell you where I'll be."

"Whoa," she says. "That's intense."

"Sort of is, I guess."

"You, like, *totally* trust me."

"I do, Jo."

"Aw, you're such an *awesome* friend." I can imagine her zoning out in her own little peace-love-marijuana world while I try to tell her the specifics of my vacation plans.

Jodi may not have been the best person to entrust with this after all.

"I'll just e-mail you with the info," I decide. "Like what plane we're on and the name of the hotel in Miami..."

"Wait! *We're? Miami?* Who is this 'we' and why are 'we' going to Miami?" Nothing like a secret to snap Jodi back to reality. Before I can even reply, she's guessing. "I know...it's that guy. From high school. MC Loser or whatever he calls himself. You're jetting off to have an affair with him in Florida!"

"Nice that you think so little of me, but no."

"Oh. Sorry."

"S'okay." I smile, because it's not like I haven't fantasized about it. "Kat and I are going to enjoy an impromptu mini–spring break."

"Oh. Really."

From her tone, I realize just how big I've screwed this up. "Jodi...it's not like that. Don't get mad. We didn't exclude you on purpose or anything...we just decided tonight! We were a little bit drunk! At this crazy chick's sex-toy party..."

"Oh, really."

"Ugh," I groan. "You don't *know* her! You weren't invited!"

"I guess I'm just a third wheel to you guys, now that I don't teach with you two anymore. I *knew* one day you'd just *discard* me. I just didn't know it would come so soon."

"Jodi, you haven't taught with us for eight years." Ah, the drama that is Jodi Moncrieff. I backpedal and sidestep and do all sorts of fancy verbal dancing, but it seems to be of no use.

Finally, I just appeal to her mothering instinct, Jodi's kryptonite. "Jodi, how *could* you go to Miami? And leave your three precious girls like that? You can't stand to be away from them for even one day, you know that. Plus, Lee wouldn't let you. He's kind of controlling, right? Likes to know where you are all the time, likes you home, cooking meals and stuff..."

"Fuck Lee!" Jodi shouts, waking her dozing husband. I can hear her muffled conversation with him. "Not you, babe. It was something on cable. Go back to sleep. Lauren, are you there? I'm taking the phone upstairs."

The cabbie pulls into my driveway and I ask him to let the car idle while I wrap up this call.

"You know, I've got a grandmother in Miami," Jodi says, back on the line.

"That's a nice non sequitur."

"Yes, whatever that means," she says. She slows down her words and pronounces each distinctly. "I've. Got. A. Grandmother. In. Miami."

"That's. Nice," I try, playing her game.

"She's very old. So old that she might die. Any day now."

"That's too bad," I add, aiming for a sympathetic tone.

"I think I should visit her. One last time. Because she's practically on her deathbed, you know."

My heart starts beating fast.

Of course!

Jodi is the best liar I know.

"Lauren, are you there? I better wake Lee and tell him that I just got this *awful* call from my grandmother. She's *very* sick. She wants to see me one last time. I *have* to go to Miami…"

"Tomorrow!" we shout, united in blissful deceit.

MIDLOGUE

LADIES AND GENTLEMEN OF THE JURY, I could bore you with the details of how I managed to sneak out of my house at 5:30 a.m. that Thursday morning, deceiving the Hadley School District, my husband, my children, and my babysitter, among others. Lawyers could postulate an in-depth analysis about how I *felt* about it all. A psychiatrist could lecture to you about women and their midlife crises, the way completely respectable, law-abiding citizens could just turn all *Thelma and Louise* at the mere mention of Botox.

But I've been a juror, remember, and I know that your time is precious.

So, I'll just tell you that, in the movie version of my life, the Clash's "Should I Stay or Should I Go" would be playing as I entered my dark and sleepy suburban split-level home at approximately 11:22 p.m. on Wednesday evening, having just finished making the call to Jodi. That one call that turned her from a mere witness to an actual accomplice, I guess you could say. But that's for another jury to decide down the hall, and so I will not speculate.

Instead, I will admit that I packed a small carry-on as best I could in the darkness. And although I could not locate my favorite beach cover-up anywhere, I eventually went to bed. I awoke and dressed in the blue-gray morning fog, left a note on the kitchen counter next to my car keys, and slid out the front door to await Kat's arrival in my driveway.

You see, once the decision to bolt was made, everything just fell into place. The old Lauren, the me from the time before jury duty, would have kept ongoing lists on her iPhone of the pros and cons of such an adventure, had she even entertained the thought at all. She may have surfed the web in the school library, searching for online support groups for teachers on the verge. She would have asked other people's opinions, stopping coworkers in the faculty lounge to ask if they had ever taken leave of their senses. When did they do it, and for how long? What were the consequences?

But here's the funny thing about taking leave: you just do it. All the thinking and planning and worrying and wondering grabs its wings and takes flight. And you know what? Watching all of that day-to-day sameness fly right out the window?

It feels really fucking good.

Ladies and gentlemen of the jury, I would prefer to admit that I feel some remorse.

I regret to say that I do not.

I would like to say that I have reflected on, and learned a great deal from, all that has occurred.

I regret to say that I have not.

And so, without further ado, I shall submit into evidence an accounting of the rest of my week.

Or what I recall of it.

And, Your Honor, I would just like to mention here that all songs from the soundtrack of my life that week are listed on my Facebook page and are available for purchase through iTunes. Enjoy!

CHAPTER 15

Thursday

"I HAVE A SURPRISE FOR YOU," I say with a smile, getting into Kat's Mini Cooper and throwing my luggage in the backseat.

"Jodi called. She's running late." Kat glances over at me. "Was that your surprise?"

"Yes! Why'd she call you? I told her it would be more fun if she just showed up at the gate, ready to go. I thought you'd love it."

"She said she didn't want to wake anyone in your house with a call. She probably texted you or something."

I check my phone and see that she has. Then I reach into my bag and pull out a CD case.

"New mix?" Kat asks.

"Miami mix, baby!" I pop it in and '80s music fills the small space. "You know how I love the mixes!"

With little traffic so early in the morning, we make it to Kennedy airport in no time, park the car, and get our boarding passes. Jodi calls Kat to say she's at the airport and is parking Lee's car. He would have been suspicious if she said she was taking a cab, so she insisted on driving herself, to fit best with the dying-grandmother story.

A few minutes later, Jodi enters the terminal looking like a famous person who is trying hard to be nonchalant. She's wearing a wide-brimmed, white sun hat and enormous black Gucci sunglasses. She's got layers of gauzy material wrapped around her delicate frame. Gladiator sandals wind their way up her ankles.

"She's gonna have to check that." Kat motions to her huge suitcase. "Who brings that much stuff for two days?"

"It's shoes and bras, mostly, I can tell you from experience."

"Bras?"

"Yes. Apparently, there are different kinds for every outfit. Racerback, push-up, push-up racerback, strapless underwire… there's quite an education to be had, traveling with Jodi."

"It's like last night all over again," Kat jokes. "By the way, I have a little bit of a headache. You?"

"Not too bad. I bet Leslie's feeling it hard, though."

"Should I make a lame joke about 'hard' or no?"

I give Kat a look just as Jodi gets to us.

"Hi-yyy!" She kisses us each on both cheeks with a "mwah!" sound. "Why aren't you guys dressed up? We're going on vacation!"

"Because airplanes are cold," I say.

"Because I don't own shit like that," Kat adds.

We wait while Jodi checks her luggage and then we head through security.

Jodi is busy unraveling the laces on her gladiator sandals, so Kat and I take turns going through the metal detector, waiting for her on the other side.

"Excuse me? Ma'am?" a security officer calls. I don't look up from where I am retying my sneakers until he says it again, this time in my ear. "Ma'am."

"Uh, y-yes?" I stammer, looking to see if he's confusing me for someone else.

"Come with me, please." I glance at Kat, who shrugs. Then the officer motions toward her. "You, too."

"Jodi!" I call. "We're being examined."

She removes her sunglasses and watches with wide eyes as Kat and I are led into a privacy cubicle off to the side.

"Let's hope there's a cavity search," Kat remarks. "That would be a fun way to start the trip."

The officer hears Kat's comment but does not smile. "Ladies, sit, please."

From a gray plastic tray, he removes and holds up two items. One is a pair of handcuffs trimmed in pink fur. The other is a tube of lipstick. He waits.

I'd know that lipstick anywhere.

And it ain't lipstick.

"Kat!" I proclaim in mock horror. "You actually *bought* that from Candy Cox?"

"What?" she asks, looking to me, then to the items. "No!" she exclaims, realizing what I mean. "Officer...I have no idea where those things came from—"

"Well, I do," he says, cutting her off. "These here," he says, shaking the handcuffs, "were in the blonde's pocketbook."

"I—"

"And this interesting device," he says, holding out the mini-vibrator, "was in the bag belonging to...Kat, is it?"

"Ugh!" she groans. "Leslie!"

"What?" I ask. "Her dad's that top lawyer, is that what you mean? That we should call *Leslie* for legal counsel?"

"No!" Kat muses, a small smile playing on her lips. "Leslie *gave* us this shit as party favors last night! That's why they were in our bags."

"Ohhhh!" I exhale. "That's funny," I decide, and we start cracking up. Kat is laughing so hard that tears roll down her cheeks.

"Fucking crazy bitch!" she says fondly, recalling Leslie from last night.

"Um, ladies. I don't think you understand. This is a serious matter. A matter of national security."

This has us laughing even harder. "Yeah, I'm a regular bin Laden!" she cackles. "Taking down democracy with my lipstick vibrator!"

"Locking up freedom with these plush, Playboy Bunny handcuffs...that don't even lock!" I add for good measure. "My metal nail file is more menacing!"

"Hello!" Jodi calls, her hat visible just above the rim of our cubicle. "I'm going to Miami with or without you two losers, just so you know. See you at the gate."

"Maybe!" I joke, still trying to catch my breath.

"Please, officer," Kat says benevolently. "For your significant other, gifts from Lady Hoochie. Now, if you don't mind releasing us, we've got a plane to catch."

The announcement tells us to fasten our seatbelts, secure all items under the seat in front of us, and turn off all electronic devices until the captain tells us it's safe to power on again. Kat puts headphones into her iPod and slips one ear bud under her hair, concealed from any Gestapo-like stewardesses. Jodi passes out gum and opens her bible, *People* magazine. She runs her hands lovingly over the glossy pages and begins to read.

The plane creeps along the runway. The captain tells us that we are now next in line for takeoff and reminds us to turn off all electronics until we reach our climbing altitude. This is Kat's signal to hide the ear bud once more.

I check my e-mail before shutting off my phone, finding three correspondences of note. The first is from Doug.

Subject: Jury Sequestering
From: dworthing@corporatebranding.com
Date: April 13
To: laurenworthing@gmail.com

Hi Lauren. Saw your note when I woke up. Can't believe the judge called you so early this morning and demanded that your jury be sequestered. Immediately! That seems a bit extreme for a civil case like that, with low-profile clients and all. Unless it's more than you were letting on? I know that, as per your instructions, you can't tell me anything now, but if you are allowed time to call and check in today, please do.

I'm sorry that we haven't had time to connect. Sorry, too, that you are tangled up in this case, cut off from your life. I know you don't always love your job, but I bet you wish you were back in school right now. Ha.

Thanks for taking a cab to the courthouse and leaving us with your minivan and the car seats. I will make sure that Laney does some grocery shopping today while the kids are in school and that she takes Ben to Little League tonight.

By the way, do you have the number for Becca's
friend Ainsley? She says she has a playdate
with her but it's not on your calendar. Oh,
right, you can't call me. I'll find it somewhere.

I know jury duty sucks. But maybe they'll
settle early or something? So you can come
home and tell me what the kids like to eat
for lunch? Ha again. Not panicking too much
here…just the right amount, I think.

—D

Oh, I'm so ashamed of myself.

Sort of.

He bought the story! And now he's got no choice but to be an active parent! Sometimes you've gotta do what you've gotta do. Doug has to work late and cancel our romantic dinner? Fine. Understood. Things happen. Just like I've got to have my pretend jury sequestered and lie my way to sunshine.

Luckily, I already lined up Jackie to babysit tonight (Laney's not a fan of overtime), otherwise this little getaway really might not have been possible.

The second e-mail comes from Dara, the secretary in the main office at Hadley Middle School. She's asking for paperwork confirming my prolonged absence due to jury duty. She's asking that I drop it by. Today. At my earliest convenience.

Okay, now that one has me a bit rattled. I send off a quick reply, my fingers nervously striking the letters on my phone. I'm hoping that once she learns of my sequestration, she'll get off my back.

Although, now that I've sent a response, I'm not sure jurors are allowed to have their cell phones when sequestered.

Maybe she won't think of that.

The third e-mail is self-explanatory:

```
Subject: Re: Hi
From: lkatzenberg@yale.alumni.edu
Date: April 13
To: laurenworthing@gmail.com
```

You are a baaaaad girl, Mrs. Worthing. Skipping school, lying to your husband, getting Botox, going to Boston for the day. You're much more fun than I ever remembered you being in high school. Middle age really agrees with you.

So, what's it going to be today? How about visiting another old friend?

```
Subject: Re: Re: Hi
From: laurenworthing@gmail.com
Date: April 13
To: lkatzenberg@yale.alumni.edu
```

Can't today, old friend. Am on my way to Miami. ;)

I hit "send" and power off just as the plane accelerates. Kat grabs my hand and I grab Jodi's on the other side. I close my eyes as we take off, hope and fear churning together in the hollow of my stomach.

"Christ, Lauren," Kat swears as we wait for Jodi's bag to come around the carousel at the Miami International Airport. "Could you get off that thing? You're like iDicted to your iPhone."

"I'm just checking my messages," I say. "But that's pretty good, actually. I'm gonna use that line. iDicted."

The balmy, sweet-smelling air of southern Florida envelops us as we exit the terminal and hail a cab.

"This is a*maz*ing!" Jodi cheers. "I love you guys! I love us!" We tell the driver where we're headed and sit back in the cab, rolling down the windows and admiring the palm trees. Jodi begins unwrapping herself like a mummy, letting go layer upon layer of cotton, until all that's left is a bandeau top and miniskirt.

"How did you do that?" Kat demands. "How the fuck does she do that?" she reiterates, turning to me.

"It's a gift," Jodi concedes.

"So, are you going to visit your grandma?" I ask Jodi.

"Are you kidding me?" she says. "Of course I'm not!"

"But...why not? She only lives a few miles from the hotel, I thought."

"Yeah, and she has dementia and won't know if I'm there or not. If anyone in my family asks her, 'Oh, how was your visit from Jodi?' she'll probably say, 'Jodi? Who's Jodi?' So, why waste the time? I'll send a basket of oranges with a card."

"A demented grandmother as an alibi. I love it." Kat nods approvingly.

I try to finish replying to Lenny's e-mail without them noticing, which of course fails miserably. He suggests that we stay at the Delano, but I tell him we already made reservations.

"You love him," Jodi teases. "He's your pretend boyfriend."

I smile and ignore them, finishing my e-mail and putting the phone away.

"It's not funny, you know," Kat says. "Adultery."

I think of Kat crouched on a stool in her classroom closet, wasting her money on calls to a psychic hotline, her husband running off. "You're right," I say, taking her hand. "It's not funny at all. I'm an insensitive jerk to flirt with Lenny, after all you've gone through."

"Me?" Kat asks. "I don't care about you flirting in front of me. I mean because of Doug."

She has a point.

I haven't given much thought to that aspect of my flirtationship.

"But, you *can't* think of your husband if you're, like, fantasizing about some other guy," Jodi explains, like it's simple math. "That's just a buzzkill." She readjusts her bandeau top. "Anyway, it seems completely harmless. As my grandmother always says, 'There's nothing wrong with looking, as long as you don't touch the merchandise.'"

"Yeah," I say, "but she's delusional!"

"Just don't touch, Lauren," Jodi reiterates.

"All the thrills without the chills?" Kat jokes.

"Story of my life," Jodi says cryptically, as the cab pulls up in front of our hotel.

CHAPTER 16

WE QUICKLY CHECK IN, change, and head down to the cerulean water, edged with sand the color of a light suntan. We walk as far as we can from the more crowded part of the beach and choose a nice, secluded spot. An attendant sets up three lounge chairs facing the sun and orders some lunch for us. Jodi gets a margarita, the thought of which makes both Kat and me queasy. "Tonight we'll join you," I promise her. "We require a few more hours of detox first, though."

It's only 12:30 p.m., and we're sitting by the aquamarine ocean. I close my eyes and listen to the soft surf, the seagulls overhead, and my own shallow breathing. "I can't believe we did this! I am chillaxing!" I declare.

"Mmm," Jodi concurs, flipping through the pages of yet another tabloid magazine. Her BlackBerry buzzes and we all jump. She picks it up from the plastic side table and examines the message. "You've got to be kidding me! An 'emergency' text from the PTA. Urgent committee chair meeting today at two o'clock, regarding T-shirt sales." She flings the device into her bag with disgust. "I am on vacation, people, now leave me alone!"

"Damn straight," Kat adds. "I'm going to sleep."

After lunch, I end up reading Jodi's tabloids and then pass out in the sun for most of the afternoon.

I wake up to the sound of Kat thumbing away at her BlackBerry. At first, I think I'm still back with her behind the bushes outside Leslie's neighbor's house. Then I see the sun hanging low in the sky just behind a palm tree and remember where I really am.

A sudden memory of the horrors of the night before flashes across my frontal cortex and I groan.

"Hello, Sleeping Beauty," Jodi sings. "Nice bruise you got there on your knee."

I look down to see that the toilet incident in Leslie's lav did in fact leave a colorful memento.

"How'd you get that?" Kat asks, looking up from her keypad.

"Oh, you know, this and that," I say.

"I can't believe you guys are cutting school!" Jodi says. "This is just like *Ferris Bueller's Day Off*." We then spend several minutes debriefing about how we left things at school, with Kat filling Jodi in on her more-than-slight problem with the *di*ministration and Psycho Mom. I ask their opinion about Martha and how I think she's onto me.

"Classic paranoia," Jodi dismisses. "No one cares about you nearly as much as you do; I've learned that the hard way. Not even your lover boy, MC Little Douche Bag or whatever his name is."

"MC Lenny Katzenberg," I clarify. "And I bet he has been thinking about me. I probably received a few playfully naughty texts from him while I was sleeping."

I check my phone to find that there are no playfully naughty texts from MC Lenny.

"Bad reception?" Kat asks.

"Mm," I say. Although I did get another e-mail from Doug.

"Sunset yoga," a soothing female voice sings from across the sand. We stop our conversation and turn in the direction of the sound.

"She's over there," Jodi points. "Follow the harem pants."

"Sunset yoga," the woman calls again, this time much closer to us. "Starting in five minutes."

"Hey," Kat calls back, standing and stretching. "How much for me and my friends?" Kat is a certified instructor for vinyasa and hatha and about fourteen other types of yoga. When she's not discussing astrological and psychic energies with Varka, she's perfecting a pose and meditating.

Or she's drinking and cursing. There's a fine balance.

The woman comes closer. She's a toned, tan, tiny sprite of a thing who makes even Kat look normal size. Her legs are hidden beneath flowing pink pants, but her muscular torso is on full view in a string-bikini top. "It's free for hotel guests," she smiles, twisting her long blond hair into a knot on the top of her head. "Right over here." She points toward an area a short walk down the beach. "And we provide the mats. All you need to bring is some water and your chi." She looks like the yogi version of Shakira, abs and all. She carries a stick of burning incense in her right hand.

"Let's try it! Sounds fun!" Jodi says.

I am not convinced. Exercise is one of those things I like to avoid as much as possible. Especially when hung over and already sweaty. "I'm thinking that upside down is not going to be my favorite state of being," I say, "but you guys go on."

"We said we'd do everything together on this trip," Kat reminds me.

"When did we say that?"

"Just now." She half smiles.

"Funny. Fine," I say. We gather our things and follow the harem lady and a trail of woody incense down the beach. She nods her approval and tells us that her name is Debbie.

I preferred Shakira.

Jodi picks up our conversation from where we left off. "How was that party, by the way? You guys didn't say much about it."

"Just typical girls'-night-out stuff," Kat mumbles, adjusting the beach bag on her shoulder and hiding behind her towel.

"Yeah...just...you know, pole dancing, dominatrices, dildos, and a little bit of a lesbian lovefest...very suburban, boring, nothing to report." I grin.

Jodi's eyes go wide, and Kat hits me on the arm. "Lauren!"

"Holy crap hell! Do tell!" Jodi rhymes.

"What?" I say to Kat, who squints menacingly my way.

We reach a shady spot on the beach under some palm trees. Ten blue mats are set up, and several other participants have already arrived. We drop our belongings in the sand and grab three spots at the back of the group. Jodi positions herself between Kat and me.

I'm not going to feel bad. I mean, this is Jodi. It's not like I'm going to spill Kat's secret to the whole world.

"I think it would be good for both of us, actually, Kat. To unburden ourselves," I say, stretching.

Jodi looks at us with really fake sincerity, because she's so thirsty for gossip that she can't even pretend that she isn't thrilled. "Yes! Unburden."

Kat pulls her hair off her face and tucks it into a hat, buying time. "Well, *I* really think we should begin by discussing my friend's *awesomely sexy* dance moves, which inadvertently left our hostess with the need for six stitches across her left cheek."

"Touché," I say.

"Ouch!" Jodi says.

"Welcome." Debbie smiles, palms pressed together over her heart. We mimic the pose. "Let us begin with a series of sun salutations."

I work my way through the movements, and then, when I think it's safe enough to talk, continue the conversation, sotto voce. "Although, *I* think the better story is how *my awesomely sexy* little friend here got the new *female* school board president drunk, and then fooled around with her in the guest bedroom."

"Nice!" Jodi says, peering up at Kat through her legs, in a Downward Dog pose.

"Did I mention that this female that Kat fooled around with is also a girl? Like Kat? A *female woman girl*?" I say, my face turning red as the blood rushes to it. I move from Downward- to Upward-Facing Dog.

"Yup! Caught it the first time!" Jodi says. "Katy Perry, here she comes!"

"Hey, that was my line!" I add enthusiastically.

"Shh," warns a man in a Speedo in the row in front of ours. He moves into Warrior II and we follow suit, remaining quiet for a few minutes.

The ocean is peaceful and still as the sun begins to drop lower in the sky. A slight breeze moves across the beach and cools me down. The palms rustle overhead and I feel more relaxed than I have in a long time.

My mind has a moment to empty. But just as I try to imagine a clear, blank slate, a question pops into my head that I cannot ignore. "Kat," I whisper. "How do you know that Leslie needed six stitches?"

Jodi and I both look at Kat. She's holding a beautiful Tree pose, but what I see before me is a classic double pause followed by a triple fidget. I've caught her at something.

"I'm just guessing," she says, trying to stay balanced.

"Bullshit." Surprisingly, this comes from Jodi and not me.

"Ladies, if you cannot be quiet, I will have to ask you to leave the group," Debbie says, pseudo-sweetly, biceps flexing. I remind myself that underneath the calm façade is the body of a woman who could seriously kick my ass.

"Fine." Kat tilts her head skyward and stares at the darkening blue expanse for a moment, neck arched, liked she's stretching. She sighs. Then she turns toward us. "This morning I friended Shay on Facebook. She told me."

"Really? Why would you do that? I thought the goal was to distance yourself from the crime scene, not leave your fingerprints all over her, metaphorically speaking."

"Do you know how many people probably friended Shay after she won the election?" Kat says, expertly switching her Tree pose to the other leg. "On Facebook, I'll hardly stand out from her admiring crowd."

This is true. It's probably a nonissue, I think, relaxing into Pigeon pose. I close my eyes, the sun's glow trapped inside my lids, turning my inner vision a bright tangerine. Inhale, exhale.

Kat clears her throat as we stand up and switch positions once more. "Of course, now that Shay's asked me to be her PTA liaison to the faculty, I guess we'll be spending a lot of time working together. Afternoons, evenings. Perhaps just the two of us." She raises an eyebrow meaningfully.

"Kat! Are you joking or are you insane?" I shout.

"Shh," Jodi says, looking around apologetically. "You're kind of yelling, Lauren."

"I don't care! Ever since Peter broke up with her, she's been, like, on a mission toward self-destruction. She's *completely* lost it!" I turn my head to Kat, maintaining my Warrior pose, if not my composure. My arm reaches out in her direction, accusingly. "Do you have a death wish? I mean, we left town because of *your* little tryst with Shay last night."

"Eagle!" Debbie cries desperately.

We ignore her.

"Newsflash, Lauren. You have it backward: *I* did *you* a favor."

"Um...keep it down, psycho yogis," Jodi adds. "Let's play nice and have fun here. I came for a *break* from stress!"

We let that sink in. I turn away from Kat and face the ocean once more.

"Namaste and all that shit," Jodi adds.

Lowering my voice to the level of one appropriate in yoga

class, I try for a softer, albeit still defensive, tactic. "Kat, do you really want to lose your job and perhaps cause a scandal for Shay Greene and her whole perfect family?"

"My job *that I hate*, you mean?" Kat yoga-yells back. "And why does Shay get to have it so easy? Everything's so perfect, huh? Maybe *her* life needs a little bit of messing up like mine!"

"Happy Baby!" Debbie cries. "Happy Baby, everyone!"

I lie on my back, grabbing my toes with my hands. "You didn't just say that, Kat." I'm trying to relinquish some of my anger by rocking back and forth in the pose. "You want her to go down *with* you? In some sort of suburban *Desperate Housewives* scene, where you guys are found making out in the janitor's closet at the elementary school? I know you are hurting, and maybe this all seems like fun in your head, but are you really that demented?"

"It doesn't even matter what I do, Lauren. There's a nanny cam somewhere that will ruin both Shay's and my life anyway, remember?"

"You're right," I concede. "But that doesn't mean you should just give up on having a future that's drama-free. Your past has been chaotic, true, but your world doesn't have to resemble a nighttime soap opera forever. You deserve better, Kat."

Her eyes hold mine for a second. I can just about see through them, into the machinery of her brain as gears shift and slide into place.

"Guys! People are staring," Jodi says. "Get up." I look around and notice that Kat and I are the only two morons still on our backs in Happy Baby pose.

"I thought you *liked* people staring at you," I say to her. And before I can think better of it I add, "Bring on the paparazzi! Let's get famous for nothing!" I'm on a roll now, truth-telling pouring out from my pores, and it feels freeing. "Three kids and no excitement, so…"

"That was a secret!" Jodi protests.

"Ooh…time to *unburden*," Kat snarks.

"And speaking of secrets, *Lauren*," Jodi adds, "you're basically cheating on your husband."

"Which is not much different than basically *stealing* from yours," I say.

This is not what our beachy vacay is supposed to sound like.

This is certainly not what sunset yoga in SoBe is supposed to look like. We glare at each other in stunned silence, having never fought like this before.

I'm suddenly not feeling quite so free.

I change my mind; honesty sucks. I wish I could stop time and rewind the clock, put Pandora back into her box.

"That's it! Good-bye," Debbie says, managing, despite everything, to be holding the most perfect Half Moon I have ever seen.

"Kumbaya?" Jodi calls, trying to make amends with Debbie as we gather our belongings and quickly step away from the group.

"Well, that went really well, Lauren, dontcha think?" Kat accuses. "Now my chakras are all misaligned!"

I pivot on the sand and face her. "This is not only *my* fault, you know. First, you got kicked out of school and now Jodi just got us kicked out of sunset yoga! Which I didn't even want to participate in, I might remind you."

Digging my toes into the sand, I wait for a response.

No one speaks.

I look at Jodi, who looks at Kat, who looks at the ground.

Now that we're silent, this would have been the perfect time to join the yoga class.

"Um, ladies...if I may?" a man calls out.

I turn my head in the direction of the voice, which holds the slightest hint of southern charm.

Jodi takes one look at the guy and shakes her head in disgust. "No, you may not."

About ten feet away from where we are standing, tucked inside a sunshade cabana, sits the offending individual. He's wearing faded shorts and a ripped T-shirt, a Kangol summer-style fedora, and mirrored aviators. From his chin hangs the scraggliest looking beard I've ever seen. It's long and unkempt and kind of grayish blond, like an old man's pubes.

An overstuffed army-style duffle bag rests at his side, probably containing all his worldly possessions. He looks like Nick Nolte's character from *Down and Out in Beverly Hills.*

"What is he, homeless?" Kat whispers to us.

"Don't get too close. Ignore him," Jodi instructs. "And I'm not talking to you, Lauren."

"One, I'm sorry. I should not have lashed out at you like that.

You want to get famous, go for it. Two, I thought we were on the good part of the beach," I say.

"I thought so, too, until you yappers showed up, ruined yoga over there, and made me all tense in my private beach cabana," the man says. Then, pointing at Jodi, "I agree with her. You guys are giving me some serious agita."

"I don't need your agreement!" Jodi calls back.

"I thought you said we were supposed to ignore him!" Kat says.

"I'm merely *telling* him that we are ignoring him!" she explains.

"What if he wants to eat our small intestines with a spoon?" Kat asks.

"Then we'll give him Lauren."

"Ha," I say.

"I'm a practicing vegetarian, ladies...no worries about cannibalism from me. And yes, I heard all about your little drama, since you were whisper-screaming it to the whole of South Beach."

Jodi's shaking her head in wonder. "He's got, like, Spiderman's hearing."

"Batman's," I correct. "You know, like *bats*?"

"Maybe spiders have great hearing, too, for all you know." She cannot be wrong.

"Are you two really going to fight about something this stupid?" Kat demands.

"Yup," the man calls. "I think they are."

"Listen here, you motherfucking Fu Manchu—"

The man interrupts what is sure to be one of Kat's most colorful diatribes on record. "All I'm saying is, Mercury is in retrograde, and..."

Kat stops. She turns her head to the side just the tiniest bit, to see if she heard him correctly. "All right. You've got ten seconds."

He scratches his beard, like he's seriously thinking about what advice to dish out.

Then he looks up and begins pointing. "To you, the black-haired girl, I say: stay away from trouble. As my great-granny used to tell me back in Missouri, you don't shit where you eat."

"See?" I say, nodding along with the random man's words of wisdom and hitting Kat on the arm. Hard.

"I'm Kat, by the way," she calls back.

"Nice to meet you, Kat. Please keep your dick in your pants."

"Fuck you," she retorts, one corner of her mouth turned up in a devilish smile.

"Lovely," Jodi says. I'm not sure if she's referring to the beach bum or Kat. It kind of doesn't matter.

"And you," he says, pointing at me.

"Moi?" I look over my shoulder to see if he's mistaken me for anyone else on the beach.

"Yes, blondie. You're not so unique, you know. Everyone feels the way you do. Wanting to cut school, call in sick, take a break."

"I'm not ill; I'm on jury duty," I clarify. "You only eavesdropped on part of the story."

"Well, I caught the part about those little texts. That are not from your husband, I'm guessing."

"I might not be married, you know," I call back. Then I whisper to Jodi and Kat, "I'm really not liking this guy."

"I can see that pretty diamond sparkling in the fading sunlight, my friend," he replies.

"Shit, he's going to rob us," Jodi says.

"I'm not gonna rob y'all!" he says, sounding very much like a character from a movie who is, indeed, just about to rob us. "I've got kids, too," he adds, motioning to Jodi. "Lots of 'em. And I've got paparazzi. Lots of 'em."

"Go slip into something more comfortable—like a coma," Jodi says. *Like a coma?* I think. She gets up and faces him. It's like she's practicing for a scene for which she'd win Best Actress in a String Bikini in a Dramatic Role. "You've been *spying* on us and now you know all this *shit* about us and you're *slimy* and you're *freaking me out!*"

"That's it. Time's up. I'm calling the cops," Kat says, grabbing her BlackBerry from her beach bag.

His face—what little of it is visible—registers alarm mingled with something else. Is he laughing at us? He gets up and saunters toward us, palms in surrender mode, his voice taking on a stage whisper. "No, no! Don't call the cops! It's cool. Really! I'm sorry for upsetting you. I'll explain!" He smiles and pulls his sunglasses down to his nose, flashing some gorgeous baby-blue eyes at us, dimples creasing his cheeks. "Will you let me explain? Sans police?"

Kat drops her phone. My mouth hangs open. Jodi takes a step forward.

The beard and the Kangol and the sunglasses and the dimples. The baby-blue eyes, and all those kids. All that paparazzi.

"Hey," he says, sticking out his right hand toward Jodi. "I'm Tim."

CHAPTER 17

IT'S TRULY AMAZING HOW QUICKLY Jodi's repulsion and fear can be replaced with full-on lust.

"Hi-yyy," Jodi coos, straightening her shoulders and tossing her auburn waves theatrically. "I'm Jodi."

Then she shakes hands with world-famous actor, two-time Academy Award–winner, and legendary hottie Tim Cubix like it's the most natural thing in the world, like she's just been waiting since seventh grade for him to show up and fight with her on the beach. "And this is Lauren," Jodi adds, motioning in my general direction without letting go of his hand or shifting her gaze from his. "I believe you've already met Kat."

How can Jodi form words at a time like this? Kat and I are having a much harder time keeping our shit together in the face of this astonishing bit of news. We manage to be calm for about a half a millisecond before gathering together in a hug and shrieking. Then we jump around in a circle of elation and share the discovery with each other.

"Ohmigod!" I scream.

"I think I just called Tim Cubix a motherfucker!" Kat cries excitedly.

"Shh!" Tim Cubix smiles, motioning us to come sit under the cabana. "Be subtle, could you, maybe?"

"I can't! I just can't!" I gasp. "You're too real for words!" I'm having the weirdest sensation standing next to the physical being of such a renowned celebrity. It's almost an out-of-body experience, like he's pulled me into one of his movies and I'm no longer living in my mundane world.

I feel like I'm in that scene from *The Wizard of Oz* when Dorothy opens the door to her house and emerges from the black-and-whiteness of Kansas into the Technicolor of Munchkinland. "It's just...I can't stop screaming!" I scream.

"Well, try, please or else I'm gonna have to vacate," Tim Cubix says, looking over his shoulder and up the beach. The crowd has thinned out considerably now that it's getting late in the day, but there are a few stragglers like us in a cluster of chairs a ways down the beach. "I'm in no position to draw a crowd."

"So, then why are you even talking to us?" Jodi asks. Plastered to her face is a dreamy smile that she can't seem to make disappear. She's trying, though. It just won't budge. "Not that I'm *complaining*."

Jodi's boobs peek out from the triangles of her brown crocheted bikini top as if to say that they aren't complaining either. "Maybe if we call you Lex Sheridan, no one will notice you!" she says.

Tim actually laughs good-naturedly at Jodi's bizarre suggestion.

"Who is Lex Sheridan?" I ask.

Jodi checks with Tim via eyebrow communication. He nods his head like, *go ahead, tell them,* and she continues. "Everyone *thinks* Tim got his start in *Fly By Night,* in which he plays the superhero vampire, Black Dawn."

"Yeah, yeah, we know," Kat says. "And that was such a surprise blockbuster that Hollywood just kept making more of them, with *Dawnbreaker* and then *Night Stalker* and *Black Dawn Redux.*"

"See, but here's what you ladies don't know," Jodi says. "Tim's big break was playing a male-nurse-slash-bodybuilder in *Afternoon Delight!* That was my favorite soap opera in middle school, and those six weeks with that character were the best ever. The writers hit him with an ambulance so he died in front of his own hospital."

"Hence Lex Sheridan." Tim smiles.

"Hence!" Jodi says.

"Holy *Dawnbreaker,*" Kat says, plopping herself down on the sand. "I'm sitting in Tim Cubix's shade."

I wonder if I can think of him as merely "Tim" or if my mind will only allow him to be a first and last combo, like Michelle Obama or Jacques Cousteau. I try it out. Tim, Tim, Tim. Just Tim. Bring him down to earth, Lauren, or you'll never be coherent again.

"Who me? The homeless beach bum?" Tim's smile is all creases and dimples and loveliness.

"Yeah, well...from a distance..." Jodi starts.

"And even from close up, actually..." Kat says.

"What? I look awful?" He's coy, he's playful, he's flirtatious. I'm officially besotted. He takes a seat on the edge of his beach chair and we all swoon as Jodi sits down next to him.

"Well, the beard... You do, yes," Kat braves. "But that doesn't mean we don't love you."

"It's true. We love you, Lex Sheridan," I say. I am a moron, officially. My skin instantly flushes pink and I feel a little bit dizzy. I join Kat on the sand.

You know how girls used to cry when they saw Elvis? Or scream in sheer terror over their love for the Beatles? I'm like that on the inside. Little teenaged versions of me are in my head screaming and jumping up and down and having a festival of sheer euphoric insanity. On the outside, I'm trying to keep it together for the sake of my own thin reputation.

I pinch myself on my forearm to keep the tears at bay.

Yes, I am that stupid.

"Well, if it makes you feel any better, I love my fans, too."

Which is nice of him to say. Even if it sounds totally canned.

He pauses for a second, as if debating what to do with all of us. He puts a hand on his leg as if about to stand, and I think he's planning to bolt.

Because if I were this movie star right now, surrounded by the somewhat unstable trinity of ladies made up of Kat, Jodi and myself, I'd be like, *what the hell did I get myself into here and how can I quickly extract myself from it?*

But then Jodi invites Tim to join us for a cocktail, ordering a round of strawberry mango smoothies for us from the hotel's beach waitress. He sort of shrugs to himself and settles back in his chair, pushing down the brim of his Kangol.

Kat and I drag over a few stray chairs and circle around him.

"See, I *knew* not to get you an alcoholic beverage." Jodi says to Tim, clearly loving this moment. Then turning to us, she adds, "Lex is not drinking much these days."

"Spoken like someone on a complete *People* magazine diet," a bemused Kat murmurs.

"The *Afternoon Delight* fan is right. I've got another shoot coming up in a few weeks, and I've got to drop, like, twenty," Tim explains.

"Speaking of which," Kat adds, "aren't you supposed to be on set right now, in the Everglades or something? Right around here, I think." Jodi gives her a look. "What? Maybe I can be an *expert*, too. It just so happens I read one of your tabloids on the plane. And Tim? Can I call you Tim?"

"I would prefer if we call him Lex," Jodi says.

"Call me Tim." He nods, smiles, and dimples us, all in one swift move. A hot chill passes through me, the kind that in grade school meant that someone had just stepped on the site of your grave. It's exciting and dangerous all at once.

"Okay, Tim," Jodi says, sounding disappointed. "If you say so. But if you ask me, it lacks something."

"Cheese," Tim says. "It lacks cheese."

Kat continues. "You never did answer our question of why in the world you would get in the middle of our bitchfest."

Tim glances over his shoulder, first left, then right, and then stares off down the beach for a while. I start biting my cuticles in the stillness.

Then he sighs. "I know I just met you ladies, but I feel like maybe I can trust you." He stops there and seems to make some sort of decision. "What the hell. I listened to you for long enough to know your stories, right?"

"Tim Cubix is stalking us," Kat says, shaking her head in disbelief.

"So I know how you are, shall we say, on the lam—" Tim continues.

"On the down low," Kat adds.

"MIA," Jodi says.

"Pulling a *Thelma and Louise*," I manage before turning bright red again and shutting my mouth.

"So, anyway. My point is this," he continues. "With one call, I could tell *your* husband"—Tim looks at me—"or *your* husband"—he smiles at Jodi—"or your soon-to-be-ex-husband—"

"Oh, he wouldn't give a flying fuck," Kat responds.

"—just where you are and what you're really up to," Tim finishes. Then he looks directly at me. "Ms....Jury Duty, was it?"

I can't believe it!

"Tim Cubix is blackmailing us!" I testify.

"Shh," he orders, looking around again.

"Holy *Fly By Night*." Kat shakes her head disapprovingly.

"This is so exciting," I decide, taking a sip of my yummy non-alcoholic, lo-cal smoothie. It's like my life really *is* a movie!

"I must apologize for my friends, Lex. *Tim*. It's just that they spent last night pole dancing and making out with women, and now, meeting you, they've come completely undone," Jodi explains.

"I did not make out with anyone! She did," I say, pointing to Kat. "Not that there's anything wrong with that. To clarify," I falter, wondering why I can't just shut up.

Kat gives a half wave as if to acknowledge that she is the mock lesbian of note.

Under these new circumstances, I just can't stand the thought of arguing with Kat and Jodi. I lean over and take Kat's hand in mine and squeeze it. She squeezes back.

I think we're good. For now anyway.

I'd like to apologize in some small way to Jodi as well, but she's far too obsessed at the moment with Tim. Which, in my mind at least, means that all is temporarily forgiven.

"Sooooo," Jodi purrs, moving as close to Tim as she can without actually mounting him, "what's the scoop? Why aren't you at work right now in the Everglades?"

"'Cause I'm hanging with you lovely ladies!" he tries.

"Bullarkey," Kat states.

"Fine," Tim says, putting his hands up in an 'I surrender' gesture. "Would you believe me if I told you that I'm...pulling my own little *Thelma and Louise*?" He pulls down his sunglasses for a second and winks a baby blue my way.

"Um..." I begin. Even Jodi and Kat seem to be at a loss for words.

"It's true. I needed a getaway. My agent booked me back-to-back on these projects even though I asked him not to, so, between work demands, and the paparazzi, and Ruby, and the kids—"

"A shitload of kids!" Kat adds. "Some natural, some adopted!"

"—I just...heard this little voice in my head telling me to slip away for a few days. I know it's not *right*. I know that my manager is going ballistic right now. I've put him in a tough spot. But he'll figure it out." He scratches the back of his left hand as if there's a strong itch there that just won't go away.

"And Ruby?" Jodi asks, her bikini triangles quivering in excitement. "Have you told her where you are?"

Ruby is Tim's longtime girlfriend, a mega movie star in her

own right, whose humanitarian efforts helped promote her to a leadership role in UNICEF. Together, they've been dubbed Rubix Cube by the media.

"Yes and no. I mean, I live for her and my family. Really I do. But I needed a break from my hectic life and she understands. We are texting, keeping in touch. But she doesn't know I'm in South Beach."

"So...you're just like us!" I say. "Technically, *we* could blackmail *you*."

Everyone looks at me.

"Not that we ever would," I add quickly.

"Don't worry about it," Tim continues, smiling. "The cameras will get to me first and spoil everything, just you wait."

"You need a disguise," Jodi says. "Something to make you incarnito."

Tim studies Jodi for a moment, but doesn't try and correct her malapropism. I instantly like him for it.

"I have a feeling hanging out with you guys might do the trick, actually. No one really looks at a group of middle-aged women in a hotspot like this. I think I could blend in."

"Thanks? So, you're blackmailing us *and* using us," I decide, warming up to the idea of this movie star as a real person. "And insulting us."

"Sort of." He nods. "Awkward question? Could one of you guys get my room key for me at the front desk? My manager always books my hotels, but since I'm not talking to him, I just showed up here and did it myself, from my cell phone. Then I realized I was kind of screwed. I can't just walk up to the desk and check in under my own name, see. The cameras would start flashing in ten seconds. I'd be found out and sent back on the first flight."

"Like you broke your parole or skipped out on bail." Kat nods.

"Just like."

"Have no fears," Jodi says, standing. "I'll get the key. What name did you use?"

"Tom Cruise."

"Seriously?" Kat asks.

"Yeah, he and I have this longtime running joke with hotels, where I check in as him and he checks in as me. It's hard to explain."

"Sounds pretty basic," Kat says.

This whole scenario is striking me as more than a little odd. Fine, it's true that Tim would have trouble getting a room without being discovered in an instant. But we just met him like ten minutes ago. How could someone at his level of celebrity hang with regular people like us? And three women, no less? Something isn't adding up. But it's so much fun that I decide not to dwell on the fact that this all feels like a little too buddy-buddy too soon.

Jodi grabs her stuff and heads to the lobby. "I'm off," she says, looking like a Hollywood starlet again, with the hat and the sexy cover-up, the big sunglasses and the metallic beach bag. I can tell she's loving this whole thing. I mean, she's about to pick up the key for Tim Cubix's hotel room, which suddenly makes her famous by association, which is almost like being famous herself. "In the meantime, why don't you guys take him upstairs?"

"Can't," Kat says, looking at her watch. "Look at the time. Five forty. I've got a massage booked with Clooney in twenty minutes."

"Cool!" I say.

"Joking," she says back, rolling her eyes. "C'mon, Tim." She snaps a towel at him. Let's hit the showers."

Man, is he fucking gorgeous or what? As we ride up together in the elevator, I have to steady myself against a wall as another heat wave travels through my body. I look for any signs of distress from Kat. Complete normalcy. No twitching, no hives.

Intellectually, I know Tim Cubix is just a *guy*. But my reaction is visceral. I might break down at any moment. Like he's the Mona Lisa and the painting is hanging in my house. It's both utterly fabulous and, at the same time, it's unsettling to look it in the eye.

As we enter the hotel room, a call comes up from the lobby. "Hello?" I answer in a British accent.

"Oh, sorry, wrong room," Jodi says.

"No! It's me, Jo, with a disguised voice!"

"Freak. Tell Lex that housekeeping hasn't gotten to his room yet. They didn't believe he was Tom Cruise, who, apparently, always stays at the W when he's in town. They say the room won't be ready for a while, but tell him not to worry. I have my ways and I'm gonna use 'em." She disconnects without saying good-bye.

I tell Tim the news of what happens when you are not a famous person and you check into a hotel pretending to be Tom Cruise. How sometimes you have to wait.

"Mind if I just freshen up in here?"

"Yeeea—uhhhhh...!" a stunned Kat and I reply in unison, our four eyeballs watching his every move.

So now Tim is "freshening up" in our bathroom. Kat and I are unpacking our things and watching E! on television, the volume turned up so we can hear it over the rush of water.

"Hey, Kat." I smile. "Tim. Cubix. Is. On. TV. And. In. Our. Bathroom!"

"Taking a shower!" she adds.

"He's probably naked!" I scream, on the verge of tears again.

"Shh...I sure as hell hope so. Otherwise, that's weird, right? Why would he shower with his clothes on?"

"Because we are sitting here fantasizing about him right on the other side of the door! Duh!"

"It's locked."

"People know how to pick locks."

"Well, unfortunately for us, we don't."

A knock comes as we are debating whether or not we could— and then should—try to open the bathroom door with our credit card–like room keys.

"Coming, Jodi," I say, opening the door.

Only it's not Jodi.

Standing before me is Lenny Katzenberg. All six feet, two inches of him, with the biggest smile I've ever seen. His hazel eyes hold a flicker of devilish charm and his hair is noticeably more salt-and-peppered than it looks in his videos. He's wearing worn Levi's and a rock concert T-shirt, just like he does on camera.

He looks better than great.

"Lauren!" he announces, pulling me close to him in a bear hug. "What a surprise! What are you doing here in Miami?"

He smells like cinnamon and oranges and pine trees.

"What am I—?" I begin, as he releases me.

"Kidding. I got your e-mail this morning and knew: this was it. It was like you were telling me without telling me."

My heart starts to beat wildly, not out of lust, but rather in a full-on panic attack. "And...what, exactly, was I *not* telling you?"

"That you wanted me to come to Miami!"

"Because...?"

"Because." He nods his head solemnly and takes both of my hands in his, looking in my eyes. "Exactly."

Holyshitholyshitholyshitholyshit.

The bathroom door opens, and a towel-clad Tim emerges. His hairless torso is rock solid and dripping wet. It takes all the strength I can muster not to reach out and lick him.

I am a sick woman, surrounded on all sides by temptation.

"Hey," Tim says, noticing the open door to the hallway and speaking to Lenny. "Could you decide in or out, and close that behind you? Thanks." He picks up his duffle bag from one of the beds and takes it back into the bathroom with him.

"By the way, you look familiar," Tim Cubix says to Lenny Katzenberg, before shutting the bathroom door once again.

Lenny cocks his head to the side, evaluating what just happened. "Was that...?"

"Tim Cubix, yeah, yeah, yeah, big effing deal," Kat says, coming over to us. "Get over it. I mean, you came down here to get laid, right? Not to stargaze."

"Kat!" I say, shocked more by the idea of Lenny getting laid than by Kat's complete rudeness. Am I to be the lay-er?

"I'm Kat, if you haven't figured that out by now," she says, putting her hand out to shake Lenny's. "Lauren's best bud."

Lenny releases my hand to shake Kat's, then looks around the room, waiting for me to say something.

"Lenny! Wow, I mean, this is really..." I trail off, not sure *what* it is or how to feel about it.

Kat fills the awkward silence.

"Oh, you're probably looking to see who else we're hiding in here. Bono was hanging out, but he had to go. Some forest he had to save somewhere, big tree emergency. And Ashton Kutcher took a Snickers from the minibar and owes me four bucks! Famous people, I'm telling you." Kat sounds confident but starts pulling nervously at her curls.

Getagripgetagripgetagripgetagrip.

"Hi-yyy!" Jodi sings, the front door slamming behind her. "I got you an adjoining room. Only now you are known as Mr. Moncrieff of room 1215." She stops talking and takes in the scene of me standing awkwardly between Lenny and Kat, Tim nowhere in sight. "Well, isn't this *interesting*." One of Jodi's perfectly arched eyebrows is perfectly arched in surprise.

We all stand around silently. Lenny adjusts his duffle bag on his shoulder and coughs.

"I got it!" Tim hollers, stepping out of the bathroom fully dressed. He towels off his hair and points at Lenny. "I know where I know you from! You're that YouTube rapper! *Love* your stuff, man!"

Everyone relaxes. A hearty guy handshake follows and it is agreed that Tim and Lenny will bunk together next door.

"Well, that was bizarre," I sigh, sitting down on one of the beds.

Jodi makes sure that the door between our room and theirs is locked. Then she comes and sits down next to me.

"Which part, specifically?"

"The Lenny coming to see me in Miami part!" I say. "I mean, not that the me-being-in-Miami part isn't bizarre, or the us-being-here-with-a-gorgeous-movie-start part isn't even more bizarre," I add. "I think I'm getting sick. I think I need to lie down."

"Lauren, the Lenny-coming-to-see-you part is probably the least bizarre of them all," Jodi says.

Kat nods, coming to sit. "You're beautiful. And you're funny. Putting aside the fact that Lenny's pulled a dick move as an accessory to potential adultery, he's not wrong about you."

"I don't believe you." I put my head on a pillow and pull the blanket up to my shoulders.

"Believe us. We wouldn't hang out with you if you were boring and ugly," Jodi says, stroking my hair.

Jodi's so-called logic makes me smile, as always.

"See?" she says. "Such a pretty smile."

"So…" Kat begins. "What are you going to do about Lenny, exactly?"

"Sleep with him," I mumble into the pillow.

"What!" Jodi shrieks.

"No!" Kat says.

"I mean, he did come all this way for me. It's the least I can do." I grin.

"Oh, thank God, she's lying," Jodi says to Kat.

I reposition myself on the bed. "Ugh! Truth is, I have no idea what I'm going to do. I mean, for all my daydreaming, I never thought of a moment like this one actually presenting itself. I just had these blank fantasies of us...like...on a mountaintop."

"Like in *The Sound of Music*?" Jodi wonders aloud.

"Or hanging together at a club," I continue. "You know, when you go to have your picture taken in front of a blue screen and they Photoshop the background in after? My daydreams are nonspecific like that."

"Sexy." Jodi smiles.

"You crazy slut!" Kat adds.

"Jeez, you two!" I say, hurling pillows at them. "What do you want from me? I feel like I'm back in high school and my friends and I are planning for my loss of virginity."

"You planned it?" Kat asks.

"You didn't?" I ask back.

I lie back down and readjust the comforter. "I'm a flirt. That's all I've ever been. A big-talking, daydreaming, romanticizing, cock-teasing good girl. I never thought I'd ever have to deal with the nitty-gritty of infidelity."

"Oh, it could get nitty..." Kat singsongs.

"And gritty..." Jodi adds melodramatically. I ignore them.

"I guess I'll have to talk to him, figure out how I feel. I don't know. He's so adorable. But...shit. How old am I?" I sigh. "Kat, could you open the minibar and pass me a tiny bottle of alcohol?"

This whole thing is actually making me miss Doug. Right now I crave the safety of a real-life, stable relationship, even one as distant as ours currently is. I wish I could ask *him* what I should do in this situation.

I know, I know, this seems completely counterintuitive. I'm just not used to making big decisions on my own. Doug's opinion is so strong, so sure, so ever-present. Even when I don't ask for it, he gives it to me. Like, every day for the past decade or more. "Those shoes make you look like a librarian," for example, as I'm heading out the door to work. Or, "If you washed your car every once in a while, I might take a ride somewhere with you."

Oh, that's right. It's all coming back to me now. All the tiny criticisms and how they build up until they became a wall around me. *Screw you, Doug*! my head screams. *You and all your little barbs can just go to hell.* "I'm just being sarcastic," he's said when I call him on his nasty attitude. "You're too sensitive, Lauren. They're jokes."

Sarcasm, my ass.

I climb off the bed, slide open the door to the balcony, and step outside for some air. I swear, it's hard to breathe around Doug sometimes, even when he's 1,200 miles away.

But then I think about how it used to be between us, in those first years of our relationship and marriage. He was so easygoing and thoughtful, so sweet and funny. Where did he go? And where am I?

"So?" Kat says, stepping outside with me and handing me the world's smallest rum and Coke.

"I think it's time for me to call my poor, unsuspecting husband."

Jodi wishes me luck and goes to take a shower. Kat and I turn off the TV to ensure complete silence while I'm on the phone. She busies herself by mixing more tiny cocktails in plastic cups.

I close my eyes as Doug's cell phone rings, imagining myself in a different hotel room for an entirely different purpose.

"Lauren!" Doug answers on the fourth ring, sounding relieved. My heart gives a small tug in his direction.

"Hi," I sigh. I don't know what to say. *I sort of miss you? I'm having fun without you, behind your back? Lenny Katzenberg is here with me in Florida and I'm pretty sure he wants to do the nasty with me?* "How are the kids?"

"Fine now."

"Fine...*now*?" I ask. "But, like, not fine before now?"

"We just had a little babysitter situation. Jackie had to cancel at the last minute and I'm still in the city. She didn't want to call and bother you and I didn't want to call and worry you, so I handled it myself."

He sounds proud of his efforts, but I'm not convinced. "Could you elaborate? On how you handled it? Without me?"

"Why do you sound mad, Lauren? There was nothing you could do. Relax, it's fine."

I'm not mad; I'm furious. With myself.

"But who did you call? Were the kids freaking out? What about Laney? Were they by themselves? Is Jackie okay?" My mind immediately travels to the worst-case scenario, in which my children are alone in the house and have decided to turn on the oven, run the bath, and light some matches for fun while downing bagfuls of peanuts and almonds. "Why didn't you call me?"

"Because you're *not home*, Lauren. Because there was nothing you could have done."

The fact that he's right only makes me feel worse.

Kat, lured by the sounds of my distress, comes out onto the terrace to pour me another tiny cocktail. I down it in one gulp and wipe my mouth with the back of my hand.

"I called Mrs. Hunter from next door," Doug continues.

"The one who killed her cat?"

"They were never able to prove that."

"Did it hang *itself* in the basement, Doug?" I am losing it now. "Did it?"

"It may have been driven to suicide, yes," he says in an even tone. "That's what the police report concluded, at any rate."

"How does a cat...?" I stop myself. "Is she still with Ben and Becca?" I ask in horror.

"No, no. Jackie volunteered to get the kids off the bus at three thirty, so I sent Laney home early. But when Jackie didn't show up on time, I called Mrs. Hunter, who brought the kids to her house for a snack."

"Dear Lord."

"Then I spoke to Jackie, who, by the way, didn't sound remorseful at all and who we will never again use as a stand-in babysitter."

"But...she's always been so responsible! Isn't she getting a teaching degree?"

"Whatever, Lauren. I don't know where you find these people."

"Craigslist." I turn my back on the view from the balcony and lean against the railing. In the glass door, I catch a reflection of myself, blond hair loose in the balmy night air.

"Anyway, I had to call Laney, who has a class tonight, but she was able to send her roommate with our house key to babysit until I get home. Diana, I think her name is."

"You *think*?" I bark.

"I'm doing the best I can, Lauren!"

"I know," I choke, willing myself not to cry.

I'm the only person I know who takes a small vacation and ends up on a huge guilt trip.

"You okay?" Doug asks, his voice softer now.

"Mm-hmm," I mumble, small tears rolling down my cheeks. Right now, I want to smell my son's hair. I want to bury my head in my daughter's warm neck. Have I strayed too far from them and Doug, from my life? I take a deep breath.

"Can you tell me where you are? When you're coming home?"

"Saturday," I whisper.

"You're sure? The case will be over by then?"

"I'm sure." I say. "Done on Saturday."

"Okay, then." It sounds like he's smiling. "That's manageable. I'll just pretend you're on a business trip," he jokes. "One of those teacher's conferences in places like upstate New York, or Pittsburgh!"

Or Miami.

"I'm sorry, Doug. I'm so sorry," I say.

"Lauren, it's something you *had* to do," he reminds me. "Don't be sorry."

The fact that he's being nicer and sounding more sympathetic than I've heard him in months gives me pause.

Is it because I'm away? One of those absence-makes-the-heart-grow-fonder things?

Or because I'm supposedly sequestered? Which must suck if you have to do it in real life?

Or because I sound distraught, which I am, by the babysitter's abandonment of the children I abandoned first?

Or...is he distracted by something else? Working late, canceling on me and the kids, never wanting to go out and have fun with me anymore.

Maybe that distance I'm feeling in my marriage isn't entirely my fault. Maybe it isn't entirely imagined.

I glance at the adjoining door between our room and Lenny's, and wonder, is Doug hiding something from me? I mean, it doesn't seem all that hard to cheat, lie, or steal from someone you love. Jodi can do it. Tim Cubix can do it. If I could do it, couldn't Doug?

"Doug. Is there anything you want to tell me?" I ask.

There is a slight beat and then he answers. "Nope. All good here."

His lighthearted sincerity is all I have to go off of. I make a judgment call to believe what I hear, to put my faith in the man I married twelve years ago and who I know so well.

I only hope he still has faith in me, when this crazy leave of absence is done.

"You know," I say. "This...jury duty thing. It *is* something I had to do, actually." I take a hearty sip of my latest rum and Coke and let myself relax a bit.

"Oh, and Lauren, before you go. The strangest thing. I've been getting these cryptic messages from a Martha Carrington over at the middle school. She seems to think that you were released from jury duty on Tuesday morning...?"

Fuck me! I try not to get frazzled as I stare at the sun setting over Miami, and start yelling into the phone, thinking fast. "What's that, Doug? You're breaking up! Damn this cell phone. The bailiff is calling us right now...I shouldn't be talking to you...Tell Martha I'm at a hotel in an undisclosed location and that we're about to have pizza delivered to our rooms...I'm bunking with a woman named Carrie...not allowed to watch TV or turn on the radio...like the OJ case...highly sensitive matter...I love you...I gotta go!" I finish, opening the sliding glass door and tossing my cell phone onto the bed as if it's on fire.

CHAPTER 18

"THIS IS ROCKIN'!" TIM SCREAMS over the beat of deep bass, giving me the thumbs-up sign and drinking his alcohol like a good boy. He has been completely transfigured. Back in the hotel room, Jodi used her professional makeup kit to transform Tim. Then we accessorized him to the hilt so that no one can even tell there's a person under all the stuff.

It's amazing what a hat, sunglasses, and a hairy mole can do to change one's appearance.

"You're like the Artist Formerly Known as Tim Cubix!" I yell back.

"Shh." He chuckles, swaying slightly in the tide of the crowd. "Don't give it away. I love being anonymous!"

"That's why the Clevelander is so perfect for us tonight," I add. "It's easy to get into and it's filled with tons of trashed nobodies!" I'm finding that the more I drink, the easier it gets to just hang with my movie star.

Even though he's in disguise, he does not want to hit the usual high-end Miami hot spots tonight.

"When I party, I'm not looking for an attitude, but a vibe," he says. "And this place has got it."

"Woo-hoo!" Kat says by way of agreement, coming over to us with Lenny in tow. Alcohol has made her soften a bit toward Lenny. "Although I still think he's a prick to pick on a married lady," she assured me, before pulling him onto the dance floor a few minutes ago.

"Have you seen the women's bathroom?" Kat asks us.

"I regret that I have not," Tim notes.

"Well," she continues, clearly tipsy, "it is, like, stocked with great stuff! There's hairspray to use and all, and condoms, but then there's also a full-on candy bar! With gum and mints, and...these!"

she says, producing enough Blow-Pops for us to each take one. Which we do. Enthusiastically.

"Hey, where's Jodi?" Kat asks. I gesture toward the raised dance floor, where she is dancing to Pink's "Bad Influence" with the huge, blacker-than-night bouncer.

"Ooh...let's join her!" We push our way through the crowd of spring-breaking twentysomethings until we reach the front.

I have managed to avoid any solo time with Lenny, thus avoiding having any sex with him. So far this strategy has worked.

Lenny and the Artist decide to watch from the sidelines as Jodi, Kat and I have a blast dancing our asses off. Lenny stands a good three or four inches taller than Tim, and I realize that the movies make him seem bigger than he really is.

Kat's request for the Weather Girls' "It's Raining Men" floods the dance floor with bodies. We are suddenly surrounded by tons of people, a circle forming around us. We take turns busting out moves and dancing with strangers, as onlooking dancers hoot and applaud.

Jodi disappears momentarily and comes back with MC Lenny, who takes center stage with ease. He breakdances, moonwalks and gyrates around Jodi, who smiles and shakes her butt at him. Then the bouncer finds Jodi again and Lenny is left dancing solo.

He looks my way and I feel my heart lurch. I know I shouldn't dance with him. Dancing is the first step toward my romantic downfall. I lose all inhibition when confronted with disco. It's like, gimme a drink, play some Gloria Gaynor, and watch my pants magically disappear. There are several college men from the class of '92 who will attest to that.

I shake my head at Lenny. He makes a sad face.

Poor Lenny. So far, I am not worth the price of a plane ticket.

I watch him find a new dance partner, a perky blonde who looks like me twenty years ago. I momentarily feel a pang of jealousy. Partially for him, but mostly because I wish I still looked like her.

The thought makes me panic. Where did the time go? I mean, one minute I was twenty, and in the next, my lifespan has doubled.

The issue is, I don't *feel* forty. I still feel twenty, or maybe twenty-five, and I think I always will. That disconnect between my biological age and the one I feel inside is what's so confusing. Most of the time, I walk around thinking I'm young. It's not until I look at this girl dancing with Lenny that I remember that there's an entire *generation* of adults out there that are younger than me.

Which is what I'd call a buzzkill.

But then Kat grabs me and forces me to dance with her as a circle forms in the center of the floor. I pretend to push Kat into the circle for a solo and she pretends to push me back, because we're lame like that.

A few guys move in to breakdance a bit. We clap and hoot and raise our fists in solidarity with them.

Then Lenny enters the circle and Kat and I whistle at him as if he's a stripper. He winks our way and then presses his torso against the floor, moving his body up and down in waves.

"Go Lenny, go Lenny, go Lenny!" we cheer. Without so much as bending his knees, he pops back up and busts a few more moves for the crowd before bowing and then disappearing back into the circle. "That was awesome," I gush at Kat. "If Doug did that I would so have sex with him right now."

"You'd fuck a guy for doing the worm?" Kat asks dubiously. "That's all it takes?"

She stares at me, then adds, for effect, "*The worm.*" She stops before saying the rest, which I believe would be something to the effect of: *Your life really is sadder than I thought.*

Kat doesn't understand, because she hasn't been married to the same man for over a decade. She doesn't understand that a man who breakdances is sexy, and a man who flirts with you online is sexy, and a man who follows you down to South Beach and drops everything *just to be with you* is sexier than hell. She doesn't understand how incredibly, overwhelmingly sexy a man can be when he does for you all the things that your husband just *doesn't*.

I push my way out of the circle and go in search of Len.

When I find him, I lean into him with my whole body, my hands pressed firmly against his chest. His heart is beating fast. He looks down at me with something like laughter, but then sees my expression. His face turns serious, matching mine, his eyes asking me something like *now* or *yes* or *really* and I know that if I don't act fast we'll end up speaking to each other and the last thing I want right now are words.

So I kiss him.

And I am instantly on fire. And then the club starts spinning and I'm standing—I know I'm still standing—but I feel like I have tilted sideways and I can't get enough of Lenny, and yet I know I need to stop, all at the same time.

Everything around me fades away, all sound, all movement, all people, and there's only us.

There is something electrifying about slipping my tongue into the mouth of another man. There is a current, a charge, that makes it very hard to break free.

Until a moment later, when all sound and movement and people come rushing back and remind me of who I am and what I am doing.

And that there's only one way for this to end.

I shove Lenny away from me. He looks confused and reaches out for my hand. I slap it away.

"Don't ever do that again!" I snap.

"Me?" he asks.

"I was talking to myself!" I yell. "But, yeah, now that I think about it, you, too!"

I turn and push through the crowd, hoping to forget the way anger and heartbreak distorts his handsome face.

I need to leave. I need air. Even though the Clevelander is an outdoor club, the place is making me feel claustrophobic.

I need to push this woman out of the way, this woman who is talking to the Artist Formerly Known as Tim Cubix.

"Hey, Artist!" I call. "I've got to get going!" I put my hand to my ear in order to gesture a telephone call. "Tell Jodi and Kat to call me, will you? I'm going to take a walk back to the hotel."

Tim excuses himself and comes my way. It's so loud in the club that he has to shout in my ear. "Lauren, you look wigged out." I feel his warm breath on my neck and I think I might just pass out. Give up and pass out right here. Because, really, these amazing men are too much for one suburban housewife and middle school teacher to handle. In the future, if ever I find myself in need of a small adventure, I should just keep it simple and go in search of a high-end European toilet.

"Um..." I begin. "Kissed a man...not my husband...might pass out...need backup...girlfriend 911...job, husband, children all driving me insane...loved you in that *Macbeth* remake set in Portugal..."

"I'm not gonna lose ya!" Tim Cubix assures me, sounding like a commander in a Vietnam War movie. "No girlfriend left behind!"

He scoops me up and carries me over his shoulder like a wounded soldier, pausing here and there as he scans the crowd for my friends.

Instead, he finds a seat for me at the end of the bar and plops me down on the high, backless stool. Brushing some sweat from his brow, he sighs. "Too crowded. For now, you're just going to have to settle for me."

At first, I think he means that I should kiss him instead of Lenny, and I want to shout, "Uncle!" I've had enough, I give up. And then I come to my senses; he means he'll stand in for Jodi and Kat. "I'm not sure I can explain," I say. "But, you know, thanks for playing."

Tim smiles, a big full-on grin. "What? You think because I'm a guy, I can't relate to whatever it is you're going through right now?"

I consider this. "It's more the movie-star factor," I say. "You make me feel really uncomfortable. Physically. Like my insides are actually melting into a gelatinous mess."

"Jeez."

"I know," I say, "It isn't pretty. Just trying for truth here."

But instead of walking away from le freak that is me, Tim Cubix starts talking.

"My eight- and six-year-old sons, Slim and Leo, they're always fighting these days. Wrestling and getting into each other's space. One will be like, 'Dad, he's hurting me!' and the other will be like, 'He started it,' and I'm like, *Can't you just stop touching each other for five minutes, people?* And the big girls, Leyla and Bette, same thing...my house has, like, a thousand small forest fires everywhere. You think you have it bad, Lauren? No offense, but I've got six children, *three times* as many as you." His eyes are wide and he's holding up six fingers as proof of the math, in a Nixon-like pose. It's comical, but I try not to laugh, because I want to keep our heated debate on track. It's the first time I've felt really comfortable around him and I don't want to break the spell.

"No offense, Lex Sheridan, but you've probably also got *ten times* the staff."

He orders us some water from the bartender. "True, but the other day Ruby caught one of our nannies using her straightening iron and was really grossed out. And in terms of discipline or love, no hired help is a substitute for a mom or a dad."

I can't believe it. Ruby Richmond has a babysitter as hair-centric as mine!

Which means I'm totally missing the point of his tutorial.

"Ruby and I have tried everything with the kids, from star charts to special days with just one of us, and we'll hit on a strategy that works for a while, but nothing seems to work consistently. It's like as a parent, I'm a magician, a tap dancer and a parole officer all in one."

Got it. So the Rubix Cubes know that raising a family is exhausting and not always particularly rewarding. I open my mouth to speak, but Tim just keeps on venting.

"Plus, we're trying to toilet train the twins, now that they're turning three. Bubba is all right with it. He's an easygoing little dude. But Didi *just won't take a shit*. She holds it and holds it, driving me and Ruby nuts, until we think we'll have to take Deeds to the hospital. Then, finally, she'll go into the bathroom and close the door behind her and strain and cry until she's landed *the biggest dump you've ever seen in your life*. Didi actually clogs our toilets."

I am rendered speechless.

"Not to mention, there's all the usual stress of parenting with the added scrutiny from the paparazzi. I might be fiercely angry with my child, but, in public at least, I have to look like the perfect father. Leyla likes to go to the children's shoe store for the helium balloons, you know? And so we left the store one time and she accidentally let go of the balloon and, naturally, started to chase it. *Into traffic* on Wilshire! I grabbed her arm really hard and yanked her back from the curb. My heart was beating wildly, adrenaline rushing. I could hear the paparazzi calling after me, and so, in the middle of making sure my child was unharmed, and simultaneously wanting to scream at her and smack her butt, I had to think, *Remember, the cameras are flashing*."

"Is this my breakdown or yours?"

"And then, there's always the issue of fidelity," he says, raising his eyebrows knowingly.

"You're quite the conversationalist." I'm mesmerized by his dimples and will continue to say anything to make the man smile, even just the teensiest bit. Score.

"Every few weeks, *Star* magazine or *People* or TMZ.com runs some piece about how I was caught cheating, or how Ruby is flirting with some celebrity on the set of her new movie and I'm jealous. They make up quotes, attribute them to 'someone close to the actor' or 'sources say.' It's all bullshit. Ruby and I aren't married, but we have made a commitment to each other and to our children. Sexual fidelity may or may not be a part of that equation, but that's for us to decide. So the point I want to make to you, Lauren, is that your life is in your hands. You're a grown-up, making mostly good decisions. Parenting sucks, fidelity sucks. *Sometimes.* But isn't that real? Isn't that messy and awful and confusing, and therefore, worth every bit of the struggle?" He says it like he's asking himself the very same thing, like he's rehearsing for the biggest role of his career. We're both drunk enough to have tears in our eyes. "Isn't it beautiful?"

I blink mine away and nod my head. "I kissed Lenny."

Tim swallows a gulp of water. "Shocker."

"And there's no erasing that, no Superman reversing the globe to make time rewind, to undo the event. And now I'm scared."

"Scared of what?" Tim Cubix, posing as Dr. Phil, asks.

"Of...well..." The music is still blasting, a typical Eminem rap, and I align my thoughts with the heavy beats of his refrain.

I'm scared of liking the kiss,
I'm scared of wanting more,
I'm scared of losing Doug,
that he won't love me anymore...

I'm scared of so many things; those are only the ones that rhyme. It's all there, and Tim sees it in my face but doesn't make me speak it out loud. Instead, he pulls me into a brotherly hug. "Own it. Reflect on it. You'll figure it out."

Spoken like Dr. Grossman.

CHAPTER 19

TIM FLAGS DOWN JODI and waves her over. He debriefs her quickly, then disappears back into the crowd, giving me a thumbs-up and a wink.

I tell Jodi the whole story, how I went in search of Lenny and how I kissed him, and how Doug and I don't get busy very much these days. "And when we do, it's so boring and mechanical that I just don't even see the point!" I blurt, my face growing hot under her scrutiny. As close as we are, my friends and I hardly ever talk about the specifics of our marital sex lives. "And kissing Lenny was...amazing."

"*That's* your problem?" she asks. Like I'm complaining about a stick of bubble gum having lost its flavor. "Welcome to the real world, Lauren! Where married people fall out of lust!"

She finds an empty stool and perches herself next to me at the end of the bar.

"Here's the thing," she says. "Let's just follow this through to its end point, to the worst-case scenario, or best-case scenario, depending on how you want to look at it."

"Best case," I say.

"Well, best case, in your warped little mind, you and Lenny fall *madly* in love and you have this *amicable*, easy divorce from Doug. Lenny *loves* your kids and you live happily ever after in some sort of Barbie Dream House version of real life."

I'm already sad just hearing the word *divorce*. "That sounds more like worst case to me."

Jodi shakes her head at me. "No way. Worst case is the same scenario, only it's ten or so years down the road and you realize that you no longer want to have sex with Lenny either. That he's become your new, old Doug."

"But I like my old, original Doug. I don't want to grow tired of anyone else."

Jodi reaches across the bar, grabs a maraschino cherry from the bartender's garnish setup, and pops it in her mouth. "Exactly. So, my point is, *marriage gets old*. It's the nature of the beast. Lee had all this dental work done once and, for a while there, the thought of kissing him really skeeved me out. And, meanwhile, we hired this gorgeous electrician—named Fabio, I swear—and I was having all these lustful thoughts about Fabio's plugs and my sockets and shit. So all of this is going on and I'm like, Jodi, what are you going to do? Have *sex* with the *electrician*? Really? Just to feel a momentary charge? I mean, Lee's a bit of a gonif, and his family is totally dysfunctional, but I love him to death. I would never want to hurt him. So, instead, I waited it out. And after Lee got his bridge permanently replaced, and he smiled at me during Lindsay's travel soccer game one Saturday, it all came rushing back. I felt like jumping his bones in the back of my Escalade. Ebbs and flows. End of story."

I mentally wade through the muck of Jodi's story until I find the clear stream in the middle of it. "So…I get it. It's not Lenny!" I tell Jodi.

"Then, who is it?" she asks, confused.

"No, I mean, that's what you're telling me, right? It's the *idea* of Lenny."

"*Oh!* Of course, that's what I've been saying all along," she agrees, popping another cherry into her mouth.

I miss the promise of new love—or lust, at any rate. It's that completely unexplored, exciting, flip-flop in my stomach, first kiss, "high school high" feeling that my life has been missing.

I crave that spark that Doug and I misplaced long ago, that spark that happens when you connect with someone new, when you enter into some territory you have not yet explored. Doug and I used to have that static electricity, like a feeling of being pulled by the same orbit around any room we were in. We loved touching each other, or even thinking about touching each other.

Now it's just a peck on the cheek in the morning and some vanilla sex a few times a month and on most of the major Jewish holidays.

Don't ask.

Jodi passes me a drink and I take a sip. "Skinnygirl margarita," she explains. "My fave."

I find Lenny dancing with a young blonde again. They are laughing about something. He towers over her and has to lean down to speak to her. She stands on tippy-toes to catch his words.

Kat notices me and Jodi watching Lenny. She waves tentatively in our direction, then gives me a thumbs-down sign.

I plaster on a smile and wave back. Is she trying to tell me that Lenny is bad news? That she doesn't like the new song that the DJ is spinning? "I'm going to fill Kat in on the drama, okay?" Jodi says. I shrug in response, which she accepts as my acceptance of her blabbing to Kat.

I have to wonder, could that excitement still be there with Doug? Or is the feeling only present in the danger, in the newness, in the this-is-not-my-husband factor of someone like Lenny?

Some young girl bumps into me and spills her drink on my shirt. "Sorry!" she giggles. A guy with a baseball cap on backward helps to steady her and gives me a wink. I wonder if the girl's mom knows what she's up to tonight.

I take another sip of Skinnygirl and study Lenny. Breakdancing, charismatic, YouTube-sensation MC Lenny. He's the life of the party, the polar opposite of Doug.

Why won't Doug ever dance with me? At bar mitzvahs and weddings, why does he stand against the wall, arms folded across his chest, and shake his head no? Anger bubbles up so quickly that it surprises me.

Before I know what I'm doing, I'm drunk-dialing my husband.

"H'lo?" Doug picks up. He sounds groggy, and I realize it's after 11:30 at night. But now that I've got him, I can't let go. My words come out fast and sort of slurred, but I feel a clarity I haven't in years.

"I love to dance, Doug! You *know* that! When we got married, you led me to believe you did, too. I thought you were a fun guy, a guy to grow old with like those couples on the dance floor that move together as one! But...you lied! So, I need you to tell me you'll dance with me! Right now!" I realize how that sounds and try to explain. "I mean, not that you'll come dance with me right now—oh—this isn't coming out right...but anyway, it's of utmost importance!" I guess I'm pretty buzzed, because a swarm of bees have taken up residence in my head.

"Where are you?" This is Doug's response.

"In a hotel. Sequestered. I told you before."

"Uh-huh." He sighs. "With all that noise in the background. Dancing."

"No!" I backtrack. "I'm not dancing *now*. You're confused."

"*I'm* confused." He laughs, unmistakable irony lacing his tone.

"Well, maybe I'm *tip*sy." I have to shout a little to be heard over the crowd as it cheers for something that I can't see. I try to get a grip, recall the lie. "Yes, Doug. You see, I'm sitting here with my fellow jurors in Alden, with nothing to do and nowhere to go. Of course! We raided the minibar and now we're playing some music because we aren't allowed to put on the television." I pause and try to hide a burp. "We happen to be a very lively jury."

"I see," he says. "A very lively jury. Indeed." He either coughs or laughs, I can't tell.

"Yes. And this...jury. They've got me really thinking. This case, it's about...infidelity...a wrong turn...I can't say more. And I'm deliberating right now, I mean, we're in the midst of these very emotional deliberations, and I can't help but think of us."

"Cunts!" some guy yells at a group of women who have just walked away from him at the bar.

"What was that?" Doug asks.

"Bailiff asked us if we wanted *pints*. Of beer." I move away from the center of the courtyard and try to find a quiet corner.

"How does this court case involving infidelity remind you of us?" Doug asks softly.

"I wonder...if the woman in this case had no choice. For the past twelve years, her husband left her alone a lot of the time, you know, with work demands, lots of travel. She raised these kids all by herself, when she wasn't working, and she had this horrible babysitter who often used her ceramic straightening iron!" I explain. "And then the husband didn't even make *an effort* to romance her! No dancing, he said, no time or money for vacations. He would criticize her and the children and all that they were doing wrong, but never compliment her as a mom or wife for all that she was getting right. I would imagine she was really bummed out, living with a man like that, a man who sucked the joy out of her life. Maybe this woman had no choice but to commit adultery with"—I fish for a descriptor that is not "YouTube rapping sensation"—"the tennis instructor. Maybe she was forced into fantasizing about a guy who was much more fun than her husband. Dreaming of a different life, a younger life. Maybe she had to stray, to save that little piece of herself that was dying more and more each day." I wipe my eyes with the back of my free hand.

I scan the crowd for Lenny and find that he's not with the blonde anymore. He's talking to a perky redhead who I immediately decide is a ho. What the fuck? Is Lenny just a crazy flirt, throwing all the spaghetti against the wall to see what sticks? Or did he really come here for me?

Choice A: Cheat and go back home. Choice B: Give up on my marriage. Neither one seems all that great. I conjure a third option. Choice C: Give away the man I love to flirt with and try to make it work with the man I still probably love. Let Lenny find someone really available.

Which he's kind of doing anyway.

"Asshole!" I say, partially into the phone, watching Lenny do the cabbage patch dance with the redhead. Then I remember Doug. "I mean, the tennis instructor. The wife ultimately killed him. He *really* had to go."

"Lauren, are you there?" Doug shouts. "I can't tell if you've been listening to me."

"I'm here," I sigh, turning my back on the crowd and sitting down on the edge of the pool. "But I haven't been listening."

"I love you and I *will* dance with you from now on. I just...suck at it; it's embarrassing. A forty-year-old guy doing the Macarena. But I will try, for you. Not, like, all the time, but occasionally...I'll dance. I won't ever sing karaoke, though. But I promise to go easy on the kids, especially Ben. I just need you back. From...jury duty. So we can talk, for real, face-to-face. Please," he begs.

"Face-to-face," I repeat. I remember my forehead and wonder if Doug will notice.

"Saturday night. I don't want to end up like that husband in the court case. Or the tennis instructor." I can hear him smile.

"Saturday night. At Jodi's dancing event at her temple? It's a date."

"Lauren, I love you," he says. "I want our life back." He sighs. "Good luck deliberating."

"Oh, I'm pretty sure I've made up my mind now," I say, wondering whether Doug knows we are speaking in code.

"That's good. That's great!" Doug declares. "And Lauren?"

"Yeah?" I giggle, high on a newfound interest in my own husband.

"Send my love to Jodi and Kat, would you?"

CHAPTER 20

SOBUSTEDSOBUSTEDSOBUSTEDSOBUSTEDSOBUSTED!

How does he know?

What does he know?

I am trying to find my partners in crime to tell them that we've been found out—somehow, to what extent I'm not sure—but the crowd has grown so thick with bodies that it's hard to see past the person in front of me, much less around the whole space.

So instead I grab some strapping young college boy and ask him to dance. Maybe I can have a good time in Miami without damaging my marriage any more than I already have.

The funny thing is, I think, shaking my hips and trying to get into the music, is that Doug didn't sound mad. Not at all.

Maybe I misunderstood him. Maybe what he really said was, *Let's buy a cat.*

It is certainly possible, with all that noise and all that alcohol coursing through my bloodstream, that I misheard him. Right?

The guy I'm dancing with is twenty-one, tops. He's youthfully skinny, with long arms and a pronounced Adam's apple. He's looking at me really strangely. "Where you from?" he asks, trying to make polite conversation.

"New York!" I shout. "You?"

A shadow crosses his face, and then he breaks into a huge grin. "Mrs. Worthing?" he asks. "I thought that was you!"

"Johnny?" Second period. Sixth-grade English. About a decade ago. Fourth row, second seat. B-plus student. "Johnny Dawes?" I'm going to be sick.

He laughs. "It's Jon now."

"Of course it is." I nod solemnly, not wanting to laugh in his cute (very cute, maybe even sexy—stop it, Lauren, for God's sake, he was your student!) face. It's amazing how boys do that, grow up and become men. Men like Jon, here, with all these muscles peeking out from under the short sleeves of his T-shirt.

I am foul and awful and horrid.

We're still dancing, though I've reined in the gyrating and am now doing a 50's-style sway. I'm going to look uncoordinated and uncool, but that's better than being pegged as a cougar. The song is a sexy rap number. Usher's lyrics "I want to make love in this club / in this club" float past me and I cringe in humiliation.

What would be worse? To stop dancing or to pretend this is normal? I go for normal. "How's your mom?" I shout over the noise. *How's your mom?*

"She's fine, thanks."

Which one of us is going to stop the madness? Unless. I look at Jon's face. He's giving me the eye. It's like he's *into* me.

Don't get me wrong: I *want* to be wanted. Just not by a twenty-one-year-old who could never tell the difference between the homophones *their, there* and *they're*.

At least he's legal, I think. Neither one of us really has anything to hide. It's just a harmless dance.

Except that I'm married and I used to be his teacher.

"Hey?" Jon asks. "How come you're not in school?"

Oh, and that.

I jog my alcohol-soaked brain for an answer. "I'm here on a conference, with...some other teachers." Which is sort of true.

"Cool." He doesn't really care. "I go to college in Massachusetts," he says, "with those guys." He points to where Jodi is dancing with two beautiful specimens of fraternity life.

"Oh, that's my friend with them! I've been looking for her!"

"Hey, I think that friend of yours is giving Steve and Patrick her number," Jon comments.

"No, I'm sure she isn't," I counter. Jon shrugs.

So now I'm curious. I turn to see that, indeed, Jodi's BlackBerry is the center of that little group's attention. She holds it as they all talk and dance at the same time. She's smiling and laughing and typing something on her phone.

"Do you mind?" I call out to Jon, gesturing that we should dance our way over to them.

"Hi-yyy," Jodi says, enveloping me in a one-armed hug.

"Hi?" I say. "I have a weird question for you?" I decide to hold off on telling her about Doug, since I've decided not to trust what I think he said.

"O*kaaay*," she purrs. Her pink floaty top moves back and forth with the music, and her hips sway slowly. "Say hi to Pat and Steve. They go to Harvard." Johnny Dawes goes to Harvard? This really is a parallel universe.

"How nice for them. And Jon," I add, smiling over at these boys. "Hey, Jon, come here and meet my friend Jodi."

"Mrs. Moncrieff?" Jon asks, clearly shocked by his double-whammy of good fortune. Van Halen was right: *I'm hot for teacher.*

"What the fu—?" Jodi says, stopping herself short from dropping the whole f-bomb in front of one of her former third graders. "Johnny Dawes?"

"Hi!" he says, smiling in a way that reveals the little boy underneath all the years.

"It's Jon now," I say.

"Nice one, Lauren." Jodi whispers.

"He's legal, not jailbait," I assure her.

"Oh, good. Now I feel much better," she says sarcastically.

"Hey, Jon says that you were taking down his friends' phone numbers just before. On your BlackBerry."

"What?" Again, she looks at me like I'm crazy. "*Oh!*" She laughs and takes her phone back out of her tiny purse. "The boys from Harvard here said that they thought I was hot. So, first I told them that they were correct, *naturally*. And then I told them that I'm old enough to be their *mother's much younger sister*."

On the screen of her BlackBerry glows an image of Jodi's three daughters, taken last summer on the Cape.

"I was like, this is Jossie, and she's eight, and Lyndsay is six, and my baby Dylan is already five! Can you believe it? And here they are skiing, and here they are at the ballet recital..." she says, flipping through the pictures.

We look up at Steve's horrified face. "You mean...you're... MILFs?"

"And they were my teachers back in Hadley!" Jon adds.

Steve immediately grabs Pat and Jon and heads for the exit as Jodi and I die of laughter.

"Bye, Johnny!" I call. "See you at homecoming!"

....

I make the definite decision not to tell her or Kat what Doug said. Why spoil her good time?

Plus, if I heard him correctly and he's not buying the kids a cat, then what does he know, exactly? That we're together. So what? Maybe he thinks we're all hanging out at some hotel in New York City or something. Atlantic City, maybe.

I quit deliberating any more and decide to believe that.

We find Tim, Lenny and Kat together by the bar, where we agree to do just one more shot of Jäger. I swallow my pride and tell Lenny that he looked great dancing with those women.

"One of them called me Justin Timberlike!" Lenny laughs. Then he gets kind of pensive. "Can you and I...take a walk for a minute?"

"Um...sure," I say. A half hour ago, I was sort of dreading this conversation. But the fresh alcohol moving steadily through my bloodstream creates a blurry sensibility that makes it all okeydokey.

"So..." he begins. I think he's going to bring on a breakup speech, which my ego can't handle right now.

"I've been thinking and I've decided that you should totally keep flirting with strangers tonight," I jump right in. "I mean, unless you just want to keep playing the field and fuck that redhead over there," I sort-of joke.

He balks, confused. "Who?"

I point her out. He shakes his head quickly back and forth.

"That's Kelly! She's my half sister's college roommate. I just ran into her by accident and had to give her a big hello. Random, right?"

"So random," I say, trying to backtrack, but Lenny won't let it go that fast.

"You're disgusting, Worthing. She's, like, twenty! On spring break!"

"Oh," I manage, flushing slightly. These spring breakers are really confusing.

"In case this wasn't *clear*," he says, his voice rising, "I came here for you."

"But—" I start.

"And, in case this *also* wasn't clear, you haven't given me the time of day since I arrived. Until that intensely amazing sucking-face session, which ended with you pushing me away." He's angry now, his hands gesturing broadly. "Maybe I should just text you right now and you'll eagerly respond. But in person? Nada."

His indignation makes me squirm; it's hard to find something to say in response. *You're right? I lured you here and now I'm avoiding you like in some adolescent game? I'm so sorry for leading you on? I had no right to toy with your feelings like that? Look at what a mess I've made?*

And then, just as Lenny starts walking away from me, I find my way through this emotionally foggy mess. "Wait a fucking minute, Lenny!"

This stops him dead in his tracks. He turns, his shoulders drop. He waits. "What?"

"What? How about *this*!" I'm feeling some nice rage myself now. "I. Didn't. Ask. You. To. Come. Here. *You* did this, not me!" He bows his head and comes closer to me, until I'm eye-to-eye with his chest. I take my pointer finger and star poking him with it. "I flew to Miami to *avoid* real life, to get away from everyday dramas, to have a fun vacation with my friends. *Not* to have sex with you! Honestly!" The music has stopped for some reason and the whole club is staring at the two of us.

"Make some fucking noise, people!" Kat calls, just as some cheesy Top 40 starts up again.

I try again, softer this time. "We were just flirting. I thought you knew that." I shake my head and try to pin down all the contradictory emotions I'm feeling, but they are on a moving target. "But still, I guess it's no excuse. We're both adults. I should have known better, I should have thought ahead to where flirting with you could lead."

Lenny takes my hand away from where it has been stabbing him and steadies it with his own two hands. "Lauren. How long have we known each other?" He stoops down and looks me in the eyes.

"Since second grade. I can't do the math on that. Even when I'm sober."

"A long time. So long that I know just how bad you suck at math. You cried after every quiz in Mr. Grady's fifth-grade class."

"For the record, he was an asshole."

"Agreed. And maybe me, too. Maybe I've been an asshole for coming here, for putting you in this position."

He stops and I stare at him. "You mean, you aren't going to

follow that up with some kind of teaser, like, 'But if I could get you into *any* position...'"

He laughs. "I'm trying really hard to be aboveboard here, Lauren! Don't remind me of all the dirty things I *could* say. That's how we got into this mess to begin with."

"So...we *both* fucked up here?"

"Yeah."

"Well, mostly you did." I smile.

"I'll accept that extra dig only because I get to hang out with Tim Cubix and talk shop."

"I'm going to miss flirting with you," I say, going for honesty. "I kind of don't want that to be over. Bad as flirting is, for us and for my marriage and stuff, I can't deny that it is...really fun. Truth is, I kind of want to keep you *and* have my life back."

Which I cannot believe I am admitting to anyone, least of all Lenny, but there it is. In vino veritas.

"You dream big," Lenny laughs. "A woman who wants it all." He puts on a fake voice about an octave higher than his normal one. "'Waiter, I'll have a stable husband with a side of dirty flirting, please, medium-well.'"

It's embarrassing, hearing your own desires splayed out like that, spoken back to you in jest. But he's right, of course. I tried to bend the rules to fit my whims. I craved midlife with a shot of adolescence.

"So. I can't sleep with you. Not here in Miami. Not ever!" I exhale, perhaps letting air into my lungs for the first time since Lenny showed up today. "Which is good! It's feels so *right* not to have sex with you."

"I wish I could say the same," he says.

"Can I ask you something?"

I interpret his pause as a yes and continue. "Why me, why now?"

Lenny looks over my head like the answer is somewhere out on the dance floor and he just has to stop it from breakdancing long enough to stand still.

"Because I finally had the guts."

I burst out into laughter. "Oh, sure! Lenny Katzenberg lacked the courage to kiss me in high school! That's a good one."

"Lauren," he says. "How stupid are you?"

I decide not to answer that.

"Do you remember all those times we were alone together as seniors, working on the yearbook?" I nod. "So, then, do you remember moving away from me every time I tried to kiss you, or make any type of move?" I shake my head.

"I thought you, like, hated me or something. That you merely tolerated my presence. You always shivered with disgust when I 'accidentally' brushed my hand with yours as we passed the scissors and stuff back and forth."

I roll my eyes. "I wasn't shivering with *disgust*, dumbass!"

"Oh."

"We could have been a thing!" I realize, twenty years too late.

"Talk about your bad timing."

Lenny and I both bow our heads in silence, sharing a melancholy nostalgia for a teenage lovefest we never got to have with each other.

"Some things happen for a reason, I guess. Or don't." I smile sadly.

Lenny shrugs with his whole torso, shoulders reaching up to his ears. He holds it like that for a moment before letting the tension release. "Bottom line? In the present time, even with all of this shit between you and me, I'm really glad I'm here." He kind of ruffles my hair in an uncle-ish way. "You?"

"Jury's still out on that," I say.

We make our way back from our heart-to-heart, strolling around the far side of the pool in the center of the Clevelander's courtyard.

"Do you see that?" Lenny asks, gesturing across the pool to where Jodi and Tim are seated at a round table. Although we cannot make out what's being said, Jodi is clearly giving a piece of her mind to some guy with a Mohawk and lots of gold jewelry. We quickly push through the throngs of drunkards and reach the table.

"How dare you?" Jodi scolds, now standing and facing this very large, fierce-looking man. "You have no right taking pictures of us!"

"Lady, I was just getting a shot of..." He trails off, trying to come up with an excuse. "The pool?" he finishes.

Jodi tosses her long hair defiantly. "You were not! You took a picture of me and my friends here, and I don't appreciate it one bit!"

"Jodi..." Tim begins, trying to calm her down. Kat arrives at the table just as we do.

"Forget it, Artist. Once she starts..." Kat shakes her head. "You just gotta let her go until she's done."

"Wow, she's worse than Ruby!" he laughs.

"Lady, your ass is beautiful, what can I say?"

"My...?" This stops Jodi. "You were taking a picture of my ass?" Her tone is noticeably softer. "Not a picture of..." She trails off before saying "my friend Tim Cubix here?"

"Yes, ma'am." He bows. "It's a beaut. I have a collection on my wall and yours is gonna go front and center."

"Well." Jodi smiles. "In a perverted sort of way, I'm more than slightly flattered."

"That's my girl," Kat jokes as I join her at the table.

"Now, if you could just..." he says, motioning for her to move left a little bit. Left, toward Tim.

"Jodi! He's lying! Paparazzi alert!" I call out. Jodi immediately pushes Tim out of the way and poses for the shot alone, with her hair covering her face, unrecognizable. Then she grabs Tim's arm and they push their way toward the exit as Kat, Lenny and I follow close behind.

"Hey!" I say, tapping the arm of the bouncer Jodi danced with earlier. "Could you maybe throw that asshole over there into the pool?" I point to Mohawk, who's fiddling with his phone.

"For Jodi? I'd do anything!" he yells back.

"And make sure his phone goes in with him, please, sir!" Kat adds. "Bastard!" she yells toward the paparazzi, giving him the finger.

Outside the Clevelander, we gather by the far side of the courtyard gate and peer over the railing as the dude, his Mohawk, and his phone go overboard. Jodi and Tim high-five each other as we all jump into a cab idling on the corner.

"When that guy gets dry, he's gonna come looking for us. I know the type. Plus, he's got friends, so he'll just send out an APB till I'm found," Tim says, leaning back in the taxi, which still hasn't moved. "Fucking bummer."

CHAPTER 21

"WHERE TO?" THE CABBIE ASKS.

"Tommy's Tattoo Parlor," Tim instructs. "You know it?"

The cabdriver nods and pulls away from the curb.

The ride is a silent one, as we each assess our own blood-alcohol levels and try to regroup.

"I'm sorry," Jodi says to the darkness.

"It's okay," Tim says, knowing the apology is meant for him. "You didn't know. You have no reason *not* to trust people."

"No, I mean, I'm sorry for buying those tabloids for all those years, for feeding the media's frenzy and for contributing to what almost happened to you tonight."

"It is a serious pain in the ass," Tim concedes. "But it's bigger than just you, Jodi. Way bigger."

"I just want you to know that I'm starting to get it. That maybe being famous isn't the point..." She trails off. "I'm not making sense. But that was kind of scary."

"Agreed," I say, nodding. "And, Jo, you're making perfect sense to me." I wink. "Now you know: the grass is fucking brown."

"Huh?" Everyone turns to me, the nonspecific question asked in chorus.

"You know, like the opposite of the 'grass is always greener' idea," I say by way of explanation, mostly for my own benefit. I needed Lenny to show up at my door and say, *Here I am if you want me.* Jodi needed someone to try and take her picture for profit. None of it feels all that great, once it happens.

Except maybe for Kat standing up to our principal. That's got to be a pretty satisfying sensation.

"What time is it?" Kat asks.

"Like twelve forty-five." I yawn.

"What we need is some blood soup!" Lenny says. "Like they drink in Korea, to refuel. To get rid of all the toxins."

"I've got a couple of hair elastics, a Tylenol sinus pill, and a few packs of Barbie chewies if anyone wants," Jodi offers, digging through her oversized metallic clutch.

"This is it," the cabdriver announces. "Ride's on me."

We start to protest, but he waves us away and winks at Tim. "See ya later, *Black Dawn*."

"I guess that disguise wasn't as ironclad as we thought," I muse. I watch Tim as he looks into the mirror lining one side of the tattoo parlor and scrapes the mole off his face.

"It's all good," he says, nonchalantly. Like he's reading a line from a script. I start to wonder, what the hell?

"So...why are you hanging out with us, again?" Kat, Lenny and Jodi are off flipping through books, deciding which tattoos they would get if they were getting tattoos.

"Because," he shrugs. "You're regular people. I can't even remember the last time I was with normal, non-Hollywood types, except for my family and some guys I grew up with, that is."

"*Okay*."

"It's like this. You know how you think it's fun to hang out with me?"

I nod.

"Well, it's the same for me. I've been gone so long from normal, I'd just like to be around it a bit and hope some of it rubs off on me."

He finishes removing the hat and mole and uses some cleanser on the counter to scrub the remaining gunk off his face. "Plus, I like MC Lenny. I have a project I want to pitch to him. Tommy!" he shouts with a smile, upon seeing a compact, completely bald man emerge from the back.

"Cubix! How you been?" Tommy gives Tim a handshake–arm bump. His muscular arms are covered in tattoos and several earrings pierce both ears. He reaches for something from a packet on the counter and puts it in his mouth.

Tim laughs. "Still sucking toothpicks, my friend?"

"Not sucking them. *Chewing*," Tommy clarifies. "Like twenty, thirty a day. Only thing that keeps me sober."

"Amen." Tim nods. "Good for you."

"So?" Tommy waits.

"Long story. Bottom line is, I bonded with this fine group here, and now we're kind of on the lam from some paparazzi at the Clevelander."

The rest of the group has joined us. We line up and make our introductions, sounding like some warped von Trapp family siblings.

"Hi. I'm Lauren, and I'm pretending to be sequestered on jury duty."

"I'm Kat, and I just told my employers to go fuck themselves."

"I'm MC Lenny, and I got on a plane for her—" he points to me—"only now I'm going to have to heal my broken heart in a rap song and broadcast it for the enjoyment of the masses."

"And I'm Jodi," she purrs. "My grandmother is not really dying."

"Super," Tommy says, clapping his hands together like he's heard it all before. "Now, who wants some ink?"

It's just a pretty little one. It didn't even hurt that much. Jodi, Kat and I all got them. But I'm not showing you where, so just drop it.

"I hate to say this, but I think we have to go top shelf or go home," Tim says as we exit out the back of Tommy's shop. We're standing in a deserted alley, waiting for a ride from Tommy's friend. It's close to two a.m. and although I should feel tired, I don't.

"What do you mean?" Lenny asks.

"Well, I know a few exclusive clubs that will let us in no problem. They offer all types of security for...people like me. No cameras, no reporters, no worries. Either that, or back to the hotel directly, so we won't be spotted or followed."

"I'm not going back to the hotel!" Jodi protests, speaking for all of us.

"I'd like to watch the sun rise," Kat adds.

Lenny nods. "I'm down with that."

"So, okay, then. We'll have Tommy's friend take us to a place I know."

"What's it called?" I ask.

"I just told you. A Place I Know."

"Celebrities are so cool!" Jodi says, as a soccer mom–style minivan flashes its lights at us and comes up the alley.

"*This* is our ride?' Lenny wonders aloud.

The driver's side window rolls down, revealing a gorgeously sultry woman with pouty red lips and cascading black hair. She looks familiar. She winks a blue eye at Tim.

"Oh, c'mon!" Tim scoffs. "Tommy!" he calls. "Where the fuck are you? You did this on purpose, right?"

"Hi, babe." The woman smiles, her voice thick and low. "You coming or what?"

A second-floor window opens and Tommy's head appears, toothpick stuck between his lips.

"Funny, no?" he calls down to Tim. "I had to do it. Great gag. When I saw her act about a month ago, I thought, if I ever run into Cubix again, I'll have to make introductions. Just didn't know I'd get lucky so soon!"

"You are an asshole, you know that?" Tim yells back. But I can see his smile as he shakes his head back and forth.

"See ya round, Rubix Cube!" Tommy calls before slamming the window shut.

Now I get it! The driver looks just like Ruby Richmond.

"Climb aboard," she instructs in that very low voice. "Nice to meet you all. I'm Dixie. Dixie Normous."

A Place I Know is hidden between a bodega and a shoe store a few blocks from the beach.

"It's like Hernado's Hideaway!" I decide.

"Olé!" Kat adds.

"Wait one minute, there, darlings," Dixie scoffs, when we thank her and make our good-byes. "I'm not leaving you; I'm just parking the van. I have to spend some more time with my delectable husband!" She throws her head back, revealing humongous tonsils. She leaves us on the curb, her laughter carrying down the street like pebbles tossed into in the gutter, reverberating hard and deep.

"That was fucking scary." Tim shudders.

"Yeah. Freaky-deaky." Jodi makes a face.

"It's not the fact that she's packing balls," Tim clarifies. "It's just...she looks so much like Ruby."

The inside is a bit of a shit hole, which I find disappointing. But then Tim leads us out back, to a lush, overgrown garden lit by lanterns. Ambient music fills the air. I can hear muffled chatter from different corners that I can't quite see.

"See? Discreet," Tim explains. "There are these pockets of seating areas that kind of wind their way through here and down to the beach."

"Now that's more like it!" Jodi smiles, taking a seat on a swinging bench tucked to our right. "I think I could fall asleep right here," she adds.

"I can't tell you how many times I've done that," Tim notes. "There are blankets and lounge chairs for serious crashing. Great big hammocks and tiki torches perched on the beach."

"Beach looks awesome," I say, yawning and settling down next to Jodi.

"I think I'll head down there," Lenny says, like it's some sort of invitation. I start to formulate all those same excuses in my mind, upset that I'll have to explain it all again to him. Why I can't go to the beach with him, how I'm trying to make things right again with Doug. But then I see him looking toward Tim and feel really dumb.

"Len and I still have to work out a few deets on that deal I mentioned to him earlier, back at the Clevelander. It's still kind of hush-hush. You guys don't mind if we leave the party?"

Kat waves them away with a tired hand and curls up on the bench next to Jodi's and mine.

The guys head down the path lit with flickering candles, Tim giving a little wave to us in the darkness.

Then I pass out.

CHAPTER 22

Friday

"WHAT? HELLO? ARE YOU THERE? Is anybody there?" Jodi emerges from the trees and heads toward me, cell phone in hand. "Can you hear me now, fucker?" she yells into the phone before disconnecting.

"Could that phone be any more annoying?" I ask, struggling to sit up against a beanbag. "Ugh, my mouth tastes like vomit."

"Yeah?" Jodi asks, staring at me, unamused. "Do you know why that is, Lauren? That's because you threw up for, like, twenty minutes last night."

"Oh. Sorry," I say.

"Don't apologize to me. Dixie was the one who coached you through, holding back your hair and singing to you and shit before she had to go to her performance at the Roxy."

I stretch and look around the deserted courtyard that we have camped out in, noticing the gray early morning light as it softens the edges of everything. The reasons for having slept outside on this lounge chair are not immediately clear to me, but the stiffness in my shoulder blades announces quite distinctly that I shouldn't have.

I realize that I'm shivering and grab a fleece blanket near my feet, wrapping it around my shoulders and tucking my hands safely underneath. I must have used this same blanket last night, because it smells faintly of my vomit.

At least, I hope it's my vomit.

I try to warm up, but the blanket is wet with dew. I'm suddenly filled with this jetlagged, homesick feeling reminiscent of summers spent camping in Maine.

I've always hated camping.

My gaze finally rests on Jodi, who looks completely pissed off. "Why so bitchy this morning, Jo?"

"Because of this call!" She shakes the phone in the air over her head. "I'm here to rest, goddammit, to sleep late. At home, my kids wake me up at this exact time every day. I needed to *skip* sunrise this morning, thank you very much!"

Just as she completes her tirade, her phone rings again. "Jesus!" she exclaims into the microphone.

"I don't think it's him," I joke. My head feels like it's floating above me somewhere, slightly disconnected from the rest of me, and I wonder if perhaps I am still a little bit drunk. It's certainly possible. I could use some Visine, a cup or four of coffee, and a toothbrush.

My body stings and I remember the tattoo. My head stings and I remember the Botox. My eyeballs sting and I remember the Jägermeister.

When this trip is done, I'm going to have to plan a real vacation.

I begin making elaborate plans for the day. First order of business: go back to the hotel and take a long, steamy shower; then call down for an extravagant feast from room service and, lastly, indulge in a nice afternoon siesta on the beach. I don't think we'll go out tonight; maybe just head to Nobu or something for a sophisticated meal and then rent a movie and hang out in bed. Like an old-fashioned, girls-only sleepover. No drinking for me tonight, thank you very much, and no MC anybodies or famous movie stars to derail the status quo.

I'm thinking about trying to stand up.

I'm thinking about trying to stand up and go over to Jodi, who is now crying into the phone.

"But, that can't be! It's...impossible! This wasn't supposed to happen!" she's yelling amidst her sobs. "I *am* calm! I'm fucking calm, Mom!"

Jodi is anything but calm. "Yes. No. Of course! Anything you need, Ma. Anything at all. I'll take care of all the arrangements. You don't have to come down from New York. That's why I'm here," she concludes, giving a quick, furtive glance my way.

Then Jodi is listening again to her mother's words, tears rolling quietly down her cheeks, the remnants of her mascara bleeding in blue-black lines. "Mom, I know," she sobs. "I know I was her favorite grandchild."

I head down to the beach to wake Kat, Lenny, and Tim with the news.

"She really *died*?" Kat asks, scratching her head and sending her curls flying. "No fucking joke?"

"Who died?" Lenny mumbles, eyes still closed.

"Jodi's grandmother," Kat answers.

"Ironic!" he coughs out. "Like rain on your wedding day."

Kat laughs from her hammock and I'm glad. She doesn't seem to hate Lenny that much this morning.

"Poor Jodi," Tim yawns, swinging in a hammock nearby and finishing a text to someone.

"You're still here?" I ask, turning to face him. The comment comes out with more bite than I intended, and it hangs unanswered in the air between us. I try to backtrack, but now that the thought is there, I can't stop wondering about it. "Not to be rude, I mean, we've loved your company...but...*why*, again?"

Tim seems momentarily at a loss for words, adjusting his hat and looking left, right and over his shoulder like he did when we first met yesterday on this same beach. "Does every encounter have to have a purpose?" He smiles. "Can't it just...be?"

"Is that Scientology?" I ask.

"I don't know about you, Lauren, but I truly believe he's here because *I'm* such awesome company." Kat tries for her usual sarcasm, only this time it falls flat.

I look at Kat, who looks back at me. Then we both study Lenny, who crosses his arms in front of his chest like he, too, is waiting for an answer.

Because here's the truth of the matter. Under scrutiny, in the critical, morning-after light, it's apparent: We're cool. But we're not *Rubix Cube* cool.

"It's like I told you yesterday. I needed a break from my so-called reality," Tim offers.

"And *we're* your choice of vacation destinations? Seriously?" Kat pushes.

For the first time since I've met him, Tim looks uncomfortable. "It's complicated, okay?"

"Complicated how?" Lenny probes.

Tim motions for Lenny to follow him. "Guy to guy?"

Lenny stretches and locates his and Kat's shoes under a

nearby daybed. "Um, okay," he agrees, giving a backward glance our way as he heads toward the surf behind Tim Cubix, slipping on his classic white Adidas sneakers as he goes.

"Those Superstars?" Tim asks conversationally.

"Yeah," Lenny says. "I'm a collector."

"Me, too!" I hear Tim say before their voices disappear with them around a corner.

Kat and I make our way back up the winding path. "What do you think that was about?" Kat asks.

"I dunno...maybe Tim and Ruby are having some problems after all?"

"That might explain the 'guy to guy' thing," Kat agrees. "But, still, I don't think he'd confide about something personal like that to a relative stranger, even if he does like Lenny's performance art. Tim had this female stalker once, I remember. Needed to go to court, get a restraining order, everything. He's really *not* like us. Something isn't adding up."

"Yeah, only, yesterday we were too drunk to notice or care." Yesterday, anything was possible. We left our jobs, families, and responsibilities in the dust and flew down to Florida without much planning, and without remorse. Yesterday it was possible to bump into one of the most famous actors of all time and party with him. Today, we find ourselves with a dead grandmother, several hangovers, and an elusive celebrity with unclear motives.

At the back entrance to A Place I Know, we find and immediately begin to console Jodi, who is crying on the phone again. "Lee," she mouths, rolling her eyes skyward. She turns back to her husband's call.

"Of course I saw her yesterday," Jodi insists while sobbing into the phone. "She seemed perfectly fine. I mean, fine for someone ninety-three years old and basically *unconscious*." She listens to Lee's response as we sit on either side of her on a teakwood porch swing.

"No, she didn't know I was there. I felt like...like I was sending her love from afar. Like my presence was felt even when I wasn't in the room."

"Which was never," Kat whispers.

"Be nice," I answer.

"My sarcasm is worst in times of distress," she shrugs. *We're in for some morning, then*, I think.

Jodi disconnects and looks at us, eyes tired. "I have to keep lying about this! Concocting new webs! It's going to drive me insane, I tell you." She takes a deep breath. "I mean, it's one thing to lie for pleasure. It's another thing entirely to lie out of necessity."

"So tell the truth," I venture.

"Ha," she responds, not even hesitating to consider the possibility. "The truth, meaning that I'm here with you? Lauren, even if I wanted to talk truth, I don't see how that's even possible without dragging *you* into a boatload of shit."

Except that Doug already knows. Maybe. Some of it. All of it?

Then she stands and stretches, reaching for her bag. "Well, I guess I better get going."

"By yourself?" I say. "No way. We're all for one and one for all."

Kat nods. "The Three Musketeers take Miami's Golden Girls."

"Where are Lenny and Tim?" Jodi asks. We do our best to explain the conversation we had with Tim and how it led to a guy-only talk.

"You were inquisitioning him?" Jodi asks, horrified.

"That's one way to put it," I counter.

"Hey, guys?" Kat calls down to the beach from our spot along the path, catching Lenny and Tim's attention. "We're off!"

"Where are we going?" Tim calls back.

"The hotel?" Lenny guesses, their voices coming closer.

"*We?*" Kat and I ask in unison.

"Nope. Hebrew Home for the Aged!" Jodi yells.

The guys have jogged up from the beach and are panting slightly when they reach us. "At least, Kat and Jodi and I are going there. You don't have to come with us." I look at Tim, in particular, while saying this last part. It's one thing to take Tim slumming at the Clevelander. It's another monster entirely to drag him to the bedside of a dead nonagenarian.

Tim seems to agree. He hesitates, then looks sideways at Lenny.

Lenny puts an arm around Tim and pulls him close in what looks like an act of either aggression or camaraderie. It's hard to tell which.

"Of course we're coming! *Right*, Tim?" Lenny says.

Tim struggles a bit under Lenny's grip and produces a tight smile. "Sure! Love it! Sounds like a blast."

"Such a good guy, that Tim Cubix," Kat sighs, watching him shake some sand of his pants and disappear inside the now-deserted club. Lenny and I sigh right along with her.

"Yeah," Lenny agrees, a hint of chill in his tone. "Unique, that one."

CHAPTER 23

"HEY, I'VE ALWAYS WANTED to solve the Rubix Cube!" the cabdriver
says, cracking himself up. Tim winks theatrically at us as Jodi gives
the address.

"I'm just warning you: it's not that nice a place," Jodi offers,
probably as an advanced apology to Tim. "I mean, it wasn't my
grandma's home or anything. She just had to move there last year,
after her mind started to really crumble." Tears well up in her eyes
again. "Before that, she lived in this sweet little apartment overlooking the bay. I used to love spending Christmas vacations there
with her."

I put one arm around Jodi and try to comfort her. "Jo," I say,
"you have to know that none of this is your fault. Don't feel guilty."

Kat hands Jodi a mini packet of Kleenex from the depths of
her man-pockets. She never carries a purse but still manages to
have on her a surprisingly stocked bar of requisite womanly para-
phernalia, producing lipstick, breath mints, or Visine like a magician doing sleight of hand.

"Yeah," Kat says. "There's no shame to be had, just because
you said you'd visit your grandmother but you didn't and instead
hung out all night drinking with *It* magazine's Sexiest Man Alive of
both 1997 and 2002, then she died the next morning with no family
there beside her."

"Not helping," Lenny stage whispers across the cab as Jodi
starts wailing.

"Sorry, Jo. I'm terrible at sympathy. This is why I wasn't a
good kindergarten teacher!"

"As your next career, I wouldn't consider undertaking, then."
Tim smiles.

"Maybe tax collector?" Lenny asks. "Dentist?"

"Maybe everyone should just shut up," Kat barks back.

"Good times, people. Good times," I joke. "Let's keep it light. We're in Miami, after all."

"With my grandmother!" Jodi adds. "Who is actually really dead!" She stops crying and looks out the window. Turning back after a moment, she stares at me, wide-eyed. "Lauren. I am never going to tell another lie for as long as I live."

I bite my tongue so as not to say something rude, like, *I think you just told one right now*, and instead take her hand in mine. "Okay, Jo. That's a big statement to make. But I know what you mean." Among all the other lies floating around the Moncrieff home, I think of Jodi's cash-back habit and wonder if she can really live in complete fiscal honesty with Lee, working within the true budget of their finances.

It's possible. I mean, in the past twenty-four hours, I've learned a thing or two about myself that I don't particularly like either. There are definitely some things I'm going to try and change when I get back to New York. So, if I can do that, maybe Jodi can, too.

I smile at her sort of crookedly. "I'll help you do your best if you help me do mine."

"No lying," she states.

"No cheating," I add.

"No flirting on the side," Lenny adds.

"No more psychic hotlines!" Kat hoots.

"No more alter egos!" Tim declares.

"Whatever, Lex Sheridan," Jodi jokes, smiling for the first time all morning.

The cab pulls up a circular driveway and stops in front of an institutional-looking, white concrete façade. A few sad palm trees frame the peeling columns out front. Jodi sighs.

We all pile out into the now-bright, humid sunshine. Lenny goes around to the driver's window with some cash.

"Hey, MC Lenny!" he says. "Love your YouTube videos." He takes the cash before they shake hands. "It's a real honor!"

The driver honks and waves at us as he pulls around the circle and out onto the street.

Lenny turns to Tim. "That was weird, right? Being recognized, first by you and now that guy?"

Tim shakes his head. "Nah, man. Better start getting used to it. Your work is already known...and I got big plans for you."

Kat and I exchange bemused eyebrow raises. Then we escort Jodi through the electronic, hospital-like doors and into the frigid air-conditioning of the old age home.

"Hi-yyy," Jodi purrs halfheartedly to the receptionist. "I'm Sonia Goldberg's granddaughter. She..." Jodi makes elaborate gestures with her hands to denote *moved into the great beyond without me by her side.*

The receptionist jumps up quickly, sparing Jodi the need to explain any further. "Of course! Follow me this way."

She motions our group to a set of double swinging doors off to the left of the lobby, only then looking from face to face.

"Are...all of you...*relatives*...of the deceased?" She pauses on Tim.

"Why, yes, ma'am, yes we are." Tim nods and tips his hat, southern charm and con man all in one. He turns to us and smiles, giving a look that says: *Watch and learn, people. This is how you excel at daytime television and suck the blood from unsuspecting New York mobsters while playing a superhero. This is how you get through those double doors. Nice and easy, with a little swagger.*

The receptionist pauses and gives an uncertain grin in return. "My," she says, unable to utter more than one syllable in the presence of such infamous hotness.

I plaster a fake smile on my face and smooth down my hair. Kat tries to appear taller. Jodi begins wailing full force, as Lenny comforts her, saying, "There, there, cous'. I know just how you feel."

The doors swing on their hinges, and we have made it through to the other side. Covert high fives follow all around.

I pat Tim on the back. "I think you almost earned a third Oscar nod just then."

He winks and tips his hat again, mimicking his actions almost exactly from a moment ago. "Aw, shucks, ma'am, it was nothin'."

"I can't believe I already broke my resolution to stop lying," Jodi complains. "That crying was complete bullshit."

She leads us around a corner and into a room shrouded in darkness. A frail figure rests there, outlined under the thin white sheet. In the dim light, I can make out some old photographs in gilt frames on the bedside table, of a young woman dancing. Each image finds her in a different costume, from a dramatic ball gown to a fringed flapper dress. This must have been Jodi's grandma. In the largest photograph, she poses with a handsome man who must have been her husband.

In the corner of the room sits a huge basket of oranges, still wrapped in cellophane and tied with a bow.

Then the real tears come.

I know it's not nice of me, but while Jodi and the Hebrew Home's staff are discussing next steps for the body, I slip into the deceased grandma's bathroom and freshen up. Under the sink, I find individually wrapped soaps and a few packages of denture-safe toothbrushes. The only eye drops I find are prescription ones for glaucoma, and I decide not to risk it. In the absence of deodorant, I find Gold Bond talcum powder and rub it under my arms.

It is decided that we will eat breakfast while Jodi's grandma is being "prepared" or whatever.

"What happens now?" I ask, as we exit the building and stand around uncertainly.

"I don't know," Jodi admits. "I guess my mom will take care of it all from here. I better call her."

We start walking down the circular drive and, at the main road, turn left. The staff suggested we dine at a Denny's about a half a block up, which had gotten Tim all excited.

"I can't remember the last time I ate in a Denny's!" he says again, as we approach the huge yellow-and-red sign.

"No way, mom!" Jodi shouts into the phone. We are about to enter the restaurant. Kat has her hand on the handle and gives me a look asking *what should I do*? I shrug in return. She moves back from the door and we decide to wait it out in the parking lot, since Jodi's phone call has gotten increasingly louder.

"That's...gross!" she complains. "I'm *sorry* I'm not being *mature* enough for you, mother, but...really...I don't see why I have to be the one to escort her home! All by myself!"

Lenny coughs loudly.

This is followed by silence as Jodi listens to the response and shakes her head back and forth. Then she speaks again. "Fine. Just remember what happened when I had to dissect a frog in sixth grade. That's all I'm saying." Then she hangs up and looks at us staring at her. "What?"

Tim is the only one brave enough to approach Jodi, probably because he doesn't know any better, having only met her yesterday. "You okay?" he tries.

"Oh, don't use any of your smooth southern acting charm on *me*!" she spits. Tim's eyes go wide as she continues. "This was supposed to be a little *vacation* for me, you know. Some time off from my family. But now, that's all a *fantasy*. Because, now I have to make sure my grandma is packed in *dry ice* so that I can take her back to *New York* with me...later today!"

"Sucks to be her," Kat whispers.

"Sucks to be *her*?" I ask Kat, annoyed. "You mean, it sucks to be *us*. I have news for you, Kat. This is Sympathy 101 and you're now enrolled. We're all flying back with her."

Kat looks over her shoulder, to where Jodi and Tim are talking it out. "You mean...party's over?"

"'Fraid so." I nod. "Time to deal."

CHAPTER 24

BREAKFAST IS A SOLEMN AFFAIR as everyone slumps further into his or her own contemplative shell. There is little of the joking, fun-wheeling aura of last night. Four hours of sleep can do that to you. So can guilt, remorse, confusion, and possession of a corpse.

I notice Lenny staring at me over a pile of pancakes, and I squirm against the pleather banquette. "What?" I blurt.

Everyone jumps at the sound. Lenny pulls his lips in tight, and cocks his head to the side, studying me. "It's just...you look different than you did yesterday. Like...less angry," he decides.

Less angry?

Jodi pipes in, stabbing the air with a fork full of sausages. "He's right! And...your eyes look bigger!"

"Are you guys messing with me?" I ask, scanning their faces for signs of irony.

"Huh," Kat says. "It's like...your forehead or something is different. Maybe you slept funny?"

I did sleep funny all right.

But wait, did Kat say...my forehead? I start to smile and am about to tell them my about my "secret" doctor's appointment from Tuesday. It will feel so good to share the news. And to think, it's actually working! People are noticing!

Tim winks at me and interjects before I can speak. "Um, ladies and gents, I think that's what we in Hollywood would call Botox."

"No!" Kat and Jodi say in unison. I plaster a big fake grin on my face in response, trying to hide my embarrassment at being called out.

"Yeah, yeah, I did it," I admit. "So...how do I look, really?"

Kat, Jodi and I head to the bathroom, where I try to inspect my forehead in the lousy fluorescent lighting.

"Huh," I say, looking closely. It really is pleasantly smooth and wrinkle free. My eyes do seem to have opened up a bit, probably because the skin above and around my brow has tightened and raised.

"It's a miracle!" I cheer. "I love this stuff!" I'm totally converted to the dark side now. Looks like I'll be tutoring quite a bit in order to feed my injectables habit.

Jodi pats me on the back and reminds me that she's four years younger than me. "But eventually, if I ever start looking as bad as you did, I'll get the name of your guy," she concedes.

"Gee, thanks."

"What is this?" Kat screams from behind her bathroom stall.

"Are you okay?" I ask, as Jodi shouts, "What happened?"

"I. Have. A. Fucking. Tattoo! On my inner thigh! Under this bandage! Right here!" she yells.

"Can I see?" Jodi asks, banging on the stall. "Open up!"

"No!"

"You don't remember?" I ask the Obvious Question, but still, I'm kind of surprised. I thought I was way more inebriated that she was, and I recall getting the tattoos.

"We all got them," Jodi adds. "I copied Tim's."

"You did?" Now, that part I don't remember. I can only hope she doesn't have Ruby's doodles on her back. Or worse, a sketch of King Tut's sarcophagus. Tim has one on his arm. He showed it to me last night. Kinda creepy.

"Yeah. I inscribed my daughters' birthdays next to my C-section scar."

"In hieroglyphics, like Tim?" I wonder.

"No, idiot. In pink and purple."

"Kat." I knock gently on the yellow metal door. "Come out."

"It's mortifying. I can't. I'll never come out again!" I peer through the seam where the door meets the frame. Kat is perched on the toilet tank with her head in her hands.

"It can't be that bad," I soothe. And then I whisper to Jodi, "Do you remember what her tattoo is?"

Jodi shakes her head, clueless. "Something about astrology, maybe? Or yoga?"

"I. Can. Hear. You!" Kat calls.

"Oh, wait! I'm having a vision!" Jodi announces proudly. Then she saunters over to the stall where Kat is hiding and knocks lightly on the door. "Hello, Kitty?"

"Fuck me!" Kat says, exploding out of the stall, past us, and out into the restaurant.

Jodi can't stop laughing. Bending over slightly, she runs into the stall. "I think I just pissed myself!"

"Why?" I ask. "What's so funny about saying 'Hello, Kitty' to Kat?"

"Dumb ass. That's her new tattoo! It's a white-faced, chubby cat with whiskers, a huge pink bow, black eyes and a yellow dot nose. I sketched it out for that guy Tommy. It looks like something from Kimora Lee Simmons' line of jewelry! Hysterical!" she calls out from behind the stall. I hear her flush and blow her nose. "I'm crying again, but this time, it's from comic relief. I really needed that!"

I manage to get her back out into the restaurant and to our booth in one piece. Only Kat is at the table waiting for us, the guys nowhere in sight. "Meow," Jodi declares, holding her juice glass high for a toast.

Kat holds out her middle finger in response.

Out in the parking lot, Tim and Lenny are speaking animatedly. Tim leans against the trunk of an old car while Lenny paces in front of him.

"It's your responsibility to tell them," Lenny argues.

"No, it isn't. I don't have to do a damn thing if I don't want to. I only mentioned it to *you* because I thought you were cool," Tim says.

"Mentioned it? Like it was just something in passing? An oversight that you conveniently forgot about?" Lenny barks. "And don't say something completely juvenile, like, 'I thought you were cool.' Unless you've been cast in the part of a seventh grader, perhaps?"

"Whoa," Jodi says.

The men both turn their heads at the sound of Jodi's voice, and instantly clam up. Tim scratches his four-day stubble with vigor while Lenny continues pacing.

"Anyone want to tell us what's going on?" I ask.

"Nope," Tim says breezily.

Lenny motions with his pointer finger at Tim. "You—" he starts. "Arrgh!" He grunts in frustration, never completing the thought. "Where are they, huh?" he asks Tim, his hands gesturing wildly around the parking lot. "Come out, come out, wherever you are!" Then he gets up in Tim's face. "You've got some nerve."

"Oh, that's rich." Tim shakes his head back and forth, a smile creasing the corner of his mouth. Cutely, I might add.

No, Lauren, I scold myself, not "cutely." Lenny and Tim are fighting and, no matter what, you must root for Lenny to win. Even if Tim is larger-than-life and amazingly adorable.

"*I've* got some nerve?" Tim repeats, like they are practicing cheesy dialogue in some Clint Eastwood film. "What about you?" Tim looks around. "Actually, what about *all* of you?"

We stare back at him. No one says anything for a few beats. Then I turn to Tim. "What about us?" I wonder.

Tim sighs. "Nothing, Lauren. Just forget I said anything."

"Can't do that." He looks at me and I smile. "Listen, Macbeth. You're very cute and very famous and I'm just trying to keep it all together around you, so no, I haven't had much nerve until this point. But now I'm going to *demand*—" my voice shakes a little bit on the force of the word, but I push past it—"that you tell us exactly what's going on."

It's perhaps my imagination, but I sense Jodi and Kat moving in on either side of me, like bookends giving me support.

Lenny clears his throat. "Tim's got bodyguards."

"Well," I say, sort of caught off guard, "naturally, he's got bodyguards. I don't see what—"

"No, I mean, *here. Now.* Watching us, making sure we're legit. The whole time we've been hanging out with him, he's been faking this friendship with us—"

"Now, wait a second there, Len!" Tim jumps in. "That's just not true."

"So you *don't* have secret security guys watching us right now?" Jodi asks, moving a step closer to Tim.

Jodi and Tim bonded last night, certainly more than either Kat or I did with him. Lenny, too, with his YouTube connection and all that Hollywood talk. Depending on Tim's answer, they have the most to lose.

"Jo, it's...different for me," Tim tries, looking contrite. "I'm not like you, I mean, not anymore. I can't just walk up to people on the beach in Miami and become fast friends! I have to be cautious. About everything I do."

"So, you lied to me! To us," she declares. "You probably planned this whole thing, to *practice* being a normal person for some upcoming blockbuster role." She puts her hands up to show that she's making quotation marks around her next words. "'Logan Price *thought* he had it all,'" Jodi says, mimicking the voiceover guy from the movies. "'The perfect family, the perfect career. But one crazy night in Miami changed all that.'" She stops, gathering her thoughts. "It's like...like, we were your *research*. Your rats!" She walks right up to Tim. I think she's going to punch him, slap his face, or spit at him. Instead, she reaches up and knocks Tim's hat right off his head. "That fedora makes you look fucking stupid!" she cries. And then she storms off down the street.

Kat, Lenny, and I chase after her, leaving Tim—and his elusive bodyguards, wherever they might be hiding—alone together in the Denny's parking lot.

I've got to hand it to Jodi, she does have a flair for dramatic exits.

The next few hours pass by in a blur at the funeral home. There is paperwork to watch Jodi complete. There is the body to consider. There is transportation to the airport to arrange. There is Tim Cubix's betrayal to replay like a scene from a bad movie. Kat and I sit patiently while Lenny works the phone and changes all of our flights to match the one Jodi and her grandma are scheduled for.

"It's all set," Lenny sighs, throwing his phone down on a plush, crimson velvet banquette. "We're sitting together on the three o'clock. I was able to do pre-boarding and everything."

"Thank you!" I say, relieved that it's all taken care of.

"Too bad," Kat adds.

"You know," I begin, turning to Kat, "I'm kind of tired of your moping about this. Jodi's grandma *died*. I mean, I'm bummed, too. I could have used another day on the beach. But, you've got to admit, Kat, it's pretty selfish of you to put this trip before your friend's needs." I pause. "What's the big deal? I mean, it's not like you have anything to go back to..." And then I stop. Lenny is shaking his head, and Kat has turned away.

Because that is, of course, the issue exactly. Kat has nothing to go back to. No husband, and perhaps even no job. Only divorce proceedings and résumés on the horizon. Plus, perhaps, the leakage of a local, minor sex scandal to clean up.

"Damn," I whisper. I put my hand out to touch her arm but she shoos me away.

"You're right, Lauren. I have nothing."

"That's not what I meant—"

Lenny chimes in. "She was only saying that—"

Kat stands up and shakes her hair in disagreement. "Just...I can't...give me a moment alone, okay?"

She moves across the room and enters a chapel door on the right. Based on the organ music and the sign on the door, there seems to be a funeral going on inside. But I'm not about to tell Kat that.

"We're in deep shit," Lenny declares.

"You think?"

"Oh yeah. Didn't you notice? She didn't even curse at us. Not once."

He's right, and I'm left with silence and more than a few goose bumps. Kat's marriage was wrong from the start, but even so, getting out of it will be painful.

"Peter left her *and* spent their savings, you know," I tell Lenny, reminding myself of the horror of it all.

He nods. "She mentioned that. It explains a lot of the hostility."

"Some of that's just Kat. She's always been kind of thick-skinned and quick with the insults."

"She's trying to be tough. But she's so *sad*, Lauren. Can't you see that coming through?"

I take a deep breath and consider this. How much have I really paid attention these past few days? I mean, to anything other than myself? I thought this little trip might heal me—heal all of us—and make the hurts just magically disappear. Like a twenty-four-hour cure-all. But now I have to go home and face Doug and Laney and Ben and Becca. I have to go back to work on Monday and face my homeroom, grade papers, read *Johnny Tremain* aloud for the eleventh time.

I'm not sure I can stomach it.

Jodi has to go home to a grieving family, and face all her lies with Lee.

And Kat will return to…what?

Jodi emerges from a back office looking ten years older than she did yesterday. A white-haired man in a suit and tie emerges behind her, rolling a pine box on a gurney. Jodi closes her eyes for a moment, then opens them, her gaze on me. "Okay. Let's do this."

I put Lenny in charge of retrieving Kat from the depths of Melvin Kantor's funeral, and hustle out behind the coffin. A large woman, clad in tight leggings and an ill-fitting Florida Marlin's T-shirt, waits next to a van idling in the parking lot.

"You the granddaughter?" She squints at Jodi in the hot sun.

"You the driver?" Jodi squints back.

The woman holds up a walkie-talkie and speaks into it. "I got her," she confirms to whoever is crackling on the other end of the line.

Jodi gets into the passenger seat while Lenny, Kat, and I pile in to the back row. I try not to get freaked by the presence of Sonia Goldberg in the back, but it's hard to ignore her.

Our silence is broken by the driver. "It's one o'clock right now, and your flight is at three. You need to stop at the Loews Hotel, I hear, before going to the airport, right?"

We confirm that, yes, we'll just need to stop for about fifteen minutes to pack our things and check out.

"Schedule is tight. I'll take Collins, then," she concludes, sitting back and turning up the Latin salsa on the radio. I can tell that she's satisfied in the way that drivers are once they have mentally mapped out their route.

We stare out our respective windows. It's another glorious day here, and I feel some regret over not being able to enjoy it. Kat is sort of right about that, much as it makes me feel like a douche—Lenny's got me using his favorite word—to admit.

We go over a bump and the casket rattles slightly behind us.

A strange euphoria overcomes me. I don't know why, but ever since I attended my first funeral when I was thirteen, I've always felt very much alive in the presence of a dead body.

I know it's morbid to think like that, but I can't help it. Sonia Goldberg is making the sun shine brighter for me today, putting the world—with all of its contradictory desires—in sharper focus. It sounds odd, but I whisper a small prayer of thanks to her, for reminding me of the joys of living.

I want to tickle my children and hear their giggles of delight. I want to hug Doug. I want to try again.

As much as I was looking forward to the flight down here, I'm now equally anticipating the flight home.

And then the van slows down.

And then the van comes to a crawl.

And then, the van stops.

The swell of traffic seems to have come out of nowhere. One minute we were cruising, and the next, we are enmeshed in a jam of epic proportions.

"What the fuck?" Kat asks.

"And...she's back!" Lenny says, clearly pleased to hear Kat spew an expletive.

"Not sure," the driver says with a shrug. "I'll radio in and see whassup."

"This is bad," Jodi mutters to herself. "Very."

The four of us hold a collective breath as the driver asks for details. "Yeah, I'm on Collins!" she calls into her device.

"You where?" a guy shouts back through the radio.

"Collins, man, Collins!" she yells, pounding on the dashboard for emphasis.

My euphoria has been replaced with dread. Lenny looks calm, but raises his eyebrows at me in question. Kat is sucking a curl.

"You going to duh parade?" the disembodied dispatcher's voice crackles back.

"Whah parade?"

"Oh, this is too much!" Jodi exhales in exasperation. "Are you two for real?"

"Forreal," Lenny smiles. "Dat's how you say it. Forreal." He motions across his body with his hand splayed wide, like a homie in one of his videos.

"Jesus Fucking Christ." Kat shakes her head.

I try to calm her down, although my own heart is beating wildly. "I know, it's making me anxious, too."

"No, Lauren! I mean, walking right beside our van is Jesus Fucking Christ!"

All heads turn to follow Kat's pointer finger. Indeed, strolling a few paces in front of us is a man in a long, white, flowing robe, with stringy brown hair extending down his back.

Jodi rolls down her window and sticks her torso out. "Hey!" she calls. "Hey...Son of God!"

The man turns toward the sound of her voice. Spotting her waving at him, he waves back and smiles. "Yes, my disciple. What may I do for you?"

"Can you, like...tell us why there's so much goddamned traffic?"

"And why you are dressed like that, and what the hell is going on here, and, oh, about a million other things," Kat adds conversationally.

"I do not believe that God almighty has damned the traffic." He pauses and smiles at his own little joke. "But I will guess that the swell of cars is caused by the closing this afternoon of Collins Avenue."

"Closing?" Jodi calls back, echoing what we are all thinking.

"Yes, for the Gay Pride Alliance costume parade. It is...heavenly. You may be stuck here for a few hours until the road is reopened. They are preparing the parade of floats now." He bows and continues on his way.

"Fuck those gay motherfuckers and their gay motherfucking parade!" Jodi swears.

"She's really someone's mother?" Lenny asks no one in particular.

Kat slides the van door open on her side and jumps out. "I'm going to get a better look, just see how bad it really is up there," she says. "Back in five."

Lenny gives us a half wave and follows her out into the heat.

"Great," I sigh. I scoot over to the middle and tap Jodi on the arm. "You okay?"

"Just don't," she whispers, pulling her arm away from me. "I know you mean well, Lauren, but please. Don't even *try* right now." She sinks lower in her seat and takes out her BlackBerry. "I better e-mail my mom."

Given the choice between sitting in the thick silence of the van or going out into the thick Miami heat, I pick the latter.

Which is a choice that changes everything.

CHAPTER 25

I'M WALKING NORTH, weaving my way delicately between hordes of parade-goers, sunbathers, and tourists lining the avenue. Some groups of performers have assembled themselves in clumps here and there, dressed in elaborate flamenco costumes and other outlandish, garish (and, in one case, ass-less leather) splendor. It looks more like Carnival in Rio than any gay pride parade I've ever seen in New York.

Again, I find myself regretting that we'll have to leave Miami so soon. I would have loved to watch the full entertainment and all the floats go by.

I stop in front of an art deco hotel to let a crowd of tie-dyed and jean-short-wearing hippies pass. In that moment, a white Hummer-style stretch limousine pulls up next to me and honks "La Cucaracha."

I turn toward it and smile, anticipating a bunch of Elvises or Marilyns will emerge.

Instead, a window toward the back of the vehicle rolls down halfway, and a man's hand emerges. He's pointing to me. I do the obvious and point to myself, too. The hand makes a thumbs-up signal.

I am not approaching an unmarked vehicle like that, no matter how intrigued I might be. And intrigued I am. I shake my head back and forth. The last thing I need on this trip is to be abducted.

The tinted window rolls down a few inches more. The man's hand comes back out, this time waving a fedora.

I'd know that stupid hat anywhere.

Then, just as quickly, the hand and hat withdraw and the window slides back up.

I approach the vehicle and knock. "Okay, Tim. Let me in."

The automatic locks release. Without thinking much beyond

Well, this should be interesting, I pull on the handle, jump in the Hummer, and slam the door shut behind me.

It takes a moment for my eyes to adjust to the darkness inside the cavernous limo. I can make out three figures. I assume that the smaller one is Tim and the other two—big guys sitting around the side of a U-shaped seat—are his bodyguards.

I sink into the black leather and enjoy the air-conditioning. "Well?" I say, deciding to play it really cool as my heart beats out of my chest. "You wanted something?"

Tim turns on a small light overhead. His dimples crease in a sort of sad smile. He looks tired and worried at the same time, as if he's been left without a tour bus in Lithuania and can't see a way out of it, like he did in 1999, in a riveting performance of my-wife-played-by-Katie-Holmes-is-dying sort of a way.

I almost feel bad for him.

"Look, Lauren," Tim begins. "You are perhaps the sanest one of the bunch—lying to your husband and dabbling with infidelity notwithstanding—and so I thought it would be best to choose you as the one to hear me out."

I consider this, mentally scrolling through my coconspirators, and nod in agreement. I don't trust myself to actually say anything, so I bite my tongue and wait.

Tim nods back. "Good. So, here it is." He takes a deep breath and asks the bodyguards to give us some privacy. Once they have left the vehicle, I feel more at ease. Tim senses this and begins. "I'm down here to shoot a movie in the Everglades."

I shrug. "Okay, I believe that. Kat was right, then."

"That's not the interesting part." He shakes his head ruefully. "This movie I'm doing. It's about this ordinary guy who finds himself in extraordinary circumstances. Without boring you with too much plot, suffice it to say that he ends up being falsely accused of killing his own son, and now he's on the run from authorities while trying to prove his own innocence."

"Like *Presumed Innocent* meets *The Green Mile* meets *A Few Good Men.*"

He nods. "Only totally different. Because it's set in the Ever-glades."

"Cool," I say, thinking the opposite.

Tim grants me signature smile number three, the one with a hint of irony.

"Fine, you got me, I think it's kind of a dumb premise. But I'm sure you'll be great in it. Continue."

"Anyway, the dude is forced to literally live in the wild, hiding out in the jungle-like terrain of Southern Florida's preserved wet-lands. He spears fish and eats mangrove crabs and oysters to survive."

"Now, that is cool," I add. "Very *Cast Away*-ish."

"Yeah. Except not, because it's set in the Everglades." He sighs, seemingly annoyed. I know the clock is ticking here on getting to the plane, so I hold my thoughts and let him continue uninter-rupted. "Anyway, there's this one scene where the guy comes up against a crocodile, and he has to fight it for survival. In the script, the man and beast both walk away from the confrontation scarred, but alive. I liked that. I thought it was perfect symbolism for what happens later in the movie, during the courtroom drama scene. It's actually one of the reasons I signed on to the project in the first place. That scene *moved* me."

Here he pauses and I say nothing, certainly not what I'm thinking, which is to burst out into a Jack Nicholson–style *You can't handle the truth, crocodile*!

"So on Wednesday morning—just two days ago—I'm in my trailer, and I'm getting psyched up for that scene, because we're scheduled to shoot it at nine. Only my assistant comes in and hands me a revised script. I get this bad vibe, you know, as she passes it to me. Sure enough, I flip through it looking for the changes. Now there are snakes hanging around with this croc, and my character has to kill them before even battling the croc. Like it's a video game and you have to get past snake level before kicking it up to croc level. I mean, ultimately it's not that big of a deal, since I get to have final say on how the scene plays out, but now I'm torn."

He looks at me like this is a significant moment. Like, at this point in the story, I'm supposed to laugh or cry or gasp, only I don't know which response to give. I settle on the truth. "So?"

"Snakes!" He scratches the back of his left hand with his right, just like he did yesterday, and I realize this is the reason why. He can't stop the itch coming from inside, and it has something to do with this very issue. "I fucking hate snakes! They creep me out big-time! It's, like, one of the *only* specifications in my contracts, all caps: NO SNAKES, and this douche-bag director knows it."

I can't help smiling at his use of the term *douche bag*. Lenny would be so proud. Quickly, I realize what that smile must look like to Tim, though, so I try for moral support. "Guy's clearly a douche."

"Right?" Tim shakes his head sadly. "So, I was about to remind him of that line item and ask that we return to the original, scripted, snakeless version. Until." Here he pauses, lost in thought. "Until I thought, what if this character is afraid of snakes, like I am? Then suddenly, the director's rewrite is actually much better than the original. The added depth provided by this snake-killing scene heightens both the physical and the emotional stakes for my character, bringing him to a place he never knew he could go."

"It's brilliant," I say, the English teacher in me kicking into high gear. "Because then the scene possesses both internal *and* external conflict."

"Exactly." Only, he doesn't seem happy about the revelation.

"Great, so you solved the problem!" I say.

"No, because suddenly, *I* was conflicted. I knew what was best for the film. But it wasn't what was best for me. Lauren," he says, his eyes filled with pain. He's pleading with me not to think less of him as he makes this admission. "I couldn't do it. I just couldn't green-light those serpents. I needed time."

"So?"

"I walked off set yesterday morning."

I can see that he's rattled, admitting this. "That's pretty big, huh?" I sound like Georgie, coaching a child who has just read aloud for the first time.

"Never done it before. Real dick move."

I try to think of something proactive to say while my mind is processing this new information: Tim Cubix is *afraid* of something? I settle on, "What's next?"

He leans back into the leather seats and considers this. "Big press due to come on set tomorrow. I know I have to be there. Everyone's losing money as is, each day I'm not there filming. If this story gets out, it will go national."

"*Inter*," I say. "International."

"Fuck." He looks my way with ironic grin number five. "Fucking snakes."

I'm starting to warm again toward Tim, the vampire superhero with an actual Achilles heel, but then my smile turns chilly as I consider what he's not admitting. "Snakes or no, you really lied to us."

"In a way," he concedes again, this time with regret. He scratches his scruffy beard. "I wish I hadn't done it that way, but I just didn't see any other choice at the time."

I can see it pretty clearly from his point of view. But I have to think about what Kat would say, how Jodi would respond. "*And* you used us."

"As a disguise, of sorts, yes. I needed to regroup, and you guys just happened along, yelling at each other at the perfect time." He smiles genuine smile number one.

I wanted to stay mad at him, really I did.

But the thing is, I'm not only a somewhat sane person, I'm also the kind of person who likes to give others the benefit of the doubt.

And who can hate a genuine movie star who genuinely hates snakes with such conviction, I ask you?

So, anyway, as I sit in his stretch Hummer limo, *Tim Cubix is apologizing to me*. Do you understand how bizarre that is? And how huge? He's *sorry* for lying to us. His intentions were self-motivated, but weren't ours as well?

As if sensing my hesitation, Tim adds, "It wasn't one-sided. You guys used me, too, you know."

"For your fabulousness?" I joke.

He laughs, a deep chortle. "As Kat would say, Absofuckinglutely."

Something is still troubling me, though. "How do I know you're not lying to me right now? I mean, you *are* an actor." I don't mention that I've privately nicknamed and catalogued all of his expressions.

"I hate when people say that. It's like you can't possibly ever be considered truthful if you lie for a living."

"When you put it that way..." I joke.

"Yeah, it sounds really bad." He stops to consider what else to say. "I guess you just have to trust me, right? Isn't that what friends do?"

"Oh, so now we're friends."

"I hope so, Lauren. I really do like you nutballs." Spoken like one who knows us pretty well, I think.

"Oh, what the hell." Even if it is fleeting, I'd rather have this moment with Tim under false pretenses than not have it at all. I put out my hand and we shake on it. "It's all good."

Now that we're back to being allies, I debrief Tim on our dilemma with Sonia Goldberg. "There's a massive gay pride parade blocking Collins Avenue, and then there's a plane that's supposed to take off in one hour and twenty-five minutes...with us on it!" I summarize.

Tim signals to the bodyguards, who get back in the car, and the three of them, together with the driver, try to figure out what to do to help us.

Tim pauses from his conversation for a second and lets his gaze drift out the window.

Something in the parade catches his eye, because the next thing I know, he's barking orders to the bodyguards and forming a plan.

"What?" I ask, excited in a clueless-puppy sort of way. I'm completely happy about his strategy and I have no idea why!

Tim turns to me, his blue eyes sparkling and devilish. "It's Dixie! She's the key!"

"She's got the key? The key to what?" I call, but Tim's not listening.

Instead, he continues to shout directions at his bodyguards, Tweedledee and Tweedledum. They ask me where the van with Jodi and Sonia was last seen. I quickly rattle off the cross street, and the two burly bodyguards take off in that direction, pushing against the tide of pedestrians as quickly as they can.

Then Tim Cubix exits the limo, grabs me by the hand, and leads me toward the middle of the parade. In that moment, I feel like we're starring together in some action adventure–romantic comedy mashup film and I'm long-limbed Cameron Diaz!

But this is real life, which makes me short and makes me worry for Tim's safety for a moment, knowing he's truly bodyguardless and truly in the middle of a full-on city parade. "Are you scared?" I ask.

"Nah!" He smiles. "I'm loving this!"

"Good!" I say. "Me, too!" I feel young and dangerous and sexy, and at the same time, I feel completely safe. I have no idea what Tim's up to, but I suddenly trust him with my life, since he's trusting me with his.

"Call Lenny and Kat and have them meet us here," Tim shouts over the din of the crowd.

"Where's here?" I yell. Tim points and I follow his finger's line, up and over the feathers and boas, and onto Dixie's float.

I stare at the scene in disbelief.

We could not have planned a more brilliant escape plan than the one floating before us now.

Dixie is cross-dressed as Ruby Richmond again, only today she sports an army-green tank top, tight black shorts, and a huge utility belt. Her hair is pulled back in a high ponytail. The float is covered with ancient-looking artifacts and caskets, with men dressed in fatigues trying to shoot at her from behind crates.

"Dixie!" Tim shouts as we jog alongside her float. She cocks a .22-caliber in his direction, which I can only hope is also a prop. She sees us and drops the weapon.

"Hi!" she says, extending her hand to Tim, that rich bravado carrying over the random noise of the crowd. "Get up here, stud!"

Dixie Normous is dressed up as Ruby Richmond in her most fulfilling role to date: the video-game-to-big-screen character Jenni Bale: Crypt Ranger.

"This float is about to get one more casket." Tim winks, hoisting me up after him.

Securely aboard, he explains to Dixie the disaster that has been our morning. "So, bottom line, we're in a bit of a bind and we need to hitch a ride with you to get Sonia Goldberg's remains up the avenue. Can you handle it?"

Dixie's full lips pout in concentration as she takes it all in. Then she blinks once, and flashes a brilliant Ruby-like smile at the crowd. "For my life's leading man? You know I'll do anything!"

The float is making steady progress up Collins Avenue. Kat and Lenny get my text, and, a few minutes later, they are running alongside us and hop on. The four of us stand atop the float and wave to the crowds and cameras as we scout for signs of Jodi, her grandmother, and the bodyguards.

"This is surreal," Lenny voices for all of us.

"Sort of like that time we shroomed senior year," I add.

"At Disneyland. I remember it fondly. I thought you were Goofy."

"I am!"

I've never been in the midst of so much action. Standing on the float gives us a great view of the whole stretch of road, the beach one block over, and swarms and swarms of festively-attired people. Voices call out to us as if we actually belong on the Crypt Ranger float.

We've reached the middle of the parade route, it seems, where bleachers and a bandstand have been set up. News vans with camera crews from local television stations are parked down a side street. Our float slows down and then stops as the parade's MC announces our arrival. Surprisingly, he's dressed in a suit and tie.

"That man is rather formal for this occasion, no?" I ask Dixie.

"That's KD Lang," she points out. "Always dresses like an undertaker, what can I say?"

"Ladies and gentlemen," KD begins, "may I present Dixie Normous as Ruby Richmond as Jenni Bale: Crypt Ranger!" The crowd explodes into deafening cheers. Dixie cocks a machine gun and sprays fake bullets over everyone's heads.

"And...who's this?" KD continues, noticing our famous companion. Tim waves tentatively at her. "Why...I believe that Ruby brought her delicious family man, Tim Cubix, along for the ride today!"

The crowd goes nuts. Dixie grabs Tim and smacks a wet kiss on him, and I am reminded of Kat and Shay at Wednesday night's fortieth birthday party.

"Great costumes, Rubix Cube!" KD winks. I wonder if she knows it's really Tim with Dixie.

The float lurches forward an inch and is about to start moving again, when we hear shouting behind us. "Hold that float!" someone calls. The chant picks up voices along the way and pretty soon everyone around us is cheering it: "Hold that float! Hold that float!" It's like we're at a baseball game when everyone starts in on "Let's go, Yankees!"

Kat and I rush to the back of the float to see what's up.

Coming toward us are Tweedledee and Tweedledum, bearing Sonia's casket high over their heads. Behind them I can just about make out Jodi's auburn head as the sun glints off it, walking unsteadily on last night's strappy, high-heeled sandals. Her feet must be killing her.

People part to let them through as the bodyguards heave the plain pine box onto the float. We take Jodi by the hands and get her aboard. Some of the actors around us help move the casket so it's safely positioned toward the middle.

Jodi looks like she might faint. We find a crate for her to sit down on. Someone passes her a canteen of water. After taking a deep gulp, she scans the street below. Finding Tim's bodyguards in the crowd, she blows kisses at them and then mouths "Thank you."

One of them puts his hand over his heart. The other waves her gratitude away, as if carrying a casket ten blocks in ninety-degree heat is no big deal. He's dripping sweat like rain.

"Okay!" Tweedledee shouts, hitting the side of the float like it's a tractor. "Start her up!"

Our float starts its gentle glide again.

Music begins as the next float in line takes center stage. It's the Beatles' "Twist and Shout" and it makes me want to dance, only I'm not coupled off. Kat and Tim twist into each other, leaving Lenny to dance with Dixie. He gives a shrug my way and goes for it.

I take a seat next to Jodi and put my arm around her. "It's going to be fine." I say. "I'm like ninety-seven percent sure."

I can't help but notice that the big guys are going to remain close to Tim. They each move to one side of the float and act as our personal escorts up the avenue.

It takes another ten minutes to get to the Loews. The end of the parade route is near and the crowd has thinned out substantially at this point. I can see our hotel's mammoth white façade and do a mental cheer that we've made it this far.

Tim motions to Lenny. A whispered huddle follows, Lenny bending down quite a bit in order to get eye-to-eye with Tim. I notice Lenny nodding his head in agreement as Tim passes him a slip of paper. The conversation ends with a handshake–arm bump, hug, slap-on-the-back combo, the likes of which I've never seen.

Then Tim turns to us. "You guys jump off here and go pack," he instructs. "I'll have my driver meet you outside the hotel in fifteen minutes."

"But what about…" Jodi begins.

"My guys will get Sonia safely off this thing and into the Hummer. You'll all drive together to the airport. I'm staying in Florida, for work." He looks at me and smiles. I give him the thumbs-up. He's got to go back on set and deal head-on with whatever problems he's got. *It's that kind of day for all of us, Tim,* I want to say. *A day to face the snakes in our lives.*

Tim stops and looks at Jodi, taking her by the hands. She looks away, somewhat theatrically. I think I see a hint of a smile under all that lovely red hair, but I can't be certain.

"I know you don't trust me anymore, Jo," Tim says, as we all hang on his every word and her every response. "I know you probably can't even stand me. So I'll promise on Lauren's good name instead of mine. I *promise* to take care of your grandmother."

Jodi tosses her hair over one shoulder and looks Tim in the eyes. "Whatever, Lex." She pretends nonchalance, but her eyes are brimming with tears.

"Thanks for trusting me," he says. Then he leans over and kisses her on the forehead.

"Aw," Kat coos.

I think I hear the sound of a camera's click, but that would be impossible to make out over the rush and roar of the crowd. Wouldn't it?

CHAPTER 26

IF MY LIFE STORY WERE A MOVIE—which I now sometimes like to believe it is—here's what you'd see this minute, flashing across the screen.

You'd see adjoining hotel rooms, in which three women and one man (in their mid-to-late thirties, all rather attractive) frantically fling their belongings into suitcases. They emerge from the hotel lobby a bit frazzled and pile into a white Hummer-style stretch limousine. One woman, wearing a huge white sun hat, black Chloe sunglasses, and layers of gauzy material, opens the back of the vehicle. She extends a perfectly manicured hand out to touch the plain pine box.

After a dramatic pause of a few seconds, she slams the trunk closed and slides into the limo next to her friends. Collective Soul's "Hollywood" plays loudly as the camera pulls wide, showing from a bird's-eye view the limo as it makes its way along the highway to Miami International Airport.

"Tim made sure they'd hold the plane for you," the driver says as we reach the airport. I notice that we're not at the traditional arrivals and departures gate. In fact, magically, we're on the tarmac.

The belly of a commercial 747 hovers overhead. We scramble out of the car and quickly make our way up the steps and into the cool, recirculated air of the plane. "Thank you!" I call after the driver. "Please tell Tim how much we appreciate all of this!"

The driver tips his hat in acknowledgement, before moving the vehicle out of the way of the giant metal bird.

Because of our distinctly Hollywood entrance and the high we're all feeling from the ride, we're expecting an equally glamorous welcome on the jet. Maybe applause from the other passengers, or at least some champagne from the crew. Instead we are greeted with forty-two rows of icy silence. Apparently, people don't like when their plane is delayed, even if it is for a dead grandma and her unconventional entourage.

Awkwardly, we move past the fabulous people and down the walk of shame, finding our seats in the middle of coach. Jodi sits by the window, pressing her nose to the glass. I assume that she's watching her grandmother being lifted into the cargo hold along with all of our luggage, which can't be easy for her.

"You holding up?" I ask.

"What the hell just happened?" Jodi asks. "I mean, really!" She doesn't seem upset so much as shocked.

I shake my head with the absurdity of the past twenty-four hours. "I don't know, Jo…but it would make a fantastic movie, dontcha think?"

"Gum, anyone?" Kat asks, extending a new pack of Juicy Fruit and smiling wide.

It's only after takeoff that I realize I have no idea what I'm heading back to.

As soon as the captain announces that we are free to move about the cabin, Lenny comes up the aisle from his seat to find us. He stretches his arms overhead and yawns like a baby lion. His hazel eyes crinkle pleasantly and the lines between his eyebrows crease with character. He's holding that pose to really enjoy the stretch, giving me an unguarded moment to enjoy the sharp angle of his chin and the perfect symmetry of his face. When he's done, his eyes lazily open and meet mine, looking, as always, like he's just heard the funniest joke and he can't wait to share it.

He really is cute.

Cute from afar, I mean. There is to be no touching.

"So…" Kat begins. "What were you and Tim talking about back on the float?"

"I could tell you, but then I'd have to kill you," Lenny jokes.

"Seemed pretty profound," I add. "Especially since you hated him a few hours ago and then suddenly you're doing the arm-bump with him."

Lenny pauses and considers what to say. He turns to the guy in the aisle seat across from ours. "Hey, buddy?"

The man's got to be in his mid-to-late twenties. He takes his headphones off and looks up. A smile of recognition lights up his face. "MC Lenny?"

"Yeah, dude, that's moi," Lenny says. "Switch seats with me?"

"Cool!" the guy says, grabbing his gear and exiting the row. "You working on anything now?"

"Yeah, actually, I just landed a little project with Tim Cubix," Lenny says, winking our way.

"Excellent! Can't wait to see it, man."

Lenny moves aside to let the guy through. "Twelve C. I'll move my stuff in a sec." Then he sits and stretches his legs into the aisle. Seeing the three of us staring at him, he adds, "What?"

"Please elaborate," I say.

"You'll kill me, but tell all to a random stranger who just happens to know who you are?" Kat adds.

"Figure of speech," he says. "Not literal murder."

Lenny then tells us how Tim's been working on a project to help Haiti recover since their devastating earthquake a few years back. "His goal is to build twenty new schools, to replace some of those lost by the earthquake," Lenny says. "And to significantly raise the country's standard of education from where it had been before. Train teachers, recruiting from within Haiti, and empower the citizens through education. The program is called Build a Better Future."

"I remember when he made that announcement," I say. "It got a lot of press."

"Yeah, it did. But since then, the Future program has been sort of forgotten about. What with so many other initiatives in and around Haiti. At least, that's what Tim was telling me."

"So...let me guess." I smile, an idea forming. "He wants *you* to spread the word?"

Lenny nods.

"No shit," Kat says.

"Actually, Tim wants to create a song with an accompanying music video celebrating the completion of the twenty schools, to be released around Christmastime. Proceeds from the sale will go toward building even more schools, and other facilities, like homes and community centers. Tim said he's been in touch with a few rap singers and other musicians who agreed to take part in the work, but no one has stepped up to run the project." Lenny scratches his head for a moment and then adds, "It's the craziest thing, but…Tim wants me to spearhead it. He wants me to write the song and produce the video."

"Oh, Len…" I say. My eyes fill up with tears and I feel like an idiot. "No more accounting!"

"I know, right? It looks like Build a Better Future is the break I've needed to get out of a real job and into a dream one. Saying it aloud like this makes it almost seem true."

"Like 'We Are the World'!" Jodi says.

"Like 'Feed the World'!" Kat adds.

"Ooh!" Jodi says, interrupting our cheering. "Brainstorm!"

"What?" I ask.

"Can't tell. I want to talk to Len privately and see what he says first. And then I'll surprise you guys."

"Shall we rendezvous by the coffee urn in the back of the plane?" Lenny asks, already standing.

"Sounds lovely," Jodi says, stepping over me and Kat to get to the aisle.

Kat sighs. "It's nice that at least one of us has got something good lined up."

"You call the school yet? Talk to Martha?" I ask.

"Nope. Chicken," she says. "You call Doug yet?"

"Bwack," I say, trying to sound like the chicken that I am. Then I remember what Doug said to me last night on the phone. I quickly replay the conversation for Kat, to see what she thinks he meant.

"Wait, wait, wait," she says, shaking her head, "He actually said, 'Say hi to Kat and Jodi for me'?"

I nod.

"You sure? I mean, it was loud in that place. Maybe you misheard him and he said something like, 'I hide my cat in jury duty.'"

"What does that even mean?" I ask.

"I have no fucking idea. It sounded better in my head."

"Blue chips? Peanut mix?" a stewardess asks, pushing her cart up the aisle.

Kat turns to her with urgency. "Do you serve shots? Like, of very strong alcohol?"

"Kat," I say, "drinking won't solve our problems."

"True, that," she says, taking a few of the mini bottles offered up by the stewardess. "But it's fun anyway."

I put my hand on her wrist. "Please don't." She looks over to me and drops the bottles onto her tray, where they clink and roll around. "I need your help. Your sober, *real* help with this one. Doug knows something; I'm not sure *what* he knows, and I'm not sure *how* he knows whatever he knows. Plus, Martha's been calling me and e-mailing me and leaving messages with Doug asking as to my whereabouts. If the woman could text, she'd be doing that, too. I lied to my family, I lied to my employers. I think I might be coming home to a blitzkrieg."

"Maybe," Kat says. "But then again, maybe not."

A few minutes later, Jodi and Lenny return from their conference. Lenny immediately sits and takes out a notebook, flipping to an open page and writing quickly.

He laughs aloud to himself. "I've got the best song picked out..."

"Lenny, surprise, remember?" Jodi says. Still standing in the aisle, she asks me to fish her camera out of her bag and hand it to her. "Come on, Len, let's do this."

Lenny rolls his eyes and sighs, finishing whatever notes he was jotting down. "This takes some time, Jo, some planning and careful thought. I know it looks effortless, but it's not. It's hard work."

"Whatev, dude," she says, rolling her eyes right back at him in mock exasperation. I have no idea what they are planning, but if it involves Jodi, Len and a camera, then gyrating hips and a gangsta beat can't be far behind.

Len nods to himself, content with some thought, before he stands and moves with Jodi toward the back of the plane.

A gloomy New York sky greets us as we make our descent. Jodi gets teary-eyed as we say our good-byes at the baggage carousel. So much bonding has happened in the past day that it's really hard to see our small group go their separate ways.

Some security guards are consulting with Jodi about the plans for transporting her grandmother to a funeral home in Westchester. I think about Sonia Goldberg's funeral, planned for Sunday morning, and then remember our original plans for Saturday night. "Jo, you're not still planning to participate in the temple event tomorrow night, are you?" I ask.

She looks confused, then upset. "Of course I am!"

"I just thought, what with your grandmother and everything, you might have, you know, changed your mind about dancing?"

"Lauren," Jodi says, stepping closer to me. "Tomorrow night is probably even *more* important now that my grandmother is gone."

I'm not sure why that is, but I'm not going to argue. I nod instead. "Right. Well, then, Kat and I will see you there."

"And Doug?" Jodi asks.

"Depends on how much he hates me right now," I say. Just thinking about seeing him makes my stomach ache.

I turn to Lenny and try to shake his hand, formal but polite, like people who've just met at a technology seminar and now hope to keep in touch.

"Hug me, douche," he says, enfolding me in a giant embrace.

The fact that this statement brings tears to my eyes shows just how demented I am right now. I know that I can't go back to having Lenny as my dirty pen pal, and I'm not quite sure that I am ready to just be his friend. So this feels like a real farewell.

"I guess this is it," I say into his shoulder. "See you at the next high school reunion?"

"Oh, I'm pretty sure we'll be seeing each other sooner than that," he comments cryptically.

"Shake," Kat instructs, putting out her hand toward Lenny in a farewell gesture.

"I thought you hated me," he says.

"Nah, just hate what you stand for. Stood for. Tried to do," she says awkwardly, which is unlike her. "You know what I mean. Now that you aren't trying to break apart Lauren's marriage, you're growing on me."

"Aww...you're making me blush," Lenny jokes, grabbing Kat into a bear hug so big that she momentarily disappears. She emerges flushed, and tries to hide her embarrassment by grabbing her luggage and heading toward the exit.

I don't know if I've ever seen Kat blush before, not even when she told me about kissing Shay. MC Lenny's mystical charm.

I give Lenny a final wave and start following Kat, since she's my ride.

"You guys…" I hear Jodi call. She sounds weird, like something's not right. Kat stops near the exit and turns. Lenny and I turn, too. "You guys!" she calls again, louder this time, more frantically.

I spot Jodi leaning against a small sundries kiosk, looking like she can't stand up. I drop my bag and run across the length of the luggage-claim area to where she is. "Jodi," I ask, propping her up against my arm, "what happened?"

"Can you breathe, can you see? Are you hallucinating?" Kat asks, coming up behind me.

"Should we call the paramedics?" Lenny asks. Turning to me, he says, "Sit her down so she doesn't pass out and crack her head wide open on this tile."

I comply.

We all sit on the floor in a small, close circle, looking for signs that Jodi is okay. "Say something," Kat pleads.

Jodi shakes her head. She moves her hand instead, handing an object to us in the center of the circle.

It's her iPad. I put out my hand and catch it. We all look down.

EOnline.com is staring back at us, with a huge, full-color photo making the news headlines of the day.

It's a picture of us.

"Oy," Jodi says, finally speaking.

The headline reads "Tim Raises Awareness." Under that, the picture shows all of us atop the Crypt Ranger float. Tim, Dixie, me, Lenny, Jodi and Kat…all of us.

"What are we aware of?" I ask.

"*That's* your question," Kat says.

"Um, one of?" I clarify. "I mean, obviously, there are other, more pressing issues to deal with here, like the fact that *our cover is so blown* and *we are so dead*."

"But, naturally, you ask whether our efforts were humanitarian in any way," Lenny says. "Because you're generous like that."

"Exactly. Thank you," I say, giving Kat the finger.

"Oy," Jodi says. "Oy."

"Ditto that," Kat says, "and add a couple Hail Marys."

Kat and I will lose our jobs. Jodi and I will lose our husbands, our children.

Okay, maybe I'm being dramatic, but I've got to believe MasterCard at a time like this: The price of fun is truly priceless.

"I thought I wanted to be famous," Jodi says, finally moving away from Yiddish expletives.

"And so you are," I say. "Infamous, at any rate."

"Oy!"

"It's a pretty clear shot, actually. And we all look like we're having a blast," Kat says. "I really like it!"

"Here." Jodi shoos away her beloved iPad. "You can have it." She excuses herself to the bathroom. "I need to try and wash the guilt off my face."

Lenny intercepts the device and reads the blurb aloud. "*Rumors that Tim Cubix walked off the set of his latest picture,* Croc of Lies, *prove false after all. Cubix's manager explained to E! that when Tim got word of Miami's gay pride parade, he rushed to be by the side of his longtime friend—and Ruby Richmond impersonator— Dixie Normous. Dixie is a well-known figure in South Beach, beloved for her long legs, big lips and even bigger commitment to the legalization of same-sex marriage. 'I'm a humanitarian who happens to be an actor, not the other way around,' said Cubix, when asked about his choice to leave the production set for a day. 'The director of the film was in full support of my decision; he's not a snake like some other people in Hollywood. And this film's gonna rock!'*"

I smile. *Tim, your secret is safe with me*, I think.

I take another glance at the tabloid. Was that really us, only a few hours ago?

Kat's right, though. It's a great shot.

"And what about same-sex marriage?" I ask, looking at Kat.

"I'm all for it!" she says. "As long as I don't have to marry anyone of any sex anytime soon, it's cool with me."

Good answer, I think. Supportive but noncommittal in any personal way. "I knew I heard someone snapping photos this morning," I say.

"There was tons of press there, actually, come to think of it. I'm sure we're plastered all over the Internet by now," Kat says, seemingly bemused by this recent turn of events.

"And how do you think we're going to explain this to the Hadley School Board?" I ask.

"Tim needed us?" She shrugs, hearing how that sounds. "I dunno. We'll figure something out."

"And what if Lee sees this?" I ask, thinking of Jodi's husband and kids happening across this image on the web. "And…Doug?"

"Jodi needed us?" she says. "Jodi needed Tim?"

None of it sounds convincing.

"Oy vey," I say, for once agreeing wholeheartedly with Jodi.

CHAPTER 27

IT IS SIX O'CLOCK AT NIGHT. I stand outside the front door to my house, keys in hand, almost ready to come face-to-face with my husband. The truth is that even though I know Doug knows that I was with Jodi and Kat, I still plan on lying to him a little bit about the events of the past two days.

My logic is plain and simple. I took leave of my senses, and now I'm back. I have no interest in burdening Doug with details of my kiss with MC Lenny Katzenberg. That's in the past. I tried it, I didn't like it, I'm done with cheating. I'd like to spare Doug the humiliation and rage over one tiny indiscretion. And I'd like to spare myself the pain of having disappointed him, which I know I have.

I suppose I'm a coward. I'd like to avoid a big ugly scene where we yell and scream and cry. I'd like to think that, because I made a mistake and learned from it, I'm bringing my better self back to the marriage, and that's all Doug needs to know. I'd like to think that we can move forward together, without me having to acknowledge disloyalty from the recent past.

Right now, as I hear his footsteps moving solidly across the hard wood floors on my living room and approaching the front door, I like to think that that we can work this thing out nicely by just brushing it all under the carpet.

Doug opens the door, his face steady and unreadable. "Lauren," he says. "There you are." If he's surprised to see me a day earlier than expected, he doesn't show it. He pushes the door open further to reveal a police officer standing to his right.

Clearly, Doug has other plans for me.

....

I am seated on the living room couch, feeling much calmer now that I know the children are fine—at the park with Laney as we speak—and that, apparently, Doug doesn't want to have me arrested. Yet. But that's as much as I know.

I look to Doug for clarification, and he shushes me with his eyes. It's the same look he gives me when I'd like to rip into my mother-in-law during some perfectly awful Hallmark holiday, so I know it well. In those situations, Doug usually steps in, and here he does the same.

I eye the police officer, taking in his sandy buzz cut and bright blue eyes. He looks very young, like he's fresh out of the academy.

Doug and the officer are both standing, and I instantly wish I was, too, so that they wouldn't have this advantage of height over me. Doug begins speaking and comes over to sit near me, which is a nice touch, a showing of solidarity. "When you didn't show up for work today, Lauren, Martha Carrington over at the middle school called me at work *again*."

"Buh—" I begin. Doug holds up a finger to silence me. It works. Especially since I wasn't sure what I was going to say after the "but."

"But," he says, looking from me to the officer and back again, "as I told her many times, you have been sequestered for the week by the Alden County Courthouse and were expected to be released from your case tomorrow." His mouth is saying the words but his eyes are telling me that he knows this to be complete bullshit. There are some perks to a twelve-year marriage, and speaking volumes without actually talking is one of them.

"Yeah, buh—" I try again. The finger goes up, my mouth shuts.

The officer steps in now, to continue telling the story. "But Mrs. Carrington, working off her own information, seemed to believe that you had been released from jury duty several days ago, and that, since that time, there may have been some foul play involved in your more recent disappearance."

Martha gave me up to the feds!

I am quite certain now that I will never ever get the position of English chair.

Doug is looking down at his hands as the officer speaks, so I can no longer read his expression.

"Further, this Mrs. Carrington felt that your husband knew of your whereabouts but was covering up the real story with falsehoods."

Oh, and Lauren? Say hi to Jodi and Kat for me.

How can I make my face look completely startled by this revelation? I make my eyes wide and fake a gasp, which seems a bit too false, even to my own ears.

The policeman takes my outburst for an authentic bit of emotion. "I know, I know," he says. "It seemed farfetched to me, too."

I smile, and shrug it off as if to say, *What a crazy world we live in, right?* Feeling better, I stand and shake his hand before leading him out of the house. "Well, thanks so much for coming, officer..." I say.

"But then..." he says. My right hand meets his extended left hand, and I realize there's a folded piece of paper in it. He shakes it to let me know I should take it.

I open the tri-folded white page to find an exact copy of my jury duty release form, signed and dated on Tuesday. The officer clears his throat. "I decided to just call the courthouse and ask about your role as a juror. Turns out, Mrs. Carrington was correct; you were released on Tuesday. And it only took me about five minutes to clear that piece up!"

Well, doesn't he seem awfully proud of himself for getting off his ass and making a phone call.

"Oh yeah, that," I say, completely busted.

I need to sit. I hold my hands up to my eyes and try and push back the tears that are forming. I don't want to cry because of Martha. I must not let this officer see me break down. I remind myself that these are tears of anger, not sadness, and that helps me get a grip.

I'm angry for getting caught like this, and I feel like a complete fool for thinking I could just get away with such a stupid scheme in the first place. But mostly, I wish I didn't feel like I had to lie to Doug throughout this whole adventure, first to get down to Miami and now again upon returning.

I wish I could have seen some other way to get what I wanted without sneaking behind Doug's back. Because that's really what was corrupt about this unorthodox vacation choice of mine, the lying to Doug part. Not the cutting-school part; I see that now.

No. My inability to share my plans—and worse, my feelings— with my spouse is the real crime in my leave of absence.

I worry that my marriage will just crumble before my eyes, a house of cards collapsing, and yet I can't see any way to hold it all together.

Doug and the officer continue talking as I try to collect myself. Doug leads the policeman into the kitchen and I wonder, is he offering him coffee *now?* But then I hear their footsteps on the stairs and wonder if he's giving a house tour.

I mean, we'll probably get divorced and have to sell the house, but it seems a bit premature to show it off for sale at this very moment, doesn't it? What kind of a cold husband offers up the family home before the divorce papers have even been drawn up, I ask you?

I look around the living room as if I'm seeing it for the last time, and think, *I wish I had spent more time here with the children.* I love my home and, even though they sometimes drive me crazy, I love Ben and Becca. I feel safe here, in this warm family room that Doug and I created for our little family. For a moment, I have trouble remembering why I felt I had to run away.

The longer Doug and the officer are gone, the more I wonder what type of trouble I'm in with the police. Am I about to be charged with child abandonment, for leaving the kids with Laney? Or is he here to arrest me for a work-related crime? Do people get thrown in jail for leaving an uninspiring substitute teacher in charge of their English class for more than three days? It seems unlikely, although, based on my experiences over the past few days, I'd be hard pressed to say that anything is really unlikely anymore.

I imagine I'll be arrested any minute now, as soon as the officer is done looking in my walk-in closet or whatever he's doing. I hope Doug remembers to tell him that we've got central air now, too. That's a nice selling point. Then I mentally slap myself back to reality. Tears roll down my face, regret mixed with humiliation and fear. I wonder how long I'll be locked up and what my sentence will be: community service? Or something real, like a few months in one of those country club–like women's facilities in Bedford? Maybe I can plea insanity and get placed in an outpatient psychiatry program, with other upstanding citizens: moms, wives, and teachers who just went off the edge one day like I did, and only looked back after it was too late.

Although, I've got to say, I'm not feeling all that much regret right now. What did I really do wrong? I mean, sure, I lied to my employer and my family. I drank a lot of alcohol and peed in someone's bushes after gouging her face with my heel. I got on a plane and hung out with a bunch of cool people, famous, infamous, and non-famous alike. I kissed a man who is not my husband, after watching him do the worm. I got a tattoo and danced on a parade float.

Instead of acting forty, I acted like a college freshman on her first spring break.

But! I also helped some friends in need. Kat was going off the deep end with the psychic hotline. After kissing Shay Greene, she needed to vacay pronto, and thanks to me, that was possible. And when Jodi's grandmother died, who was there to make sure the body could get on the airplane in a timely fashion? Well, Tim Cubix did that, really. Tim Cubix *and me.*

Tim Cubix and me.

That cracks me up in like ten thousand different ways.

I can't wait to tell Doug all about it.

Then I remember I can't, and I feel lousy all over again.

When Doug and the policeman don't return after about eight minutes, I start to freak out. I wonder if Doug is trying to blackmail the guy by showing him my meager jewelry collection, or teaching him how to hack in to a popular pay-per-view porno website for free.

I stand up and move around the downstairs, trying to locate where they are on the second floor. I hear murmuring above me from the far side of the kitchen and know that they are in the office over the garage, where we keep the computer.

Creaking on the back stairs lets me know that the men are coming down to the kitchen. I grab a magazine from the pile of mail and pretend to be flipping through it at the center island, casually, as they enter the room.

"So," I say, gathering my courage. "Do you need to take me down to the courthouse or something? Book me on charges of abandonment or reckless endangerment or cutting class or whatever it is you're here for?"

Doug's head snaps up and he looks at me with sheer confusion. The police officer does the same. "*You*, Mrs. Worthing?"

"Yes. Me," I say, feeling very brave, holding my chin high in the air, like an actress playing the role of a falsely convicted death row inmate about to be taken to the electric chair.

"Well, I can't see why I would do that." He laughs uncomfortably, shifting his eyes toward Doug.

Doug shakes his head and locks his eyes on mine. "Lauren. Martha Carrington thought you had been *murdered*. The officer came here to question *me*."

"*What!*" I drop the magazine. Doug's finger moves to silence me again, but I won't stay quiet, not this time. "I'm not dead!"

The officer laughs. "Yes, well. I can see that."

"Not dead *yet*," Doug mumbles, raising his eyebrows at me.

The officer clears his throat and looks chagrinned. "Well, thank you for presenting me with your very alive wife, Mr. Worthing. It seems that I won't be needing you to come down to the station with me after all."

I wait for him to leave, but he's pretty rooted to the spot. I look up, wondering what the holdup is. Then the officer looks at me.

"Mrs. Carrington was quite agitated when we spoke on the phone yesterday. She said you had been acting erratically—calling the school and then hanging up in the middle of a conversation, hiding your face from her at the doctor's office—and she feared that you were in an abusive relationship, too fearful to reach out for help. I'll give her a ring once I get back to the station, but I think you should call her yourself. Once she knows the facts, I'm sure she'll be much relieved."

The facts? The last thing I want Martha to know are any and all facts.

Although she did try to, you know, save me from Doug, the wife-beating murderer. Which is nice of her, in a completely misguided way.

The cop seems embarrassed, and I wonder exactly what Doug was showing him upstairs. But then his words confuse me. "I just wanted to say...my cousin Bill is trying to marry his longtime boyfriend, and, well, even though I think it's kinda weird for a guy to marry another guy, I don't think it's my place to stop him, if that's what he wants."

"O*kay*," I say.

"So, I just really wanted to thank you for your hard work in raising awareness and all that money to help support gay rights."

I want to say, *What you talking 'bout, Willis?* But I catch a look from Doug that says, *Just go with it*, so I plaster a smile on my face and nod imperceptibly. "Why, yes, of course. It's my pleasure."

He's not quite through with me, yet, though. "And I was really sad about the earthquake in Haiti. So terrible, what happened."

"Indeed," I say, reaching to the floor and retrieving the magazine I had dropped, my thumb pressed into a cover shoot of Ruby Richmond. "May I show you the way out?" I gesture for him to follow me, and we exit the kitchen together and head down the hall toward the still-open front door.

The officer turns to me one last time. "So, when you get that autograph for me of Mr. Cubix and Ms. Richmond, could you just make sure the inscription reads: *Look who's dead now*? It's my favorite quote, from *Black Dawn Redux*."

I swallow my surprise. "Absolutely!" I chirp. "They will be just delighted to do that for you, officer!"

Then I close the door behind me with my full weight and turn, sighing with relief.

Doug is already there, standing in the hallway, which makes me jump with surprise. He does not look happy.

"You left a paper trail a mile high, Lauren. Every time you bought something and charged it to our Visa card, I knew where you were and what you were doing, okay? Lunch on the beach at the Loews Hotel, Miami? Drinks at the Clevelander? No big mystery. Not to mention, you wouldn't be able to use your cell phone all week long if you were really sequestered! Now, do you mind telling me what the fuck is going on?"

CHAPTER 28

MY MOUTH IS WIDE OPEN and I'm really, really, really thinking about spilling my guts and telling Doug the whole truth and nothing but, till death do us part or whatever, when the door opens and my kids sort of tumble inside with Laney.

"Hi!" I cry out, staring into Ben's and Becca's round, blue eyes, both smaller versions of my own. I grab Ben and hug him to me. "I missed you guys so much!"

"Mom!" he shouts. "You're back!"

Becca joins the chant. "Ma! Ma!"

"You got taller," I tell him, letting him go and measuring him against my torso. He beams with pride. Then I pick up Becca. She smells like sugar and Play-Doh and is even pudgier than I remember her being on Wednesday.

Nothing makes me love my children more than being away from them for two days.

"Ah! You are home!" Laney sighs, looking totally wiped out. Her hair has leaves in it and has been pulled out of its ponytail, into a sort of rat's-nest halo. Although there are bags under her eyes, she looks completely delighted to see me, and immediately begins handing off the children like batons at a relay race. She props open the door with one foot, afraid that if it closes, she might never be allowed to leave.

"Becca ate some Doritos at the park. She needs a bath tonight because she didn't get one yesterday, and she has some paint stuck in her hair. See?" Laney points to the offending bits of blue, then inhales in order to finish the rest of her diatribe. "Ben is hungry and ready for dinner *now,* and also he needs some help with his spelling because he has a test tomorrow. Becca's teacher called and said she has been bullying some of the boys on the playground. Bye!" She waves, grabbing her giant pocketbook, which probably has something of mine stuffed deep inside.

"Thank you!" I call. "Have a great weekend! See you Monday!"

This last comment stops her short. She turns around on the steps leading to the driveway, shaking her head. "Not Monday. It's my vacation next week. I'll see you the week after, remember?"

I try to rack my brain for some sort of clue, a memory of a conversation, letting me know that I'm not hearing this information for the first time.

"South Beach, Miami. Remember? With my girlfriends? For spring break?"

Oh, the irony.

Laney must have told me this, might have even asked my permission before scheduling the trip, though she doesn't always. But something about it doesn't feel right. How could I forget a huge issue like my babysitter leaving *for a week*?

As if sensing my hesitation, Laney continues. "It's the same time as your school vacation," she prods. "You told me I could go." Now she's pouting, arms crossed defiantly across her chest.

This is what it's going to be like to have teenagers, I realize. I'm not going to like it.

"What day is today?" I ask no one. Doug has taken the kids into the kitchen and hasn't even been a part of this conversation. I now step all the way outside to address Laney. "My school vacation begins the week after, on the twenty-fourth. This Monday is only the seventeenth."

"Oops!" Laney says, not seeming the least bit regretful. "See you in *two* weeks, then!"

Great. As I watch her disappear down the driveway with her huge pocketbook bulging, I feel almost certain that my favorite cover-up is going to Florida after all.

Once the children are asleep, I find myself alone with Doug in our bedroom. I pretend to busy myself with unpacking the rest of my bag.

"So..." Doug begins. "Are you going to answer my question or not?"

The old Lauren certainly would have given in by now. She might have cried, or begged for forgiveness, or apologized a thousand times over. Although, who knows what the old Lauren would have said or done, since she probably wouldn't have taken leave in the first place, right?

The post-Miami me decides on an offensive attack, albeit in a loud whisper so as not to wake the kids down the hall. "I might ask you the same. What the hell is going on here, Doug? What could you have possibly said to that police officer when you disappeared upstairs to make him think I can get him an autographed picture of Tim and Ruby?"

"Tim and Ruby, huh?" he says, a dimple creasing his left cheek. "Those are some familiar terms you're using for mega superstars."

He is really handsome, my husband. And, so far, he hasn't yelled at me, or given me the silent treatment, or marched right out of the house. So far, he hasn't done any of the things that I thought he would do. He's surprised me. He's been patient, even in the face of being questioned about my alleged disappearance and possible murder.

"Lauren, it's time," he says, looking tired, looking sad. "You need to tell me."

And so I do.

Well, everything but the kiss.

When your husband of twelve years listens to your story, the one in which you do not act like the good mother, teacher, daughter, or wife that you have always been, you cry. You cry because, for the first time in a long time, he's listening.

He listens, and he hears you. And he says that he doesn't know how you grew so far apart so fast, and that you're not the only one to blame. He tells you how much he missed you, not just while you were on leave but for months and months before then. He tells you that he's so anxious about work that he doesn't know how you are going to make ends meet. You tell him that you recently spent a lot of money frivolously but that you'll tutor and make it up somehow. But you make it clear that you are keeping the shoes, the bag, and the sweater. He tells you that the Botox looks okay, but he would prefer you grow old naturally and gracefully with him.

You tell him that, sometimes, you can't breathe. That life as his wife and as the mother to these beautiful sleeping children and as the teacher to these sixth graders feels claustrophobic and stifling. You tell him that, sometimes, you're not sure who you are anymore because you're only defined by your relationships to other people.

When your husband of twelve years tells you that he loves you, truly, madly, and deeply, whoever you are or think you are, but that if you ever pull another stunt like that he really will kill you, you kiss him.

And then you have sex with him.

Twice.

CHAPTER 29

Saturday

I HAVE NEVER BEEN SO EXCITED to talk to my principal in my whole life. I've been up since six a.m., just waiting.

"Do you think I can call her yet?" I ask Doug from my perch at the kitchen island. "Do you? Do you?" The clock reads 9:01 a.m.

"I think four coffees is about three too many," he says, handing me the phone. "You're shaking like a Chihuahua."

I flip over the middle school faculty handbook, which lists everyone's home phone numbers. I have committed Martha's number to memory after staring at it for the past few hours.

"Lauren!" she says, picking up on the first ring. She sounds quite jolly for a Saturday morning. "I heard from that nice police fellow! You've been found!"

I laugh along good-naturedly before taking a deep breath and replying, "Well, to tell you the truth, Martha, I've never been more lost."

We agree to meet for coffee in an hour, at a local spot called the Grind. "My treat. There are some things I should probably explain," I say.

"Me, too," she says.

The line goes dead, but I find myself still holding the phone to my ear. Did I hear her correctly?

I spend that hour driving Ben to a basketball game and taking Becca to gymnastics.

"Mom, tie my sneakers and put some more air in my ball,"

Ben demands as we head out the door. He stands in the foyer like an invalid, waiting for me to get him ready for his activity.

My body moves toward his out of some remembered, instinctive reflex. Then I pull back, willing myself not to blindly obey.

Instead, I cross my arms and give him a knowing look.

"What?" Ben asks. "Oh, right. *Please*," he adds.

I shake my head. "Try again."

"She wants you to do it yourself!" Becca explains, reveling in the fact that she can simultaneously score points with me while upsetting her brother.

Ben gives me a long stare, which I hold, until he breaks the trance by dropping the basketball on the wooden floor and bending down to tie his laces. Next, head still down, he picks up the ball and heads out to the garage, where we keep the air pump.

My children hop out of the car, listen to their coaches, and play nice with the other members of their teams. It seems that, as long as my children are busy and apart from each other—and slightly afraid of me—this day will go smoothly.

There is a silver lining to this trend of overscheduling one's children, I'm telling you.

The Grind is dark and slightly grimy, and it has that heady smell of freshly ground coffee beans. I inhale deeply and move past the students from the local college who are lining up for their morning Joe and a homemade flaky croissant. Before I had kids, I liked to come here and grade papers on weekend mornings. The scent of coffee would get trapped in my hair; I would pull it to my face and relive it for the rest of the day. Someone should make a perfume that smells like the Grind, because I'd totally wear it.

It's no surprise that Martha is punctual, arriving at ten o'clock on the dot. I watch her for a moment before revealing my location in the back of the cramped, beatnik-inspired space. She readjusts the stiff, black pocketbook on her arm and then hesitantly touches her hairsprayed coif.

Martha is nervous.

I get her attention by standing, calling out her name and waving, a big smile plastered on my face. I am not sure what to expect from her today, but an offensive attack of kindness can't hurt.

I have already purchased us two coffees and some blueberry scones, not really caring what she'd like to eat or drink.

"Lauren!" Martha blinks at me, and I think there might be tears in her eyes. We stare at each other for a moment as I wait for her next move. As I've mentioned, Martha's age slides somewhere between fifty and a hundred and fifty, depending on the occasion and how the light hits her. (Her oldest look is under fluorescent lighting while disciplining a child; her youngest look is at sunset while disciplining a parent at the annual school picnic.) Today, perhaps because I'm seeing her completely out of context, perhaps due to the fact that she's wearing jeans and a T-shirt, she looks more youthful than ever before.

Martha grabs me in an awkward embrace, my torso bending toward her while my butt hovers over my wooden chair, hands pinned to my sides. When she lets go, I sort of fall right into my seat.

"Well!" I say. "That was a bit unexpected."

"Yes," she agrees. "It's odd for me to admit, even to myself, but it seems that I am happy to see you alive." She smiles sadly.

"Gee, thanks."

"The thing is..." she begins, and then, thinking better of it, stops herself.

I am intrigued; I want to know where this is heading. "Please, continue."

"I...I get the sense that you despise me. Don't shake your head at me, Lauren, and try to deny it. I see it in your eyes, have always seen flashes of hatred there. And I just want to know *why*." She rubs her hand against her forehead, as if she's in pain from all this thinking, and instantly I know: Botox! That's why she looks so much younger today, and that's why she was at Dr. Grossman's on Tuesday.

The world truly is full of surprises.

Then I remind myself: *Focus, Lauren. Tell her why you hate her.*

And then, *Why do you hate her?*

If there is one thing I have learned this week, it's to cut through the bullshit and be honest, with myself first, and then (mostly) with others, even if that means I'm not going to come out looking perfect. I'm thinking of Lenny. I'm thinking of Kat, and Jodi, and, for the most part, of Doug. "I hate *you* because you hate *me*!"

There. That was easier than I thought.

Though now that I hear it out loud, it sounds really stupid and childish.

Like we're middle schoolers.

"This is about the department chair position, isn't it?" Martha twitches.

A week ago, my answer would have been a quick yes. But now, with everything that I've experienced and reflected on this week, I have to stall for a moment, to consider my response.

I tear off a corner of the scone and try to chew. It's stale and dry and I end up coughing bits of pastry into the space between us. *Cool, Lauren, keep it cool.* I imagine myself at the Clevelander with Tim Cubix, crying together over the way life is messy and, therefore, beautiful. I sip from the coffee cup and answer. "At some point I guess it was about that job. But now, it's about so much more than that, you can't even imagine."

I tell her just enough about my trip to Miami to make it sound more like a soul-searching weekend at a retreat in India than the complete and utter pleasure bender that it was.

"I can't imagine wanting to escape, hmm?" she says, her hands folded tightly over the pocketbook in her lap. "Lauren, do you even know anything about me?"

Only that you were fashioned in a mad scientist's lab, put together from parts of an old Buick LeSabre and several defunct administrators, then sent to my school to try and ruin my good time.

She blinks. "That's what I thought. Nothing."

And so, I look at her more closely and begin to wonder. Is she married? There's no ring. Does she have children? Or cats or dogs, a backyard, a foot fetish? Where does she live?

I don't even know how she takes her coffee, and I don't even care that I don't know. I never asked.

Who's the hater, now, Lauren?

"Mrs. Worthing—" she begins, and I think, *Great, we're back to that.* "I thought you were being abused."

"Well, in a way, I was!" I say, trying to explain my point of view, to have her really understand me for once.

She is not amused. "I thought the recent changes in your behavior had to do with signs of personal distress."

"But they were! I was distressed!" I counter.

She shakes her head and keeps speaking over me. "I observed you, I asked around. And then, when your husband covered up for you like that, I thought you were in trouble with him, like I had been, once, with my husband. I called the police because of genuine concern for your well-being. Someone once did the same for me and it saved my life."

Well, piss on my leg and tell me it's raining. I try to imagine her being afraid, being hurt, being in danger. I try to see beneath her cool surface, to the origin of the twitch, to the crack beneath. It's hard to fathom. "Really?"

"I don't make a habit of lying."

Yes, bad habit.

"I'm so..." I begin, about to say "sorry," but then I look up from my awful scone and see that she has *emotion* on her face.

I think of her cyborg-like manner, the distance she has always kept from me and everyone else at school. And for the first time, I realize that living that way must be very lonely, and possibly, very sad.

"I'm so glad you told me, Martha," I say, reaching across the sticky wooden table to take her hand.

She smiles sadly, wiping a few stray tears on the back of her brown sleeve. "You're still not getting that promotion, you know," she says. "Even if you are being nice to me."

"Look at you, cracking the jokes."

"Except that I'm being serious."

I have to remember who I'm dealing with here.

"That's fine," I say, taking my hand back, relieved that we are at least talking about it. "I was more embarrassed than anything when you passed me over. In truth, I don't think administrivia is really my thing."

Martha stands to alert me that our meeting is coming to a conclusion. I do the same. What I want her to say is, *Oh, I think you'd make a fine administrator, but I just couldn't afford to lose you as a classroom teacher since you show so much brilliance there.*

Instead, her cool formality is back, as firmly in place as her hair. Martha dumps the untouched coffee and scone into the garbage bin and adjusts her pocketbook awkwardly on her shoulder. Then she turns to me and smiles. "I agree, Lauren. Administration is not your thing."

We walk together toward the front of the coffee shop, me licking my wounds and Martha lost in thought. I push open the glass door and hear the bell chime overhead. The dewy spring air smells like rain.

"Oh, and another thing, Mrs. Worthing."

I roll my eyes and face Martha. "Call me Lauren, *please,*" I beg.

She nods curtly. "Another thing, *Lauren.* You will write up and then sign a report detailing how you spent your week's leave. This will be shared with the superintendent and placed in your permanent personnel file. Should you ever disappear on us again, you will be terminated."

I swallow, and look at the ground, concentrating on the flecks of glass shining in the pavement. Now that I hear my job truly is in jeopardy, all I want to do is keep it safe from harm.

I think.

I picture Martin and his antics, and the never-ending parade of essays and homework just waiting for me to collect, grade, and return.

Doug needs me to work. Maybe even I need me to work. But do I want it to be there, at the same middle school where I began my career?

I think of my tiny notebook with just one promising research idea scribbled inside.

I really need to put in a call to Georgie.

"And you will be docked for three days' pay. Monday and Tuesday, as we know, were actually spent on jury duty. The other days will not be covered by the district."

I wonder if Martha is a fan of Tim and Ruby. Now there's a plan: I could just go around town handing out autographed pictures in lieu of taking responsibility or managing any fallout from the week's adventures.

Instead, I shake Martha's hand. "Of course. Consider it done."

Even with all of the reprimands and punitive actions taken, I walk away feeling completely relieved. Why? Because Martha doesn't seem to know anything about Kat's role as my accomplice.

CHAPTER 30

I PICK UP MY CHILDREN from their activities and bring them home to rest and play. Doug and I challenge them to a huge Wii Sport competition in the basement, girls against boys.

"Mom, you suck at golf," Ben says merrily, as he watches me sink the ball into the water four times in a row. "Just forfeit."

"Never!" I say. "I will never give up. And use the word 'stink' instead, please."

"Sorry," he says, quickly and with sincerity.

I smile back and give him the thumbs-up while holding the Wii remote, thereby sending another golf ball off a cliff and into the water.

"You're better than me, Mommy," Becca says. Which is true. We're so going to lose this game.

"Let's switch to shooting those ducks and balloons out of the sky," Doug suggests. "Mom's really good at that one."

We play silently for a few minutes, each of us concentrating on racking up as many points as possible for our team.

Then Ben turns to me. "I missed you," he says.

"I'm glad you came back," Becca adds. Her particular choice of phrasing makes me wonder if she was worried I might not return.

"Oh, Bec, the best thing about going away is coming back." I put down the remote and pull both children to me, and inhale the warm, slightly puppy-dog smells trapped in their hair. "I'm sorry I had to go away in the first place."

I look at Doug while saying it.

"I think we need to set some new house rules about how we talk to each other and how we treat one another, okay, guys? So that everyone stays here and stays happy," Doug says. "We'll have a family meeting tomorrow night at dinner, when Mommy and I have more time."

"Okay," I say along with Ben and Becca. I know that not every minute with my family will be as warm and tender as this one. But it's nice to have this one, right here and now.

"Who wants to come with me to pick up the new babysitter and a pizza?" he asks, looking at his watch.

Temple Beth El is aglow with spotlights as Doug and I pull in to the parking lot. It's clear that there is an event here tonight, and that it's going to be huge, like the opening of a new Target in a strip mall.

Doug hands the car keys to a valet wearing a robe and fake beard.

"Jesus, they are taking this fundraising effort really seriously, aren't they?" Doug asks as we walk up the steps of the midcentury-modern temple, a red carpet cascading under our feet.

"Moses, you mean."

"The party's theme tonight is *Dancing with the Stars,*" I tell Doug. "Jodi's pretending she's not that into it, but I think it's her dream come true." At the top of the stairs, we stop, greeted by life-size cutouts of each of tonight's Beth El "stars." Six members of the temple's congregation pose and smile with cardboard stiffness. I put my arm around "Jodi"—tight black dress, high heels, auburn highlights, hand placed defiantly on one curved hip—and Doug snaps a picture of us with his phone.

And that's when I see her. Well, not the *real* her, but her like-ness, right next to Jodi's frozen self. I can almost hear her calling me a bitchwhoreasshole through clenched teeth.

Even in cardboard, Leslie scares the crap out of me.

I grab Doug by the arm and try to lead him out of the building. "We have to leave. Go. Home. Now."

"What is it, her gift? Just bring it to her another time," he says. "I'm not driving back fifteen minutes for something you forgot."

Thing is, seeing Leslie, I realize that I forgot my balls.

I try another tactic. "Might vomit. Very ill. Chills. Legionnaire's disease."

"You mean, like, from a cruise?" Doug is studying me hard.

"Ballots here!" a voice calls from a table set up nearby. "Buy some extra ballots for tonight's fundraiser."

Despite my desire for immediate flight from the building, Doug and I walk over to the table and give the volunteer our names. She hands us an envelope containing our tickets for entry to the ballroom and two pink ballots. "You can buy extras if you'd like," the woman explains. "They are two for ten or four for *c-c-chai*." She spits the Hebrew word for eighteen with a good deal of throaty phlegm.

"Ah, *there* you are! I've been looking all *over* for you!" Jodi calls, grabbing me by the arm and pulling me inside. "Doug, go find Lee and help him with the cameras. I need Lauren's help getting ready."

I fake-smile and wave good-bye to Doug as Jodi drags me into the peachy, plush interior of the Beth El ladies' room.

And just like that, I'm trapped. Trapped in temple.

"Jo," I say, collapsing into an overstuffed armchair and trying not to panic, "do you know Leslie Koch?"

"Yeah, sure. She's one of the crazy bitches who's dancing with me tonight." She leans into the glass and applies more makeup to her already flawless look. "I don't know her all that well, really. But the word is, she had some sort of accident the other night and now her face is all fucked—" She stops midcurse and turns, lip gloss wand extended toward me as an accusation.

"Up," I say. "Fucked up. What did Kat say? Six stitches?"

"That was *Leslie Koch's* sex-toy birthday party? With the kissing of girls and dancing round poles?"

"And the gashing of hostesses...yes, Jo!"

"That means...*your* dominatrix is the president of *our* sisterhood!"

"Small world," a chilly voice from behind a bathroom stall says. A flush follows.

Jodi mouths the word "Leslie" to me, and I mouth the word "Duh" to her. I have my hand on the door handle and am about one second away from freedom when Leslie's words stop me.

"Always running from the scene of the crime, aren't you, Lauren?"

I let go of the door and turn to face what's left of Leslie's face.

Her entire right cheek is covered in gauze held in place with surgical tape. The rest of her face is masked in huge sunglasses. She slides them up to her hairline and lets them rest there, so that Jodi and I can have a good, long look at the full horror.

And look we do.

It's really so much worse than anything I could have imagined. Her eyes are rimmed in purplish green and the whole top half of her face is puffy. "Did I...did I also break your *nose*?" I whisper-ask.

She merely nods.

Then she reaches up and removes the gauze from her cheek, displaying a gnarly, jagged line of stitches caked over in dried blood.

"Yikes," Jodi says.

That's when I notice the bandages on Leslie's hands. "What happened there?" I ask, gesturing to the Band-Aids covering both palms.

"When you knocked me to the living room floor, I broke my nose against the coffee table and then cut my hands on some shards of glass from a broken, *priceless* Baccarat vase that you will have to pay for."

I try to remember that scene from Wednesday night, and shake my head. "I'm really sorry about hurting you with the heel of my shoe, Leslie. Really, I regret it more than words can say, and I'm hoping I can find some way to make it up to you. But the rest I didn't do. The coffee table had been moved out of the way, to make room for the pole dancing."

"According to who?" she asks, moving in so close that I can smell the kosher hors d'oeuvres on her warm breath. "It's your word against mine, Worthing, isn't it? Everyone at my party *saw* you gash my face. Everyone *saw* you and Kat run for the door, and everyone—"

"That's because you were calling me a—" I cut in, in my defense.

"I was a *wonderful* hostess through and through, and you shat on me!" She steps away from me and toward the sink, where she calmly dispenses soap into her hands and begins to scrub between the bandages. She looks at us reflected behind her in the mirrored wall. "Who do you think a jury would believe?"

Jodi and I stand there, mouths open, trying to take in the fact that I'm being fucked sideways.

Yes, who would a jury believe?

"But—" I begin. "But—you said you had the whole thing

caught on tape! From a nanny cam!" Not that this would help my case exactly, but at this point I think it must be better to have proof of the terrible acts I really did do, rather than being framed for the awful things I didn't.

Leslie smiles with half her mouth, like that character from *The Dark Knight* after his face melts and he turns all evil. "Maybe I have it, and maybe I *lost* it."

"'Shat' is such a weird word, isn't it?" Kat says. "I never like how it sounds." We all turn toward her voice.

"I slipped in unnoticed at some point during her tirade," she explains. Turning to Leslie, she adds, "Quite a performance. I only hope you can be as convincing out there in the ballroom tonight."

Leslie stays cool. "Well, if it isn't Lauren's little garden gnome."

"A short joke! How original," Kat says. "Jodi, don't you have to get out there now? I think you're on first." Jodi and I move toward the door like lost sheep finally collected by our loving shepherd.

We are out in the hallway when we hear Leslie's parting words. "Oh, Kat? Make sure to slip Jodi some tongue when you kiss her good luck tonight. I know how much you like the pretty ones!"

Which can only mean one thing: she's seen the videos.

"Wow, she's got a dark side I never saw at Sharing Shabbat," Jodi says, shuddering. "Not to mention, she did that Keratin treatment on her hair this week, and now she looks like a drowned rat."

"That's what you noticed about her appearance, Jo?" I ask. "Her newly straightened, processed *hair*?" Then I turn my attention to Kat. "You okay?"

She reaches for her phone and begins tap-tapping in a way that's reminiscent of the gestures that preceded our trip to South Beach. "Oh, I'm just awesome," she says. "Fan-fucking-tastic." She turns away from us, her phone glowing ominously.

"No more trips, Kat!" I joke, but she waves me away, half-listening.

Then I turn my attention to Jodi. "*You* going to be okay?" I ask, worried that Jodi might have lost her focus before her Big Night. The three of us walk toward the ballroom together as crowds of people are being ushered to their seats.

"I'm fine," she says, taking a deep breath. "My whole family is here to support me, and you guys are here, and I've been practicing this for months, and now I get to do it in my grandmother's honor." She pauses, tears in her eyes. "It's going to be a beautiful evening. Nothing can spoil it for me."

"Amen to that, ladies," MC Lenny says, swooping down over our little huddle and making me jump.

"Lenny!" Jodi smiles, embracing him. "I was getting worried!"

"Because...he's *supposed* to be here?" Kat asks, putting her phone into her bag.

"That's what I was wondering." I quickly scan the hallway for signs of Doug. This is very wrong. I feel faint. I glare menacingly at Jodi, who seems oblivious to my pain, her arm tucked neatly into the crook of Lenny's elbow.

By making her plans for tonight, whatever they are, Jodi has unwittingly fucked with the space-time continuum of my universe.

"See, Lauren?" Lenny says, turning toward me. "I told you at the airport yesterday that I had a feeling I'd be seeing you again soon."

"Oh yes, I see!" I smile painfully and take two baby steps away from him. "So very soon!"

"And why is that again?" Kat asks.

Lenny smiles. "Ah, Kat. How I've missed you."

"Don't tell them, Len. I want it to be a surprise until the very last moment!" Jodi says, jumping up and down like a cheerleader. "Lee and the kids don't know, my parents don't know, only the rabbi does...it will be a*maz*ing." Motioning to Kat and me, Jodi says, "Now, you guys go in and let me work with Lenny, here."

Great. My husband and my crush at the same temple event with a woman who wants to kill me. I'm not a very religious person, but I've got to believe that Someone is seriously testing me.

CHAPTER 31

I'M NOT SURE WHAT I EXPECTED, but the temple's ballroom is underwhelming. Try as they might, there is little a decorations committee can do to hide the fact that the place was constructed in the late 1960s, with parquet wood floors, low-grade ceiling tiles, and few windows. Fifteen or so large, round tables circle the dance floor, each draped in a gold tablecloth. A lone, sad-looking mirror ball dangles from the ceiling.

I find Doug wilting patiently in line behind mostly old people at one of the beverage stations set up in the dank corners of the room.

Kat slinks off to say hi to the side of the family that binds her to Leslie.

"Would you care for some Mt. Eden chardonnay?" Doug says, handing me a plastic cup with a urine-sample-sized amount of yellow liquid in the bottom. "Apparently, it's being rationed."

Doug and I are good. We had a heart-to-heart followed by makeup sex.

Then why do I suddenly feel so ill at ease around him?

"Lauren." Doug clears his throat, as if he has something important to say. My stomach clenches involuntarily.

"Mm?" I say, downing the entire shot of wine in one gulp. It's sickly sweet and will probably give me an instant headache, but I hold my cup out for a refill anyway. Doug takes the bottle of wine from the bartender and fills my glass to the top.

"Promise me something." He places the bottle back on the bar and meets my gaze.

"Mm," I say, taking a kosher egg roll from a passing waiter and popping it into my mouth. It's hard to swallow with my heart lodged in my throat.

"No matter how tempted you might be…"

"Mm?" I ask, taking giant gulps of wine while scanning the room for signs of Lenny.

"...do not bid on or purchase *anything* at tonight's auction."

"Oh!" I exhale. "I can so promise that!"

Doug does not look convinced. "You say that every time we attend one of these functions, and then you drink some wine and peruse the silent auction table, and the next thing I know, we've won a three-hour tented party with a DJ."

"In my defense, that was a good idea. But I did not see the fine print that read 'Good only on a Tuesday between the months of December and March.'"

"And...?"

"And there was no way of knowing that Making Moves LLC was bankrupt and would fold the following week."

Doug gives me a lopsided smile. "You know what I mean."

"Fine," I say. "No bidding and no buying. I swear."

We move toward our assigned table, where we are seated as guests of distinction with Jodi's family. I give my condolences to Jodi's three daughters, who are all dressed in shades of pale pink perfection, one prettier than the next. Lee is setting up a tripod that's cradling a video camera directed at the center of the ballroom. He makes one final adjustment, then takes Doug's arm in a masculine, handshake-like greeting.

"Dudes! How the heck are you?" Lee's laid-back manner is reflected in his casual dress of jeans and an untucked button-down. His blue eyes sparkle as he surveys the room.

"So sorry about Sonia," I say.

Lee nods solemnly. "She was quite the lady. Jodi's family will miss her. On one side, she had a Holocaust survivor, and on the other side, a Ziegfeld Girl!"

My mind flashes back to the Hebrew Home for the Aged in Miami and the images of Sonia in elaborate dance costumes crowding her room. I have a pretty good idea which history was hers.

"Oh, also, Mazel Tov!" I add, kissing Lee's cheek and sitting next to him.

Lee reaches for a huge camera outfitted with a telephoto lens and begins to fidget with it.

"Hi-yyy!" Jodi, making the rounds, has arrived at her own table.

"Hey! My beautiful wife. I made a plate of apps for you." Lee motions to a mound of kosher egg rolls to his left.

"Ugh! Are you *crazy*? I've been too nervous to eat all *day*, Lee, *you* know that."

"I do." He winks at us, head nodding in agreement. He then raises a glass of water to toast her. "As I was saying: to my beautiful, skinny wife!"

Jodi rolls her eyes, her anxiety palpable. "I *can't* take another *minute* of this. I'm going to get *changed*."

"Changed?" Doug whispers my way.

"Yeah. The dress she has on now is just for the 'meet and greet' portion. She bought something off the Internet for the main event."

"I think I'm starting to like this evening a bit more now," Doug says.

Leslie enters the room and scans the crowd, no doubt looking for her family, with Lenny walking in right behind her. I hide behind Doug's shoulder.

A man with an elaborately decorated tallith grabs a microphone and stands on the podium set up at the front of the room.

"Ladies and gentlemen, welcome. I am Rabbi Cantor—and, no, I don't sing!" There is a smattering of tired laughter from around the room; he probably feels compelled to tell the joke every time he introduces himself, poor guy. "If you will take your seats, we plan to begin the evening's festivities in about five minutes."

"Awwwright," Lee says, rubbing his hands together. "Time to do one last check on my AV setup."

Kat stops by on the way to her assigned table, waving hello to Jodi's daughters and then to Doug. "Shalom," she says. "You guys have room for me at your table?" she asks. "I'm flying solo. I decided not to invite the estranged Peter tonight, for reasons linked to his obvious douchebaggery."

Doug smiles back at her. "Hi, O'Connell. How was your trip?"

Kat looks at Doug and, without missing a beat, says, "Mr. Worthing, I don't know what the eff you're talking about. Excuse me for a moment, will you?" Then she pushes past a nearby couple and disappears from view.

Now, that's one way to avoid the truth. I guess she'll be sitting at her assigned table instead of squeezing in with us.

Doug and I settle into our seats as the lights dim. Someone pulls down a video screen, and the rabbi speaks into the microphone again. He takes a small slip of paper from his pocket, unfolds it, and puts on his bifocals. "If an MC Lenny could please come up to the front?"

Lenny is dressed in dark-washed jeans, crisp white shirt and a midnight-blue velvet blazer that instantly sets him apart from the rest of this crowd. He adjusts a neon-yellow yarmulke on his head that reads *Livin' on a Prayer* in Hebraic-type font. He sort of leaps onto the podium and grabs the mic from the rabbi, easily moving into a greeting of "Yo, yo, yo, Temple Beth El! The *Jews* are in the *house!*"

This gets a tepid response, with only slightly more applause than Rabbi Cantor's joke about his own name. Lenny smiles at the crowd and changes course. "What I mean is, what's up? *Mah koreh?*"

"This kid, he's Jewish?" Lee's great-aunt leans over and whispers to no one in particular. "He's some kind of entertainer, like a magician?"

"He's an accountant," I clarify. "With a penchant for popular culture."

She shrugs and waves her hand across the space, like it doesn't really matter what I say; she's already decided that he's an ass.

Lenny continues. "As many of you may know, this week, we lost a wonderful member of our Jewish community, and the Moncrieffs—located at table nine, can I get a spotlight on them, please, thanks—lost a beloved member of their family. That is why Temple Beth El would like to dedicate tonight's events to the memory of Sonia Goldberg, beloved great-grandmother, grandmother, mother, and friend." He pauses as real applause fills the room. "Jodi?"

Jodi emerges from behind the ballroom doors. The spotlight finds her and there is a collective intake of breath.

Because, ladies and gentlemen, she is breathtaking.

Picture a petite version of Cindy Crawford with a dash of Fran Drescher thrown in for attitude. Toss in a black-fringed micromini spandex dress, fishnet stockings, and patent leather fuck-me pumps, and you've got one-tenth of the idea.

"This is a memorial?" Jodi's great-aunt asks. "For my sister, Sonia?"

"And so much more, Aunt Elaine," Lee adds.

With a hand from Lenny, Jodi manages to step up to the podium without showing much of her black lace underwear. Under the spotlights, her makeup sparkles and her hair cascades in a shiny burnt-red mane. "Thank you all so much for coming this evening to support us here at Temple Beth El." She pauses and lets her gaze travel meaningfully around the room, milking this moment for all that it's worth. "As Lenny just mentioned, we lost my grandmother this past week in Miami."

And then we found her, I feel like adding.

"It was a tremendous blow to us all, softened only by the fact that I had traveled to Florida to see her the day before."

"As they say, timing is everything!" Lenny adds over Jodi's shoulder.

Jodi is only momentarily flustered by this unexpected out-burst and quickly silences Lenny with a death stare before turning back to her adoring fans. "As many of you know, my grandmother, Sonia Goldberg, was a Ziegfeld Girl in the 1930s. She was passionate about Judaism, gardening, and borscht-belt comedians."

"Which is why Morris eventually left her," Great-Aunt Elaine adds, none too softly.

With tears welling up in her eyes but not quite ruining the mascara, Jodi comes to her conclusion. "And so, I have asked my very talented friend here, MC Lenny Katzenberg, to put together a video montage with musical accompaniment as a dedication to Sonia's rich and varied life." Applause follows, with standing ovations. "Lenny, if you will?"

"Of course, Jodi," Lenny says, taking over the coveted spot at the mic.

And so, the lights dim once more and the video begins.

Surprisingly, it begins with an image of the entire Cubix-Richmond family, seated on a couch in what looks like the living room of their home.

"Lex Sheridan!" Jodi calls out to the darkness, to Lenny, to the screen, to God.

"Is this a service announcement from the United Nations?" Great-Aunt Elaine wants to know.

"Yes," I say.

"Hi, Jodi," Tim starts. "My family and I would just like to express our deepest condolences to you and your entire family. It has been a privilege and a pleasure to get to know you, and I'm sure so many of the people in that room tonight can attest the same. Yours may not be a household name, but trust me, you *are* famous to those who love you and need you so very much in their lives."

Jodi scans the crowd and catches my eye. I wink and give her the thumbs-up simultaneously. I see Kat across the room doing the same.

"And, Jodi," Ruby says, "the Richmond-Cubix foundation would like to help support your temple's efforts to assist impoverished orphans in Somalia, and have decided to pledge fifty thousand dollars in Sonia Goldberg's name to this great cause."

"Thank you, thank you!" Jodi says, blowing kisses at the screen, although there's no one really there to respond. I'm pretty sure her thanks are for the notoriety as much as—if not more than—for the funds.

"Have a wonderful evening!" Slim, Leo, Leyla, Bette, Bubba, and Didi say, waving as the camera fades out.

A low murmur of voices starts humming around the room as people ask, "Was that really...?" and "How does Jodi...?"

Jodi's mom reaches across the table to tap me on the arm. "What was that?" she asks. "Do you know anything about it?"

"Not a clue," I say.

Doug smiles. "Ditto here."

I whisper to Doug, "See? Isn't it kind of fun to lie like that?"

"To Jodi's mom, sure. To each other? No, not at all." He takes another sip of kosher wine and grimaces as it goes down. Turning back to the crowd, I notice Doug watching Lenny.

I'm paranoid, certainly. I mean, *everyone* in the room is eyeing Lenny. He's over six feet tall and is standing at a podium with a spotlight in his face and a microphone in hand. He's just brought Rubix Cube to Temple Beth El, for crying out loud. Everyone is watching him for a reason. And that reason has got nothing to do with me.

Right?

MC Lenny is hushing the crowd and tapping on his computer to bring Sonia's video onto the screen.

The sound of Sister Sledge's "We Are Family" fills the room

with its familiar disco beat, and I feel a little disappointed in Lenny for selecting such a conventional tune to accompany the memorial montage of such an unconventional woman like Sonia Goldberg. Then the music begins to blend with something else, and suddenly, a rapper's voice sings out "You could never be replaced...to have one more dance with you, Mama..."

I've never heard this song before, but it's perfect for this moment. Tears fill my eyes.

The lights come up to thunderous applause. "Thank you, MC Lenny, for that heartfelt homage to Sonia Goldberg." Lenny gives a wave and a curt bow from the front of the room. He then goes about dismantling his electronics. "Now, to the main event!" Rabbi Cantor cheers.

"Give it up for the main event, people!" Leslie calls, standing on her chair, wobbly. Her husband gently pulls her down.

"About time," Great-Aunt Elaine yawns.

I try to make eye contact with Lenny, but he's not looking up. I lose track of him on the other side of the ballroom as the lights dim once again.

"I want to thank you all for coming tonight for this *very* special event. As you know, each year, the temple tries to find creative ways to raise funds to support our community. This temple provides so many Jewish individuals and families with cultural and educational activities, from our wonderful preschool to our bar- and bat-mitzvah programs to our adult learning and travel opportunities. Why, this year alone, we visited Israel, Turkey, and Boca!" Cheers and whistles follow from table six. "Okay, Dave, that's enough. We know how you like those Turkish baths!" More hoots from table six ensue.

"Enough," the rabbi continues. "Let's get to the moment you have all been waiting for." People begin to applaud, but the rabbi holds up his hand to delay them. "First, I need to say thank you. Without these seven brave and talented volunteers from our very own Beth El congregation, this night would not have been possible. They have each been matched with an appropriate dance partner and teacher, with whom they have been practicing and preparing for several months now, taking time away from their families in order to learn and grow.

"Now, many of you may *think* you know what is coming, because you enjoy watching the television version of this event and are familiar with the concept. But believe you me, you have never seen anything quite like this. Ladies and gentlemen, from the glamour of Hollywood straight to the Beth El ballroom: Welcome to *Dancing with the Stars of David!*"

Thunderous applause, of course, follows his words. There is no holding back; Great-Aunt Elaine, getting a second wind, stands and starts stomping her rubber-tipped cane against the floor. People go as wild as possible in God's house, some even standing up or putting their fingers near their incisors to whistle.

"Jodi's gonna rock!" echoes through the room just as the lights go completely dark and the first couple enter the room. Lee, realizing he has spoken too loudly, grimaces. He whispers to Doug and me, "She's on second."

"I know," I whisper back. "I'm a little bit nervous for her."

"Relax, she's a pro," Jodi's mom says. "I put her in dance competitions and pageants from the time she was three, like JonBenét."

"That's scary," Doug says.

"No, actually, it explains quite a lot," I say. Like one's personal quest for fame and fortune. Imagine being told your whole life that you were a star? And then you didn't become one. Unless you pretend that chairing the book fair for the PTA is akin to being Miss Universe.

Not that becoming an educational guru like Georgie was quite as big as that for me, but still. I can identify with the feeling of unfulfilled ambitions.

I find a roving waitress and request a double shot of Baron Herzog chardonnay.

Having downed that like it was Gatorade after a four-mile run, I motion to Doug. "I'm going to the bathroom quickly, before the first so-called contestant."

Doug looks up from the photos in his hand and manages a pained smile in my direction. Lee must be showing off pictures of his new Porsche again.

In the hallway, I run into Kat, who is deeply focused on her preferred mode of communication, typing furiously on her phone. "How's Shay?" I ask in annoyance, sure that she's flirting with disaster.

She stops what she's doing, slowly crosses her arms across her chest, and gives me a Look. "And how's Doug?"

"What?" I pause, deciding how to answer. "I told him."

"Everything?" she asks, her green eyes probing. "About Lenny?"

I squirm. "Not quite."

"Hmm," she says. "That doesn't please me. And it doesn't please me that Lenny's here tonight. I had to leave the ballroom because your little love triangle, combined with Leslie's presence, made me feel all goosebumpy. See?" She shows me the hair on her arms, which is indeed sticking up at attention. "Like Tim said, Mercury is in retrograde, and it causes mishaps with travel and communications, and delays of all sorts. Plus, lots of anger."

I stifle a laugh. "Kat, really? *Mercury is in retrograde?* This explains our trip to Miami and Leslie's erratic behavior, I suppose? Oh, I see. Forget Shay for the meanwhile. Is that what Varka told you, as you were busy texting her just now? Does Varka agree with Tim Cubix's astrology?"

Kat looks up through her curls and I know I'm right.

"Kat! Lemme guess, for twenty-seven dollars a minute, Varka has an explanation for everything, like, that our trip got messed up because Jodi's grandma died, and that we were delayed in the parade traffic because Mercury was moving backward. Ah, it all makes perfect sense now, of course! I want to know, Kat, did I kiss Lenny because of the alignment of the planets?"

Kat has found a loose thread in her sweater and is very busy unraveling it. I back off for a second and try to pinpoint what's really upsetting me.

"Kitty-Kat," I sigh, my tone softening, "I just hate to think that you find comfort in some pretend astrological psychic instead of in me and Jodi, in the real world right here."

She shrugs. "We all have our ways of dealing, Lauren."

It's true, of course. Kat finds solace in the reading of the stars, Jodi by coming up with ways to be rich and famous. And I choose refuge from my real-world problems by creating an alternate-reality relationship, one devoid of responsibility and filled only with pleasure.

"Varka and I are just saying, this won't resolve itself. We think you need to spill it all to Doug."

"Oh, *we* do, huh?" I say. Then Kat and I both turn our heads at the sound of a rustling to our left.

"Don't worry, Kat," Doug says, standing behind us in the hallway, partially hidden by a fig tree. "She just has."

The bottom falls out of my stomach.

"I came to find you guys and tell you that Jodi's on next." Doug walks back toward the ballroom and pushes his full weight against the doors. "Oh, and Lauren?" He stares at me for one quick moment, the look on his face registering tremendous hurt, disappointment, and white-hot anger. I've never seen anything like it before. "Fuck you." Then he's gone, absorbed into the darkness of the temple ballroom.

"Shit!" Kat says.

I follow Doug, and Kat follows me, bursting through the doors and disrupting the show. Applause is dying down and I hear MC Lenny introducing the next couple. "Hailing from Little Odessa, Queens, and Big Odessa, Russia, please give it up for stay-at-home mom Jodi Moncrieff and professional Arthur Murray dance instructor Rudy Cryzinski!"

"Hey, MC Lenny," Doug calls, his voice coming from some point between tables eleven and twelve in the far right-hand corner of the room. Every head turns at the outburst. "You are officially a scumbag!"

Doug finds his way to a glowing red emergency exit sign. He pushes against the secure door and disappears into the night.

The wailing of the alarm matches my growing sense of absolute panic.

What have I done?

And, more importantly, what am I going to do about it now?

CHAPTER 32

I FOLLOW MY HUSBAND out into the chilly night, is what I do.

"Lauren!" I hear Jodi call, but I can't go back in there and cheer for her, not while my marriage is disappearing out the back door. I follow Doug around to the parking lot and realize what he's trying to do. Escape.

"Lauren!" Kat calls, running after me.

"Lauren!" Lenny calls.

"Lenny, just go back inside, will you?" I hear Kat say. "Stay out of it. Jeez."

"Moses, don't give the man the keys to our car!" I huff, catching up to Doug at the valet station. "He's been...sipping kosher wine!"

"Fine, I'll walk," Doug says, starting out of the lot and onto a neighborhood street, hands deep in his pockets, back hunched.

"I'm coming with you," I say. It's hard to keep pace with him in my new Louboutin heels. I end up taking very quick, little steps, but still fall a few feet behind.

"Don't," Doug says, stopping midstride and turning abruptly toward me. "Just. Don't."

"But—" I begin. "I want to talk!"

"You know what? Maybe *I* don't want to talk to *you* right now, okay? You had plenty of time to talk to me in the last, oh, twenty-four hours or so, and you didn't. We've had, like, our whole *lives* to talk, and you chose running away instead of telling me what's really going on!"

He's yelling at me and holding back tears at the same time.

"You *lied* to me, Lauren! You very quietly, very deliberately lied by hiding the truth."

I'm crying as his words register. This trip to Miami was meant as a hall pass, a get-out-of-jail-free card. But adult life is not a middle school hallway where you can languish while cutting gym class.

"I wish I had just told you the truth." I have snot and tears everywhere.

Doug studies my face. "But you don't wish that you hadn't kissed him." It's not a question.

What would have happened if I had *not* kissed Lenny the other night at the Clevelander? I might have always wondered, always fantasized about him. I probably would have kept up the flirtation when we came back to New York, letting Lenny's attention continue to undermine my marriage. But now, with that behind me, I'm officially released from the silly spell of pretend infidelity.

"No," I say. "I don't regret it."

"Nice," Doug spits. He starts to walk down a hill and into town, away from me, away from the lights of the temple.

"I needed to know, Doug!" I say. "I acted completely immature, I understand that. And I'm not proud of what I did, but, at the same time, I know it was sort of the right thing to do."

"How can you say that?" he asks, still walking away.

"Because, in the end, it brought me back to you."

He turns and faces me one more time. "That's such twisted logic! You had to kiss somebody else to come back to me? What are you, a senator?" We are screaming so loudly that a light comes on inside a split-level home; a curtain on the second floor pulls back to watch us.

"I love you, Doug. But I'm not perfect."

"I knew that already," he says ruefully. "You didn't have to go so far out of your way to prove it."

He wipes his face with the back of his shirt and then runs his hands through his hair. He inhales a ragged breath while I wait. Then he seems to make some sort of decision.

"Go back, Lauren. Watch Jodi. I'll be at Starbucks down the hill. I need some time alone."

I stand in the middle of the sleepy suburban street until I can no longer see his silhouette under the streetlamps.

I am shaking all over by the time I get back to the Beth El parking lot. I'm not sure that I made my point clearly, but at least for now, it seems like Doug won't bolt.

I guess that's the most I can hope for after being so stupid. So incredibly juvenile and stupid.

"I've got the keys to your car," Kat says. "Give the word and I'll track Doug down for you, hit him with the vehicle, drug him with painkillers, and keep him as your love prisoner until he forgives you." She's been waiting on the temple steps for me, but now she stands to gives me a hug.

"You'd Kathy Bates him for me? Full-on *Misery*?"

I pull back and squeeze her hands, tears welling up in my eyes. Kat's ridiculously corrupt mind, coupled with her wicked sense of humor, always yanks me back from the brink.

"You know I would," she says. "And not just because it would be fun."

We walk together back toward the temple, my body feeling tired and physically bruised. "We talked a little," I say. "I think it will be okay. I mean, I *hope*," I add, as an afterthought.

"I'm sure it will be fine," Kat says, not sounding at all sure.

The guests are just getting settled back into the ballroom after the impromptu fire drill caused by Doug's hasty exit. Kat and I take seats at Jodi's family table.

"Sorry," I mouth to Jodi, who is coming toward me with concern on her face.

"You okay?" she mouths back.

I shake my head in an awkward maybe-yes-maybe-no way. She nods knowingly, then closes her eyes, rolling her neck side to side and trying to prepare for the dance.

The voice announcing the couple this time is Rabbi Cantor's. "What an exciting evening we're having, Congregation Beth El! Luckily, the fire department's services were not needed, and so, without further ado, we shall return to *Dancing with the Stars of David*!"

"Where's Lenny?" I ask Kat.

"Gone," she says. "Took his computer slideshow and hightailed it."

I feel bad about that; Lenny keeps getting caught in my life's dramas. I'll have to send him an e-mail to apologize.

"Do not send him an e-mail to apologize," Kat says, reading my mind. "He's cool; I talked to him a bit outside before he left. But I doubt he'll be hanging with us anytime soon. Which is probably a good thing, no offense."

Jodi takes her position on our side of the dance floor, one foot behind the other, left hip facing her partner, Rudy. Her head is turned away from him in a dramatic frieze. Rudy is waiting on the other side of parquet tile, looking like a gymnast ready to mount a pommel horse.

Jodi stands still like that for a good ten seconds, as the music takes its time to start. In the still air, her mom whispers to our table, "She was always such a graceful dancer."

I suddenly have a flash of Jodi in another place and time. I imagine her at five, in her first tap recital, hair curled and piled on her head. At ten, learning all of Paula Abdul's and Janet Jackson's choreography to perfection. At fifteen, starring in her high school's version of *Chicago*.

Picturing Jodi through the ages is a good distraction for me at the moment.

Their music finally begins. It's a pumped-up dance song with a heavy bass at the onset. Jodi saunters across the floor in long, sexy strides, and meets Rudy in the middle. Quickly, she throws her right leg onto his shoulder.

"Yowza," Great-Aunt Elaine says. I couldn't agree more.

He catches her by the ankle and spins her around so she is facing our table. Underwear be damned, the woman is wearing lace spandex bike shorts under her dress! It is sheer genius, having the double effect of hiding her privates while also providing extra tummy support.

One can only hope that Leslie has been as wise.

Jodi continues to silence the crowd with the technical difficulty of her steps combined with some sort of freakish flexibility. At the start of the routine, people cheer and clap whenever the couple shows off a great new move. But with each passing minute, the room grows quieter and quieter, lost in the beauty of their dance.

She catches my eye for a second, looking really upset. Is she hurt? Has she twisted her ankle? I scan her legs for signs of fatigue or injury, but her step still seem confident and finessed. Jodi's years of experience on the stage must be telling her something.

Her uncertainty brings me out of the moment and makes me worry about Doug. I picture him sipping a grande skim latte, staring off into space as teenagers and old couples file in and out of the coffee shop, the minutes passing unnoticed.

I hope he will wait for me.

Suddenly, Jodi looks my way again. She is definitely trying to tell me something. Does she want to give up? Has she torn a ligament? But she's come so far. I can't let her stop now, not when the memory of Sonia Goldberg, Ziegfeld Girl, hovers over the room.

"What's up?" I ask Kat.

"Dunno. Looks like she's upset about something."

"Cheer louder!" I insist.

We stand up. As the music comes to its final moments, I feel like Béla Károlyi at the '96 Olympics, telling Kerri Strug to stick the landing, despite her injury. Stick the landing! Stick the landing! I feel so moved that I say it aloud, Russian accent and all: *"Stick the landing, Jodi!"*

The music bangs out a final note. Jodi slides into a full split, arms raised above her in a V for victory.

Needless to say, the girl sticks her landing.

When it is all over and she's finished smiling and bowing, Jodi comes over to our table. She has her death-stare radar set on me and Kat, completely pushing Lee and his bouquet of calla lilies out of the way so she can reach my chair ASAP. I see the daggers in her eyes, and my first thought is not that *she* had been injured, but that for some reason, *I* am going to be. I steady myself for a coming assault, although for what I can't imagine.

"*I totally fucked up!*" she whisper-screams to me and Kat. "*Did you see how I missed those first few steps? I can't believe it! How many people do you think noticed?*" She takes a deep, rattled breath and looks at us intently.

I am relieved that nothing is, apparently, my fault. Beyond that, I have no idea what she's talking about. Her dance was flawless. Also, last time I checked, this is not the real *Dancing with the Stars*. It's not the Olympics, or even the Olympic trials. Not even close. But Jodi is too far gone for this type of logic; the truth doesn't matter to her.

It's time to muster up some serious attitude.

I give Kat a look, saying, *me first*.

Then I take Jodi firmly by the arms and make sure to give my most penetrating gaze. "You were fucking awesome, are you kidding me? You danced circles around Rudy!"

"You're a star!" Kat adds. "Friggin' gorgeous, too."

"You're definitely going to beat Leslie!" I say, on a roll now.

"Beat her, or *win*?" Jodi snaps back.

"Hey. Isn't this a fundraiser?" Kat asks.

"And isn't my marriage sort of falling apart while I'm trying to cheer you on?" *In this somewhat ridiculous event*? I think.

Jodi turns away from us, a tear in her eye. "I'm sorry, guys. I don't know why I'm being like this."

"Because," Kat says. "It's something that matters to you. Something special, that sets you apart from all the other moms."

Leslie's name is announced, along with her dance partner's.

"Yeah, but," Jodi says. "Who cares?" She tries to smile. "I mean, *besides* from me, who cares about this stupid competition?"

"We do," I say, surprising myself. "If it's important to you, it's important to us."

Jodi leans into me and Kat and hugs us, one bony arm around each of us. "How fucked up am I?"

That question is too big to answer directly right now, so I don't. "You're going to win," I say. "I promise."

I stare down at the two pink ballots I received at the start of the night, and begin to hatch a plan.

It's only once I'm standing in the lobby with cash in my hand that I remember my promise to Doug. No bidding and no buying.

I stop, considering.

Perhaps there's a way to fill out ballots in Jodi's favor without actually, you know, *purchasing* them, thereby keeping my promise to Doug as well as the one to Jodi.

Stuffing my money back into my clutch, I quickly head into the ballroom one more time, looking for my favorite partner in crime.

"Ballots!" I whisper to Kat, pulling her away from a tall, dark and handsome waiter. She doesn't look amused. "Grab all the ballots you can find!"

"What are you doing?" Then, taking in my crazed look and my hands full of pink slips of paper, she asks again, slowly, as if she knows the answer perfectly well. "What. Are. You. Doing?"

I dig through my clutch for a pen, and, finding two, hand one to her. "We're filling 'em out." I scribble *Jodi Moncrieff* on my two and look around for more. "*All* of 'em."

As Leslie starts her number—a surprisingly non-sexy, nonbitchas dance to the Talking Heads' "And She Was"—Kat and I move stealthily out of the darkened room and into the hallway, collecting and filling out the pile of extra, pink ballots that sit unguarded at the now-unmanned check-in table. When both my fist and mouth are full of paper, I slink back into the ballroom and stuff them into a waiting ballot collection box.

And then I go out and gather some more.

Of course, the voting is not supposed to be done until all seven of the contestants have danced. But, do people always wait until the end of a trial before deciding who is to be awarded compensation? Of course not. So, let's just think of *Dancing with the Stars of David* as a huge car accident, and rightly find in favor of Jodi Moncrieff.

When I approach Leslie's table, another idea forms, this one perhaps even more brilliant that the last.

"Hey, Kat," I whisper, standing in the corner behind table seven. "Come here."

She moves through the darkness and joins me, pushing her mop of curls from her flushed face. "Yo. This is fun!"

"Leslie's family is here."

"Yup."

"I mean, no one is at the Koches' household right now. It's sleepy. It's *empty*."

"You sound moronic."

"I'm trying to make a point!"

"So make it!"

"Shh!" someone chastises.

I point to the ballroom doors and Kat follows behind me. Right before exiting, we get a glance at a not-too-flattering shimmy of Leslie's rear as she jitterbugs across the floor.

The light seems bright in the hallway after slinking around the dim outer rim of the ballroom. I squint at Kat. "Thanks to us, Jodi's going to win this 'dance competition,' right? So she doesn't need us anymore this evening. I figure we have about forty-five minutes to get Doug, drive down to Hadley, get the nanny cams, and come back to Beth El by dessert."

Kat is blinking her green eyes at me, shaking her head back and forth. She speaks very slowly. "So...you mean...we're planning a *stealth recovery operation* involving the *breaking and entering* of

Leslie's home residence, while working under the *alibi* of having been at *Dancing with the Stars of David*?"

"That's exactly what I'm saying!"

"Now, that's what I'd call a Saturday night!" Kat tosses me the keys to my car. "Let's collect your husband and commit some petty larceny!"

"I was thinking more like, let's help save our own asses."

"Yeah, that, too," she says, the glow of her BlackBerry lighting up her face as she starts tapping. "Totally."

CHAPTER 33

I LEAVE KAT AND THE CAR idling while I run into Starbucks to (hopefully) retrieve my husband. My heart lifts at the sight of Doug seated at a round table in the corner, staring out a window.

There's hope, then.

I quietly exhale, letting out air that I'd probably been holding in since he emerged from behind that fig tree at the temple.

Don't fuck this up, Lauren.

He doesn't notice me, so, before announcing my presence, I take a moment to study him in profile.

His skin, usually a deep olive, looks washed out under this lighting. His eyes have developed creases in the corners, matching the wrinkles in his rolled-up shirtsleeves. He reaches up with one hand and rubs his stubble absentmindedly.

Doug shaves twice a day with a four-blade razor, and still, it's not enough.

I love that I know that about him.

I approach his table and say the first thing that comes to mind. "I'm an idiot."

Doug shakes his head in agreement. "True as that may be, it's not an excuse."

"No, it's not an excuse." I pull out a chair and sit across from him. He lets me, which I take as a sign to continue. "I could say that I was drunk. Which is true, but, again, it's not an excuse."

He continues to rub at the stubble on his jawline. "I hate that you kissed him. It disgusts me, and I'm not sure how or when I'll ever get that image out of my head."

I nod. My eyes well up with tears, but I say nothing.

"But I think...I hate *more* the fact that you deceived me. That you came back from Miami and told me everything *but* that. I have to wonder, if I hadn't overheard you talking to Kat, would you *ever* had told me the truth?"

I am not sure what to say to this.

"And then I have to wonder, what else are you keeping from me?" His bloodshot eyes hold mine.

I think about the position as chair of the English Department, that infamous job I did not get and now don't even want.

I think about how tired I am, keeping track of everyone's schedules, of constantly buying ridiculous birthday presents for ridiculous birthday parties, of washing dishes and folding laundry that my hired help doesn't.

I think about the ways in which I sometimes ignore my children's bad behavior, giving in to their whines and complaints just to shut them up.

Just to make all the noise stop.

These are among the few details I overlooked in my original confession to my husband.

"There are a few things," I begin. "Nothing as bad as the Lenny issue." I can't bring myself to say, "kiss" to Doug.

"Things like...?" He arches his eyebrows.

"I *may* have visited Georgie Parks."

"*Professor* Georgina Parks? At Harvard?" he asks. "When?"

"Wednesday." I shrug, a smile forming on my lips. I try to bite it back.

"Why did you do that?"

"Because of a sweater." I'm sort of laughing now, hearing how it sounds, remembering the week. I brush a tear away from my eye. "It's a long story."

"I've got time," Doug says, folding his arms across his chest and leaning back in the chair.

"No, you don't," Kat says, materializing by our side. "Should we want to successfully rob Leslie's house with any amount of grace, time is definitely one thing we haven't got much of."

Doug stares at her, incredulous. He looks to me for an explanation.

"Plus, you can't just sit here and mope," Kat argues. "Well, I mean, you can, but it will continue to suck."

"She's right," I say. "Come on. I'll explain everything in the car."

"Everything?" he asks.

"With Kat as my witness," I say, holding my palm out flat, like I'm taking an oath.

"You're about to become one of us!" Kat grins.

Doug hesitates, still deciding what to do. "And what is that, exactly?" he asks, following us out onto the street and getting into the passenger side of the car. "Werewolves? Criminal master-minds? Complete freakazoids?"

"A little bit of all of the above," Kat decides, buckling herself into the back. "If you also add in the fun factor."

"Legally, you should sit in Becca's car seat," Doug says.

"Original." Kat extends one middle finger his way before answer-ing her phone, which has just begun to ring.

Am I wrong to love a series of diversions that momentarily take the focus off of my recent infidelity and compulsive need to fabricate and obfuscate?

Definitely not wrong, I conclude, turning on the radio. I select an XM station with a heavy enough rap element to complicate Doug's ability to think clearly.

Kat listens intently to the voice on the other end of her phone as I pull out of the parking spot and make my way through the quiet streets of Elmwood. I decide to skip the traffic lights on the main road, preferring instead to take the highway three exits south to Hadley.

"Excellent!" Kat says, disconnecting and dropping her phone back into her handbag. "Don't be mad," she says to me.

"*Okay*," I say, making eye contact with her in the rearview mirror.

"Shay's going to meet us there."

"*Okay*," I say, trying to remain calm.

"Shay Greene?" Doug asks. "Newly elected Hadley School Board president?"

"That'd be the one," I say.

"You guys know her?" Doug asks.

"Mmm-hmm," Kat adds.

"Part of the week's festivities," I say.

I mean, how much truth does one *really* have to divulge to one's husband?

And then I decide: all of it.

I exit the highway and pull onto the streets of Hadley. "Kat fooled around with Shay and it was caught on Leslie's nanny cam, and also I swung around a pole and gashed a hole in Leslie's face, plus I sort of got to third base with a toilet." There. That should explain it.

"Which was also caught on nanny cam," Kat adds. "The face-gashing part, anyway. And Leslie's threatening to blackmail us with it. And maybe sue Lauren. So we're going to get the evidence and destroy it!"

"Is that why Leslie had that bandage on and those huge sunglasses? It looked like she had cataracts removed after falling down a flight of stairs," Doug says.

"Nope," Kat says. "Us happened."

"Though she's totally lying about the black eye being my fault," I add.

"True, that," Kat confirms. "Which is another reason why we need the videos."

"A regular Watergate," Doug says, looking out the window. I am pretty sure the corners of his mouth turn upward when he says this.

I cut the lights on my car as we pull onto Leslie's street. Passing by her house, I park at a bend in the road a little ways down, which Kat refers to as the official rendezvous spot. Sure enough, there is a gold Mercedes S class waiting for us in the darkness.

I flash my lights and Shay emerges, wearing skinny black cargos, platform booties and a wrap cardigan.

Doug rolls down the window on his side. Shay leans in, enveloping the car in her flowery perfume. "I've got the security code for the alarm." She grins. "Meet me by the basement entrance." She drapes one fold of her long sweater over her shoulder and hurries down the block.

"Who *are* you people?" Doug wants to know.

"We're members of the elite Hadley Union Free School District," Kat explains, once we're all assembled by the French doors leading out onto Leslie's terraced, overly landscaped backyard. "Merely welcoming our new school board president into the fold. Now someone hand me a credit card."

"This won't work," I say, digging through my wallet and handing her a plastic card.

"Because you maxed it out this week?" Doug wants to know.

"Good one, Mr. Worthing!" Kat says. "You just might prove to be better company that Lenny."

"Who's Lenny?" Shay wants to know. "Kat, you don't need that. Just pick up the mat. There's a key underneath."

"A YouTube rapping sensation," Kat jokes, pretending to swoon. She finds the key and hands me back my card. "This is going to be the easiest breaking and entering I've ever done."

"How many have you done?" I want to know.

"Not MC Lenny Katzenberg?" Shay asks.

"Yes, MC Lenny Katzenberg!" I say.

"Four or so," Kat says. "If you don't count college."

"He's so cute!" Shay gushes. "I *love* his videos. Especially that one about Obama, did you see that one?"

"Great," I concur. "One of his all-time best."

"Can everyone just shut the fuck up about Lenny Katzenberg, please?" Doug shouts. "And is that a cat I see, on the other side of the door?"

"Oh no," I say. "Here we go with the cats."

Kat opens the door, and Shay slides in to quickly turn off the beeping alarm. We follow her to the front hall, where she opens a closet and deftly punches in a series of numbers.

"I house-sit sometimes." Shay shrugs, noticing our silence. "It comes in handy."

"I'll bet," Doug says. Turning to me, he adds, "Let's move out of district. On Monday." A gray tabby mews from the corner archway leading into the kitchen. "And someone lock that thing in a bathroom."

Shay does.

"Yes, my husband is afraid of house pets," I confirm to Shay and Kat as we plan out a strategy for canvassing the house.

Doug, scratching his legs furiously even though the cat is now securely out of the way, volunteers to be our watchman.

I turn to him and sigh, reaching up to kiss him on the forehead. "You're not allergic. We had you tested, remember?"

He shrugs and goes out the front door, hiding behind one of the huge columns. "I'll alert you with a bird call if I see someone approaching," he says.

"I can really see MC Lenny's appeal," Shay says. "Now, let's get cracking, shall we?"

Eight minutes later, the entire house has been canvassed for hidden cameras, with most of our search focusing on the living room and the guest bedrooms.

"I found one in an air purifier," Shay says, calling down from upstairs. "From the room we were in, Kat."

"Score," Kat says, simultaneously finding and removing a small camera from the back of an air freshener that was plugged into a socket in the living room.

"That's going to be mine!" I say.

"Good," Kat says. "Then we located the most incriminating two. Let's get out of here."

"Wait." I say. "I need to check Leslie's bathroom before we go."

I pass Shay on the curved staircase. "Try a mirror!" she suggests. "Or, like, a clock radio? But hurry!"

I enter the oversized bathroom and begin to look around. I notice a small Renuzit room freshener and grab it. For good measure, I also take the goose-necked vanity mirror sitting on the counter next to the sink. And one of those plug-in night-lights.

"We good?" Kat asks as I hurry down the plushly carpeted stairs.

"I guess," I say, surveying my armload of random items. I don't know whether to hope that I've got a recording of my actions or to hope that Leslie doesn't put hidden surveillance in her bathrooms.

"Then, off with the lights..." Shay says, hitting a switch in the corner. "And I'm going to reset the alarm...and...go!"

We head en masse back through the dining room and out the French doors. Kat locks them and slips the key back under the mat while I reshuffle the items cradled in my arms.

My silk shirt sticks to my back and I realize that I'm sweating.

"Well done, everyone," Shay says, always the leader. "I'll upload the video at home and let you know what we've got."

From the other side of the glass, I can just barely hear Leslie's cat meowing loudly in protest from his powder-room prison.

"Back to temple, people!" Kat says as we head through some bushes and around to the front of Leslie's property line. We signal to Doug, who meets us at the curb.

Kat stops at our car and turns to say good-bye to Shay, kissing her chastely on both cheeks. "You're the balls, Shay. Thanks a million."

"Lotsa fun," she says, closing the trunk of her luxury automobile on all the stolen goods. "Hey, we should all hang some time. Go for drinks?"

"Um...maybe!" I say, pushing Kat into the backseat and slamming the door before she can respond.

CHAPTER 34

"WELL, THAT WENT OFF WITHOUT a hitch," Kat says, settling into her seat. She checks her phone. "Jodi says not to worry and that she's praying for us."

"*Might have* gone off without a hitch," Doug says. "Conditional tense."

"What are you talking about?" I say. "We were brilliant in there! Like the A-Team or something." Doug's always such a glass half-empty to my glass half-full.

I accelerate as we get on the ramp to the highway, slightly annoyed and buzzkilled by my husband's underwhelming response to what is clearly a coup for Team Lauren.

"I agree that you got some of what we came for, and that that part of the mission was a complete success," Doug starts. "But..." He trails off.

"Out with it," Kat says.

"First. Why did you steal all that stuff? When Leslie notices that her mirror is missing, won't she become suspicious? Won't that make her want to look at the footage that was recorded there earlier? Or, perhaps, other footage?"

"But see, my dear Watson," I explain, using my Sherlock Holmes voice, "Leslie won't *be able* to see the footage because we stole the cameras and the recording devices that held it!"

"But while you were inside Leslie's house, I started thinking. Doesn't all the information get backed up?" he asks.

"That's why I took her iBook laptop!" Kat exclaims. I reach my hand up from the steering wheel so that Kat can give me a high five from the backseat.

"See, we've thought of everything." I say.

"The Cloud," Doug says, shaking his head. "The Cloud."

"Oh. My. God. The Cloud." Kat echoes. I have no idea what they're mumbling about. Then Kat starts moving her hands in sweeping, circular motions, like she's conjuring a phantom from the air. I watch for a second in the rear view mirror and begin to understand.

"You mean...all the data in Leslie's house is automatically backed up to some server in cyberspace?" I ask slowly.

"Instantly, probably," Doug says. "And what about the rest of the nanny cams?" he asks into the silence. "The ones we *didn't* take? The ones that probably recorded you running around Leslie's house just now?"

His words hang in the air as Kat and I consider this. It's lucky that I know where I'm going, because I need to do it on autopilot; my mind is completely transfixed with an image of several nanny cams recording my removal of several *other* nanny cams. I'm sure we didn't get them all; we weren't even trying to.

As I pull into the parking lot of Temple Beth El for the second time tonight, I have to wonder: Just how brainless are we?

Kat pulls out her BlackBerry and begins tapping away.

"I hope you have a direct line to God," I joke, handing my car keys to Moses.

"Trust me," she says. "Shay's Godlike."

"At this point, do we have any other choice but to trust Kat?" Doug says, taking my hand and leading me back up the temple steps. "And Shay?"

I squeeze his hand tightly, smiling at his use of the plural pronoun. "Not really," I admit. "But it doesn't bode well that our fate rests in the power of their texting."

Big-band music echoes through the temple hallways as we enter the building. "Perfect timing! It must be the dinner and dancing portion of the evening," Doug says.

"Act nonchalant," Kat says, air-kissing us good-bye as she pushes through one of the sets of double doors. Doug and I wait a beat before doing the same. We try to get to our table, but are immediately engulfed by partygoers boogying across the parquet floor.

"Wanna dance?" Doug asks shyly.

Our phone conversation in Miami comes rushing back to me. He remembers.

I nod eagerly. We embrace and sway together slowly, not caring that the upbeat tune calls for something more like a Lindy than a waltz.

When the song ends, we take our seats for dessert.

"So?" Jodi asks, sliding her petite tush onto my chair with me. I scoot over to make room. She looks from me to Doug. "How'd it go?"

"Great! Good," Doug says, clearly trying to make up for his sobering, rational point of view in the car. "No problems. It went off without a hitch, to use Kat's words."

"*Ex*cellent!" Jodi purrs. "And," she asks, looking from me to Doug and back again, "are you two co-pathetic?"

"Copasetic?" Doug asks aloud.

"Great!" Jodi concludes. "Now if only my night could run as smoothly." She scans the room, appraising the competition one final time. "That trustee over there with the toupee and the cane is surprisingly light on his feet."

"I have a feeling you'll be happy with the outcome, Jo," I say, smiling inwardly.

Chocolate mousse in a Star of David chocolate-molded cup is set in front of each place setting. Jodi eagerly moves back to her chair to devour her dessert, speaking to her daughters and me between bites.

"You know, girls, you should be very proud of mommy and learn from my example. I worked really *hard*! I was so *nervous*. But now it's all behind me and I'll always have the *memories*." There's nothing quite like watching Jodi wax philosophical. She stares off to the middle distance above Great-Aunt Elaine and sighs. "It was a *once*-in-a-lifetime event, and I'm just *glad* I got to participate in it."

"So, you don't care anymore who the winner is?" I have to ask.

"No! Of course I still *care*," she scoffs, pouring herself an extra large glass of Mt. Eden pinot noir from a half-empty bottle on the table. "You do think it'll be *me*, don't you?"

Lee comes over to the table and takes a seat to my right.

"You look relieved," Doug says. I nod my head in agreement.

"Nah, Worthing, just proud of myself." He digs into the mousse. Mouth full of foamy dessert, he explains, "I decided to buy a few extra ballots, to, you know, secure the outcome." His voice drops a level and he nods in Jodi's direction. "The competition this year was *fierce*. All the men from morning minyan are voting for Morris."

Luckily, Jodi's too busy retying her daughters' hair bows to notice our whispering.

I think of all the ballots Kat and I already filled out in Jodi's favor, and wince inwardly at the unnecessary expense Lee just doled out.

"How many did you buy?" Doug asks.

Lee holds out his palm. Five isn't bad, I think. Unless he means fifty?

I'm about to do the mental math on that when a screech comes over the microphone.

"Everyone, if I may have your attention at the front," Rabbi Cantor says into the mic. "It's time to announce the winners!"

The lights flash several times as all the dancers are called to the center of the room. Jodi's nervousness is suddenly palpable, at least to me. She stands straight and confident, holding her partner's hand, just like couples do on the real *Dancing with the Stars.* But she is rolling her ankles around, fidgety. The rabbi takes the cordless mic from its stand and approaches the dancers, who form a horseshoe around him.

"Let's give all of these fantastic dancers another round of applause!" he begins. "Their hard work paid off tenfold tonight. I know that I myself have not been quite so entertained since Morris and Sylvia Glickstein's wedding!" Some cackles come from the far right corner and the rabbi turns his attention to them. "Remember that klezmer band? Incredible."

"Get to it, already!" Elaine calls out.

Doug, as bored as Jodi's relatives, notices a book of matches on the table bearing the slogan Temple Beth El: Where Judaism Is on Fire. He slumps over his chair and starts lighting matches, dropping them into his sweating water goblet right before burning his fingers.

The panel of three judges is introduced: Norman, the temple president; Rebecca, the director of the preschool; and Rabbi Cantor. True to reality-TV doctrines, the judges begin to heckle and generally mess with the minds of all the contestants. The bottom half of Jodi's face is smiling while her eyes glow with hatred, as each judge says something slightly off-color and derogatory to each participant.

"Of course, Mrs. Moncrieff missed her calling, choosing predictable family life over a scintillating career on the Las Vegas strip," Rebecca, the preschool director jokes.

What's more insulting: being told that your life as a stay-at-home mother is unfulfilling or that your level of talent would have qualified you only for *Vegas*?

I imagine Jodi blowing off each judge's head with nothing more than the fierce red light emanating from her eye sockets. Bam! Bam! Bam! Like a scene from *Star Wars: Battle of the Temple of Beth El.*

Doug lights another match and lets it burn down. The smell of sulfur fills our corner. "Find something else to do," I whisper.

At long last, the award ceremony officially begins, and Rabbi Cantor once again takes possession of the microphone. "First of all, I have to say that, thanks to your enthusiastic voting, the temple has set a new record for fundraising, collecting over ten thousand dollars in one night! This is unheard of, especially during an economic crisis like the one we are now experiencing." He pauses, removes his glasses, and wipes away a tear. Putting his glasses back on, he takes a deep breath and continues. "Also, I have to say that it was very difficult to pick a winner. You are all winners tonight, and so these certificates will reflect that."

Uh-oh. A sinking feeling develops in the pit of my stomach.

"What does that mean?" Doug asks. "*All winners*?" We watch as the charred remains of a paper napkin float down to the table.

"Bad sign!" Kat says, crossing the room and crouching by my chair. "Very bad!"

"So, the first certificate goes to Morris and his partner, Svetlana. For the best moves by anyone under—and over—the age of sixty-five!" The man with the toupee and cane graciously accepts his certificate by kissing it, then Svetlana.

The crowd goes "Ooh!" and a woman who is presumably his wife calls out, "No tongue, please, Morris!"

"Next, never to be outdone, is Gary and, again, the lovely Svetlana. Gary, rumor has it that you signed up for *eighteen* extra dance sessions. Is that true?"

Gary grins from ear to ear like a schoolboy and nods, giving a thumbs-up to the rabbi.

"The guy danced *in a chair*," Lee says, clearly disgusted.

"You are the most dedicated to the art of the dance!" the rabbi says. Gary steps toward the rabbi, who shoos him away. "Now, don't move a muscle! We'll bring the certificate right to you!" Good-natured laughter follows.

This whole awards ceremony is starting to remind me of Little League. Last spring, Ben won the certificate for Most Punctual Player. He wanted to know if that meant he had scored the most home runs. Shamefully, we told him that it had.

It seems unlikely that we can fool Jodi in this way, though neither Kat nor I is beneath trying.

"And now, for the best dance couple! They showed us how to swing like the pros. Their combined experience and enthusiasm could not be matched."

Kat takes my hand in hers and we squeeze hard.

Rabbi Cantor stalls for maximum drama before announcing the winners' names, and I think, *Did he say swing*? That doesn't sound like the dance style of Jodi's choreography, exactly.

"Leslie and Javier, this one's for you!"

Fuck.

Fuck, fuck, fuck.

Jodi's jaw drops as we all watch Leslie—sunglass-wearing, evil beyotch Leslie—claim what should be Jodi's prize.

"Shalom, people!" Leslie calls to the crowd, pumping her fist in the air. "God bless you!"

"I thought that the older gentleman was much better than this fatty," Great-Aunt Elaine says, to no one in particular. Lee gives her an odd look. She quickly adds, "But, of course, Jodi was the best!"

"Of course!" Jodi's children, mother, Lee, Doug, and I add.

Finally, after the tin man gets his heart, the lion his courage, and the scarecrow a brain, Jodi is given the award for best costume. People applaud enthusiastically as she graciously accepts the certificate, waving the white paper over her head like a surrendering general after battle.

"Yea, mom!" Jodi's daughters cheer.

She walks toward us with a sad smile on her face, and hugs her youngest daughter to her chest.

"Oh well..." I begin, "I guess it wouldn't have been fair to have just one winner."

Her flat palm silences me. "Just stop."

"Okey dokey." I sink into my seat next to Firestarter.

Kat tries to console her with humor. "It could be worse: the dance duo of Deborah and Devorah could have tried to hit on you."

Jodi immediately bursts into tears. "That's true! They didn't even try to hit on me!"

"Nice job, honey," Lee comments absentmindedly, patting Jodi on the back. "You'll always be my superstar." She pushes past him and goes to sit with her mother, who immediately begins force-feeding her chocolates.

Lee turns his attention to Doug and leans toward him, whispering. "All those ballots I bought. What a scam!" He shakes his head in a combination of disbelief and admiration for the slippery fundraising techniques of his beloved temple. "They didn't even count 'em!

"Not to mention the fifty-thousand-dollar donation that Jodi brought in from Tim and Ruby," I add. "That should have guaranteed her the win."

Doug picks up a lit candle and starts to let the melting wax drip onto his hand. "Temple fundraising is like voting in Florida."

Lee doesn't respond. "I mean, Jodi wasn't the only one they fucked over tonight," he muses.

"Huh?" we ask in unison.

"I think I just bought enough ballots to finance next year's trip to Israel." He waves to the rabbi halfheartedly.

"Did you really buy fifty?" I ask.

"More like five hundred," Lee says, raising his eyebrows, seemingly shocked at his own generosity. "At five bucks a pop."

"Ouch!" Doug and I look down at his hand, now red and blistered.

Lee, still watching Rabbi Cantor from across the room, shakes his head sadly. "No kidding, dude. No kidding."

CHAPTER 35

DOUG AND I MAKE OUR GOOD-BYES and head to the parking lot. We are almost to our car when Leslie appears out of nowhere. Alone. Shrouded in dark glasses and night.

"What do you want?" Doug asks, stepping in front of me as a human shield from whatever animosity Leslie might hurl my way.

"To apologize," she says simply.

I'm speechless.

"Really?" Doug asks, incredulous but not unkind.

"Yes." Leslie removes her glasses and meets my gaze. Yeegads, she looks even more ghastly than before. Her skin is settling into a green-and-purple tie-dye design where it isn't covered in bandages. I try not to wince in horror and imagined pain. Then she adds, "I— I fell."

"I *knew* it," I say. "There was just no way I could have—"

"Well, hold on there, bimbo," Leslie says, starting to sound more like herself. "You still ruined my party and caused me to get six stitches across my left cheek, basically leaving me for dead on my living room floor."

"I *apologized* and I *tried* to help! But you were so mean and Kat wanted to leave and I was drunk and—"

Leslie cuts me off again. "And, Lauren, I have a serious, *serious* drinking problem, which only exacerbates my bipolar disorder."

I don't know what to say to that.

"So, sometimes, I'm a major bitch." She shrugs. "A rage-aholic, as my team of doctors says."

I just stare at her.

"I'm working on it, really I am. I mean, for starters, I found God tonight," she says, gesturing back toward the temple. She smiles absentmindedly, probably thinking about her sweet, holy victory on the dance floor.

"But has *God* found *you* yet?" Doug asks under his breath. I nudge him on the arm to shut him up.

She snaps back to attention, eyes flashing. "Now, *that's* the kind of stimuli that could send me right over the edge," she hisses, teeth clenched. She's really trying to control her emotions, I'll give her that much. It's bizarre, like watching the Incredible Hulk as he goes through his transformation.

"Men are such jerks," I say, trying to defuse her anger by blatantly dissing Doug.

"Hey!" he says.

"Total Neanderthals," she agrees, seemingly soothed, at least for the moment.

"You were saying?" I prod.

"Oh, yes." She smiles with the half of her face that can still move freely, clears her throat, and pulls her back up straight. "As part of my twenty-four-step program, I'm asking for your forgiveness."

Then she bows her head. Like, in a genuflectionish way. And awaits my response.

Several days ago, my drunken clumsiness sent her to the hospital. And less than one hour ago, I entered her home illegally, stole her goose-necked vanity mirror—among other nonessential items—and locked her cat in a bathroom. And now the woman is asking *me* for forgiveness.

"Uh..."

"Of course she forgives you," Doug says. "Because *everyone* makes mistakes, right?"

I grimace at Doug's obvious use of irony.

"Right, Lauren?" Doug continues, as Leslie looks on, somewhat confused. "Whaddaya think? Does *everyone* get a second chance tonight?"

"I'm a big fan of forgiveness," I say, looking at Doug. "You know, across the board. Like, for everybody."

"So?" Leslie asks. "Are we good here?" She glances from me to Doug and back again. "I have no idea what the fuck you guys are talking about, but I've got to get back in there and apologize to approximately twenty-six other people." She takes a crumpled list out of her décolletage and scans it for names. "Kat's next."

"Yeah, we're good," Doug says, looking at me. "As long as you stay on the straight and narrow."

"Oh, I will," Leslie says, putting her bandaged palm up toward the blackened sky. "It won't be easy, and I've learned some tough lessons these past few days. But believe me, Doug, it won't happen again."

I nod my head in agreement and take my husband's hands in mine. "Believe me and Leslie, Doug. It *won't* happen again."

CHAPTER 36

Sunday

I WAKE UP WITH A SERIOUS case of the Sundays. It's an illness that has plagued me since my first days as a student teacher more than fifteen years ago. I thought it would remedy itself in time, or at least lessen in intensity, but it has never abated. What's worse is that, in recent months, it has actually intensified.

If you are a teacher, you know what the Sundays are. Heck, maybe this illness even translates into different fields of employment, but having never been anything but a teacher, I wouldn't know. The Sundays are, in short, a series of small panic attacks that leave me feeling nauseated, anxious, and depressed, all at the same time, knowing that Monday is just around the corner.

Have I graded the quizzes? Have I read the short story that I've assigned to the class? Did I ever get back to the three parents who were upset with the grades I "gave" their children (since they only "earn" As)? Sundays are like a wakeful SAT dream: I'm naked, late, and sweating, standing in front of twenty-five sets of eyeballs that won't look away.

The only thing worse than Sunday is the entire month of August, which is like one long Sunday, as I count down the lovely days leading up to September's arrival.

I think today may rival any other Sunday on record. An intense feeling of fear, combined with a despondency I can almost taste, makes me groan. I pull the duvet up high over my head to block out the faint morning light seeping through the sides of the bedroom curtains. It seems to be raining, which only adds to my gloom. Doug stirs next to me.

"Doug," I whisper. "I think I've lost feeling in my toes."

"You're fine," he says, rolling over.

"I'm not fine. I have some kind of stomach bug."

"Get up and make the kids pancakes," he mumbles.

"But that's your job!"

"You owe me. I'm sleeping in."

Hard to argue with that.

I place my pillow against the headboard and sit up against it. "It's just...I don't want to go back to work."

"Are we really doing this again? Now?"

"I know you think that all I did was lounge around in Miami, but there was more to it."

"I know you did more than lounge, Lauren, believe me."

I let that comment slide. It's going to be a while before we truly get past The Kiss. Doug needs to have a chance to vent. I get that. So I hold my tongue and try to seamlessly move on from our awkward silence.

"I'm talking about Wednesday. When I went to see Georgie."

"So we're really not sleeping anymore, huh?" Doug sighs, propping up his pillow next to mine.

"And what she said completely threw me."

"Which was?" He rubs his eyes awake.

"That she's all about the freedom to choose."

"Choose what?" Doug asks.

"Exactly," I say.

"I'm choosing to go to the bathroom," Doug says, pushing aside the covers.

"And I'm choosing to let you make the pancakes, since you are so good at it."

"Just because I'm good at it doesn't mean I like it," he says over a forceful stream of pee. Now, that's part of the problem with marriage right there, I think. What's wrong with closing the door? I think it would greatly help to keep romance alive if we all just silenced the sounds our bodies made in front of the ones we love most in this world.

But wait.

What did Doug just say?

Just because I'm good at it doesn't mean I like it.

Could that be it? The tagline summarizing my entire educational career thus far?

I scan my brain to try and remember what else Georgie said. I come up with a nugget: That it's no wonder I needed a break from teaching, because I take it so seriously.

What else did she tell me?

Something like, the answer would come to me if I opened myself up to the possibility of "it," whatever that might be, and that maybe I am not the master of my so-called master plan.

As I put my feet into my slippers, a hint of an idea flashes across my cerebral cortex.

I suddenly need to get Georgie on the phone.

But of course I can't, because it's Sunday.

Damn you again, Sunday.

I text her and hope for the best.

When the phone rings a few minutes later, my heart leaps in anticipation of the Great and Powerful Oz, but it's not. "What time do you need me before the funeral?" our new babysitter, Carrie, wants to know. She worked out so well last night that I asked her back to help out today. That way, Doug can attend Sonia Goldberg's funeral with me.

"Eleven thirty," I say.

"Can I bring some art projects over? My little sister loves them," Carrie says. I will myself not to love Carrie too much, because I now believe that, like every babysitter I've ever had, she will eventually disappoint me and my children.

"Sounds like a great plan." I pull the blanket up over the sheets to make the bed, cradling the phone under one ear.

I am about to make the kids' beds, too, but then I stop myself. Today may be the end of my school leave, but it's also the start of a New Order in the Worthing household. Today, my children will do some housework.

"Kids!" I call from the hallway landing. "Come up here, please, and make your beds!"

For someone on leave from the darker side of life, I'm sure spending an awful lot of time around dead bodies.

Well, really, just one dead body in particular.

And today, we're putting her to rest.

I shake some of this morning's rain off my jacket and hand it to a woman behind the coat check at Stillman's Funeral Home. Doug gives her our umbrella and takes the claim ticket. We follow the signs for Sonia Goldberg and make our way down the hushed, softly carpeted yellow hallway.

"Hi-yyy," Jodi says, embracing me as I enter the family visitation room to the side of the chapel. She's wearing a tight black floor-length sheath à la Morticia Adams.

I had a theory and now it's been proven: Jodi owns a sexy ensemble for every occasion.

"Hi, Doug," Jodi purrs, hugging him next.

Before letting us go, she leans into us. "I am so hungover," she whispers. "I got totally trashed after they announced last night's winners! And guess who I drank with?"

"Can't imagine," I say.

"Rabbi Cantor," is Doug's guess.

"Well, Kat, of course," she says. "Kat…and Leslie."

"Leslie Koch?" I blurt.

"One and the same!" Jodi says. "She apologized to Kat, and then we did shots of Manischewitz. Well, Kat and I did. Leslie won't drink anything purple anymore. It's part of her—"

"Twenty-four-step program?" Doug guesses.

"Anyway, she's coming today to pay her respects." Jodi reaches into the deep V of her dress's neckline and pulls out a small packet of Tums. She pops two in her mouth and offers the roll to us.

I wave her offer away. "That should be interesting," I say, hoping Leslie isn't on to us yet.

We make our way down the line of mourners in the Moncrieff-Goldberg clan, saying hello to all the people we just saw last night, and head into the chapel.

Kat's seated alone, about ten rows back. She waves us over with a halfhearted hand in the air. She appears to be sucking on a lollipop.

"Blow Pop, actually," she says, when I ask her what she's got in her mouth. "Trick from the Clevelander. Keeps me from puking."

I slide into the wooden pew and put my arm around her. Her face has a greenish tinge. "Kat, you've got to stop drinking so much."

"Brilliant plan. You've solved all my problems."

Too much sarcasm so early in the day can mean only one thing. "Peter?" I guess.

"I'm serving him with official divorce papers tomorrow. And I have to go back to school to deal with the *di*ministration. So, yeah, I'm just trying to keep my food down."

"The Sundays." I nod.

"Yeah. Worst part of the job," she says. "Besides the, you know, teaching aspect."

Doug, who has been silent until now, clears his throat. "Why don't you quit?"

I swivel my head around to face him. "Her or me?" I ask, knowing the answer.

"Lauren, not everything is about you," Doug says, sounding just like my mother. I hate when he does that.

"I need money, Doug. That's the problem." Kat starts chomping on the lollipop with her incisors to break through to the gum.

"Like teaching is the only way to make a living?" he asks. "You can't waitress or something for a while?"

"Would you want me to serve you the pasta special? Really?" She smiles and chews a big wad of gum. I imagine her spilling Alfredo sauce on customers she doesn't like. Often.

"Fold T-shirts at the Gap. Work in a bakery." Doug is chock full of creative solutions for Kat. I'm sitting in the middle of them, wondering, why isn't he letting *me* off the hook? How come Kat gets to bake and I have to go back to teaching, tomorrow and probably forever?

An orchestral version of "Wind Beneath My Wings" interrupts my thoughts. Before I can get into another fight with my husband, the Moncrieff-Goldbergs come through the door and take their seats in the first row.

Slipping in right behind them is Leslie Koch.

Given our new peace pact, I smile and wave in her direction. She turns to me and time slows down.

You know that thing people do in movies, where they hold up two fingers, point them in their own eyes, and then aim them right at you? It's a menacing, foreboding gesture that means *I'm watching you*. Well, that's exactly what Leslie does when she sees me. And then, just as Rabbi Cantor is about the begin the funeral service, she sits down at the end of a row across from me and mouths the word "Meow."

I do believe that we are fucked. Again.

....

"I want to quit," I say as Doug and I get into his car, metaphorically ripping the Band-Aid off quickly. We are getting into line for the police-escorted procession down State Street and to the quaint Jewish cemetery about ten minutes away in North Elmwood. "Also, I do believe that Leslie is back to hating me. Well, this time it's *us*, really, you included."

"Why?" Doug asks, turning to meet my eyes. He adjusts the wipers and the rain slides out of view.

"Well, for starters, because we broke into her house last night while she was dancing her ass off."

"No, Lauren." He places the sign from the funeral home on the dashboard, letting other drivers know we are part of this convoy of cars. "I mean, why do you want to quit your job so badly? You are a great teacher."

I smile sadly. "Just because I'm good at it doesn't mean I like it."

"Since when?" He pulls out of the parking lot slowly, making a right hand turn behind Kat's black VW Beetle.

"Since...I don't know." I think for a moment, watching businesses and strip malls pass by under gray skies, their neon signs blurred by the rain. "It's just so...predictable."

"You really wanted that promotion."

"Actually, no," I say. "I wanted to be the department chair because it seemed like the logical next step. I liked the idea of teaching a lighter course load, and of spending more time in other teachers' classrooms, helping them. You know how I love to teach teachers. Maybe even more than I love teaching children."

"So, why not apply for positions as the English chair at another school?" Doug asks. "It's the right time of year for job hunting in education; I bet you could land something great."

I am already shaking my head no before he even finishes the complete thought. "Because, here's the thing: I don't want to be an administrator. That's one of the things I realized this week. I would absolutely *hate* to be Martha. I am terrible with scheduling and overseeing a budget. I don't want to have to discipline people. I just want to..."

"To what?"

"Fold T-shirts at the Gap?" I joke.

"Lauren!" The way he says my name makes me feel like I've just been scolded by my father.

"Why is okay for Kat and not for me?"

"Um…let's see." He's angry now, and the car jerks sideways as he takes one hand off the steering wheel to count reasons on his fingers. I clutch the underside of my bucket seat and keep my wide eyes staring at the road. "Number one: you have a Harvard education."

"Smart people can work in retail."

"Not you. Number two: Kat is in crisis. Her husband is a dick and her marriage is falling apart."

"Maybe I'm in crisis, too!"

He puts both hands back on the wheel and turns to me, his eyes dark and unreadable. "Are you?"

I take a deep breath. "No," I say, feeling stupid. "I just needed a break. A mini vacation from my monotonous, tenured life. A small leave of absence. But I'm back now." I feel a wave of regret pass over me as I admit this.

It's really Sunday, after all.

"Kat also told off the principal. Right?"

"Yes," I concede.

"And it wasn't the first time?" Doug would make a good prosecuting attorney.

"Like maybe just four other times?" I say in a small voice.

"So she's in deep shit."

"Deep Shit, Arkansas," I agree, laughing to myself. Doug looks at me funny. "It's a line from *Thelma and Louise*." I wave my hand dismissively. "Forget it. Inside joke."

We arrive at the cemetery and park behind the other cars. Kat joins us, and we walk together toward the burial site. The grass is soft and wet and the heels of my boots keep getting stuck. Doug holds a massive umbrella over the three of us and we huddle underneath.

"I'm thinking bakery," I whisper to her. "You need to work in a place that smells comforting. Kneading dough and puff pastry is a way to heal."

"I'm thinking that Leslie's going to stuff me into an oven and fry me like in *Hansel and Gretel*."

"She gave you the death stare, too?"

"No, on the way to our cars, she said, 'I'm going to stuff you in an oven and fry you, like in *Hansel and Gretel*.'"

"That's pretty clear, then."

"Yeah. I'm safe for the moment, though. I don't think she followed us to the cemetery."

Sonia's plain pine box is already suspended over the deep hole of earth. We say a few prayers—well, Doug and I say them and Kat gives a hearty "Amen" at the end of each—and then the coffin gets lowered slowly down on a mechanical platform. Which is weird to watch and somber all at the same time.

Jodi is crying now, as is her mother and father, and her daughters and even Lee. I didn't know Sonia, but I know what it's like to lose your grandparents. I mourn for Jodi's family and I mourn for Sonia. Her life seems like it was filled with love and rich with interesting opportunities, and I guess that's all we can ever hope for. To live long, and to live well.

The sound of a cell phone ringing in close proximity to me jars me from my silent contemplation. Kat jumps and fumbles for the offending phone in her coat pocket.

"Turn that off," Doug whispers.

"I'm fucking trying," Kat says through clenched teeth.

When she looks at the caller ID, however, her eyebrows raise and she pushes a button on her screen. "Hello?" she whispers, stepping away from the crowd and our protective umbrella. She moves quickly under a tree a few feet away and continues talking on her cell as Doug and I and the entire Moncrieff-Goldberg family watch incredulously.

Rabbi Cantor clears his throat and regains the group's attention. "Now we have reached the point in the service that represents the family's final act of honoring their deceased loved one. "Al mekomah tavo beshalom," he says, then hands a trowel to Jodi's father, to spill some dirt onto the coffin.

This part of a Jewish funeral always gives me the creeps. I shudder inwardly and watch as the spade is passed to Jodi's mother and then to Great-Aunt Elaine.

"She shaves her *what*?" Kat calls out from under the tree. "No fucking way!"

I continue to cringe and shudder, but not because of the sound of spilled earth on a plain pine box. Doug coughs and I take out some tissues and sniff into them, as we try and cover the sounds of Kat's wicked cackle.

The service ends a minute later and people make their way back to their cars. "Shivah will be held today at the Moncrieff home in Elmwood, and then for the remainder of the week at the Goldbergs' apartment in Queens," the rabbi says.

Kat meets us on the hill as the crowd disperses. She shakes her damp curls out like a dog coming in from the rain and splatters me with water as she ducks back under my umbrella. "Subtle," I say. "Holy."

"Holy shit." Kat is grinning from ear to ear. "You have *no* idea."

CHAPTER 37

AS MUCH AS I'D LIKE to hear the details of Kat's telephone conversation, my priority right now is to get out of the rain, which has crossed over from light drizzle to heavy downpour.

"Tell me later!" I shout over my shoulder as I break away from Kat and the rest of the crowd and make my way behind Doug to our car.

"But...it's important!" Kat calls back. "And really funny!"

"I can live with the suspense!" I say, shooing Kat back to her own car.

Doug's phone starts buzzing in his pocket. A shadow crosses his face as he looks at the screen. "Gotta take this," he says. "Work." He presses the phone to his ear and slides into the driver's side, slamming the door shut.

I'm about to go around to the other side of the car when I realize that I haven't said good-bye to Jodi. There is a black limousine a few cars ahead of ours, so I decide to knock on the window and wave a quick farewell from under my umbrella.

The black tinted glass slides down a few inches. A hand emerges, holding a fedora.

That's not Jodi's, I think.

"No way!" I laugh. I jump up and down in the puddles and demand more. "Roll down the window, Tim! I need to see your whole beautiful face to verify that it's really you!"

The automatic glass window dips lower to reveal the complete facial franchise, from twinkling blue eyes to the adorable dimples surrounding the slightly cocky grin. He even has the requisite two-day blond stubble. "Satisfied?"

He doesn't *say* the word, exactly. He drawls it, nice and slow like.

I believe Tim Cubix is using his southern charm on me.

And it works.

"Well, yes, actually, I am feeling quite...satisfied." I smile, flirting with him in a way I never could have earlier in the week. I'd like to take him home with me so we can snuggle up under a blanket and watch one of his movies while the rain pitter-patters on the roof, but I think that might be taking things a bit too far. So instead, I just babble. "You see, any old schmuck in a limousine can wave a fedora in your face and *pretend* to be a Hollywood hotshot."

The window lowers more, revealing a passenger in the seat next to Tim. MC Lenny waves a fedora at me, his lips pressed tightly together in an embarrassed smile.

I nod my head in his direction. "My point exactly."

"We had a meeting in the city about the upcoming New Orleans video, so we came by to pay our respects," Tim says, but I'm so busy watching those lovely lips move, I hardly hear what they say.

"Kat!" I call, looking out from under my big black parasol. She needs to see this. Jodi, too. I can only glimpse people a few feet ahead of me, and neither of them is in my sightline. Strange. Kat's car is still here, though. I'm not sure about the immediate family, but they probably already left. I adjust the umbrella, holding it back so that I can get a wider view of the surrounding area. "Jodi!"

Three figures in black are huddled under a tree, the same tree that Kat used when answering her disruptive phone call. It's hard to make them out through the gloom of the rain. Although my vision is distorted, I can tell that one of them is wearing a dress that reaches all the way to the ground.

"Stay here!" I instruct the fellas. "I'm going to get Jodi!" I yell the words, trying to be heard over the pounding precipitation. In response, I get a double thumbs-up. I'm telling you, they are like two peas in a pod, my Tim and my Lenny.

I pass my Doug, who is still on the phone in our car, now gesticulating wildly. I hold up my pointer finger to him, in a gesture meant to say, *One minute, I'm going to find Jodi and Kat and bring them back to that limo over there, in which sits Tim Cubix and MC Lenny*, but I'm not sure he gets all that. He merely nods through the windshield in my general direction and goes back to his call.

Whatever. His loss.

It's a slight uphill climb to my destination, and my feet are soaked by the time I reach the giant elm, my boots caked with thick mud. I've probably ruined the leather, but Tim's worth it.

"Hi," I pant, talking to the three pairs of feet meeting my down turned gaze. "I just wanted to tell you that—"

"Lauren," says a voice that at first I don't recognize. "Glad you could make it to your funeral."

"Leslie?" I ask, moving my umbrella out of the way. "Are you quoting *Dynasty* or something?" It's Leslie, all right. The sunglasses are gone and her face no longer has the bandages. Instead, a slick, Vaseline-like cream is smeared over the scar. The ointment makes the jagged line glisten and shine repulsively.

But there's more. On her head is a plastic CVS pharmacy bag, tied neatly under her chin like a bonnet.

"Hi," Jodi says. What she means is, *we're in deep doo-doo.*

"Hey there," Kat says. And what she means is, *make a run for it.*

Neither one looks all that happy to see me.

"Lemme guess," I say. "She found out about last night's intermission break-in?"

"And catnapping!" Leslie adds.

"We did not nap your cat," Kat clarifies. "We merely moved him to an isolated locale."

"Because my husband thinks he's allergic," I say.

"But he's not," the three of us explain in unison.

"May I just say, I thought your dancing was fantastic last night," I interject, trying to kiss Leslie's substantial behind and confuse her simultaneously.

Leslie considers this, nodding as if she agrees.

Kat jumps in to continue. "More importantly, had we known that you were on the verge of apologizing for your ridiculous and perverse behavior, we never, ever would have stolen your nanny cams."

"You see, we thought you were going to sue us! Blackmail us!" I say.

"Blackmail us and then sue us!" Kat adds.

"You left us no choice," I say. "Please—don't kill us. We are so very sorry."

We all freeze while Leslie ponders her next move. Her eyes are large and, at first, blank. Then they seem to fill with tears. In the intervening seconds, Kat moves closer to Leslie, which seems counter-intuitive to me. If you want to avoid being punched in the nose, I would think you would move your nose out of the way.

But no, Kat's right in there, kind of studying Leslie's face, her head cocked sideways, her nose extremely close to Leslie's jaw line, as if she knows exactly what she's going to find. She even extends her pointer finger at the red-and-white CVS baggie-bonnet and kind of pokes around under Leslie's chin, inadvertently loosening the bow.

"Fascinating," she says, stepping back toward us.

"What's that?" Leslie asks.

"You almost can't tell."

"Can't tell what?" I ask.

"That Leslie has a man beard. It requires constant attention so as not to ever appear stubbly."

"Hey!" Leslie shouts.

Kat keeps talking over her.

"Depilatories, razors, waxes, potions and lotions, you've got to be *vigilant*, right Leslie?"

We all turn to Leslie, trying to figure out if Kat's words are true.

Leslie's face is a car wreck of emotion, from first impact to crunch of metal to airbags deploying in order to keep her psyche safe from this barrage.

Kat speaks on. "Monitoring all that facial hair requires you to peer at your reflection in that goose-necked vanity mirror—equipped with nanny cam—formerly at home on your bathroom counter—several times a day, to see if any whiskers need plucking..."

Leslie lets out a deep, painful groan, much like the sound of a grizzly bear whose foot is caught in a steel trap, then lunges her full weight at Kat.

Jodi gracefully dance-steps aside to let Leslie pass, and raises her right hand overhead like a bullfighter ready to take on a changing animal. That hand then comes down on Leslie's head and snatches the plastic bag from it, whipping Leslie's neck back a little as the bag gets free.

That moment gives Kat enough time to move out of danger. Well, she's now standing behind me and clutching my forearms protectively, using me as a human shield.

"You'll have to break through Lauren first!" Kat says.

I hold my umbrella out over Kat; at the very least, I can protect her from the rain.

"Yeah...I don't think that's gonna help you," I say. "Plus, nice friend you are."

Kat whispers behind my back, "Shay's the one who called during the funeral. She watched the videos."

"Yeah, got that." This is great news, although potentially embarrassing. "Did she say how much she watched?"

"What have you done?" Leslie whispers, turning back to Jodi. Then, louder, "Look at what you've done!"

Kat and I face Jodi and Leslie, both forms now fully exposed to the weather. Jodi is wearing a triumphant grin, one sopping wet hand placed defiantly on one sopping wet hip. Leslie is crouched over, holding her head in her hands, trying to protect her hair from the rivulets of rainwater that are soaking into it.

"I'm frizzing! I'm frizzing!" she cries, kneeling on the ground, the raw grief of the moment making it impossible for her to stay erect.

Kat and I look on, confused.

"Simple fashionista science, people," Jodi explains, circling Leslie's form. The clingy black gown trails behind her theatrically as Leslie weeps on the ground, engulfed by her black raincoat and the wetness of defeat. "The well-known Keratin hair treatment is an expensive—albeit highly effective—solution for those not blessed with naturally glossy hair like mine." Jodi tries but fails to toss her hair over her shoulder, because it's now drenched and plastered to her head. "This process turns unruly, kinky hair absolutely shiny and straight. But!" Here she stops and looks at Kat and me, her eyes shimmering with knowledge. "It only works *if you keep your hair completely dry for the first four days after treatment*. No sweating, no condensation from showers, and absolutely...no...rain."

"So, we, like, messed up her hair?" Kat asks. "That's it?"

"That's not just it!" Leslie says, picking her head up and sitting back on the grass, her hair a tangled mess, some of which is now sticking to the ointment on her totaled face.

"My treatment went *beyond* Keratin, Jodi. It's way botanical and toxic, and some of the most potent ingredients come from an island in the Pacific Ocean. This magical hair-straightening treatment is only currently available in two underground locations in the United States, because it hasn't received FDA approval yet and probably never will. I can only undergo the process seven times *ever* before it will give me cancer!" She gathers her strength and stands, looking like she's going to implode. "And *you* just *wasted* one of them!"

"Wait," Jodi says. "Did you have the infamous Galapagos Straightening?"

Leslie nods.

"I am so sorry I messed that up," Jodi says. "I had no idea."

"That's the problem with your little gang, isn't it?" Leslie says, as if some deep understanding has just clicked into focus. "You always have *no idea*! You're always so sorry *after* the fact, apologizing *after* you ruin my face, and *after* you steal from my house, and *after* you destroy my hair!"

She's kind of got a point there.

"You people are so mean!"

Two points, perhaps.

"And...and...you are ruining my life!"

Well, that might be exaggeration.

"I thought that we were friends," she sighs, her voice a tiny echo of sound.

Jodi, Kat, and I are shamed into silence.

"Excuse me?" A gentlemanly southern voice calls from a few feet below the hilly knoll where we are standing. "Ladies? If I may?"

"Is that...?" Jodi asks.

"Oh yeah!" I say, snapping back to attention. "That's what I came to tell you. Tim's here. He and Lenny came for the funeral." I shrug, like, *sorry, it slipped my mind, what with all the bitch slapping.*

I lower my umbrella to the ground because the rain, of course, has stopped for Tim Cubix. It's as if his whole life exists on a back-lot Hollywood sound stage, with directors creating mood through weather and light.

We squint into the sudden glare of sun on wet pavement and watch, starry-eyed, as Tim saunters toward us in a worn leather jacket over a gray T-shirt and jeans.

"Is that...?" Leslie asks, echoing Jodi.

Tim reaches our motley crew and looks around, nodding his head at Kat, Jodi, and me while trying unsuccessfully to hide a smile. Which means I get the benefit of full-on dimples.

Sunday just got a whole lot better.

And then he speaks. "What's that saying? You can take the women out of the Miami heat, but you can't take the Miami heat out of the women?"

"Something like that," Jodi smirks. She twists the water out of her hair and ties it into a slick, gorgeous bun. "Thanks for coming, Lex. And for your generous message and donation last night." Tim waves her gratitude away, perhaps trying to make light of his embarrassment of riches. His eyes sweep over the rest of us.

"Hi," he says, extending his hand to a grotesque looking, completely humiliated Leslie. "I'm Tim."

CHAPTER 38

"IT WAS THE CRAZIEST SCENE, Doug, and you missed it," I say, sliding into the passenger seat of our car. Only, when I turn to look at Doug in the driver's seat, he's not there.

"Doug?" I call out, like he could be somewhere in our car without me noticing him, or like maybe he just didn't hear me the first time.

I get back out of the car and look down the private drive that meanders through the cemetery grounds. There are only a few cars left from the funeral procession and no sign of Doug standing about. During the pounding of the rain and the chaos of the quarrel with Leslie, I sort of forgot where I was. But in the wake of that emotional and physical storm, a placid hush has descended on the property. I gaze across the cemetery and down the soft, green hill dotted with tombstones, and breathe deeply, sending one final farewell—and an apology or two—to Sonia Goldberg.

On the third ring of my cell phone call to Doug, one of the back doors to Tim's limousine opens, and Doug steps out. He holds his cell phone up. "You rang?"

I click the "end call" button and walk toward him, my stomach roiling nervously. Has Doug been sitting in the backseat of a stretch limo with MC Lenny this whole time?

And if so, why? What in fuck's sake have they got to talk about besides...me?

It doesn't help my intestines to see that he's smirking, like he's got a secret. Or like he's very pleased with himself. Or both, like he's got a secret that pleases him very much.

Oh no, he's murdered Lenny.

He's murdered Lenny in the back of Tim Cubix's fancy ride, and now we'll all be going to jail together to live forever in one large pen like at the end of *Seinfeld*.

"...and so, while I was talking to my bookkeeper on the phone about this problem we're having making payroll this month, I looked out the window and saw..." Doug stops to look at me. "Lauren, are you even listening?"

"Nah...not really," I admit. "I'm a little freaked out right now, creating Armageddon scenarios."

"Lauren," he says, extending his hands toward mine. He clasps our hands together as we stand face-to-face, as if we are saying our wedding vows. "I have a few things to tell you. I haven't been...well, it's complicated really, but...what it comes down to is that"—and here he inhales and exhales deeply before continuing—"I have not been completely honest with you."

My first thought, bizarre as it seems, is one of satisfaction, in an *I knew it* kind of way. It's like all of my worst fears and darkest daydreams of where Doug has been these past few months have been confirmed. So, as much as I want to get angry at him for lying to me, my primary emotion is actually self-congratulatory for sensing that something was way off with us.

Then I mimic his deep inhale-exhale and ask. "Who is she?"

"My bookkeeper."

Doug's bookkeeper is a seventy-eight-year-old, white-haired librarian type who wears orthopedic shoes and smells of talcum powder and clove cigarettes. She's like Betty White's younger, less funny sister.

"You're sleeping with Dorothy?"

"Sleeping with...?" Then his face explodes into laughter as he grabs onto a mental image probably similar to the one I've just created. "My God! No! Lauren, what kind of person do you think I am?"

"A gerophiliac?"

"You just made that term up."

"Yes, I did. Right here on the spot."

"Lauren, your imagination needs a vacation. The rest of you does not. Now listen," he says, placing his hands firmly on my shoulders as if to keep me from running away again. "I've been having some...financial trouble with the company, and the bank refused to give me another loan until I'd paid back the first."

"I thought you paid back the first one in September," I say.

"I tried to." He pauses, and I watch his face as he searches for the next words. "But it turned out that I needed the money to pay the rent on the office space, and then payroll was due, and then quarterly taxes were due and, still, my clients were paying me in bits and pieces, with no one project coming in at a big enough profit margin to ever get ahead and...things just snowballed. So, no, I haven't been able to pay the bank back yet."

"Oh, Doug." I mentally begin adding up the money I spent frivolously in the past few days and estimating it at about $5,000. My stomach drops into my bowels.

"Since Dorothy is in charge of the company's books, she saw where things were headed, which was basically into bankruptcy, and she came to me one night after work with a proposition." He pauses and raises an eyebrow at me mockingly. "*Not* of the sexual nature."

"Ha," I say, meaning, *get on with your story and let's not pause for comic relief.*

"So, long story short, Dorothy has been a private investor for me since September, loaning me a good deal of her own inheritance and retirement money to help me get out from under, thus avoiding having creditors come after us and take away our house as collateral for unpaid bills."

Our house?

"Can you really be that bad at business?" I ask, rather unkindly. "And that careless? To put our home at risk?"

Doug looks contrite, but speaks defensively. "That's what you have to do when you start your own business, Lauren! Put up something of value as collateral."

"Don't snap at me!" I snap at Doug. I take a moment to compose myself, then continue at a lower volume. "You never even discussed that part with me. I had no idea."

"I know, I know." He scratches his head with his right hand. "I had it in my head that I wasn't lying to you if you hadn't asked me about something directly. I thought it was okay to gloss over the everyday accounting problems because...well, I guess I thought I could handle it myself, and that it would straighten itself out, and that I didn't want you to worry. As you well know, there's a fine line between withholding information and lying."

"Don't twist this around and make it about me!" I say. "That's not a fair comparison."

He raises his eyebrows at me questioningly.

"Okay, fine. It's a perfect comparison," I say. I look up the hill to where Kat, Jodi and Leslie are still talking with Tim.

That particular group assembled on the hill is like a study in the art of withholding information. Tim pulled a disappearing act from the set of *Croc of Lies* and didn't tell Ruby where he was. Jodi consistently skims off the fat of Lee's profitable business and uses it as her own "salary," and Leslie does everything within her power to make sure that her husband never discovers that she has more facial hair than he does. And Kat? She lied to herself, which is maybe the worst of all, by pretending that teaching kindergarten and being married to Peter would lead her to the life she thought she wanted.

Every one of us has found ways to skew the truth to fit our purposes. It's not always the moral choice, or the most mature, but perhaps, in the moment of decision-making, it seems completely necessary.

I look at Doug and try to see this mess from his point of view. "I think you didn't want me to know the truth and to judge you. You didn't want me to be mad at you."

Doug shakes his head in disagreement. "It's not anger I worried about...more like...I didn't want you to be *disappointed* in me. And I couldn't admit that I was failing. That my company was failing. That *I* am a failure."

"Oh, Doug," I say again, this time with compassion. "Your company might fail, but that does not mean that you are a failure." I put my head against his chest and hear the thrump-thrump of his heart.

"What's that you just said, Worthing? Repeat after me: nobody's a failure," MC Lenny says, emerging from the stretch limo and stretching. "Certainly not a client of mine like your husband here."

"A what?" I ask, looking from Doug to Lenny and back again.

"He's right. A client," Doug reiterates. "I saw Lenny get out of the limo with Tim Cubix, and, once my initial shock at that passed, and once my initial interest in busting Lenny's ball sack passed, too, I remembered: rapping aside, Lenny is a pretty well-known accountant in the city."

"CPA by day, RAP by night, though not for much longer, I hope," Lenny says.

"Just long enough to get me out of this jam," Doug adds.

"And...did I mention *how* I'm going to do that?" A sly smile creases the corners of Lenny's mouth.

"With some...magical accounting skills, I'm guessing?" I say.

"Including some creative restructuring of my company and another loan from a different bank?" Doug adds.

"Nah, guys. Think out of the box. Think...Hollywood," Lenny says cryptically.

And just like that, almost as if on cue from an unseen director, Tim walks over and joins us.

"Interesting threesome," Tim whispers to me, sending chills down my spine. I laugh and try to make light of his comment, because the last thing I need Doug to know is that Tim knows that I kissed Lenny in Miami. That's like TMI times a million, when a megastar's got inside info on where your wife's tongue has been before you do. Instead, I make introductions. Tim to Doug, Doug to Tim.

"Hey," Doug coughs out, extending his hand for a manly shake.

"Hey, dude. It's great to finally put the face to the name," Tim says warmly. "Your wife is a great person."

"Yup," Doug says. "Although I prefer when she doesn't flat out lie to me and then bolt, abandoning me and my kids and risking her livelihood in the process."

"True, that," Tim says. "Ruby's always on the run. Namibia one day, Cannes the next. It's *annoying*." He shrugs. "You know, women."

That shuts Doug up pretty quick.

"Hey, Tim," Lenny says, "did I mention that Doug here is a talented graphic designer with his own boutique shop in the city?"

"Really?" Tim says, studying Doug.

Doug merely nods. I want to kick him into high gear, bring out the salesman smooth talker that Doug can be when he gets excited about his work. Instead, his cheeks are flushed and he's scratching his neck nervously.

Okay, maybe that's just how I was when I first met Tim, too.

"Totally cutting-edge facility," Lenny adds, seeing that Doug might not jump in here. "He used to work with some guys out in LA at Imaginary Forces. Doug's shop can handle lots of specialized motion graphics for movie titles and trailers, plus amazing collateral materials in print, like posters and bus-wrap signage."

Lenny knows all this stuff because I complained to him for hours on end via Facebook about Doug's new solo venture and his subsequent workaholic schedule.

Now, that's irony put to good use right there.

"You serious?" Tim says, addressing Doug as if he's the one speaking the lines.

"Uh-huh," Doug says. He clears his throat, which is a good sign that he might actually speak intelligible words next. I breathe a sigh of relief as he does. "We just got Nickelodeon as a client. We hope they'll let us do all the work for the Kid's Choice Awards, but we're still up against some other agencies for that particular gig."

"I'm thinking he's the right guy for postproduction on the Haiti stuff, since I'll be doing it all in New York," Lenny says.

"What are you doing right now?" Tim asks Doug.

I'm thinking that Doug's possible answers to that question include, but are certainly not limited to: *Melting down, Freaking out, Putting my cozy Tudor on the market,* and/or *Trying to unravel a tangle of lies and get my wife to forgive me just as I have forgiven her.*

"Not much," Doug says, which is also a legitimate response. "Mourning maybe? Sitting some shivah?"

"Did somebody say shivah?" Jodi says, walking down the hill with Kat and Leslie in tow, the two of them holding the train of Jodi's dress out behind them like bridesmaids coming down the aisle. "'Cause it's at my house and I think I'm running a little late. Plus, I'm freezing! Thanks, ladies," she says, as Leslie and Kat drop Jodi's tail. "Glad we could work that out. Everyone in love again?" she jokes, scanning our faces for signs of unrest.

"Yes," Doug says, speaking for the group. "I believe we are."

"Oh, Tim, would you mind if Leslie had a small photo-op with you, after she cleans herself up a bit at my house?" Jodi asks. Tim raises an eyebrow, but nods gamely. "Wonderful," Jodi continues. "In exchange for the experience, Leslie wishes to drop any and all charges against Lauren for the 'incident' on Wednesday night."

"Really?" I say. "You...don't mind, Tim?" He shakes his head, and I turn to Leslie. "And...this is all good with you? No hard feelings?"

"I won't sue you, Lauren. But I probably won't ever be your friend again, either. No more of my parties for you."

I pretend to find this news disheartening, and shake my head forlornly. Inside, I'm thinking, *Now, that's what I'd call a win-win!*

"So, who's up for enjoying white fish and herring with Rabbi Cantor?"

"Bring it on," Lenny says. He motions for Doug to join him and Tim in the limo. Doug tosses me the keys to our car and flashes me a huge, childlike grin.

"I know all about it, Doug," I say, heading back to our Acura. "Stick with me, my friend. It turns out, life is fun!"

CHAPTER 39

"I'M GOING TO RESIGN TOMORROW," Kat tells me as we spread cream cheese on our respective bagels and move from Jodi's expansive, formal dining room into her supersized living room. Her custom-built duo of traditionally overstuffed damask sofas have been pushed aside and replaced with uncomfortable, backless wooden cubes, to reflect the Jewish tradition of depriving oneself of luxury while in mourning. We select two of these stools near a huge bay window and sit overlooking the English garden.

"That's a big day you've got planned, Kat. Divorced and unemployed all in one shot. Maybe you want to hold off for a few weeks? Clear your head first?"

Kat gives me a tired smile. "How long have I been complaining about my job?"

The answer is: for as long as I've known her. "Fair enough."

"I'm going to resign effective June, so I'll finish out the year, and give the demented-stration some time to fill my position."

"That's mature of you. It will also give you some time to think about next steps," I add.

"I've thought," Kat says. "Next steps are planned." In her usual fashion, however, she is not immediately forthcoming with the rest of the paragraph. She takes a bite of a bagel and chews it slowly.

"Oh, c'mon!" I say. "Out with it."

"Simple," she says. "I'm doing what generations of failed O'Connells do when the mainland gets to be too much. I'm going home."

I think of Kat's father and four brothers, weather-beaten New Englanders who spend entire summers on top of houses, fixing shingles and painting trim. When the seasons change, they move indoors, drinking beer in pubs until the first sign of daffodils brings them back into the light. "Home home?" I ask. "Nantucket?"

"Yeah. Ever since my mom died last year, I've been missing the island. You know what they say, pour sea salt on the wound to help it heal, or whatever."

"I think that's probably the opposite of what they say."

"Then it should definitely work for me."

I take a deep breath and let it go. "So, you're sure."

She nods, chews, and swallows. Her green eyes speak volumes of the things she can't say, retelling the stories of the decade we've spent together as teachers and friends.

"You're not just going home to drink, are you?"

"No. Yes. My sisters-in-law are opening a yoga studio in an old barn out in Cisco. The guys have been refurbishing it."

"So...you're gonna do lots of yoga?"

"Teach, dumbass. I'm going to teach yoga."

"Oh! That's perfect! Aligning the chakras and all!"

"I'm putting Varka's bull to good use." She smiles wistfully.

I hug her tightly, which is awkward with our plates of deli and our seated positions on these benches. But even with our knees rubbing into each other's, and with the promise of a calmer, more centered life ahead for Kat, I still manage to feel overwhelmingly sad.

There are so many types of loss, I realize, closing my eyes as we rock back and forth in our embrace, and so many ways to mourn.

I pull away from Kat and steady my plate on my lap, studying her face, trying to memorize it.

"I've always wanted to try this," I say, reaching out and taking one of her curls in my fingers. She looks at me oddly, but lets me continue. I pull the curl out straight, watching the hair extend far past her shoulders, testing to see how long it can really reach. Finally, I let go and watch the wave instantly tighten back up.

"I love you, Kitty-Kat."

Her eyes are brimming with tears, but she blinks them back. "Weirdo. Would you like a lock of my hair for your memory chest?"

Which is her way of telling me that she loves me, too.

I dab my eyes with a crumpled tissue from my pocket and pass it to Kat. Then I deftly change the subject.

"Oh—I almost forgot—whatever you do tomorrow when you speak to Martha, *do not* admit to being with me last week. I spoke to her about my absence and she totally doesn't know that you were in Miami."

"A benefit of her lack of Internet savvy, I guess."

"And…Shay?" I ask.

"That's it. End of story."

"Really?"

Kat shrugs. "I mean, I'm grateful that I had this week, fucked up as it was. With you and Jodi. With Shay. And now I'm grateful to be moving on, whatever that means for me."

We both sniffle ourselves back to normal.

"I, for one, am grateful for the faraway land of Nova Scotia and the wonderful smoked salmon it has given the world," Lenny says, joining us and trying unsuccessfully to fold his long body down onto one of the boxes. He gives up and remains standing, towering above us.

"Where's Tim?" I ask.

"Still talking to Doug in the limo," Lenny says. "They're just finishing up some specifics about the job."

"Thanks, Len," I say. "When you said you were going to help Doug's company, I thought you meant…" I trail off. "Like…you know…" I'm getting a little choked up just thinking about how much help he really just gave to Doug and, by proxy, to me and my family. Having a working relationship like that with Tim Cubix's production company is bigger than anything a bank could do to help Doug's finances. It will give him actual work—exciting projects—and connections to others who might require his services too.

I think our Tudor is safe.

"I know." He smiles. "It was the least I could do, Lauren. I mean, I really fucked up, coming to see you in Miami and all." He shakes his head ruefully. "I'm glad I could do something right for your family."

"Amen to that," Kat says.

"Jodi!" Lee calls, much too loud for the particularly somber circumstances under which we are here. His voice carries through the wide rooms and echoes, bouncing off the twelve-foot ceilings. We all kind of jump at the surprisingly accusatory tone embedded in those two syllables.

"Coming!" Jodi sings back, apparently not at all ruffled by her husband's bark. She sails down the stairs in yet another black ensemble, her now-dry hair fanning out behind her dramatically, recently applied lip gloss sparkling.

My curiosity piqued, I turn to the sound of their voices in the front hall and notice Claudine, Jodi's housekeeper-slash-babysitter, quickly grab her jacket out of the closet and skedaddle toward the front door just as Jodi reaches the bottom step. "I'm so sorry," Claudine says, turning back to Jodi with one hand on the door-knob, "I didn't know." Then she bolts through the front door like a drunken teen leaving the darkened playground moments before the cops arrive.

"What is she talking about?" Jodi asks, as the front door slams shut.

Lee's face as he enters the hall from the kitchen is not amused.

"Looks like there's been some hanky-panky of the domestic-help variety," Lenny whispers to Kat and me. "A little 'bend over and let me watch you clean that oven,' huh? Whaddaya think?"

"I think you really are the world's largest douche bag, Len," Kat says.

"This has nothing to do with sex," I say, putting the pieces together.

"How much do you pay Claudine?" Lee asks, trying to keep his voice neutral. Before Jodi can answer, he's speaking again, moving toward her slowly. Jodi mimics his steps, except that she's moving backward, and they dance a bizarre tango like that in a circle around the foyer. "I'm asking because I went to pay her for the week, which you usually do on Fridays, only you were in Florida. Since she came to help out today, I paid her for that, and then I counted out four hundred dollars in cash and handed it over for her weekly salary."

Jodi's big brown eyes grow bigger and more afraid, as if she's Scrooge being shown a vision of her wicked past and the conse-quences her actions will carry into her future.

The shivah has stopped midchew, as all thirty or so of the guests hang on to this dramatic display, some with Styrofoam coffee cups held aloft and frozen in time.

"And you know what she said?" Lee asks.

"Thank you?" Jodi guesses, her back now up against the silver-and-taupe wallpaper, her hands tucked behind her, clutching the decorative chair rail for support. Her body may show fear, but her voice remains solid ice.

Lee shakes his head and smiles sadly, like he's the only one in on the joke. "More like 'Oh, Mr. Moncrieff, one of those hundred-dollar bills goes to Miss Jodi's salary.'"

"She can't really be that fucking stupid," Jodi mutters to herself, anger now creeping in to claim its rightful spot behind surprise.

Lee laughs bitterly. "That's the part that gets you upset? That Claudine was dumb enough to tell on you?"

Jodi pauses for a moment and looks like she's going to cave. I think it's time to usher everyone out of this shivah so that the Moncrieffs can have their marital dispute in private. But then Jodi steps up onto the first stair so as to be seen more clearly by the crowd and strikes a defiant pose.

Who am I kidding? Jodi loves an audience, no matter the occasion.

In that momentary silence, Great-Aunt Elaine gets up from her seat in the living room and pushes her way through our little group. "Wait a second, wait a second," she says, shuffling her feet slowly. Then, once she's reached the foyer, she says, "I'm going to tell you a story."

She steps into the center of the room and stares sort of wistfully into the middle distance. "When I was a young girl, my mother gave me and my sister Sonia pushkes."

"What the hell is a push key?" Kat whispers to me.

"Maybe it's something related to Jodi."

"And why does every funeral have a nostalgic-old-lady-on-a-tangent?"

I shrug.

"A pushke is a small can or box kept in the home for the collection of tzedakah, or charity, and *yes*, it relates to Jodi," Elaine says, looking over at Kat and me and winking. "I may be slow to walk, but I am quick to hear. Anyway," she continues, "our family kept one in the kitchen, on the window ledge by the sink. We'd contribute change to it and give it to the synagogue a few times a year.

"But not this pushke; this pushke was different. This tin can was a set aside for Sonia and me to save up some money—a dime here, a penny there—you'd be surprised how, over time, it really adds up! And before you knew it, we would each have enough money to buy a new pair of satin gloves or a Billie Holiday record. Or both! All I'm saying is that Jewish women have been keeping little stashes of money on the side, hidden from their fathers and husbands, for ages. The pushke is tradition."

Jodi is hanging onto every word her great-aunt is saying, as if it's Talmudic law. When Elaine stops to catch her breath, Jodi looks triumphantly at Lee and says, "See? I was doing it for charity. And because I'm, like, *supposed to.*"

Great-Aunt Elaine walks over to Jodi and places her gnarled, arthritic hands on top of Jodi's beautifully manicured ones. The pair stares deep into each other's eyes. "Not only is it tradition, my darling grand-niece, it's your birthright. It is truly your *destiny* to steal from you husband. It's the Goldberg way. Given your insight, I'm not surprised that you discovered this secret all on your own."

"So *you* were the charity that you were giving charity to?" Lee asks, incredulous.

"Charity starts at home, Lee," Jodi says defiantly, perfectly content to stand behind her own bullshit, especially now that's it been proven to be true. Then she steps down off the stair and approaches him, her voice softer. "Lee, you treat yourself to plenty of extravagances because you have the money." She points out the window to the Porsche parked in the driveway. "But...I don't have an income. So, the fundamental question is, how am I ever supposed to treat myself to nice things if I don't have the cash with which to indulge?"

Lee looks down at the face of his beautiful, slightly corrupt wife and rolls his eyes. "Pushke or not, maybe it really is time you got a job, Jo."

"Just a little one, like part-time? Something fun and fab?" Jodi asks, her eyelids batting playfully.

I've got to hand it to Jodi. She has just managed to deftly side-step a potentially explosive argument by claiming some sanctioned, family legacy of deceit. Plus, she secured the okay to work part-time, all while making it look like it was Lee's idea.

"Knock yourself out," Lee says. Then he kisses her on the forehead and scans the crowd, sighing deeply. "Where's my buddy Jim?" Spotting his friend in the dining room, Lee waves him over and pulls him close. "Come outside with me? I need to smoke a doobie."

Jimmy fishes for something in his pocket and nods as they head out the door.

"I've got to take some notes on this," Kat says, shaking her head disbelievingly. "So that in my next life I can come back as Jodi."

"I don't know," I say, looking out the window to where Doug is emerging from the limo parked next to Lee's Porsche. "I think I'd kind of like to be Doug."

"So, what you're saying is...?" I ask Doug as we drive back from Jodi's house. The late-afternoon sun is dipping low in the sky and I can't help but feel anxious about Monday's approach.

To think how far I've traveled since last Monday, only to end up right back where I started.

Only I'm not quite the same anymore, am I?

"I'm saying that Tim basically handed me the job. We Skyped with some head of his production company who was still in her pajamas out in LA, and Tim made the introductions and was like, 'Here's the guy for the Build a Better Future project,' and that was basically it. It was insane," he says, shaking his head like he's not sure what just happened to his life.

"Cool," I say, thinking how much this past week has changed us both. "So, when do you start?"

"Next month. Lenny said he could actually use his real accounting skills to help me get a loan until then, to pay back Dorothy. And then," he says, glancing over to me while driving, then focusing back on the road ahead, "once that project wraps, you and I should plan a trip. A long weekend somewhere, just the two of us, to reconnect."

"Miami?" I joke.

"Any place but." He's not smiling.

"How about Boston?" I say, checking my e-mails and reading quickly through one I just received from Georgie.

"Boston? Don't you want to go someplace warm? Tropical?"

"Well, the reason is...I kind of wrote to Georgie this morning with an idea I had, and it seems..." I trail off as I continue to read the e-mail, verifying its contents, my excitement growing. "Georgie just offered me a job for the summer." Although I am beyond surprised to hear from her so soon, I knew it was a great idea, a

Georgie idea, a really big idea, the moment it came to me. "As a researcher and adjunct professor. At Harvard!" I say, unable to keep the enthusiasm out of my voice. "Bye, bye, middle school!"

Doug brakes too hard at a stop sign and glances my way. "Researching what?"

"Women in midlife who want to switch careers!"

"But that's...brilliant. It's you in a nutshell."

"I know! I'm brilliant! All it took was a week of cutting school to figure it out! And now I'm going to get to write a book about women like me." And Jodi. And Kat.

"Who knew that your lack of interest in your job would be so inspiring, Mrs. Worthing." Doug holds out his right palm and I slap it. "We've both failed at our jobs, and yet we're awesome," he concludes.

I read through the e-mail several more times before we pull into the driveway, and quickly jot *I accept* back to Georgie. It's a part-time gig, which is perfect for me because it will give me some time to try out stay-at-home motherhood and the perilous PTA. Georgie says I'll have to prove myself over the summer before she can offer me a more substantial salary in September. That is, if I want to continue into the fall. She says the position requires two full days on campus, but that I could stay over in Boston one night a week at staff housing and commute back and forth via train.

Good thing I've tried that train and I know it works.

And Boston isn't that far.

From New York...and Nantucket.

So, for now, anyway, it looks like I'm keeping my day job. I won't be storming into Martha's office tomorrow to resign alongside Kat, which is probably a blessing in disguise. I'll take my time and make sure Doug's project really pans out first, wait until his company gets back on its feet before I formally resign.

In the meantime, I'll get to carry that little sparkly secret around with me for the rest of the school year, knowing that I am charting a new path for my own future, and that, although it might be risky, it will certainly be rewarding.

I'd say it was quite a productive week, all in all, culminating in one of the best Sundays on record.

CHAPTER 40

LATE THAT NIGHT, DOUG AND I sneak quietly down the stairs, turning off lights as we go. I'm careful to avoid that third step, the one that always creaks and brings Becca from her bed before she's drifted soundly off to sleep.

Somehow, though, she hears me anyway. My heart drops into my stomach as I realize she's standing right behind me on the landing between the first and second floor.

"You woke me up!" she yells, her fists clenched by her side, tiny balls of rage.

"Shh!" I say. "Don't wake your brother." Doug starts to climb back up the stairs to help me with Becca, but I shoo him away.

"I can if I want to!" My daughter's got some seriously powerful lungs.

"No, you cannot!" I whisper-shout back. I'm about to get into a screaming fight with her, I know it. This will wake Ben, who will then want to play on his DSi or go on the computer. It will take me another hour to get them both back to bed, thereby shattering my precarious sense of domestic bliss and squelching any interest I might have had in having sex with Doug tonight.

Which makes me think of Tim Cubix.

Tim Cubix and star charts.

"Hey, Bec!" I say, making my voice sound full of wonder and excitement. "Do you want to draw a *star* on your *door*?" I make sure to be vague enough to keep her wanting more information.

"Why?" she asks, her huge blue eyes not quite trusting me yet. At least she's not screaming bloody murder.

"Because," I whisper, gently guiding her back toward her room. "That's what good girls do. They get stars." She nods several times to let me know that this makes perfect sense. I reach into her art supplies and tape a purple piece of construction paper to her bedroom door. I hand her a marker.

"And then, once you get enough stars, the stars turn into presents!" I explain. She nods again and concentrates on neatly making the five points. Then she places the cap back on the marker and hands it to me so she can slide back in under the covers.

I blow her a kiss good night and touch the star chart.

Because I know that, in some cases, the star himself is the actual present.

A moment later, I slip into the darkened kitchen to face the piles of mail, kid artwork, magazines, and newspapers that Doug and I still have not cleaned up, and which look like hilly landscapes against the smooth countertop of the kitchen island.

Doug joins me from the sunroom and the two of us scan the scene.

I feel like grabbing a big trashcan and dumping it all, without sorting or deciding exactly where the paper trail of our lives should go. Doug sighs, and I know he's thinking the same thing.

"The last thing I want to do right now is face this mess." I mean it literally, but it feels like a metaphor.

"We have to," he says, turning on the sharp overhead lighting. I squint. He dims it so that the atmosphere mellows.

"That's better. Where to begin?"

"Think of it as spring cleaning. We're clearing out the old baggage so that we can start fresh, with our new lives, tomorrow morning."

"That's optimistic of you," I say, picking up some old mail and looking through it.

"After today's funeral, I believe in miracles. I believe in fate, in destiny, in..." He trails off, searching for the right term.

"In the transformative powers of jury duty?" I ask, fingering a crisp, unopened blue envelope from the Alden County Courthouse. It's addressed to Doug.

"Good one," he says. I pass the envelope to him as proof that I'm not joking.

He reaches out to take it from me, but misses. We both watch as the blue envelope slowly falls in the empty space between us, as if being carried on a gentle breeze. It lands softly at Doug's feet.

"It's like the thing is *daring* me to pick it up," Doug says.

I smile knowingly.

Then, in one swift movement, I reach down, grab the envelope before he can, and rip the seam open.

After all, I've had some practice with these things.

I unfold the paper within and scan the printed information, reading aloud. "Mr. Doug Worthing...Your services are requested... yadda, yadda, yadda...County Courthouse...yadda, yadda...ten a.m. on Monday, April seventeenth."

I look up from the paper, spooked. "But...that's tomorrow!"

"Huh." He nods, a small smile playing on his lips.

"Did you know about this? Did you...*plan* it?" I ask. He says nothing. "Doug?!"

"No." He smiles.

I shake my head disbelievingly.

"Honestly!" Doug balks. "But that doesn't mean I can't enjoy your entertaining reaction to the news."

I return to the paper, my heart beating fast. "Failure to show up on appointed date...yadda, yadda...incarceration or fines!"

"Now, we wouldn't want that," he says.

"Doug! This isn't funny!" I say. "Jury duty's not a joke, you know."

"Oh yes, Lauren, that I know. Sometimes, jury duty is truly a matter of life or death." His dimples are fully creased. "Life or death *in Miami*."

"Doug!" I say. "You can't go! Laney's on vacation and I have to go back to work tomorrow, and I could really use your help."

"Lauren, I'd love to be able to assist you, really I would. But, see, America needs me."

I try to pout. I try to seem defiant, cocksure, like Jodi on the verge of getting her way.

Doug's not having it.

"First of all, do we even need Laney anymore?" he asks.

"Don't change the subject."

"I'm being serious. When the kids were small, we needed her. But now, they're in school all day. Laney's a terrible housekeeper. She's lazy and overly dramatic and..."

"Probably stealing my stuff," I conclude. I think about life without Laney. Without waiting for her to show up, without wondering whether the laundry is done, without finding out there is no more milk only upon opening the refrigerator to pour some milk. Mostly, I think about Laney sitting in my house all day, flipping through magazines and waiting for my kids to get off the bus.

What a colossal waste of time and money.

I think about what a relief home life without Laney would be.

"Can we just...do without her?" I ask, a lightness growing in my chest. "Can't we do this—raising a family, taking care of our home, juggling work responsibilities—just you and me, together?"

Doug inhales and exhales theatrically, like he's about to make a big concession. "I tell you what. I'll take the kids to the bus each morning, so that you can get to school on time. But beyond that, I can make no promises, in the short term, anyway. After all," he says, "I start jury duty tomorrow."

And then Doug smiles, snatching the envelope from my hands, a definite twinkle in his eye.

EPILOGUE

LADIES AND GENTLEMEN OF THE JURY, life is a series of trials. And whether we like it or not, a jury of our peers continuously judges our actions and bears witness to our everyday embarrassments and triumphs.

I mean, who hasn't dabbled in adultery, petty larceny, and the occasional inebriated foot-in-the-face debacle from time to time, right? Maybe you were caught in the act of such impropriety. Maybe not.

Fact: we all need to break out of our molds once in a while, so that we don't become...moldy. Stuck. Predictable. Bored to the point that we go looking for distractions instead of solutions.

And that was me.

But for all the wrong choices I made, I also learned from my risk-taking, probably a hell of a lot more than I would have learned by sitting in a real courtroom, listening to a rehashing of others' mistakes, or by hiding behind my desk in a sixth-grade classroom. By kicking up my heels this past week—both literally and figuratively—I have come to better appreciate human nature, in all its complexities and shades of gray.

Fact: No one is to me now what she appeared to be on Monday. Not even I am.

And that is why, ladies and gentlemen of the jury, your services are no longer needed. I have decided in favor of myself. I am not guilty.

Well, not guilty any more than you are. No offense. See that guy over there? He's done something he's not proud of, and yet he's lived to tell the tale. And same with the woman sitting next to you on the train every morning, and the barista who prepares your double espresso, and the piano teacher, the soccer coach, the dry cleaner. What I've learned this week is that there is a slippery slope of crimes and misdemeanors swirling invisibly all around us.

Jodi and Kat and I have lied and cheated and stolen. Turns out, we humans are all capable of outstanding acts of generosity one minute and incredible acts of mean-spiritedness the next. We are corrupt, immature, *and* fabulous. Luckily, we have the capacity to love and forgive and to support our friends and family even when they take leave of their senses.

Especially when they take leave.

In summation, this great country of America is grateful for your service as a sequestered juror in the now infamous case known as *Lauren Takes Leave*. And, on a personal note, I wish to thank you for being impartial as you listened to my side of the story, which may or may not be fictional.

I hope that, should life present you with small, open windows of opportunity, you choose to slip through occasionally, just to see what's out there on the other side. Grab control of your life by taking a vacation from it. Swim with dolphins. Invent your own cocktail. Pretend to be someone else.

Whether or not you chose to return to your place of work after that—or ever again—is entirely up to you.

And upon returning from your adventures, however innocuous they might be, may you, too, find an attentive, intelligent, attractive, and—above all—*forgiving* jury of your peers waiting to hear all about it.

This case is dismissed.

QUESTIONS AND TOPICS FOR DISCUSSION

by Julie Gerstenblatt

To invite Julie Gerstenblatt to your book club either in person or via Skype, e-mail her at jgerstenblatt@gmail.com.

Before I began writing full-time, I was a middle school English teacher. And that is why, even though *Lauren Takes Leave* is a bona fide beach read and all I want for you to say when you reach the end is "wow, that was fun," I had to include discussion questions at the end. I am used to assigning homework.

So, here's what I'm thinking you should do. Get a bunch of your friends to read the book, too, and then have a really informal book club meeting at someone's house. Or at a bar. Or, for authenticity, in Miami. You can be as committed to this endeavor as you wish. Make sure to drink a bit and to discuss a lot of other topics before getting to these questions. That's what my book group does and it works really well. In fact, try not to spend more than ten minutes discussing the novel, because a night out is a night out, and I'd hate to deny you that by bumming you out with symbolism.

Below the questions is the recipe for a great and easy cocktail favored by my book group. I call it the Literati.

Okay, here we go.

1. Have you ever felt like Lauren, Kat or Jodi? When? With whom do you most identify and why? Who are you the least like?

2. Many characters in the novel feel a sense of ennui, which can be defined as weariness and dissatisfaction that

leads to a kind of boredom or complacency. Think of what causes this ennui in Lauren, Kat, Jodi, and others, from MC Lenny to Laney the babysitter. How do they each respond to that tedium in their lives? Do you think they are right or wrong? How do you handle those feelings in your own life?

3. This book takes elements from three of my favorite texts and mashes them up. If you are at all familiar with the movies *Ferris Bueller's Day Off* or *Thelma and Louise*, or Oscar Wilde's play *The Importance of Being Earnest*, here is your chance to show off your knowledge. You can refer to the quotes that begin the novel for some guidance. Please pass me one of those homemade chocolate-chip cookies. Now discuss.

4. The novel is constructed around Lauren's week, both while on jury duty and while on leave from her responsibilities. At the beginning, middle, and end of that week, she talks directly to the reader, speaking to them as "ladies and gentlemen of the jury." What did you make of these sections and their role within the novel?

5. How do you feel about the relationship between Lauren and her husband, Doug?

6. There are many supporting characters in the novel. Discuss their roles, and share what you think of them, including, but not limited to:

Laney
Lenny Katzenberg
Tim Cubix
Lee Moncrieff
Martha Carrington
Professor Georgina Parks
Leslie Koch
Shay Greene

7. Which character changes the most, do you think?

8. The book's plot contains many twists and turns. As you were reading, what surprised you? Also, how do you feel about the ending of the novel?

9. I write with humor. Skim back through the book—what scenes or bits of dialogue made you laugh?

10. I also try to write with a purpose. I use humor as a vehicle for showing the world back to itself, by holding a mirror up to some of the unseemly truths hidden there, under the fun façade. What are the darker sides of human nature and society that *Lauren Takes Leave* highlights? (Hint: greed, infidelity, selfishness…)

11. Does your life have a soundtrack, like Lauren's? If so, what's on it? (Also, the music really is available through iTunes, and you can select the Lauren mix or the Kat-and-Jodi mix.)

12. Do you believe more in justice or forgiveness? (This is a question I stole from a deck of conversation starters used at parties.)

13. Looking back on the entire book, do you think Lauren had to take leave?

14. At this point in the evening, are you still drinking? If you are a mom, did you discuss your children, their teachers, and some local scandal? Did you try the dip? It's fantastic. Did you pick a book for next month yet? If not, check out my website for some favorite picks. I promise I won't make you read *The Importance of Being Earnest*. Oh, and thanks so much for reading *Lauren Takes Leave*.

The Literati

1/3 each of:
prosecco
St. Germain (elderflower liqueur)
San Pellegrino

The Crazy Literati

2/3 prosecco
1/3 St. Germain
(Who needs the San Pellegrino!?)

ACKNOWLEDGEMENTS

Many people helped me write this novel, although a good number of them are not aware of this fact. So, cheers to my writing gurus, living and deceased, both those I actually know and those I pretend to know: Elizabeth Berg, Nora Ephron, Helen Fielding, Peter Hedges, John Hughes, Stephen King, Sophie Kinsella, Kathleen Reilly, Roger Rosenblatt, Blake Snyder, Peter Trachtenberg, Jonathan Tropper, Lois Van Epps, and Oscar Wilde.

Special thanks to all the friends who supported Lauren and me in so many ways over the past few years. (Unlike the above, these people should be aware of the fact that I know them.) They include, but are certainly not limited to, Helen Breitwieser, Lauren Fabiano, Erica Faulkner, Anne George, Ursula Guise, Abby Hoffman, Kiki Hoffman, Howard Neuthaler, Serena Perlman, Susie Quill, Ray Sabini, Eric Seifer, Amy Song, John Talbot, and Staci Toporek. In particular, I raise my arms over my head with a boom box in hand—à la John Cusack in *Say Anything*—to shout out my love to Annabel Monaghan, Julie Seifer, Gabrielle Tullman, and Jeannine Votruba, because you guys are the best. Of course you read the book, perhaps in various stages of its development. But more than that, you spoil me with the truest kind of friendship. In grand moments like these, when words fail me, I turn to musical theater. To quote Broadway's *Wicked*, "And now whatever way our stories end, I know you have rewritten mine by being my friend."

Thanks to my family, especially my grandmother, Rose Katz, my mother, Ronnee Segal, my father, Norman Medow, my brother, Greg Medow, and my aunt JaJa. For as long as I can remember, you have provided me with the perfect environment for a (young/growing/now middle-aged) writer, one filled with unconditional love and an endless stream of entertaining stories.

Corny but true: Thanks to SoulCycle, who helped me spin my tale.

This self-published novel is not really "self" published. Team Lauren was assembled in the eleventh hour, and is made up of an incredible group of creative, insightful, and—perhaps most impressively—fast-working artists. These are the people who said yes to me, which is the best word to hear after so much no, and so much silence. Thanks to my editor, Caitlin Alexander, who made my novel better by trimming the fat and keeping the funny. To Gary Tooth, graphic designer extraordinaire, and to Liz Starin, an incredible illustrator, for taking my vision of the book's cover and bringing it to life with whimsy and artistry. To Sarah Silverton, a gifted photographer who always makes me smile, even when not in possession of her camera. And to my publicist, Amy Rosen, who, with sheer force of enthusiasm, will help bring *Lauren Takes Leave* to audiences far and wide.

And to my life's creative director, my husband, Brett Gerstenblatt, who really listened, understood, and supported me when I said that I needed to quit my teaching job and become a writer. Brett read daily chunks of the novel as I was working on it, and then sketched the original idea for the cover using only our daughter's art supplies. Thanks for believing in me and for helping me make Lauren look so good.

To Brett and our children, Andrew and Zoe: whenever I return from my imaginary world, there's no place I'd rather be than in the real and beautiful world we have created together. I love you.

ABOUT *the* AUTHOR

JULIE GERSTENBLATT is a former middle school English teacher who realized that it was time to leave the classroom when a lengthy stint on jury duty felt like the highlight of her career. As a comedy and culture writer for the *Huffington Post* and a humor columnist for the *Scarsdale Inquirer* and Scarsdale10583.com, Julie writes with candor about her life, her friends and family, and the particular demands of motherhood and wifedom in modern-day suburbia. She and her husband live with their two children in Scarsdale, New York. Although she would love to live in the city, suburbia is the inspiration for most of her funny ideas, and so she will remain in Westchester until her neighbors kick her out. *Lauren Takes Leave* is her first novel.

www.juliegerstenblatt.com